Dirty
MAFIA TORMENT

DIRTY MAFIA KINGDOM BOOK THREE

DIRTY MAFIA TORMENT

ISBN 979-8-9947836-2-7 (special edition paperback)

Published by: 3M Productions
Easton, Pennsylvania 18042
michelemannon@gmail.com

Cover Design: Deranged Doctor Design
Editor: Nia Quinn

www.MicheleMannon.com

"You may cut me with your eyes.
You may kill me with your hatefulness.
But still, like air, I'll rise."

"Still I Rise" by Maya Angelou

PROLOGUE

Renzo

Sweet oblivion beckons.

My body slackens as soft leather cuffs tighten around my wrists, holding me aloft. A lullaby called pain wreaks havoc on my mind, and I cling to it, reveling in the twisted comfort accompanying it.

Fina. Fina. Fina.

I stop struggling ... stop breathing ...

"Aiuto!" a panicked man screams in Italian. So close yet so far away. "Qualcuno venga subito."

She appears out of nowhere, a furious angel, the most infuriating creature I've ever met. Her full red lips are moving, angrily, desperately, yet it takes so much fucking effort to hear her.

Don't you dare die and abandon me forever.

She should despise me, fuck knows I've earned it. I've done a lot of twisted things, and sunk to the lowest lows while chasing fleeting highs. My world is destruction; shattering expectations and breaking hearts. It's who I am, the man I was always meant to be.

Still, she's always there, isn't she? Lurking in the corners of my mind. I told myself it meant nothing. We're tangled together, whether we want it or not, both dragged into a mafiosi world that devours the weak and rewards only the most cunningly ruthless. But Fina was never the type to be forgotten. All I see is her now—daring, relentless, waiting on a promise I never should have made.

Fina ...

Far away, people are shouting.

Far away, my mind drifts into a memory, of us and how we came to be.

⎯⎯⎯⎯⎯⎯

Eight years ago

"You're dead, motherfucker."

My brother straightens beside me, panting between curses, his face contorted with rage.

I flex my fingers. I'm the wild Beneventi, yet Sandro's boldly eye-fucking Maria DeLuca like he's a made man and not some sixteen-year-old sexual deviant, like our living room isn't lined wall-to-wall with mafiosi—men draped in dark suits, their shoes polished to a mirror shine, their eyes full of secrets and silent threats. My father's hosting this luncheon in celebration of our capo di tutti capi's birthday, and all twelve famiglie are present. Members of a rival mafia famiglia, the Cosa Nostra, are even in attendance, traveling from Italy to pay their respects to Don Lucchese.

Everyone has been on relatively good behavior—except Maria.

Still, you don't gather lifelong rivals with violent tendencies together, toss a big-breasted, blue-heeled grenade into the room, and expect a positive outcome. Disaster can strike quicker than you can say, "On your knees, Maria."

Because her husband, Don DeLuca, is Cosa Nostra.

The woman in question is presently bending over to retrieve a hair clip she's dropped. Her blue dress rides up her thighs and over the curve of her tight ass, and every man in the room—aside from her oblivious husband—gawks.

Easy conquests like the lovely Maria don't interest me. I prefer a challenge, the chase. Once she's mine, I'm down for a good fucking flavored with some pretty twisted shit, the kinkier the better.

I swore to my father I'd be on good behavior and won't turn his luncheon into a bloodbath. He didn't even demand my twin do the same.

Sandro shifts on his feet. "My dick aches so bad it might fall off."

"Stop looking at her. No one wants to see your dick rolling around on the floor or shoved down your throat."

"Speaking of dicks ..." Sandro goes stiff beside me. "Here comes one."

Massimo Grassi approaches, his stride equal parts confidence and arrogance. His father, Tito Grassi, is the most powerful capo in the Cosa Nostra, and Massimo wears that truth like an invisible fucking crown. Like Sandro, he craves control. Unlike Sandro, he has no twin to humble his ego. I sometimes imagine them locked in a room together, curious who'd be the last man standing. The thought makes me smirk, though the truth is I could outplay them both without breaking a sweat. I'm the Clark Kent of alphas, with my kryptonite being the simple truth that I couldn't care less about flexing it or chasing the Twelve's approval, especially when I can run circles around them.

Massimo's different. Wicked smart, and at sixteen already accepted into Harvard. Men twice his age respect him, even fear him. Cunning and brutal, he's a dual threat and built to rule. One day, he'll be the capo no one dares cross.

Me? I'd rather watch paint peel off walls than be part of the Life.

I offer my hand, but Massimo tugs me into a bro-hug. "Hungover as hell, brother," he informs me.

Last night's a blur of good whiskey, cigars, and women. We first painted Providence red, white, and green, and then red, white, and blue. One drink at a time, we burned the city down.

I smirk at him. "Pussy."

"Massimo," Sandro says flatly, greeting my friend like he's naming an object he'd rather ignore.

My friend smirks. "Sandro." Then he turns his back on my twin, giving me all his attention. "DJI Mavic 3. Worth every dollar."

I roll my eyes. "For a Harvard-bound fuckhead, you're clueless. Full military is the way to go. Insitu ScanEagle is built for reconnaissance. Costs more, but the battery life and range? Untouchable."

"Not easy to fly."

"Neither is graduating from an Ivy, but somehow some dickheads pull it off."

He chuckles. "I'll give you a day before you've mastered the controls."

"This a geek-off?" Sandro cuts in. "You two competing to be the next Sheldon on a *Big Bang Theory* revival? What the hell are you even talking about?"

"Drones," Massimo says, unbothered.

Sandro lifts a brow. "Toys?"

Massimo and I are locked in a heated battle over the best drones for covert surveillance. I'll argue specs and strategies all day, trading barbs and counterpoints until we've dissected every possible advantage. We both know high tech could shift the balance of power in mafia organizations worldwide. But to most old-school mafiosi, drones are overpriced toys bored rich kids fuck around with. I've no interest in trying to change their pea-brain mindset. Let Massimo be the one to drag them into the future.

"I'm headed back to the hotel," he says. "We good for tonight?"

I nod. "Meet you in the lobby at eleven."

The Cosa Nostra heir stalks off, leaving me alone with Sandro's bullshit.

"Quite the bromance," he says.

"You can come out with us if you want."

"He's the enemy."

I smirk. "He's an ally now."

"Don't kid yourself. He doesn't take you seriously. You're a distraction. A good time, nothing more."

"I'm the highlight of your goddamn day." Sarcasm rolls off my lips. "Must be a sad little life if I'm your best entertainment." The problem with Sandro, lately, is he buys into my give-two-fucks persona, missing the razor-sharp monster underneath.

One day, when I finally unleash on these condescending assholes, I'll carve my mark so deep it leaves the whole room bleeding.

Maria glances our way, and Sandro groans. "Fuuuck."

"Tap that, and you'll regret it."

He groans deep in his throat, and I study him more closely. His expression ... a smug confidence ... that been-there-done-that vibe ...

My mind races over the past few hours. We separated for a short time once, when I stopped in the hallway to listen to Don Lombardi —*The sly bastard.* "You didn't?"

"Of course he did," a voice behind us interrupts.

"What the fucking hell?" Sandro exclaims, as we both spin toward our unwelcome visitor. "If it isn't the first-rate clinger. Go get a life and stop stalking us."

"Me," I add. Because every time I turn around, Elia Seraphina Lombardi is there, hot on my tail.

She's relentless.

A teenage hellhound with her nose in our business. A girl with dark black hair, emerald witch eyes, long legs, and a flat, prepubescent chest. She's wearing a frilly pink dress fit for a princess, over what I bet are virgin white cotton underwear. The devilish cock to her head gives nothing away.

One pity wink, and now she's clingier than Saran Wrap.

It galls me knowing, while Sandro slunk off with the lovely Maria, I was preoccupied and feeling sorry for this hellhound.

Her father, Don Lombardi, a West Coast capo, was ripping her a new asshole in the kitchen, giving her a stern lecture about decorum, behavior, and the consequences of embarrassing him. He'd caught her alone with Massimo, "the enemy," and now "men are talking."

Like Massimo or any red-blooded mafioso gives a rat's ass about Lombardi's thirteen-year-old pot-stirrer.

We locked eyes from where I lurked in the doorway, and in a moment of weakness, I offered her a wink. Encouragement, recognizing her father's a notoriously temperamental prick.

One wink, and the hellhound thinks she owns me.

"The Beneventi library's impressive but lacking poetry," she prattles on in a husky, sexy voice that contradicts the little-girl-plays-princess ensemble she's wearing. All that's missing are a fucking sparkly tiara and magic wand.

"Did you hear something?" Sandro asks me.

Her sigh is overexaggerated. "You've already acknowledged me, dimwit."

What I heard was a girl with a death wish. Prowling around our home and sneaking into my father's library. She's lucky her ass hasn't yet been tossed into the Beneventi dungeon. She could spend her time reading the words written in blood on the cell walls. "Just some incessant buzzing," I smoothly reply, playing along with Sandro. "Nothing worth paying attention to."

"Robert Frost's poems should be added to the collection," she continues, unperturbed. "You boys would benefit from reading his work, especially one poem in particular."

The evil glint in her eyes captivates me.

Sandro, hating being on the losing end of a power play, ignores the warning signs and like a baited fish demands, "What fucking bullshit are you spouting now? Like I give a rat's ass about poetry."

My eyes narrow. She's positively glowing with anticipation.

"You can learn a lot from it."

I elbow Sandro in the side, but it's too late. "Like what?" The question dangles like low-hanging fruit just waiting for her to snatch hold of it.

And she does, brilliantly.

"If I were you two, I'd start with, 'The Road Not Taken.'"

Sandro stares at her, probably wondering if this annoying girl, every inch resembling the thirteen-year-old she is, with her chin cocked high and fire breathing from her nostrils, recognizes the innuendo.

But any illusions of innocence and misunderstood sexual dynamics—especially the kind involving lovely Maria—Elia Seraphina Lombardi shatters as she hammers out a final double-fisted blow.

"My advice, boys, is to stop drooling over Maria." She spins to walk away, but not before firing a parting shot.

"Take the road less traveled. One your father hasn't been down about an hour and a half ago."

—

Five years ago

THE BEDROOM'S A GODDAMN MESS.

Evidence of her struggle is everywhere; tangled sheets, a broken lamp on the floor, the slackened ropes that bind her ankles. A shard of glass rests beside her on the mattress, and I can tell she used it to pick away at the shibari rope binding her wrists.

I've got Elia Seraphina Lombardi trussed up like a flamingo ready for the fire pit.

I close the bedroom door behind me. "Miss me?"

She glares daggers. Because she can't reply; I've gagged her with a silk tie.

It'd be easy to say the devil made me do it because I never claim responsibility for anything, my motto being if the fools in my life believe they can outwit me, fuck 'em while they figure shit out. In this case, I claim full responsibility. There are consequences to actions, so my father likes to remind my twin and me. This girl needed a Beneventi-worthy wakeup call.

I get that I'm memorable, and she clearly hasn't forgotten me. In the years between luncheons, she's only gotten sharper, hungrier for my presence, and twice as relentless.

Spying on me turned into a game of dodge and evade once she caught me staring earlier. Did I use it to break up the monotony of my day? You bet I did. Teaching her a lesson became my afternoon entertainment.

I escaped to the kitchen, and seconds later, she came in for a glass of water. I took a piss, and she lurked outside the door, waiting for me to exit. When I ducked into the library, though, she was already there, seated on the sofa and pretending to read. I gave her points for that. It wasn't until she followed me upstairs like a lovestruck pup and into a guest bedroom at the far end of the hall, where no one could hear her scream, that I sprung my trap.

Did she struggle while I subdued her? Fuck yeah—I've scratches on my arm and chest to prove it. Cursed me to hell and back, too, not knowing I've been there a time or two. But to her credit, not a scream or even a whimper escaped her lips.

She's on her side now, same place I left her when I escaped downstairs to mingle, her pink feathered cocktail dress riding up over her hips.

I pause and admire my work. The rope is an intricate masterpiece, winding between her thighs, cinching her waist, parting her perfect breasts before splitting over her shoulders where it then intertwines with the other end and around the wrists behind her back.

It's my first attempt at shibari. The art form's meant to be visually appealing. But the way the rope pulls her shoulders back and showcases her big fucking breasts is so erotic, my dick notices.

Sixteen, and a stunner.

How did I miss it?

She glares at me over a shoulder, and I remind myself she's in this predicament to learn a lesson. Nothing more, but especially not because I'm designating her as my latest distraction.

I sit on the mattress beside her. "Bet you regret following me around like a desperate virgin."

Her green eyes narrow.

"Watching my every move. Stalking me." I pluck a feather from her dress. "A little bitch in heat, aren't you?" Goose bumps prickle her skin as I trace the feather across her bare arm. She's prettier now that I'm really looking at her. Curvier, with a flat stomach and legs that go on for miles.

They're bent now, wrapped up like a gift.

Good thing I don't do teen virgin.

She squirms, and the colorful ropes draw tighter.

"So tell me." I lean over to whisper in her ear. "Am I your crush or your ruin?"

She jerks her head sideways in an attempt to headbutt me.

I laugh, loving the fight in her. "Looks like you traded in your puppy dog vibe to be my little fucking pony girl. Is that what you were hoping? To be my little plaything, to be bridled and ridden?"

Her emerald eyes flash with ... interest ...

No way.

A curious fucking hellion.

"You're a virgin, right?" I demand. Not sure why I ask or why it's important. It just is, because rumors are circulating.

The Twelve are in Rhode Island for a pissing contest disguised as a luncheon. Every capo is puckered up with big guns drawn, hoping to gain favor with Don Lucchese. Because with the new succession rules come new opportunities. My godfather will nominate two men for the Twelve's vote to succeed him after his death. My father, a top earner and ruthless enforcer, will be one name, I'm damn sure of it. It's been predictably boring watching the other capos compete.

Rumors are circulating that Don Lombardi will be announcing during the birthday toasts the deal he made with Carlo Accardo. His daughter's hand in marriage for gold. *Actual* fucking gold bars. Everyone knows Don Lombardi is a gambling addict drowning in debt. Still, Don Lucchese will welcome the marriage, seeing it as an acknowledgment of the fragile peace he struck with the traitor Accardo, a former famiglie affiliate and Chicago power player, whose brother's loose lips nearly got his entire family slaughtered years ago.

My father put Pascale down.

Fast-forward to the present, where Don Lucchese has forgiven them. No doubt the wise man stacked his gold bars neatly on top of that peace.

Though rumors haven't stopped Elia Seraphina Lombardi from being up our asses. Specifically my ass—Sandro's just an innocent bystander.

Sixteen, and still a hellion.

She nods, flushed, as she struggles against the ropes.

My gaze rakes over her body. The mafiosi downstairs would be flattered by her attention. Some might take advantage of her vulnerability. If they opened their eyes and saw her like I do now, melon-size breasts, flat abs, perfectly groomed pussy hidden by the tiniest purple triangle patch ...

A picture of her forms, her in a lifeguard's swimsuit and running across a California beach. Gorgeous breasts bouncing and midnight black hair billowing in the ocean breeze.

I shake my head, regretting my horny teen years and the nights spent jacking off to old *Baywatch* reruns. Still, discovering a bombshell like Elia Seraphina Lombardi hidden beneath that horrid pink dress might be the biggest surprise of the day.

I've two choices; spring her free or peel the offensive material off her for a closer look.

No choice, jackass.

The game we've been playing was entertaining while it lasted, but it's time to cut her free. Lombardi will demand her presence for his big announcement and send men to locate her. Still, I go for cutthroat, because kindness isn't a winning strategy when dealing with a stubborn, lovesick girl.

"I'm not interested. Period. No more butting into private conversations. No trailing after me like a teenager does her first crush. No antagonizing my brother or spying on men who murder for a living.

And, as a general warning, stop involving yourself in everyone else's business. The consequences will be more severe than being bound and gagged for an afternoon." She doesn't even flinch, her expression impassive. "Stick with the children, understand? Leave me the fuck alone. Or you won't find yourself in a comfy bed next time but in the Beneventi dungeon."

We lock eyes, and I curse beneath my breath.

Is that fucking defiance I see?

I ignore the warning bells. Clasping her arms below the elbows, I help her onto her knees. She sways, and my fingers swipe across her skin. Warm breast greets me like an electric bolt to the balls.

Her throat bobs as she swallows hard. From my touch? Or the situation she's found herself in, in general?

"Enough," I grind out. "I'll ungag you, but think twice about screaming because as much trouble as this will cause me, I'll be double for you. Nod if you understand."

Her head bobs.

I can't untie the silk tie quick enough.

Her tongue darts out and swipes across her lips.

Fuck. That's hot.

I shift on the mattress, distancing myself.

"Why shibari?" I hear her croak.

I freeze. "What?"

"Why tie me up in such an erotic way?"

Bound and gagged for hours, and this is her first comment? No demands to be untied or worse, banshee screams. Instead, she questions my bondage technique? Do I pat myself on the back, or run?

Her eyes flash, and my lips draw tight.

I'm right about her. She's fucking curious, and that interests me.

"Listen, Elia," I warn her.

"It's Fina."

Well fuck me blind. "You're lucky, Fina, that I didn't anchor the tail end of the rope to the ceiling."

She looks up at the hook directly over the bed. Yeah, my father likes keeping his guests entertained. What sixteen-year-old virgin's into kink? What kind of fucking poetry is this hellhound reading?

Drawing on my inner Sandro, I face her. "Curiosity gets you killed in the Life."

She answers with poetry. "Entombed by whom, for what offence. If Home or Foreign born. Had I the curiosity. 'Twere not appeased of men."

"Jesus Christ."

"No, Emily Dickinson."

She's lost her damn mind.

Her head cocks. "You blow with the wind yet remain alive and thriving."

"Barely alive," I mutter, "and hardly thriving."

She shifts on her knees and straightens, her breasts swaying and my mind playing vicious tricks on me. "Point is, Hot Pants, you do as you will without consequences."

Until my father demands I step up.

Until my motherfucking destiny becomes inescapable.

On my eighteenth birthday, my father sat me down in his leather-clad library, the air thick with cigars and aged whiskey. His steely gaze pinned me to the chair, unwavering, as he mindfucked me. "Get it out of your system while you can." By "it," he meant all the sex, drugs, and rock 'n' roll I could handle. Understanding that numbness wasn't truly the goal. Escape. Relief. Freedom from the crushing weight of expectations was.

Because when you're Sebastiano Beneventi's son, the Life is your only destiny.

It's like my father sees straight through me, knowing my mind isn't wired like Sandro's. I'm not just some hormone-fueled kid with a rebellious streak a mile long. There's something deeper, something restless, simmering beneath my skin, a hunger for the unpredictable, a thirst for the forbidden. I crave the burn, the sting, the electrifying charge buried in the raw and the real. If curiosity killed the cat, I've died ten times over. But what'll truly kill me is the soul-crushing predictability of the famiglie. Because no matter Don Lucchese's promises of change, mafiosi will always be mafiosi. And I curse the day I'm officially one of them.

"Experiment. Test your limits," my father commanded, his voice a low growl of authority. "But don't be a stupid little shit. Don't get caught, don't get hooked, and don't fucking die. When your time's up, you'll step up as the Beneventi heir. Capisci?"

He meant proving myself, either as an earner, an enforcer—or both, if you're Sebastiano Beneventi.

The clock in my mind is always ticking, even when the weight in my wicked soul wishes for time to stand still.

She licks her lips once more, capturing my complete attention.

I smirk. "You want a taste of my dick, baby? That's why you're tracking my bed partners?"

She rolls her fucking eyes. "Curiosity is why I've befriended you."

"That's what you call this?" I gesture between us. "Befriended?"

Her sigh fills the room. "You think I'm in love with you?"

"Well ... yeah."

She laughs, and my balls shrivel at the sound.

"Why else be up my ass for years?"

Her laughter dies, and her expression sobers. "You need to marry me."

"What?" I'm not often shocked, but what the fuck?

"Not now. When I turn twenty-one. But you'll need to present your father with the idea this afternoon so we can announce it today."

Her voice is steady, yet her lower lip trembles, slight as a bird testing a wire. I spot it and the room narrows. My hand moves before my mouth does, sliding to the hollow at her throat to anchor her to the present. My thumb rests against that tiny quiver and holds it there, light enough to soothe, sharp enough to warn her away. A quieter violence blooms in my head—how much I'd love catching Lombardi alone, forcing him up against the nearest wall and bashing his head into it until he understands what flesh and blood actually means.

Fina's a pain in the ass, but no woman deserves the fate he's offering her. "A lot can happen in five years," I say, the lie flat and useless.

"So, I should ask Massimo?"

"Massimo?" I stupidly exclaim. "You're in contact with him?"

She shrugs a shoulder.

I frown. What is it about her approaching fucking Massimo Grassi for help that irritates me?

"He's my best option."

That fucking right? "But he already turned you down?"

"No. He offered me a better alternative. His words, not mine."

I laugh. "Me?"

"Sad, but true."

"You were pursuing me."

"Pursuing? Yes. Offering you my tender heart?" Her face contorts. "Absolutely not."

I'm hurt. "Why not?" I demand.

"As entertaining and deliciously wicked as you are"—she tosses her long black hair over her shoulder—"I'm out of your league, Hot Pants."

I think I'm in love.

She gives me this look, her emerald eyes slicing through my defenses, her body a weapon she doesn't even know how to use. "We'll marry, then divorce when I turn twenty-two."

I choke on my own breath. I've just been outplayed. Instinct takes over, and I quickly untie her and push off the mattress like it's ablaze. "You said you were out of my league."

"Well, I'll take you over Accardo."

Bitch-slapped. That's what this feels like, with me her bitch.

She slides off the bed, smooths her dress, then runs her fingers through her long black hair, erasing every trace of struggle. Like our wedding's already a go.

"In case you missed it, I'm uninterested in the Life."

She fiddles with the gaudy pink feathers on her dress, trying to arrange the collar so they don't fall over like wilted weeds. The more she smooths them upward, the more they spring into different directions, every which way but up.

"You're a capo's daughter, for Christ's sake. And now, suddenly, I want in?" Like I'll give up my freedom before I'm forced into doing so.

"You can continue with your lifestyle." She sighs with exaggeration. "I'm fine if we don't marry until I'm twenty-one."

"My lifestyle?" I demand.

"Come on, Lorenzo—"

"Renzo."

"Fine, Renzo. I'll spell it out for you. You spend Friday nights at Providence's Sin City and every Saturday getting high and laid at one of several nightclubs."

Jesus.

"That lifestyle."

I trace my fingers across my chin. My marrying anyone is fucking ridiculous. Being shackled to one woman? Giving up all the filthy pleasures the world has to offer? Having to answer for my habits, my kinks?

Not happening.

"My father won't agree. Not even if it's Sandro."

Her eyes flash with disgust. "Sandro?"

"It won't be me," I say in a firm tone, hoping she'll drop the idea.

She opens her mouth, the fight still in her. As much as I admire it, I'm shutting this conversation down for good.

"My father earns money. Yours pisses it away. If there's such a thing as embarrassment by association, that's how we Beneventis feel about the Lombardis. Do you really expect him to give his blessing to our marriage?"

She stares at the floor, like she'd like it to swallow her up, disappointment carved into every inch of her.

No reason for it to sting the way it does. I barely know this girl.

"Like I said, a lot can change." I open the bedroom door, signaling an end to this discussion. "Give me a few minutes before you follow me downstairs."

I walk out before she can respond, putting distance between us and the ridiculous idea I'm her salvation.

Wrong bastard to approach for help.

I'm famished by the time I reach my seat. "Where's the clinger?" is the first thing Sandro asks me, nodding toward the empty chair beside the one I'm settling into. A chair awkwardly squeezed between mine and the mafioso to my right, when it should be at the far end of the table with the other children's.

"Guess she got tied up elsewhere."

He shoots me a look.

I smirk, giving nothing away. "What did I miss?"

"Roberto Ferrara has an FBI agent in his pocket."

"No shit?" I stab an asparagus with a fork and stuff the tip into my mouth. "Don Lucchese loves strong government connections," I say while chewing.

"Yeah," Sandro replies. "Know what else he loves? Good table manners."

"Not what he told me when I approached him earlier to wish him a happy birthday. He asked about you."

"Damn it." He places his wine on the table, buying the bullshit. "You covered for me, right?"

So fucking gullible.

Finally recognizing the lie, he elbows me hard in the side.

Point made, I shove another asparagus spear into my mouth.

The luncheon is interrupted by spoons tapping against glasses, signaling the birthday toasts will begin.

Fina appears in a blur of pink.

I wait, ready to lock eyes—and yeah, offer her encouragement. Without so much as a glance my way, she takes a seat with the children.

"Can't believe that bloodhound gave up," Sandro declares. Not a huge Fina fan. She gets beneath his skin like nobody else.

I fill our wineglasses with an expensive Chianti Reserve I pinched earlier from the Beneventi wine cellar and raise mine high. "Let the games begin."

And they do, amateur hour first. Toast after toast. Boast after boast. Male egos locking horns like rams battling for dominance.

Blah. Blah. Blah.

Midway through, Don Lucchese interrupts to acknowledge my father for his financial prowess. Everyone applauds, and then, timing it perfectly, my father does what he does best, and drops another bomb. He's entering the casino business.

The room hums with excitement, the air practically vibrates. Everyone murmurs with curiosity. Except for Bible Belt Benny Manocchio. His face hardens, lips pressed into a razor-thin line, his knuckles whitening around his glass. Benny controls the South with claws buried deep in the gaming business.

Two types of men rise in rank among the mafiosi, the earners and the enforcers. My father's both, and can kill men twice; once financially, sabotaging a rival's financial assets with the click of a finger, and secondly, the traditional smoking-gun way. Today, the opposite happened. Overnight, he made every criminal in the Twelve wealthy. Not equally, of course, though no one's complaining.

And no one's dead yet.

Benny has yet to turn a huge profit. And, if he doesn't wise up and raise his glass in toast, his chance to do so is over. Hard to turn a profit when you're turning up tulips.

Don Lombardi stands.

Snickers ripple through the room, that's how much respect the bastard has.

"Don Lucchese." He raises his glass. "To ensure a new era of peace, I'd like to announce the engagement of my daughter, Elia Seraphina Lombardi, to Carlo Accardo."

Silence suffocates the room.

"Accardo's what—fifty-two?" Sandro mutters.

"Fifty-three, with the hygiene of a pig."

Judging by the reaction of those around us, we're not the only ones disgusted.

Lombardi shifts, sensing the unease. "He's agreed to wait until Elia's twenty-first birthday." With that, he sits, shoulders hunched, eyes down.

My attention falls on Fina.

She pours herself wine from a bottle that doesn't belong at that end of the table, and casually sips it. Like she's unaware of the pity-filled glances cast her way.

"In this world, that's how the Life goes," Sandro murmurs, watching her, too.

There's no middle ground in the famiglie. Escape it or let it sweep you under.

If my goddamn future wasn't so precarious, I'd almost feel bad for her.

Present

FINA. FINA. FINA.

Cold water hits my face, then I'm slapped. My head snaps to the side, and I slowly return to the present. Light blinds me as awareness creeps in.

I pushed things too far this time.

I'm hanging from a Saint Andrew's cross, arms and legs spread wide and wrists and ankles tied, knees buckled and body lax. Naked. Blood pumped full of coke, Adderall, and hell if I know what else.

The scene's a blur. I was whipped and abused, first by a kinky couple who took turns with the braided leather flogger and then by everyone watching, who joined in, tongues colliding around my dick, sucking me off, then denying my orgasm. Pure ecstasy filled with pain and pleasure. But it wasn't enough ... it's never enough.

"Tagliatelo e rivestitelo prima che arrivino i soccorritori," a man nearby exclaims.

Cut him down and clothe him.

Before the emergency workers arrive.

Did I even come before darkness disrupted the fun?

Cursing, Guiseppe, a club guard, uses a switchblade to free my wrists and ankles while a second guard, Giovanni, grabs hold of me, then lowers me to the floor.

I'm too weak to do much but twist my lips into a lopsided grin.

Scowling, they stare down at me. "Il tuo polso si è fermato." Your pulse stopped.

"Sei morto." You died.

"Come fai a vivere?" How are you even alive?

Fina ...

She wouldn't let me go. Even after I failed her ... lost track of time ... skipped out on her ... broke promise after promise ...

Blackness descends as the weight of it gnaws at my soul.

Promise me you'll save me.

But it's too late.

I'm too far gone.

1

Tina

IT'S A MISERABLE DAY.

A relentless, bone-chilling wind accompanies my father and me from the airport to downtown Chicago and cuts straight through me. Equally numbing is the dark, menacing skyscraper now a few feet away, my soon-to-be new home if my marriage to Carlo Accardo goes through.

I tuck my bright pink cashmere scarf tighter around my neck, shielding myself from the wind's bite, the Sunshine State's golden shores becoming more distant with every gust.

"Only speak when you're spoken to," my father warns. As if meeting my fiancé two weeks before my twenty-first birthday—our wedding day—is perfectly normal.

I nod, silent. Nothing I say will change his mind.

We reach the revolving glass door, and my stomach knots tight.

My father stops short, cursing beneath his breath, his attention on the street. "Goddamn it. Settemo Accardo is here."

A yellow Ferrari polished to a fine shine sits at the curb. It's expensive and pretentious, especially with the careless way it's parked, like the prancing horse on the trunk is daring other drivers to hit it. Meeting Carlo's nephew feels like another nail in my coffin, and my father's anxious expression does nothing to ease my apprehension.

"What's wrong?"

He faces me. "Just be careful around Settemo. He's not right in the head."

I blink, stunned. Is that concern in his voice? Real, genuine concern?

I'm five years old again, and he's holding my hand at the Santa Monica Pier, laughing as we eat ice cream. He kneels beside me and whispers promises about a life beyond the horizon and away from the famiglie, his kiss tender on my forehead. For a fleeting moment, I feel loved. Treasured.

Memories can be cruel like that.

A few days afterward, my mother disappeared. When I cried for her, he warned me with a hard slap and equally brutal words. "Never speak of her again."

Rumors circulate, though I never allow myself to go there. I can't survive if I do. So I bury the painful questions and save them for a future day.

My father stalks toward the glass door. "Don't forget to compliment Accardo. He eats that shit up."

I choke back the bile in my throat.

We clear security and take a private elevator to the luxury penthouse in Chicago's newest high-rise.

The Eleven—formerly known as the Twelve but minus one capo now—need Carlo's money and influence to push their casino expansion into the Midwest. That's the only reason the Accardos—unaffiliated and barely more than second-rate associates—were spared years ago, after Carlo's brother ran his mouth to the wrong people and nearly got the whole family wiped out. He died for revealing famiglie secrets, and the Accardos were left disgraced and shunned because of his actions.

Still, Carlo survived and built an empire while he waited to buy his way back into their good graces.

His money is why my father agreed to this marriage.

My father nudges my side. "For fuck's sake, smile."

I grin stupidly at the elevator camera that has him so concerned. Complacent, like I've accepted my fate.

The elevator chimes, and the door opens. My father grips my elbow and leads me inside. "Holy shit," he exclaims at the gaudy spectacle before us.

Everything is gold. From the floor tiles to window trim, the three chandeliers to the wall sconces, the furniture to the backsplash in the kitchen to our right. A life-sized statue of a naked woman with a snake curled around her bosom dominates the open living space. The monstrosity is gold—I think, maybe, real gold.

I hold my hand over my eyes like I'm blinded.

Is this man for real?

My father eats it up. "This place must be worth a fortune."

I can see him calculating numbers in his head, and the rage coiling inside me could give the golden snake some competition. "What makes you say that?" I sweetly manage to ask.

He looks at me like I'm stupid. Always underestimating me.

The promise of easy money is his drug. How to get it and how to gamble it away. Wash. Rinse. Repeat. What he hasn't done is gamble with my life. No, he simply bartered it away like it cost him nothing.

A man appears. "Follow me," he orders in a clipped tone and stalks away.

"Nice of Carlo to greet us."

"Quiet," my father snaps, expecting trumpets and getting a subtle Italian salute.

We trail behind the man, down a long corridor, and enter an enormous office that reeks of stale cologne and body odor.

I burrow my nose into my scarf. Carlo has weird beliefs, one being he believes bathing washes away a man's mojo, which affects his ability to get an erection. Sure, his bad BO is gag-worthy. But the idea of having sex with him is worse.

I get my first glimpse of him as he sits behind a desk, and he's everything I've dreaded and worse. His face is doughy and sagging, with deep lines etched from years of hard living. A patchy scruff of graying beard does little to hide the pockmarks across his skin, and his small, watery eyes sit beneath heavy lids that make him look tired and mean. He's in deep discussion with a tall man standing to the right. *Settemo, must be.*

Neither acknowledge us.

My father shifts on his feet.

"Did the commission do what you asked them to do?" Carlo demands.

"Yes. They're revising their policy as we speak," Settemo replies. "If too many investors withdraw contributions at once, the funds will be frozen for up to a year while every party is investigated."

"Excellent. Letting that much money rot in a frozen trust would bleed anyone's bottom line dry, no matter how deep their pockets. If we ever need to pull out, we'll move first."

Not known for his patience, my father clears his throat, earning the glare of both men.

"This is Matteo Lombardi," Carlo announces to Settemo. "West Coast capo to the Eleven. The man responsible for convincing Don Lucchese to pardon our sins." He practically spits out the last word, anger simmering.

A man with a grudge.

I tuck the little morsel of information away.

"Matteo, this is my nephew and heir, Settemo Accardo."

My father hurries forward, hand extended.

Settemo doesn't lift an arm, completely ignoring him, and instead zeroes in on me. He rakes his eyes over my body, bold and calculating. A chill drills down into my core. His gaze makes me feel like I've been stuffed inside a freezer in the back of a butcher shop, bodies hanging off hooks beside me.

I raise my chin slightly, defensively, aware how I look in my bubble gum pink dress, matching heels and lip gloss, and well-rehearsed smile. No way he sees past it. Arrogant men never do.

His lips twist, as his eyes darken with an emotion I can't quite put my finger on.

He's the boy who broke his toys.

I understand now why my father warned me.

"Sit," Carlo tells my father, voice cool and flat. "I've a few additional requirements before we finalize our arrangement."

My father sinks into the chair and begins reading the document Carlo has prepared. His spine straightens. "What's this?"

"A payment arrangement for your overdue debt."

Curious, I drift forward, close enough to peer over his shoulder. My breath catches.

Three million dollars.

That's my price tag?

My father slowly pulls a folded paper from his wallet. "I only borrowed ..." He squints at the faded numbers while I try to process the hurt unfolding in real time. Blood money, that's what this is, with my blood, my body, my life, as collateral. My future bartered away for cash already spent.

"My note says just under one point three million," he mumbles.

I feel like I've been gutted. Not just cut open, but carved deep enough to reach the soft, hollow places where that hopeful little girl used to live.

Carlo extends his hand. "Let me see that."

My father hesitates, then hands him the paper.

Carlo lifts it slowly, eyes hard, and tears it to shreds. "What you owe is what's written there," he says, tapping the new document without looking up. He gets off on humiliating him, doesn't he? Making a capo in the Eleven kiss his ass? Holding a deep grudge against the famiglie, are we?

My father's face turns blotchy with outrage. "We had an agreement."

"An understanding," Carlo corrects, his tone ironclad. "Things change."

I watch, wide-eyed, as my father lurches to his feet. "An understanding?" he snaps, almost spitting the words.

Stupid, stupid man.

Settemo moves closer. So does Carlo's man.

"You can't—"

"Oh my God. Those are the prettiest pink curtains I've ever seen," I exclaim, gesturing to the window behind Carlo's desk, saving my father's neck. "Did you know my favorite color's pink?"

Carlo's expression twists, the look of horrified surprise priceless.

"The curtains are gold, you stupid bitch," Settemo rumbles. "My uncle's allergic to goddamn strawberries and hates all shades of red."

Much like his questionable hygiene, Carlo's obsession with gold and loathing for anything red or pink is well documented. The moment rumors of our engagement began circulating, I began weaving pink into my wardrobe, hoping he'll recognize we're incompatible. My father hates the color too, making each outfit a double-edged strike. Every outfit is deliberate, a quiet rebellion I derive immense joy from. The news of Carlo's strawberry allergy is new, something even my online digging hadn't uncovered.

My father mutters beneath his breath as he signs the new documents, then places the pen next to them.

Carlo looks pleased as punch. "I'll expect you back in Chicago in two weeks for the wedding."

I clear my throat. The opportunity I've been waiting for has arrived. "Two weeks? Won't that be disrespectful?"

My father pins me with a glare.

Carlo files the papers into his desk, clearly dismissing us. "Disrespectful to who?" he asks, like my answer won't make a lick of difference.

"Sebastiano Beneventi."

His head snaps up.

"Father, don't you remember? You had me RSVP to his wedding invitation."

"You what—?"

I cut him off. "We can't not show up. Won't Don Beneventi take offense to your daughter getting married in the same week? He is the new capo di tutti capi, and you know how old-fashioned the famiglie are."

"You think we give two fucks about offending the man who murdered my father?" Settemo erupts, breaking his silence. "My uncle isn't waiting on anyone to break in some virgin pussy." His words are shocking, but the undercurrent within his tone sets me on edge. Sett*emo* is totally emo. A dangerous psycho to be avoided at all costs.

He steps toward me, but I hold steady. A man like him can smell fear. "You'll be headed down the aisle in two weeks if I have to drag you screaming through the church."

"But my father's walking me down the aisle."

Everyone stills.

Emo eyes me in a way that makes my skin crawl.

My father hurriedly cuts in, trying to salvage the situation. Three million in debt, and Lord knows how much more by the time Carlo is done with him, spurring him on. "She'll be too sick to travel to Rhode Island."

No. No. No. I need my wedding delayed. Extra time to plan and scrape enough money together to disappear and not be found.

Ever.

Do I want to attend the Beneventi wedding? The last person I ever want to see again is Lorenzo Beneventi. If he followed through on his damn promise instead of dishing out excuses, I wouldn't be stuck in Carlo's Chicago office, fending off three wolves like a rabbit trapped in their den.

I hate Renzo with a passion and would do anything to avoid that wedding.

Except marry Carlo.

My father speaks. "I'll send word to Sebastiano—"

Carlo interrupts him. "The reception's at his Rhode Island estate?"

"Yes."

Oddly, Carlo seems pleased.

"Perfect. While in attendance, you'll do me a favor. You do this, and I'll clear the additional debt."

"Of course. What is it?"

"Search his estate for signs of any weakness within his security. And I don't need to tell you to be discreet about it."

My father can't be that stupid. The reason the Twelve is now the Eleven is because Sebastiano Beneventi took a chain saw to a capo who crossed him.

"Deal," I hear him say. "If we add this arrangement to the paperwork."

Carlo stares him down. "Paperwork's signed already."

"And the wedding?" I ask.

"Postponed to the end of the month."

Relief washes over me. I did it. I've bought myself time. "Mind if I use the restroom?" I hurriedly say, struggling not to give my joy away.

Carlo flicks his fingers toward his man. "Show her to the guest bathroom. Your father will be waiting by the elevator."

With that, we're dismissed.

Seconds later, I enter the bathroom, lock the door behind me, and sink to the floor, overcome by relief. I bought myself time. Now I need money. A lot of it. But how?

My father drained the trust my mother had set up for me. His name isn't on the account, but the bank is in Los Angeles, his territory.

I've been gathering cash for years, pocketing loose change, stealing what I could, selling what I could. His Rolex, cuff links, even the hubcaps off his Mercedes. But it's pennies in a piggy bank when I need a Swiss bank vault.

It's enough to vanish, but not to stay gone.

And if I'm caught, that's it—I'll vanish for good.

I stand, tucking my scarf inside my bag and setting it on the vanity before washing my hands and dousing my face with water. I'm ready to return to Los Angeles and enjoy what's left of my time there. Gathering my stuff, I take a second to smooth the lace on my pink dress, and then unlock the door.

A blow slams into my chest. I stumble back into the bathroom.

Emo shuts the door behind him, a cigarette hanging from his lips, the ember glowing like a warning. His lips are pulled tight around it, his pupils pinpricks.

"I was just finishing up."

"And I'm just starting."

He lunges, fingers locking around my throat, shoving me against the wall. His grip is iron, bruising. My pulse hammers under his hand. "I thought I'd give you a taste of what you can look forward to," he purrs.

The punch to my gut is fast and merciless. Air leaves my lungs as my knees buckle. I fold in on myself, arms clutched to my middle.

He yanks me back up by my hair.

I force back my terror in favor of calm. "Carlo will notice we're gone."

He exhales a plume of smoke into my face.

I cough, eyes watering, but still meet his stare while my mind races how to escape the psycho.

Abruptly, he cups a cheek, and I don't dare move. "Not even a whimper. I like that. Make one now, and your face will be next."

It's all the warning I get.

He seizes my wrist, pinning it high above me, then presses the cigarette's tip into the tender flesh on the inside of my wrist. Heat sears my skin, and I bite my lip until it splits.

Closely, he watches me, waiting for me to break.

A pounding on the door interrupts him, and saves me.

"Not a word," he threatens, releasing me.

He pulls open the door and charges by Carlo's man.

I quickly gather my things and follow the man to the elevator. Wordlessly step beside my father, descend, and spill out onto the frigid sidewalk. We walk in the direction we came from.

Each step sends a spike of pain through my midsection, but my father doesn't notice. He doesn't care. His silence cuts deep, worse than a punch to the stomach or cigarette burn.

No one will stop the marriage. No one will spare me from what comes next. I'm a mafia princess, property to be sold, used, and discarded. A pretty token passed between men like currency. It's a world without consequences, with actions like the real-life horror show in the bathroom minutes earlier par for the course.

For too long, I hoped someone would step in. That God might intercede.

I'm done hoping and praying.

If no one's coming to save me, I'll save myself.

But first, I have unfinished business.

A fresh gust kicks up as we turn the corner, and I reach for my scarf. Like a magician, I pluck it from my purse. The cashmere billows then catches the wind like a bird sprung from its cage. I release the material, then watch it soar behind us and back toward where we came from.

"Drat," I say, my voice thin with mock frustration. "My scarf."

"Leave it," my father mutters, not even glancing back. He's walking faster now, eager to get on with his day, satisfied that the deal's been struck and his pockets are heavier.

But I don't leave it.

I turn on my heel and retrace my steps. This time, I raise the scarf high enough for the wind to carry it exactly where I need it, right behind Emo's gleaming Ferrari.

My heart thuds in my chest, but my hands are steady as I pull the small blade from my clutch and wrap it in pink. One last glance over my shoulder to ensure no eyes are on me, and I strike.

They think there will be no consequences.

They think I'll just take it.

The blade cuts deep as I carve the filthiest, most obscene, spur-of-the-moment phrase into the Ferrari's flawless yellow paint.

2

Renzo

"How do you feel about your recent flirt with death?"

My new therapist doesn't beat around the bush. Problem is I'm a Beneventi. Emotions are prey, and vulnerability the blood our enemies feed from.

"Flirting comes naturally." I cross an ankle over a knee, recline in the expensive chair, and gesture toward her desk. "Says so in one of those files."

I live by the three Ds: dodge, distract, and delay. But a fourth D, never part of the equation, landed me here—*dying*.

I fucked up, but survived.

But my father's patience is worn out.

The shrink's office is lush. Signed artwork on the walls. Harvard degree prominently displayed behind her desk. My father's taken a new approach this time; this one's less drill sergeant and more spank-bank material. The confident gleam in her eyes says she believes she'll succeed where others have failed.

Not understanding we Beneventi come with a shutoff valve. Charming mafiosi one minute and hacking men apart with chain saws the next.

No amount of psychobabble can penetrate that. Or what it takes to thrive in the Life.

"You don't want to be here."

Bing-fucking-go. "What makes you say that?"

Her sigh sounds like an eye roll. "The emergency response report says oxygen had to be administered."

Finally, something we can talk about, even if she doesn't get the answers she wants.

"I was hanging from a Saint Andrew's cross. Do you understand how much effort that took?"

She stares at me like she's trying to read my soul.

I smirk. "Closest I've come to a religious experience."

"You agreed to therapy."

"My father's persuasive."

"I can't help you if you don't want it."

"Sure you can. Depends on your definition of helpful."

She cocks her head. "What do you mean?"

I rake my eyes over her. All buttoned up, hair in a twist, makeup flawless. A woman men marry. I could have her on this desk, skirt hiked and thighs spread within minutes. No challenge there.

"You died."

"Yes."

"Did you want to die?"

"No." I unwrap a purple lollipop I stole on my arrival from a jar by the door and slip it into my mouth. Enjoying the pick-me-up from the sugar burst while Debbie Downer here tries to go deep.

She can't help me.

I've crossed the fine line so many times it's faded into the earth.

Psychiatrists get off on exploring trigger moments.

My fucking issues stem from not pulling the trigger—literally.

A few months ago, the Twelve gathered in Rome, with Sandro and me in attendance. My father demanded an audience with the famiglie heads and called out the capo of the southeast, Bible Belt Benny Manocchio, and his puppet, Emilio Conti, for their interference with the Beneventi casino expansion. Like I said, we don't have a shutoff valve. Fuck around and find out, is our family motto.

They denied involvement.

My father then hauled Conti's uncle from our rental car's trunk, handed me a gun and the incredible honor of becoming a made man right then and there.

For years, I'd contemplated this moment and how it'd play out. The dread that'd hit me. The reluctance to step up into the spotlight that comes with being my father's son.

But my mind is twisted, bent. Un-fucking-ly unpredictable.

Everyone assumes I balked. Even my father. Even my goddamn twin. No one sees the truth.

There have been whispers ever since.

Wild. Unreliable. *Weak.*

My therapist flips open a file, then clears her throat. "Your IQ is 151?"

"That what it says?"

"That's exceptionally high."

"Exceptionally irrelevant, with one exception." I take a long lick of my lollipop, then tap it against my temple. "This fucking head is a weapon. One snap and I'm not a man anymore but your worst nightmare. No remorse. No soul. Just hunger. But at least there's sex and drugs to keep the beast at bay."

She's pleased I've opened up though not taking me seriously.

Rome was the trigger moment that sent me spiraling. I hurt everyone in the wake of it. Smashed expectations, broke promises, becoming the man everyone believes I am.

I've done horrible, shitty things, and am struggling to find a way out.

The shrink leans in, still stuck on IQ. "Craving stimulation is common in the highly intellectual."

"Or maybe you're projecting. Looking for someone who shares your boredom in day-to-day life."

Her lips part. Yeah, I can psychobabble, too.

"You attended Harvard?" It's a rhetorical question with the answer on the wall.

"Yes."

"You ever meet Massimo Grassi?"

She blushes. *Interesting.*

"No."

But she's heard about him. I bet Massimo got more action on campus than the Harvard libraries.

"You're his type. Intelligent. Conservative. Blonde."

She swallows hard and shifts in her chair. "And what's your type?"

"Every type's my type." It's bullshit I feed her, and myself.

"Have you ever been in love?"

"I love a lot of things. Freedom. Drugs. Bondage. Fucking."

"Is there a woman in your life?"

"Not anymore." I frown. I burned that bridge, torched it to the motherfucking ground.

Her eyes narrow. "But there was?"

I ask myself the same thing. Was there or wasn't there? Do twenty-four hours, with a few stolen moments scattered on top, even measure up to a lifetime?

"Lorenzo ... let me help you."

I snort. "Help me?"

"Yes."

"Fine. Let's fuck."

She sits up straighter. Yet, it's too late, the flash in her eyes gave her away. "Um ... ah ... your father asked I get you sober for his wedding."

His wedding to my almost-fiancée. I seem to be accumulating them like baseball cards.

"Asked or demanded?"

"He cares."

"Love's never been the issue."

I can't pretend I'm in control, not after what happened.

The least I can do for my father after the fuckup in Rome is attend his wedding sober. But I don't need a shrink to help me with that.

I take another long lick of lollipop, then my sugar-coated lips.

Her eyes tracking the movement.

"Have you thought about what I said?"

Her words catch in her throat. "What did you say again?"

"You prefer I make it easy for you?" I toss the lollipop into the can beside her desk and offer her a smirk that ruins women. "Stand, hike up your skirt, and bend over the desk."

No matter how hard I rub the circular scar on my wrist, it doesn't fade. Just like my panic never goes away.

I should be elsewhere rather than at the Beneventi wedding right now, wasting precious time when there's urgent matters I've yet to see to. Like recruiting decoys to throw any search off my tail. Like winning the lottery or, at the very least, discovering if my inheritance hasn't been completely been bled dry.

Money is crucial to staying gone. God's blessed me with the time, and I pray a solution will present itself.

Yeah, I should be anywhere but seated in a pew inside this church and desperately avoiding *him*.

First name, heartbreak.

Middle name, excess.

Last name striking a heady combination of fear and respect in everyone around us. The kind that forces grown men into their Sunday best, the kind that turns liars into saints the second they step into church. It's a wonder the walls don't collapse under the weight of their hypocrisy.

I give in to temptation and look at the man who I counted on saving me.

Lorenzo Beneventi. Standing between his father and brother at the altar. Sinewy. Gaunt. Looking every inch like a rock god. Charisma seeping from his skin. That devil-may-care smirk still intact.

I want to claw my nails across his smug face.

Women eat up the bad-boy act, don't they? The dirty, filthy devil who makes boundaries just to break them. The bastard collects hearts like trophies.

And now he's up at a goddamn altar. A place I imagined seeing him under far different circumstances. The sight alone makes my blood boil until all I can do is keep from screaming.

He leans toward the priest, whispers something, and the poor man's face flushes crimson before he snaps back to scold him. Renzo grins like the devil himself. What kind of twisted soul pisses a priest off at his own family's wedding?

He's thinner than before, his complexion pale. Living life to the fullest has dimmed some of his sparkle. Really, he looks like hell. What has he done to himself?

My gaze collides with the asshole standing next to him—Alessandro Beneventi. He glares at me, like my very existence insults him.

I smooth a loose strand of hair off my forehead with my middle finger.

His lips tighten. He looks ready to drag me outside by the throat. His twin, mercifully, doesn't even notice me.

How I'd love to slide off a pink heel and crack Renzo's skull open. While I'm trapped, he flies free as a bird. Accountable to no one, and caring about no one, not even himself.

Death by stiletto.

The thought almost makes me smile.

My father nudges me. "Stop staring at that worthless piece of shit," he warns, clueless as always. "He'll screw anything that walks, but when it comes to the famiglie, he'll just screw you over."

A truth I know all too well. I'd rather have no hope than the hollow kind—that's the lesson he taught me. I put faith in him, and he crushed it beneath his heel. That sting runs deeper than any physical pain. I taste it still, bitter and sharp, like a bleeding wound that refuses to scab.

I drag my gaze away from Renzo. "Don Beneventi will be insulted if we don't congratulate him on his wedding," I say coldly.

"That's not the Beneventi I'm referring to."

My father's always two steps behind, incapable of seeing the real me. His blindness is a luxury I've learned to cultivate.

I release a long, exaggerated sigh, letting the sting leak into my voice. "Lorenzo Beneventi is the last man I want any contact with."

And that's true, though he's not alone in his place atop the list. Add Carlo and Emo, and you've got a full roster of men capable of tearing me open and letting me bleed out.

I squeeze my eyes shut and force a prayer. *God, I don't need love or mercy. Just money. Enough to escape. Enough to never look back.*

"Don Lucchese's funeral was the last time all us capos were together," my father murmurs beside me, oblivious.

The ceremony begins, and I stare at the pink toes of my heels for the duration, only interrupted by my father during a lull after the priest finishes a blessing. "Stroke of luck we were invited, but especially lucky the reception's at the Beneventi estate."

My thoughts turn immediately back to Chicago, and Carlo's request. My father never ceases to disappoint me.

"You can't be serious? Spy on Don Beneventi? Whatever Carlo is planning with the information you provide, we can't be a part of. Not unless you want your body parts spread out across the Beneventi golf course?"

My father grinds his teeth.

"When have you become a puppet?"

He swings toward me. I'm never this direct, and maybe that's why I'm marrying the enemy. Maybe I played this engagement all wrong? "What did you say?" he demands.

When did he become the rat who squealed on others to help himself?

When did he switch from the doting father to this weak, pitiful man?

Money. That's all that matters.

His fist curls, and I brace myself. Not even a wedding will save me if he loses his temper.

He's capable of anything ... even murdering your mother.

I blink hard, swallowing the tears that threaten. Not now. Not later either. Someday. Someday, far from here, when I have a life of my own, I'll face her death. I'll uncover the truth, then I'll decide what punishment fits the crime.

"Not all capos are present," I say, my lie thin but pointed. "Benny Manocchio's missing."

My father blanches.

Sebastiano Beneventi terrifies me, but more recently, rumors about Alessandro are circulating. How he not only took a chain saw to Benny's man but mailed his remains, piece by piece, to the remaining capos. Some suggest he's more vicious than his father.

My gaze slides to his twin.

So quick with a grin, so careless with the world. Hard to picture him holding a chain saw, much less covered in the blood of the Beneventi enemies.

Wait ... no. I *can* picture that *vividly*.

And, as far as savagery, Lorenzo Beneventi has everyone in this church beat.

My throat hitches, but I shake free from the sadness. My poor lack of judgment got me here. All those years ago, I should have chosen Massimo Grassi to obsess over.

My father ignores me through the rest of the ceremony, which is perfectly fine.

The vows are exchanged. Alessia Amato glows, radiant with her love as she cries, "I do," and hurls herself at her husband. Their kiss lingers, endless, and envy coils inside me like a living thing. Sebastiano Beneventi protects what belongs to him. Why couldn't that instinct have passed to his son?

A wicker basket is shoved into my hands, white envelopes overflowing from the inside. So many. My pulse hammers so loud it drowns out everything else.

"Give me that," my father snaps, ripping the basket away. He tosses in an envelope without hesitation and passes it along. "I hope the bastard appreciates it."

"How much?" I ask, feigning calm, though my voice cracks.

"Ten grand."

I freeze. "Ten grand?"

"Can't be the capo with the smallest offering. Not when they already whisper I'm cheap."

"Maybe the check will bounce," I mutter, too bitter to fake sarcasm and too distracted to muster anything more. Ten thousand dollars. From the cheapest asshole in the church. My mind spins, from my desperate prayer to how nine of the capos are present, to the fat envelopes, to the opportunity right in front of me. Desperate times, desperate measures, they say. I'm drowning, yet suddenly, gloriously, a lifeline is tossed my way.

"Cash," my father forces out with great displeasure. "Famiglie tradition."

That's all I need to hear.

I cross myself with trembling fingers.

Please, God. Forgive me.

And please—please—make sure Sebastiano Beneventi never learns it was me.

I'm on a straight path to Hell either way you look at it.

I pass two confession booths en route to the restroom tucked away behind the vestibule, the contribution basket overflowing with envelopes hugged against my chest.

Once inside, I lock the door behind me.

It's laughable there'd be a collection in the house of God for a man who steals and murders for his profession. Thousands of dollars stuffed into pure white envelopes, every mafioso overly generous and in competition to outdo each other in kissing their new capo di tutti capi's ass.

It seems right I take their blood money. I wouldn't be in this situation if it wasn't for their stupid rules.

I dump out the contents of my purse. My father always criticizes me for carrying a large bag, but I like to be prepared for worst-case situations.

Look who's smiling now?

But there's no time to gloat. Freedom is at my fingertips, if I can pull this off.

I stuff handfuls into my purse until it's bursting at the seams, then shove as many envelopes as I can inside my bra and panties. Then straightening my dress and smoothing my hair, I exit the restroom and head straight for the emergency exit near the confession booths.

My father, anxious to get to the Beneventi estate, had the driver park on the side street. Avoiding the fanfare over the happy couple after they exit the church and time wasted socializing with his fellow capos.

Why make nice when you're plotting to stab them in the back?

I pray his disgust at the delay I caused and his predictable impatience will have him staring out the car window with eyes off me. Yet I walk fast, heart racing for obvious reasons.

Until everything goes ass up at once.

My pink high heel snags between tiles. I'm launched forward, flailing, as I attempt to stop the inevitable, then hit the floor on all fours, my purse landing with a thud a few feet ahead.

Envelopes erupt like white lava.

Shit, oh shit.

I crawl forward, my knees and mangled wrist throbbing, and hastily gather then shove them back inside.

If anyone sees, I'm dead.

God is punishing me, isn't he?

Like he hasn't already done his worst.

Tears form. But crying won't change my life, only determination will.

Retrieving my purse, I restuff the last few envelopes. But as I stretch toward the last, just out of reach, I hear a noise to my right.

A grunt.

Ever so slowly, I look up.

The confession booth door is cracked open, revealing a man inside.

"Renzo," I breathe.

The sight mere feet from me shocks me to my core.

Wearing expensive black tuxedo pants and a crisp white silk shirt indecently unbuttoned from neck to waist, he has both feet up on the confessional window while he lounges in the priest's seat. I smell the sweet, pungent joint before I spy it dangling from his fingertips.

So many words take form. So many questions I'd like to unleash on him. Why didn't you return my calls? You're getting high in God's house? Will you pretend you didn't witness my crime?

Life's a game to him.

I was simply a distraction. Something that caught his attention until it faded.

Two words that have weighed heavily on my heart tumble out. "You promised."

Pain registers across his expression.

I relish it. Yeah, feel that? Yet it's hard not to notice how his high cheekbones are more pronounced and that he's obviously lost weight. What has he done to himself?

No. Stop it. Loathing is a much more rational reaction than worry.

I snatch up the last envelope, then scramble to my feet, hauling my purse over my shoulder and disappearing out the emergency door, just like he disappeared on me months ago.

"Fina," I hear him call out.

But I'm already gone.

4

Tina

One Year Ago

I TWIRL THE KEYS TO MY FATHER'S '66 MUSTANG CONVERTIBLE around my finger, the gleam of chrome catching the dim light. His most prized possession is now mine for the weekend. While he's away and his men are on break, I can do as I want.

And what I want is to go for a ride.

The idea has obsessed me for weeks. My taking control of the thing he worships most; his precious car at my complete mercy.

He'll never know. YouTube taught me more than enough to cover my ass, like how to roll back the odometer and erase my tracks, as if I never touched his car.

Sometimes I toy with darker urges.

Sometimes I give into them—little things, mostly. Petty sabotage. I've watered down his booze, added salt to his dinner when he's not looking, and subtly rearranged his desk. I know the passwords to his computer, phone, and the safe inside his bedroom closet. Deleting messages and changing names within his contacts, leaking his gambling debts to the other capos, skimming small amounts of cash—

45

a little here, a little there ... The list goes on. Messing with the security cameras is my favorite pastime; it drives him into hysterics when they glitch or record random images of the sky. I know every angle and every blind spot, and work them to my advantage.

Today, the urge is darker than usual. A filthy word carved into his custom leather seats, sharp, cruel, worthy of him?

But the voice of reason prevails. Resist the temptation, Fina. Take the ride. Keep the illusion. You're a mafia princess and the picture-perfect example of obedience. A woman the famiglie can point to and say, *"Her father's a fucking financial disgrace, but look at his daughter and how perfectly she carries his debts."*

I climb inside and slam the door behind me, rattling the hinges. I flip the security camera the Italian salute as I start the engine, smirking at the thought of how all my father will ever see is the loop I set, with his beloved Mustang sitting untouched in the garage and the driveway outside frozen in its empty stillness.

With a hard foot on the accelerator, I back the Mustang out of the garage like a bat out of hell, engine roaring and rubber shrieking against concrete, an adrenaline rush flooding my veins.

Until I nearly plow into a man on the sidewalk.

I slam my foot on the brake, tires screaming, the car jerking to a halt just inches from him.

"What the hell?" I snap.

The fool barely flinches, hands shoved in his pockets, completely unruffled, like near-death experiences are par for the course.

I climb out, teeth clenched. "I almost killed you."

"Then the cross-country invite would have been pointless," he replies, peeling off his baseball cap and raking fingers through his dark hair.

I freeze. Recognition strikes me like a punch.

Renzo.

I shouldn't be surprised to see him.

A week ago, I made a bold, calculated move: I texted him, inviting him to LA, out of the blue and so sudden, he's probably wondering how I even got his number. He turned me down once, back when I didn't know my own worth. But desperate times call for desperate measures, and with my father out of town, it felt like the perfect moment to lure him here.

I used what I know about his lifestyle to my advantage, promising him a good time and attaching a naked photo of me bound in playful shibari. My friend and I laughed while she worked the cotton rope around me and as I posed for pictures.

I never told anyone what happened four years ago. But I relived that moment, fantasized about it in vivid detail—even extensively researching bondage and rope playing—so I could fuel the memory, the fantasy, more fully. Cotton rope against my skin. His warm fingertips brushing my breast. That deliciously dangerous gleam in his eyes, suggesting I'm in deep, deep trouble. That there are things he can show me, filthy, dirty things I don't even know I crave yet.

It's as vivid as if it happened yesterday.

Did I think my invitation would work? Not really.

But here he is. And holy shit, he's so much more than I remember.

Inky curls, tousled and defiant, frame his rugged face. A shadow of stubble sharpens the line of his jaw. A black leather vest clings to his muscled torso, left open to reveal a trail of dark hair disappearing beneath faded, low-slung jeans. Flip-flops are the only nod to the West Coast. Part surfer. Part biker. And judging by the smirk on his lips, a total stud.

I underestimated how commanding a presence he has in person.

He sets the cap on his head and strolls up to the car. "We going somewhere?" he asks in a husky, lazy tone.

Like to my bedroom?

Like to a Hollywood sex club where he can do wicked things to my body?

He rakes his eyes over me like he's comparing the naughty girl in the photo to today's version. I'm wearing a jeans miniskirt, tight crop top, flip-flops, moody silk underwear, and a ridiculously expensive pearl necklace I purchased with my father's credit card. I wear it like a banner, a small victory in the war between his greed and my fight to survive.

"I'm surprised you came."

"Trust me," he replies. "So am I."

Okay. So maybe the pic didn't make him hard for weeks. "Still, you're here."

He skims his eyes over me like he expected bubble gum and Barbie dolls, and found a rare vintage wine. Okay, so I definitely captured his attention.

He tosses a black duffel bag next to my purse in the backseat, then hops over the door, into the passenger seat. "I'm yours for the next few days."

Pure filth fills my mind. Get a grip, Fina. He doesn't mean sex.

He smirks.

Or does he?

He nods toward the mansion on the hill. "Where's your father?"

"Chicago."

His eyes rest on me, yet he doesn't say anything. I mean, what can he say?

"The cameras are glitching again," I reassure him. "No one will know you're here or that we've left together."

His lips curl. "Glitching, huh?"

I raise a shoulder.

Then, we take off.

It's the kind of perfect California day where sunlight cascades over the hills and the ocean waves break on the horizon. The sky stretches wide above, and the crisp coastal air rolls over us. Top down and sunglasses on, my hair catches in the breeze.

The world ours to chase.

And it will be ... it must be.

"Beautiful day," I murmur, glancing his way.

He stretches his long legs lazily, head tilted back against the seat, face basking in the sun. "Beats the humidity back East," he replies effortlessly.

We're talking—it's a start. Light, easy, the kind of conversation that makes twisting him around my finger feel completely doable. Because attraction ... obsession, really ... aside, this is business.

"Ever been in the Pacific Ocean?"

"No." His voice dips into a low, seductive rumble. "If that's where we're headed, I didn't pack a bathing suit."

I can't help a smirk. The things I know about this man ... how little he cares about clothes, for instance ...

Still, beyond a few mafia gatherings and one unforgettable encounter, we don't truly know each other. I've been stalking him on social media for years, so there's that. But to say I'm prepared for the raw, dark masculinity radiating from the seat beside me is an understatement.

"How have you been?"

He smirks. Just that.

I press on. "And your father? How is he?"

"Ambitious."

A single word is all he gives me.

"And your brother?" Gag me.

He snorts. "Like you give a rat's ass about Sandro. Are we going to keep playing nicey-nice, or are we going to get to why I'm really here?"

I frown. "Nicey-nice."

He leans over, snatches my sunglasses from my face, and casually flings them over his shoulder.

"What the hell, asshole?" I shout, watching them tumble into the canyon to our right. "They were Prada." Bought with my father's credit card, one of the few rewards after he backhanded me for being sick and missing that trip to Chicago to meet Carlo. I *earned* those sunglasses.

"Now they're nada."

Fury sparks through me as I lock eyes with him. "I forgot what a self-serving dick you are."

He chuckles. "There she is. Hiding behind the niceties."

"I'm not hiding?"

"No? Then where's the girl brave enough to, out of the fucking blue, send me a daring, naughty picture, and reminding me what a budding deviant lurks beneath the princess shell?" He reaches into his pocket, pulls out a tightly rolled paper, sparks it, and draws in a deep drag. The sweet, pungent scent of marijuana curls around us. "To answer your question, I was bored shitless until that picture showed up."

"Must be nice, that luxury of boredom."

"For most, yeah. But for me? It's dangerous. Boredom brings on my darkest vices."

I tilt my head, studying him more carefully. He's a powerful mafioso's wild, rule-breaking son, yet boredom is what he finds dangerous? Fascinating.

On the surface, it's golf outings, social gatherings, the occasional mafia affair. But beneath the pretty picture he presents, his world is deliciously wicked, filled with underground fight clubs, high-end sex clubs, nights ripe with drugs, whiskey, and sin. Renzo thrives on flirting, with anything on two legs *and* with destruction. If I could capture a fraction of that life, one small nibble of that forbidden freedom, I'd feel alive in ways I've only imagined.

But freedom in any way, shape, or form is why I lured him here.

"I'm like a starved animal." He takes a long drag of his joint, then slowly releases smoke into the air. "My mind craves stimulation."

Hiding my interest, I roll my eyes. "Is that why you dull your senses?"

"I wish marijuana were the cure."

I snort. "Not just marijuana. Booze. Drugs. Picking fights with dangerous mafiosi, like Luciano Santoro?"

Silence fills the space between us.

"You keeping tabs on me?"

I bite my lip, weighing my words. I don't want to scare him off, but fear isn't a language he understands, is it? Fuck it. "You insinuated Luciano Santoro is a kiss-ass."

"He's all up in Dante Lucchese's business."

"You didn't just disrespect him, you dissed the Youngbloods too."

Everyone in the Life knows the savage way the Italian Youngbloods became made men, by luring a small army of enemies into a trap and setting them ablaze. It was twisted, gruesome, a spectacle of fire and fear, and the famiglie have been relishing every detail ever since.

Renzo takes another drag.

I've watched his life play out like a film, front-row to a starring role in a world of dark depravity. Lorenzo Beneventi at twenty-one was already a deviant. The man beside me, silently studying me, is sharper, wilder, more alive … more everything … than I remember.

He leans across the console to whisper in my ear, then gently blows smoke in my face. "You're a piece of work, know that?"

"Bet you wish we stuck to the fucking niceties?"

His laughter makes me smile. Lord, when was the last time I'd done so?

Since he knows I looked him up online, I appease my curiosity. "Explain something to me."

He relaxes back in his seat. "Shoot."

"I don't understand the appeal of underground fights."

His head pivots toward me. "Jesus. You know about them?"

Renzo rarely posts, but other fight club participants do.

I air-quote the hashtag I saw. "#unstoppable." I was shocked yet thrilled after discovering Renzo's battered, bleeding mug shot.

"You're a goddamn stalker, know that?"

I grin. "There she is."

"You want into my psyche? Fine. I fight and fuck to let out the aggression."

I swallow hard, clamping down on the wickedly delicious image of him fucking out his aggression. Wishing I'd found more footage of that online.

"Why not the gym like the other mafiosi?"

He shakes his head. "Not hardcore enough. Nothing beats a bloody battle or deep penetration, especially when I've tied her up and she's at my complete fucking mercy."

I'm pretty sure the last part's meant to shock me.

"As hardcore as snorting coke off Roberto Ferrara's girlfriend's ass before fucking her and her friend?"

He chokes on the joint.

"Don Ferrara is livid ..."

"I didn't fuck them."

I raise an eyebrow. "No?"

"Just watched," he admits, wheels churning while he figures out how I know about this specific ménage à trois. To his credit, he's quick. "I erased the picture her friend posted within minutes." He chokes out a gruff laugh. Like I disturbed his already bent sensibilities. "You obsessed with me or something?"

I pluck the joint from his fingers and take a drag. Another first with this man. "Or something."

"What, do you have alerts set with my name?"

I blow smoke, mimicking his actions, and give nothing away.

"Shit. You fucking do." His eyes spark with admiration. "For how long?"

Now that he knows—and hasn't demanded I pull over or given any signs of disgust—it's kind of exhilarating. *He gets me,* I think.

If I was fascinated with him before, I'm enraptured now.

"Why?" he demands.

I offer up a partial truth. "Just a woman in the Life, struggling to see how the other half lives. Try being a woman in this world. I wish I were someone else. Off grid, like a plumber's daughter. A person whose worth is more than a bargaining chip." I take another drag. "Someone like you, who does whatever the fuck he wants. Whose father gives a rat's ass what the famiglie think."

He silently considers me. "You think it's easy being Sebastiano Beneventi's son?"

"Hell yeah. Try being the only Lombardi child."

"We playing a game now? Who Has It Worse?" He falls back in the seat. "You're smoking crack if you think my life's rainbows and butterflies."

"One of my earliest memories of my father is when he came home one day, covered in blood and carrying a box. I asked him what was inside—thinking the blood was ketchup from the In-N-Out burgers inside the box that somehow exploded all over him. I was six, and persistent."

"Hard to imagine it," he mutters.

"I crept into his office while he slept. The box was wrapped in a towel on the floor, and inside was a man's head. It was the first time I recognized my father wasn't a plumber but a predator. I learned quickly to always be a step ahead of him or my life will end up like the head in the box."

"Your father's a hot-tempered asshole." He runs his fingers across his jaw. "And mine will have me collecting bodies in boxes after the trip to Rome next week. He'll push for me to step up. I feel it in my bones."

My eyes widen. "Step up—like as a made man?"

His lips flatten, like he's already said too much.

I hold still, watching him, waiting for more. The weed must've loosened his tongue, because he finally exhales the truth. "You think my life is mine? My old man gave me time, but that clock ran out. He made it clear; when it's my turn, I take my place. No excuses. No bullshit."

"You're worried about killing a man?"

His eyes cut to me, sharp, almost warning. "Shit. You shouldn't even know that."

I roll my eyes.

"Worried isn't the word I'd use." He pinches the tip of the joint, examines it, then drops it into the Mustang's vintage ashtray. My father will notice it eventually, and I make a mental note to toss it later. "I don't want cookie-cutter. The same dull routine, day in and day out. That's how institutions decay, how people lose their minds, drowning in the monotony of wasted days."

My breath catches. He's navigating the Life, just like me.

"I spent years dying a slow death, fueled by adrenaline, proving life outside the famiglie existed, and still came up short. Time's up. If I'm asked to step up, I will. And it's not like I shy away from violence … I thrive on it. I'll bleed, fight, obey, do whatever it takes to earn my place as a mafioso. I owe my father that much."

"What if you escape the famiglie? Disappear somewhere and start fresh?"

"I'm Lorenzo Beneventi. My fate's sealed."

"You're giving up."

"I'm being realistic."

I shake my head, a bitter edge to my voice. "Then we want different things. Me? I want out of the Life. I want a shot at living my life."

Lord, even my tone when I say the words "my life" sounds hopeless.

"So do it."

I snort, incredulous. "Now who's being unrealistic?"

He looks at me. Really looks at me. "Want to know what I'd do?"

Up ahead, a tumbleweed rolls adrift, carefree, until it snags on the roadside brush, leaving it to be ripped apart by a harsh, unforgiving world.

"Ruin myself?" I demand. "Fuck every Tom, Dick, and Giuseppe so a complete stranger I've yet to meet doesn't get the virgin bride he paid for? Hope he'll annul the wedding?" I make a face. "He'll kill me. And if he doesn't, my father will."

"You're a virgin?"

I blink. "That's what you got out of all this?" Unbelievable.

"Trust me. Fucking your way to freedom's overrated."

I scowl. This is my future he's callously joking about.

"You have a place in mind where you'd go? Abroad, preferably?"

"Yes."

"And money?"

I shake my head.

"You've time to figure that part out."

The tumbleweed I've been tracking breaks free from the brush as we speed by, and I'm suddenly lighter.

"When is your asshole father returning again?"

A flutter of excitement licks across me. "A few days."

He smiles. "Let's drive to Vegas."

My jaw drops. "You're going to marry me?"

He jerks back like I slapped him. "Marry? No fucking way."

The thought deeply disturbs him, I can see it on his face. Lord, I feel like sinking between the springs in this seat.

"Jesus. Nothing personal. I'm not the marrying type, is all."

"You said we'd go to Vegas," I grind out. "What else would I think?"

"Look. Your father runs California. Vegas is Luca Ricci's territory and a safer bet. I'll find the best location where you can get what you need—bogus birth certificates, social security cards, and several passports."

I immediately warm up to the idea. "Okay."

"As for disappearing, follow the three Ds; dodge, distract, and delay." He holds up a finger, mimicking my earlier actions. "Plant so many false leads your father's head will spin." A second finger joins the first. "Lay breadcrumbs for him to follow, far away from your actual escape route." Finger number three rises. "Use decoys dressed like you. If you time everything out, there can be a Fina sighting in San Diego, then another on the Mexico border in thirty minutes."

"I've two high school friends who despise my father."

"Lie. Tell them it's a game."

My friends know little about my family, or how important my father's position is in the famiglie. No reasonable person would aid a mafioso's daughter's escape.

"Rent a private plane in cash from a small airport. You need to be in the air soon after you leave your house. You can pick up an international flight from Denver. By the time the trail you've laid runs cold, you'll hopefully be somewhere safe."

"I don't know if I can pull it off."

He snorts.

I bite my lip, considering his words.

"Turn the car around."

My heart skips a beat. "You'll help me?"

"Yeah, I'll help you."

I don't hesitate. I jerk the wheel, spin us around, and aim northeast. Hope swells in my chest, reckless and hungry. If anyone can help me out of this Life, it's Renzo Beneventi.

"Wait," he commands. "I'll rent a car."

"Why?"

He tilts his head back, eyes rolling skyward like I'm the reckless one here. "He'll know."

"Relax," I counter. "I'll have it washed and polished to a fine shine, before I roll back the mileage."

His eyes catch the light, all dark sparks and wicked amusement.

Lord, he's devastating. A mind more devious, more clever than mine. But his laughter, low and sinful, tells me he sees straight through me ... and appreciates every twisted inch.

HOURS LATER, THE CAR BREAKS DOWN ON THE MOJAVE FAIRWAY a few miles southwest of the Nevada state border.

"No. No. No," I chant, hitting the steering wheel. Everything had gone perfectly. The four-hour ride to Vegas to pick up a fake ID and passport that Renzo had called in as a favor. The research he did on his phone to kill time, where he jotted down the private airports closest to Los Angeles, the cost to hire a plane, and contact numbers to make arrangements. Our animated discussion about the pros and cons of executing my escape, the main pro being my father underestimating my resourcefulness, and the main con being ... well, duh ... caught. When my father hacks my phone records, searching for answers, he'll find nothing. No cell tower dings—I turned my phone off at the house. No clues as to how I arranged a fake identity or transportation. With Renzo taking charge, I'll remain a ghost in all this.

I'm practically head-over-heels for this man. He's not only gorgeous, in a wildly untamed way, but wicked smart. He seems to have an answer for everything.

"He'll know I took his car."

This strikes Renzo's funny bone, and his laughter's a deep, warm rumble.

"This is a disaster."

"Fina. You riddled the cherry red paint with enough dents a demolition derby driver would applaud you. And I'm pretty damn sure you smashed the back fender while parking outside the casino."

Yeah, I was worried about the reason behind the crunching sound.

I curse my spitefulness for not being the slightest bit careful with my father's precious car, despite common sense urging me to do so. "What am I going to tell him?" My fingers tighten around the steering wheel. "He'll pound me to a pulp."

What I'm more concerned about, besides a few bruises, is that my father will realize I wasn't where I was supposed to be. That his perfect mafia princess not only escaped her cage but was plotting to destroy it.

I was close ... so close ... to freedom.

Hope is a dangerous illusion. It creeps in, slow and seductive, until it owns you. Until you learn all over again the reasons you should be afraid. It drowns out doubts and strangles caution. Leaves you open and vulnerable to the pain that always follows.

I used to stare out the window, day after day, waiting for my mother's return. Weeks and months spent hoping she would.

She never did.

My father made sure she wouldn't.

Today went too smoothly. Too easily. I let myself believe I might escape this marriage, might carve out a future that's mine. A dangerous lie I fed myself, one destined to fail.

But I do hope. I still have it in me.

I press my forehead to the steering wheel, so caught up in beating myself up, it takes a moment to realize Renzo's dead silent.

"He beats you?"

I sit up, blinking in confusion. Not at his question—sadly—but at the assumption my father, with his anger management issues and violent nature, wouldn't smack me around. My father's notorious for his temper tantrums. "Well, yeah."

Renzo makes a low, ominous sound deep within his throat, and my lips part in surprise. He never considered I'd be a punching bag? "Less now since I learned to be one step—"

"Motherfucker."

Violence rolls off him, thick, volatile, and impossible to ignore. I'm stunned, not just by its intensity, but by how wrong it feels coming from a man who lights every room with chaos and charm. The jokester. The reckless daredevil. The wild hell-raiser who bends rules like they're toys. He's the "kind" Beneventi. The one everyone whispers is the softest of the three. The least dangerous.

Some say the weak link.

I was raised as a mafioso's daughter. Spent years assessing the merits of the men in the famiglie. Tracking who holds power, who issues it, and who makes others choke on it. I never considered Renzo weak—far from it. But the look in his eyes now unsettles me, and I almost laugh. Because I see the truth within the contradiction.

His darkness doesn't just wound. It devours.

They're wrong. All of them. His muscled body's built for violence, like other mafiosi. But it's the merciless sharpness of his mind that's most lethal.

Holy hell. How do they not see the cold, calculated predator within him?

Because he hides it well.

Almost like he'd rather not be recognized.

"If I kill that fucker, all your problems are solved."

I lunge at him, catching him off guard, arms thrown around his shoulders as I scatter kisses over his cheek. He's on my side. He cares.

I don't know when it shifts. When my nipples harden against his chest. When my mouth finds his. When his eyes turn black with promise.

All I know is suddenly I'm straddling him, lips crushed to his.

God, his kiss is aggressive, his tongue torment, his lips potent.

My whole world spins.

I shift my hips, then rub my crotch against the thick bulge in his jeans.

He curls my long hair around his fingers, immobilizing me while he devours me like he hasn't kissed a woman in a long time. It's a ridiculous notion; this man notoriously goes through women like dirty socks, dirty being the key word. I've had a few clumsy kisses in the high school hallway and one less-than-spectacular groping session beneath the stadium bleachers.

I try to tug away, to remind him I'm a virgin.

If anything, my resistance spurs him on.

His kiss deepens, his tongue violently tangling with mine until I'm lightheaded. Fingers squeeze a nipple, the brief sting melting into excitement.

I arch into him with a sharp gasp. "Again. Harder."

His gaze locks with mine, those infamous baby-blue Beneventi eyes darkening to something dangerous. His palm drags slowly across my stomach, the heat of his touch searing a path upward until it claims my chest, his fingertips mapping me like a man carving out his territory. I bite my lip as he cups my breast over my bra, weighing its worth in his palm. A more ruthless pinch to my nipple sends a shock wave crackling down my spine, igniting my core until I'm trembling.

He watches me, silent and merciless, studying my reaction. His voice drops, low and rough. "What am I going to do with you?"

It's a rhetorical question.

Still, I have an answer, one he can't refuse.

I reach for my purse, dig inside it, and retrieve the shibari rope I special ordered. After the photo of me bound, I tossed it inside my purse and forgot about it.

Until now.

He glances at it, then cocks his head at me. "You carry that around in your bag?"

"Lucky you," I murmur.

I wait, with breathless anticipation, for him to react to my invitation. When he doesn't, I push harder. "To be clear, you can tie me up, then fuck me."

His jaw twitches, but otherwise, he gives nothing away. Is he shocked? Interested?

Or is he feeling too experienced for a novice like me?

He finally speaks, but not before lifting me off him, setting me on my feet, and exiting the car. "Why do I feel like this is a trap?"

I climb out, then round the hood. "It's not."

"You don't know what you're asking."

Is he testing me?

"Sure I do."

His eyes narrow.

"I studied your kinks. The spankings. Bondage. Dominant tendencies." Lord, my voice quivers when I say the last words. Not only have I followed him closely, but I inserted myself into each explicit scene. If the hot flush covering my body is any indication, I'm pretty sure I'd get off as much as he does. "You especially love restraining women." I tap his chest with the rope. "And I want to experience my first time, restrained."

I turn, press my stomach into the chrome and cross my wrists behind my back, while locking eyes with him over my shoulder.

He rubs his fingers across his rugged jawline.

I wiggle my bottom.

"This is a bad decision, babe."

I roll my eyes. "I know."

"You don't," he snaps, then taps a finger to his temple. "This fucking brain. When the switch flips, I'm all frost." He steps toward me, then leans over until his breath tickles my earlobe. "Sex barely keeps the beast at bay. You really want to tread that fine line?"

Lord, this deliciously dark side of Renzo is thrilling.

"Maybe I step straight over it?" I softly murmur. "Maybe, like in the Life, with you the only way to survive is to cross the line everyone else is afraid of?"

He hesitates.

"Or is it you're afraid? Is it because I'm a virgin?"

"Fucking hell it is."

"You never popped a cherry before?" I lick my lips, and his eyes track the gesture.

"You tell me, you little fucking stalker."

It's laughable—the answer's so straight-up obvious. Virgins aren't anywhere near the places he frequents.

"Perfect," I say. "I'll be your first."

"Fina. Fina. Fina."

I do what I must and strip. The denim miniskirt slides down my legs, the cropped shirt pulled overhead, revealing the black lace bra and matching thong. The pearls stay, draped around my neck like a challenge, glinting against my skin. I flash an inviting smile over my shoulder, then put an exclamation point on my assault. "Tie me up, Renzo, and then make my tight virgin pussy bleed all over the leather backseat."

His eyes flash, seconds before he snaps.

He grabs the rope from where I tossed it on the hood and unwinds it around his hand. Slowly, methodically, eye-fucking me with a thunderous expression ... It steals my breath.

I still, like a deer trapped in headlights, when his fingers brush my nipples, a passing caress as he expertly removes my black bra, then hooks a finger into the thin strip of my thong and tears it off me. My heart pounds as he threads the rope around my body, my skin coming alive beneath the silky weave.

"No pink today?"

"It's my day off."

He grunts, then kicks my legs apart, looping the material around each thigh, then behind my back and around my wrists until I'm completely immobile, his to do with as he will. By the time he's done, I'm vibrating with need.

"Look at you," he grinds out from behind me. "Like a fucking piece of artwork." I tense as he approaches. "Acting so innocent, the perfect mafia princess, but inside you're just as fucked up as I am."

He dips his hands between my thighs.

No hiding my excitement now, even if I wanted to.

"So wet. You crave the darkness, don't you?"

"Yes, Renzo."

He winds my hair around his fist, and the loose ends trail down his arm. With a tug, he jerks my head around, and our eyes lock. "I'm in control of your body and words. You do exactly as I say. Act without permission, and I'll punish you."

I whimper.

"Are you my fucktoy, Fina? Mine to do with as I please?"

"Yes."

"Louder."

"I'm your eager fucktoy. Do whatever you want to me."

His smile's downright sinful.

"Oh, I want, babe. I want."

He forces my head forward, and I eagerly listen, wondering what his next move will be. When his fingertips curl against my nerve bundle, everything goes on sensory overload. "Stalked me for years, haven't you?" he demands, dragging my hood between two fingers, the pressure exquisite. "Know all my kinks, you say?" His middle finger glides across my clit and through my wet center. "A little nosy perv touching herself while she looked me up on social media, isn't that right?" He roughly circles the pads of his fingers over my sensitive clit until I'm close to bursting.

He jerks my hair. "Not yet. Your first will be on my command."

Without warning, he pushes three fingers inside, raising me onto my toes, then thrusts in deeper, eliciting a small cry. It's intense, exquisitely so. My pulse races while I try not to shatter.

"Fuck. You can barely take my digits." Reverence fills his tone, and any concerns about my lack of experience and not living up to this wildly sexual man's demands vanish.

"I'll share a secret." He leans in, nips an earlobe, his fingers working me into a frenzy. "I'm harder for your virgin pink pussy right now than I've been in years."

"Please ..."

"This why you sent me that picture? You like being tied up and at my mercy?"

My knees buckle, but the rope keeps me propped upright. "God, yes."

His laughter rumbles in the air. "My virgin slut's begging to be destroyed by my thick, fat dick?"

Shaking and quivering, I clench around his fingers, wanting more, the greedy girl in me growing impatient with need. "Please, Renzo."

"Please what, Fina?"

"Please stop talking and make me come."

Silence stills the air. He releases my hair and withdraws his fingers. All my senses come alive as I wait for his next move.

A smack on my ass makes me jump, and he follows it with several others. It stings slightly, though the way I'm tied partially protects me. He presses his palm over his handprint, feeling the warm burn. I'm unsure if I like being spanked, but what I do know is, after our day together, I trust him. Blindly, foolishly so, but I do.

I want my firsts with him, even more now than in my wildest fantasies.

My breath catches, the world going utterly still at the faint rustle behind me. Then heat envelops me, his heat, as his chest presses flush against my back, his arms banding around me like iron. I'm trapped in a cage of muscle, his body stealing another demand from my lips before I can voice it.

Get on with it.

Make me come.

A calloused hand claims a breast, kneading it, while the other drags down my stomach, purposeful, hunting. My gasp splinters the silence when he pinches my nipple, sharp and electric, at the same moment his fingers breach me. Two thick digits curl deep, and my body bows helplessly into his hold.

"Shhh," he rasps at my ear, a command ripe with menace. "You wanted me quiet. So not a fucking sound from you either."

His palm grinds against my clit with every slow thrust of his fingers, the double assault short-circuiting my mind. Sparks scatter through me as my body ignites. His hard length hot against the curve of my ass, the heat of his skin branding mine.

"The backseat," I beg, breathless.

His laugh is wicked, cruelly patient. "You don't get my cock until I taste you. Until I lick your orgasm off my fingers."

My core clenches, betraying me, betraying how close I already am. God, why did I silence his filthy mouth when every obscene word he says wrecks me?

He doesn't give me what I crave. He doesn't thrust harder. Instead, he drags it out, slowing, teasing, torturing, until I'm frantic. I push against his hand, desperate, and he rewards me with teeth grazing my earlobe, his other hand punishing my neglected nipple until pain and pleasure twist into something blinding.

I bite my lip, but the dam inside me breaks. Sensation swells and crashes, sweeping me high.

"Come for me," he orders, voice raw, his lips brushing the tender hollow of my throat.

And I do. I shatter in his arms, riding wave after devastating wave, undone by his words, his lips, his masterful fingers, and the unbearable perfection of it all. My first time with a man, and he's already wrecked me.

He withdraws, spins me around, then holds up his come-stained fingers.

My lips part as his tongue sweeps across them, and the soft hum that follows is the sweetest music I've ever heard. I'll never forget that sound, or the feral gleam burning in his eyes.

His smirk is wicked and knowing, as if he understands the havoc he's wreaking inside me. Watching him lick my release from his fingers doesn't just ignite lust. It unleashes something far more dangerous. A hunger to be possessed. A need to be claimed so completely that nothing of me exists outside of him.

He's my wicked fantasy gone viral.

"Fucking hell, Fina."

Yeah, he's feeling it, too.

He licks his lips, getting every last drop.

Turning me on, so I practically swoon.

He prowls forward, and my heart rate accelerates. "I'm nowhere close to done, babe," he grinds out. Then he grips my hips, hauls me up, and with effortless strength, tosses me onto the backseat. The rope bites my skin as he climbs over the chrome, then over me, filling every inch of space until there's nowhere to run, even if I could run.

"Tell me what you think you want."

"What I want is to bleed all over you and the backseat."

His lips flatten, his eyes narrowing. "This about revenge?"

"At first, maybe." I soften, though my pulse still riots. "But now it's about me, and you."

The scowl that follows cuts deep, and for a moment I'm sure he'll spring away and leave me empty. It's a well-known fact he's not commitment material. The memory of a social media post I once read resurfaces: Lover of many, boyfriend of none.

Why would I be any different?

Something flickers in his gaze, something raw and unguarded, before he growls, "Fuck it." His mouth crashes onto mine, brutal and

consuming, but beneath the violence I taste his hunger, his commitment to this moment.

And right now, it's all I need.

His tongue thrusts deep, demanding and punishing, yet
desperate too, like he can't decide if he wants to ruin me or save
himself.

I gasp into him, reckless with a dangerous, desperate need.

"No," I murmur when he withdraws.

Then I catch his expression, and everything stills. Every wicked
thing he's thinking is there for me to see. His charm. His possessive-
ness. And as his eyes harden, even the darker side ready to destroy me.

Eyes locked on mine, he licks two fingers, then positions them
and drives home.

I raise my hips as far as the rope allows, offering him deeper
access.

He increases the pressure, and I see stars.

"You're fucking perfect, you know that?" he grinds out. "Beautifully twisted in all the right ways."

My eyes widen as pleasure crashes through me like thunder.

His gaze darkens, startling me with its intensity. "Goddamn it. I
need another taste first."

I whimper when he pulls away, my body aching at the sudden
loss. He bites his lower lip while adjusting the ropes around me,
spreading my thighs wider. When he's satisfied, a dangerous smile
curves his mouth. "Nothing between me and you now."

He pushes me back across the seat, his head lowering between
my thighs.

Then the true assault begins.

I read about this. Imagined him there, devouring me. But none of
my fantasies prepared me for the reality of his mouth on me.

His tongue is relentless, possessive, unrestrained. He licks, dives,
explores every aching inch of my pussy until I am gasping. "Oh,"
bursts from my lips, followed by a ragged, "Oh, yes."

He pauses long enough to catch my clit between his teeth. The sharp pinch makes me cry out, but he soothes it away with his tongue, easing the sting. Is this a warning of what's to come? Or the price of surrendering to such a dangerously sinful man?

My second orgasm strikes quickly, faster than I can brace for, stealing my breath. I throw my head back with a moan as he works me through it, merciless and masterful, leaving me trembling beneath his mouth.

"That was for you," he informs me, rolling to his knees as he stares down at me, his lips, mouth, chin coated in my wetness. He slaps my pussy, and the fog from my orgasm clears. Another slap, and he has my complete attention.

My eyes drop to the hand squeezing his dick.

I'm struck speechless at the sight. His dick's gorgeous. Long and thick, the head perfectly symmetrical and flushed with blood. It's pretty like the rest of him. Too pretty for the punishment he puts it through.

"That's right. Look your fill. Know what's about to break open your perfect pussy."

A low hum slips from my throat.

"I want to see your come mixed with blood dripping down me."

He grips my knees and drags me closer, stroking himself, sending a sharp, delicious heat sparking between us.

The first brush of him at my entrance has my hips shifting restlessly. His thrust comes fast, deep, and merciless, tearing a cry from my lips. Tears sting my eyes at the sudden stretch, the ache of being split apart. It hurts, yes, but the thought of him filling me so ruthlessly, so completely, sends excitement spiraling through me.

"Fuck. Fuck. Fuck," he chants, and then he does exactly that. He drives into me at a punishing pace, crashing through every barrier, forcing my body to yield and take every blessed inch.

His fingers roll over my clit, and I gasp, body caught between pain and pleasure.

"That's it. Look at my naughty girl taking my dick so fucking good."

He shifts, angling deeper, and I swear he touches places inside me I didn't know existed.

Skin on skin, raw and unprotected. The thought flashes through me like lightning. We never even discussed a condom. "I'm on the pill," I moan between ragged breaths. Hopefully he has been careful. I should have thought about this. He should have, too.

"We discussing this now?" his voice grates, breathless. "Fine. I've never fucked without a condom. Ever." He stills, just for a moment, and I swear he thickens inside me. "But with you, the thought of my seed mixing with your come and virgin blood drives me insane. Capisci?"

"Yes," I whisper. "I understand."

"Good. Now fucking hang on."

"I can't. My hands are bound above my head."

He stiffens. "You asking me to stop?"

I wiggle and thrust. "Don't you dare."

Leaning forward, he presses a gentle kiss on my lips.

I blink in surprise.

He grins. "You ready to be completely fucked?"

Why do I get the feeling he means more than the physical act?

Before I can answer, he thrusts deep, his full weight pressing into me. Again and again, relentless, consuming. My body strains to hold him. Good Lord, he is going to split me in two. But the thought only makes me want it more.

He lowers his head, claiming the swell of my breast with his lips. Marking me, owning me. His palms grip my ass and lift me, tilting my body, angling him deeper inside me until I can no longer tell where I end and he begins. Perhaps that is the point. There is no beginning or end. There's only us.

My first time is nothing like flowers or chocolate, rainbows or magic. It is gloriously painful, exquisitely pleasurable, and knowing he is savoring every second sends me soaring.

"Fuck yeah. That's it. Come for me, Fina. While I fill your sweet body with my seed."

I go off like a rocket, body collapsing around him. He drives in deeper, sprawling atop me, warmth flooding me from the inside out. Our hearts hammer in unison as we pant together, spent and trembling.

I make the mistake of thinking this is it—the kinkiest moment I've ever experienced.

He rolls up, withdrawing, then dips his fingers inside me. My throat hitches when I see the blood mingled with our come, dripping and oozing down my thighs. His eyes linger on the mess, fascinated, as if imprinting a memory for later.

Then his gaze snaps to mine. Slowly, deliberately, he drags the wet mixture across his chest, tracing circles around his nipples and crisscrossing his abdomen, like he's making a ritualistic marking. Like he is branding himself with me.

He returns to my sex, repeating the motion, leaving a sticky, slick trail across my skin.

Pleased with his work, he licks his fingers clean. The wicked, deliberate act sends a bolt of lightning straight to my core, igniting every nerve ending, like dry brush in the firestorm that is Renzo.

Minutes tick by, so many I lose count. My mind numb, my senses tangled in knots.

"Shit, you're crashing." Without another word, he frees me from the rope and tosses it aside. His hands pull my trembling body into his lap, anchoring me. "Shhh," he murmurs, his voice unexpectedly calm. "Adrenaline rush."

I melt into his chest, accepting the comfort he offers. My pulse is still wild, my body still shaking.

For a long moment, he says nothing. Then softly, "Look, Fina ..."

"I'm fine," I lie. Because I'm anything but fine. I'm already in too deep, drowning fast, desperate for him to keep holding me up. "I wanted this."

"That's not what I was going to say."

I lean back and look up at him. In unguarded moments like this, I see him clearly. The clever wheels in his mind are turning, pulling him toward a conclusion he clearly hates.

"Fuck."

My heart jumps; my fingers reflexively reach for the pearls at my throat. But they're gone, lost somewhere between the car and the desert earth. I don't need a damn necklace to prove I'll survive anymore. The weight it carried and the small comfort it gave me are no longer necessary after today. "What is it?" I whisper.

"I want to do more to help you."

I frown, not understanding. "Okay ..."

His jaw tightens. "I don't want to, but ... we're getting married."

The blunt declaration hits me like a shock wave. "What?" I spring from his lap then straddle his thighs, facing him.

"After Rome, I'll go to my father. If he agrees—"

I cut him off. "You will?" Hope bursts inside me, fierce and unexpected. Lorenzo Beneventi is untouchable. If I marry him, neither Carlo nor my father can touch me. It's why I approached him with the same idea when I was sixteen, where he didn't just shoot me down but ran away.

He curses under his breath.

"When? My wedding to Carlo is on my twenty-first birthday."

His entire body stiffens. "That miserable bastard couldn't wait to have you."

I flash him a teasing smile, trying to lighten the weight pressing down. "Won't be my first."

But he doesn't smile back. Instead, the air chills, the warmth between us icing over as if he regrets opening his mouth. As if he is already retreating.

"You sure about this?" I demand.

"Like I said earlier, I'm not husband material. Not now, not ever. Don't get your hopes up, and don't fall in love with me. We'll marry, then divorce. You'll be free. That's all this is."

The words cut through me, sharp and piercing. I hide the sting behind a sigh and say lightly, "You're so romantic."

His mouth curves into something almost like a smile, but his eyes stay bright with warning. "And you're obsessive."

I brush my lips against his, a gentle seal on our agreement. "I guess if it is a marriage in name only, there will be no more sex."

The heat flares back into his gaze, tension rippling through him. I wink, letting him off the hook, and climb off his lap.

The sun slips below the horizon as we dress in silence. The desert stretches endlessly around us, painted in reds and golds while the sky melts into night. Even as darkness falls, the world feels brighter. Possibilities I never dared imagine flicker across the horizon, promising a life I can almost touch.

My eyes drift to the backseat. "The leather is ruined," I murmur. "My father will be livid."

He laughs behind me. The sound should warm me, but it carries something brittle, something false. A warning I am too dazed from wicked sex and fragile hope to fully hear.

Instinctively, I ask, "You promise?"

He holds my gaze, silent and unreadable. A slight nod is all I get, but it's enough. "Better call us an Uber," he says flatly, and stalks away.

I cling to his promise with both hands.

Cling without knowing it is hollow.

Cling without knowing what I'm holding is a cruel lie.

5

Renzo

Present

I lie here on the floor in my father's office, eyes pinned to the ceiling like the cracks above might spell out the meaning of my fucked-up existence. Instead, all I see is her face. Her beautiful stricken expression. The fire still burning in her eyes. Her disappointment. The loathing. She looked at me like I was something deranged, something already damned.

And I am.

The truth? In a weak and impulsive moment, I caved. Chasing that high like it was oxygen. I let it crawl under my skin and hollow me out, because it's easier to feed the craving than to face myself.

They say the first step to solving a problem is acknowledging you have one. Like my efforts to escape my destiny are the issue, when it's the Life I dread.

Except the path I swore I wanted is stale and rotten. As with most things, I've grown bored with living a life of excess. Waking up in strange beds, getting off on the thrill of a punch, flashing a middle finger at the mafiosi around me—my father, my brother—believing the world I occupy is superior to their tightly rigid one.

I don't see life through rose-colored glasses. I see it through shot glasses.

And I've become exactly who they said I was.

Broken. Messy. Weak.

I've dragged everyone down with me—especially Elia Seraphina … Accardo.

My hand balls into a fist. Why the fuck didn't she run? Why didn't she take the out and disappear? She was halfway there; I'd made sure of it. But instead she put her faith in a bullshit promise from a man who'd just buried himself inside the tightest, sweetest pussy he'd ever had, then thought he owned her because of it.

Christ. I told her months ago I wasn't her savior. Thought she was smart enough to save herself.

But I was wrong.

I failed her.

And I deserve every ounce of her hatred.

"Renzo?" my father's new wife calls out, dragging me back from the darkness. Her soft footsteps approach, then I feel her hovering over me. "What are you doing on the floor? Are you okay?" The concern in her tone is a knife between my ribs.

Growing worried by my silence, Alessia nudges me with her foot.

I grab her ankle, just like I did when we first met. "Your panties red, angel?"

She wiggles free, then sinks to the floor, her wedding dress billowing as she rolls onto her back beside me. "My panties aren't your concern."

"But we were almost married."

Yeah, that's the really fucked-up part about what I've done. I pitched the idea of marrying Alessia to my father after I'd already promised Fina we'd marry. Like I could juggle two lives, play savior twice, and come out clean. My mind bent on this crazy-ass plan—marry one to free her, marry the other to save her.

In the end, I fucked them both over.

I just hope Fina never learns the truth. She deserves more than the pain I've caused her.

I turn to Alessia. "Don't you have wedding guests to greet?"

"Family is more important."

Too sweet to be a Beneventi, yet here she is. And she's glowing.

"You're happy?" I ask.

"I love him, Renzo. Desperately. So yes, I'm happy."

I give her a look. "Even with him being capo di tutti capi?"

"I know who he is, what he is. But I also know what we are."

"Kinky motherfuckers?"

Her blush betrays her, but she doesn't deny it. "We're twin flames destined to burn together."

"Sounds hot."

Her laugh rings through the library. "Oh, it is."

Nausea twists in my gut. I admire her acceptance, but it only makes me sicker.

"How's the new therapist? My father said you'd like her."

I shrug. "I like every inch of my new therapist."

"Renzo, you didn't?"

I wonder why people like sweet Alessia still have faith in me, and way more than I deserve. Yeah, I fucked the therapist. Not because I wanted fixing. Because keeping her busy with my body meant she couldn't get inside my head. Truth is, random fucks are growing old. Everything is.

Except for Fina's tight body milking me dry in the back of that car. Nothing compares, and I cling to that motherfucking memory like the undeserving prick I am.

"Bastian said you would." She sighs. "I owe him money."

I grunt. "That's what you get for betting on me."

"I'll always bet in your favor, Renzo."

Fuck. Here we go.

"She's a professional. Open up. Talk to her. Let her help."

"Open up?" I let out a low laugh, shaking my head. "What's in me isn't for the weak. Anyone soft enough to look inside wouldn't walk out the same."

"Renzo, as your friend, accept that you've taken things too far and fix it."

"I'm on it."

"Are you?"

Fucking hell. "Yeah."

She searches my face, finds nothing, lets it go. "Good."

I roll to my feet and help her up. "Better get you back to the celebration."

She stands on her toes and kisses my cheek. "Nice chatting with you, son."

I smirk. "Mom."

Smoothing her dress, she starts for the door.

"Wait," I say, my tone strained.

Her eyes snap wide.

"I'm surprised my father invited the Accardos."

"The Accardos?"

"Yeah. Carlo and his new wife."

"You mean Carlo Accardo, the guy bankrolling half the Midwest casino expansion? Your father barely tolerates him. He's not famiglia. Why would we invite him to our wedding?"

"His new bride was at the church."

Her eyes narrow. "Elia?"

Fuck. I only asked to check if Fina's okay, but I can see Alessia piecing it together. "It's her, isn't it? The one you're obsessed with. The one you chased to California, who told you to fuck off?"

Who I chased to California twice. Once, that ended with a promise, the second, that ended us.

"Elia Lombardi accompanied her father."

I stare at her like she sprouted two heads. "She's not with Carlo?"

"Their wedding was postponed. Out of respect for the new capo di tutti capi ... who I married today."

Relief lands like a punch straight to my chest. I know what this is

—a second chance. For the first time in months, I can actually breathe.

I rake a hand through my hair. *Fuck it if Sandro gets the happy ending and I get the rumors.* With that thought, everything snaps into place. Time for damage control, to silence the rumors and set the record straight—strengths, weaknesses, all of it. I'm done with this self-destructive spiral and life as I've known it. My future will be as it was always meant to be, as a productive member within the famiglie.

As for Fina, I know she hates me and that whatever we had is toast. Still, she deserves a life far from the famiglie, far from her asshole father, far from Carlo motherfucking Accardo.

I straighten, mind razor-sharp with purpose. "I better clean up, then."

Something flickers across Alessia's face, subtle, troubled. "Renzo ... she was caught roaming the estate."

I'm already moving toward the door.

"Your father's questioning her right now."

Fina

Blood polka-dots my solid pink dress as I wipe the back of my hand across my lips, gauging my surroundings and the dark, isolated room Sebastiano Beneventi's soldiers dragged me into.

Men always think roughing up a person will put them in their place. But like every other man who has put his hands on me, Don Beneventi's soldier will pay. If he thinks my stomping his shins with my heels hurts, he's in for a surprise.

Still, I recognize I'm in deep shit.

My father charged off somewhere around the eighth hole, frustrated by the Beneventis' impenetrable estate but also worried we'd be questioned about roaming so far away from the wedding celebration. He should have considered this before dragging me across a golf course in high heels.

"Have a seat," the soldier with the mean fists demands.

I square my shoulders, and as if he'd been expecting my resistance, he shoves me to the floor.

"I'm the daughter of a capo in the Eleven," I spit out. "Show some respect."

"Behave," he mutters. Because that's what mafiosi say to women, like we can't string two coherent thoughts together.

I bare my teeth, and his eyes widen.

That's right, asshole. Just you wait.

His two companions circle me, arms folded. Waiting.

Giving in to the rising terror now won't help. A busted lip is nothing compared to what my father will do to me for bringing attention onto us.

Bookcases line the walls, and it dawns on me I've been inside this room before—the library. A small desk is behind me, with comfortable sofas and chairs throughout the room. A large family portrait dominates the only bare wall, and the three Beneventi men stare down at me. Don Sebastiano Beneventi, with cold, calculating eyes; a teenage Sandro, stiff and rigid with a stick up his ass; and Renzo, with a sparkle and lively look, like life's a joke and only he knows the punch line.

At this moment, it's hard to say which Beneventi I hate the most.

But I know who terrifies me.

Lord, I stole from a man who butchered a capo with a chain saw. Who's smart and savvy, and difficult to outsmart.

Did Renzo tell him what I've done?

"I was taking a walk around the golf course. What's the big deal?"

Mean Fists points a finger at me. "Quiet."

The door swings open, and the men stiffen as their capo enters and the full Sebastiano Beneventi effect engulfs the room. Power radiates from his handsome physique. And I'm not the only one who feels it—his men stand taller, faces pulled tighter and manners on edge. Fear licks up my spine. A predator is in our midst, and I'm at the bottom of the food chain.

His attention lands on me, and I do everything in my power not to shy away.

We've never spoken. I was only a kid the last time I saw him. But the resemblance to Renzo is startling, so it's no wonder I find him startlingly attractive.

Only the most coldhearted mafioso would murder me on his wedding day, right?

His scowl deepens as he takes me in. Then, he turns his anger on his men. "Why the fuck is she bleeding?"

Mean Fists tugs his pants up and flashes his shredded ankles. "The heathen attacked me with her pink heels."

Christian Louboutin. Cost a pretty penny on my father's charge card, but worth every cent.

A second soldier holds up his hand. The imprint from my teeth is a work of art.

"She bit me."

"You too?" Sebastiano demands, frowning furiously as he gestures toward the last soldier and the dime-sized gouge in his neck.

The man flushes.

"I warned you she'd fight you."

My eyebrows raise. Because, until this moment, I thought I was so far off Sebastiano Beneventi's radar, I was a ghost.

"I also said not a scratch."

"Boss ..."

"Not another goddamn word," he snarls.

His soldiers snap their mouths shut. But now, unfortunately, I have their boss's complete and undivided attention.

"You."

I want to sink into the carpet but instead notch my chin higher.

"What do you have to say for yourself?"

"Congratulations on your wedding, Don Beneventi."

Lord, he looks ready to wring my neck.

Vulnerability is a horrible word. Because it means you're at the mercy of others. I can't help my smaller womanly frame, an easy target in a world where strength is measured by the weight of your fists or the blood on your hands. I didn't choose to be the daughter of the weakest capo in the Eleven, the man whispered about behind closed doors, pitied or mocked depending on the hour.

Everything that put me here was decided long before I had a say. It wasn't my plan to wander this man's estate, pretending I was in control, pretending I wasn't terrified. I was sent to expose his weaknesses, but all I feel is my own. Helplessness clings to me like a riptide, ready to pull me under. I hate it. I hate that no matter how hard I try to stand tall, I still feel small, always a pawn in someone else's game.

And yet here I am, under the gaze of the most dangerous crime boss, his eyes sharp with menace and something disturbingly close to curiosity.

He drags his fingers along his jaw, slow and deliberate, like he's weighing something heavy in silence.

He's going to kill me, isn't he?

And it'll take an act of God to save me.

Fat chance. You stole while inside His Divine Holiness's house.

He prowls toward me, and I swallow hard. His next words echo loudly around the room and seal my fate. "Don't think for one fucking second I don't know what you've done."

A loud commotion erupts outside the library, interrupting us.

My eyes widen in shock when the door crashes open.

And then, the most unreliable asshole on the planet bursts through.

———

Renzo

I come in swinging.

My father's main man—the bastard who shoved a syringe into my arm and dragged me off to rehab hell—is my first target. I knock him out with a single punch beneath the chin. Two more rush me. I go for the burly one first, driving my knee into his balls before slamming my elbow into the second man's gut. He stumbles but keeps coming. I count to four, then headbutt him, shattering his nose.

"Oh my God," Fina gasps.

Three down. One left.

The biggest motherfucker in the room—my father.

I tackle him to the carpet, land a few solid punches before he flips me onto my back, his arm crushing my throat.

His face hovers over mine, fury radiating off him in waves. "The last asshole who laid hands on me is buried beneath hole eight." Jesus. I *knew* the golf course on our estate was a fucking gravesite.

"Why. Is. She. Bleeding?" My voice is sharp, measured.

He clocks me on the side of the head, stars bursting behind my eyes. "You dare use that tone with me?"

I snap my teeth at him like a rabid dog. His men shift closer, waiting. "Which one did it? Who dies today?"

My father scowls. "This is about her?" His arm disappears, and I drag air into my burning lungs. He stands, smooths his tuxedo, then touches a finger to his split lip, looking almost amused.

Doubt me now, motherfucker?

"Help him up."

His man offers a hand. I ignore it, pushing myself up without assistance. My gaze darts to Fina—frozen, silent. Watching. "Who did it?" I demand.

"Jesus Christ. My man misunderstood an order and will be dealt with."

"Yeah, he will."

"He punched me." Fina wiggles a finger at my father's main man, who is slowly regaining consciousness.

I wind my foot up and ruthlessly kick him in the side, causing him to curl up like a little baby. Out of the corner of my eye, I catch Fina's smirk.

"Enough," my father orders, glaring at me, then Fina. "I'll ask again. Explain yourself."

"I was just taking a walk."

"Around my fucking golf course in high heels?" he snarls.

My eyes drop to her mud-caked pink heels. Proof that, yeah, that's exactly what she'd been doing. Snooping. Again.

Surprise, surprise.

"You've had a busy day, at my expense."

Oh shit. He knows about the money.

She holds her ground, not giving anything away. "I strive to make the most of my time."

"And you're wasting mine," he snaps. "Why were you and your father walking the estate?"

"The air's fresher than in Los Angeles."

A flash of admiration crosses his features, though Fina wouldn't recognize it. "Did you find what you were looking for?"

She shrugs.

"Cazzo. Accardo has his hands full."

Pain flashes across her face, but she tries to hide it by wiping her bloody lip with the back of her hand. The thought of marrying some repulsive old man who smells like fish and probably ruts like a pig must scare the hell out of her.

I broke my promise.

I'm the biggest asshole alive.

My gaze falls on her pink cheeks and bruised lips.

She won't even look at me.

Written me off, hasn't she?

"Call the goddamn doctor. Have him check her out." Then my father addresses a second guard. "Help her up."

"Touch me," Fina grinds out, "and you'll get the same treatment as every other manhandling prick in my life."

She gets an A-plus for bravery, though an F-minus for getting caught.

The guard steps forward, but I quickly position myself in-between them. Getting her out of this room and away from my father is the safest bet. "Hurt her, and I'll chop off your fingers, then, one by one, shove them down your throat. Capisci?"

His eyes widen in alarm and surprise. Unlike my brother, it's not every day I threaten my father's men.

I relax when he nods.

He offers her a hand up, but she refuses it and stands on her own. Chin held high, she stalks toward the door, brushing by me like I'm invisible, like I'm a worthless piece of shit. The guard trails behind her.

"Find her father and question him," my father orders the asshole who only now has shaken off the haze.

Fina stops in her tracks.

"You've got something to say now?"

Fuck. He played her, didn't he? I stiffen. Does she understands the danger she's in? The last person who stole from my father was violently dismembered.

"Matter of fact, yes."

The room grows quiet. Jesus. Prolonged silences are his move.

"I'd like to offer you some friendly advice."

"Advice?" He says it like the word doesn't sit well on his tongue. If he were any other man, if she hadn't stolen from him, I'd laugh.

As is, I half expect her to start reciting poetry, some twisted shit about violence, just to get under his skin.

She lets the silence stretch.

And in that moment, I know I'll never underestimate her again.

In a flat voice, she strikes. "The drainage pipe beneath the fence near the ninth hole is an easy access point onto your property. Your electrified fence means nothing."

The room turns to ice.

My father spins on his main man. "What motherfucking pipe?"

He stammers. "Last week, the landscapers upgraded the flooded midsection. I wasn't aware—"

"Walk the perimeter. If she's right, plug every goddamn hole, no matter how trivial. If my estate is this vulnerable again, Renzo will guarantee you regret it."

Did I hear that right? Did he finally acknowledge my ability to handle shit? Did it have to come to this for him to notice, I mean—

"I highly advise against plugging the drainage pipe."

Everyone gawks at her, except my father. He looks like he wants to strangle her.

"Why not?" I demand.

She snubs me, refusing to acknowledge me.

My father looks at me, then her. Wheels churning. Trying to make sense of the tension between us and the dynamics of a relationship he's only beginning to recognize.

"Answer him."

She sighs, like we should know her response. "Questioning my father will get you nowhere. But do you know what I'd do?"

"Go on," my father says.

"Watch and wait. What better way to discover who the real enemy is?" She spins, then hooks her arm through the guard's. "You can escort me back to the party."

Her declaration dangles in the air like a surprise wedding gift.

"Leave us," my father orders, and the other guards file out.

The door barely clicks shut before my father's fist slams into my stomach.

Pain erupts through me.

"I'm *capo di tutti capi*. No one, not even blood, embarrasses me."

There it is—the inevitable accusation. What happened in Rome months ago playing out all over again. Another chance to dig into my wounds with words sharp as blades.

"That would be fucking rich, wouldn't it?" I pant, lifting my head. "Your greatest disappointment kicking your arrogant ass?"

He touches his lip again, like he still can't believe I got one in. "If I have to lock you in the Beneventi dungeon to sober you up, so be it."

I uncurl to stand. "That's not what this is about."

He studies me, realization dawning. "Are you fucking serious? You defied me for her?"

"You assaulted a woman."

"A miscommunication. And she was trespassing."

"Still, she did you a solid by warning you."

His eyes darken. "You that gullible? What better way to escape marrying Accardo than by convincing me he's an enemy?"

I repeat her warning, wondering if he's right. "Wait and watch, and you'll find out."

"Accardo's the top investor in my Chicago expansion. He has too much to lose if he targets me—we both do."

"Why not Moretti?"

"Accardo has deeper pockets. Without him, I'll lose Chicago."

Well, shit. If I hope to talk him into somehow blocking the wedding ... "Will you give me permission to marry her?" I calmly ask, but already know he won't take me seriously—I mean, why would he?

His expression freezes. "Marry? Who?"

"Fina."

A suffocating silence stretches out. Until he laughs. "You've got to be fucking kidding me. The pussy that good?"

Annoyed he believes every decision I make is driven by vice, I give him a taste of his own medicine. "Not as good as sweet Alessia—"

He slams me into the wall so hard it vibrates. "Not another word."

I smirk, point made.

His eyes are like glass. "I need to keep Accardo fat and happy at the moment."

"And not your son."

He doesn't so much as flinch.

"You're the boss of bosses. Call it off."

He jabs a finger at me, not liking taking orders. "You pulled the same shit with Alessia."

"You're welcome."

"Stop playing hero to everyone but yourself."

What the fuck? A hero complex? Me? Is that what he believes?

Pain bleeds into his expression. "You had ample fucking time to figure shit out. And what do you do?"

Rome. It's always fucking Rome. "I didn't freeze."

"Freeze? You fucking died on me."

Right, that. "A technicality ..."

"They resuscitated you."

I rub my fingers across my jaw. "I made a mistake."

He shakes his head. "So did I by granting you your freedom."

Ouch. "I'll change."

"Right."

"Take on more responsibilities."

"Right."

We lock eyes. Yet I'm certain I'm the only one who sees me for me.

"This is my offer." His eyes narrow, then he surprises me. "Go to Rome. Work with Dante Lucchese. Learn the business. Lay off the partying, women, and drugs. Prove yourself, and I'll make you a made man."

Despite everything—the overdose; his disappointment; assaulting him, my capo, my father, on his wedding day—he's offering me what I've been waiting for: a second chance. He's handing me everything on a silver platter as if I haven't wasted years fucking around.

This time, I don't hesitate.

"I'll go to Rome."

His eyes gleam with satisfaction.

"If you allow Fina to keep the money she stole, without conse-quences."

He stares at me for a long time. Like he's trying to read my fucking soul. Good luck with that because it's as black as a starless night. Giving up, he jabs a finger into my chest. "Get your shit together and prove yourself. Be the man I need you to be. But leave that hellcat alone. No contact. No goddamn marriage. You let her figure out her own bullshit, or I'll cut off your dick and feed it to you. Capisci?"

Do I understand?

Yes. Leave her be.

As for Accardo ...

What happens next remains to be seen.

6

Tina

I RETURN TO LOS ANGELES WITH A BRUISED LIP, A WIDE SMILE, and a renewed spring in my step.

Sebastiano Beneventi's interrogation was brutal. For a nerve-racking moment, I was certain he knew I'd stolen from him. The thought still makes me shiver. What would the consequence have been? A one-way trip to the Beneventi dungeon? A shallow grave beneath the golf course?

Would Renzo have let that happen?

That question consumes me. I keep replaying the moment he burst into the library like a man possessed, took down three mafiosi with terrifying ease, and then launched himself at his father. Seeing his violent side was thrilling. He knocked the guard who'd hurt me out with a single punch. Risked his father's anger, for me.

I could've used that version of him back when I was cornered by Emo.

The answer to my question seems clear: no.

But what's that expression? Once bitten, twice shy?

Renzo has always been a contradiction, furiously loyal one

moment, absent the next. I'm grateful he showed up when he did, yet I'd be a fool to lose myself in the what-ifs.

Not when I have more urgent things to deal with, and a week to fade into the sunset.

"Goddamn it, Elia." My father's shout echoes around the living room. "Didn't I tell you to never fuck around with the security cameras?"

"I was trying to help," I holler back. "They were dirty, Father."

I smirk when he grumbles about calling system experts back to the house to fix them. I should warn the cleaning staff they'll be getting an earful.

"Headed to the beach," I call out once more. "Be back later."

"Wait. Carlo is calling about the wedding plans ..."

His eager tone twists my stomach. He's salivating at the chance to impress Accardo, ready to parrot back the information I spoon-fed him on the plane: a neat, easy-to-remember mental diagram marking the precise location of the pipe leading straight into the Beneventi estate.

Sebastiano Beneventi's a smart man, and I hope he'll take my advice seriously.

I close the door behind me.

Smiling.

It's my twenty-first birthday, and the only gift worth having is the one I'm giving myself—freedom.

By the time the dust settles, I'll be gone, gone, gone.

THREE DAYS. THAT'S HOW LONG UNTIL I'M EXPECTED IN Chicago, walking down the aisle in a church Carlo picked, in a wedding I never agreed to.

I'm cutting things close. But every *i* needs to be dotted, every *t* crossed because, once this escape is in motion, there's no turning back. It's do or die. Literally.

Tomorrow's the big day.

Speed and precision are everything. I booked a private, early-morning charter to Dallas under an alias, paid entirely in cash. From there, a direct flight to Rome. By the time my father realizes I'm gone, I'll be sipping limoncello in front of the Colosseum.

My two decoys are already in play. Do I feel bad about deceiving them? A bit. Desperate times call for desperate measures, though, and besides, if they're caught, they know nothing. Truly.

They think I'm screwing with my father again, the way I do by dressing in the clothes I wear.

One friend is already on her way to San José, decked out in the same hideous neon pink tracksuit I'll be wearing while having breakfast with my father. With all that money at stake, he'll come after me, for sure. And Carlo? Once an arrogant asshole, always one. He'll hunt for me, too, outraged that a naïve and sheltered little girl jilted him.

Another sighting places me in San Francisco, having rented a car under the name Elle Lombardo. Subtle? Not exactly. But I know exactly who I'm dealing with.

Their first stops? Obvious—LAX and San Diego. Then the bus stations, where they'll find reports of a woman matching my description catching a 10 a.m. Greyhound to San José.

I've timed everything to the minute and alternated the timing of each sighting, with the last breadcrumb in Vancouver, where I vanish into the Canadian wilderness.

A carefully crafted crumb trail.

If it weren't for the stolen money, I might not have pulled off my plan. I still can't believe Don Beneventi never noticed such a large sum was gone or suspected me. He's probably side-eyeing the Eleven, wondering why they were so stingy with their wedding gifts.

Life might never be a fairy tale, but I'm over living in a nightmare.

"Seraphina," my father bellows.

I zip my bags and hide them inside my closet. "Coming."

My father waits at the bottom of the stairs. "Goddamn it."

"What's the matter? Cameras not working again?" They are. But not for long.

The doorbell rings. Then again. And again.

My father's eyes start twitching, voice edged with panic. "What the hell is he doing here?"

"Who?"

"Motherfucking Settemo Accardo. He parked his Ferrari in the driveway."

The doorbell won't stop, or be ignored.

"Is Carlo with him?"

"I spoke with him an hour ago. He was headed to his favorite restaurant in Chicago." My father's gaze cuts toward the door, then back to me. "You answer it."

"Me?"

"No. The other idiot standing in the room."

That would be you, Daddy Dickless.

I run through the options in my head. Escape or bluster through this. My friends aren't in place, and everything's set for tomorrow. But the thought of seeing Emo makes the scar on my wrist throb.

The doorbell blares.

I swallow hard, square my shoulders, and move to the foyer to answer it.

Settemo Accardo's scowling face greets me, flanked by a few unrecognizable mafiosi.

"Well, if this isn't a surprise," I say brightly, a stupid smile plastered on my face, as if I'd long since forgotten the burn mark on my skin. "What are you doing in Los Angeles?"

"Your father home?"

He sounds *hopeful*. Like he hopes to catch me alone. Creep. "Yes, he is. Right in the living room."

Bile rises in my throat at his disappointment.

His heavy presence trails behind me, setting every nerve on edge. He smells like formaldehyde, like he's spent time in a lab full of decomposing rats. Like he pulled the short stick, then had to scour the psycho ward. The closer he gets, the harder it is to breathe.

"Settemo. I wasn't expecting you," my father says stiffly. "Does Carlo know you're visiting?"

"Carlo won't give a single shit that I'm here."

So, that's a no.

"Can I get you and your men a drink?" I offer, already moving toward the bar. "Wine? Beer?"

"Whiskey. Neat. They'll have the same."

My hand shakes as I pour. I listen closely, trying to read the undercurrent in their voices, to guess the reason for the unpleasant surprise.

It can't be good.

So the question really is, how bad will it be?

My father clears his throat. "How long have you been in Los Angeles?"

"Few hours." Emo's tone is clipped, sharp.

Confusion still edges my father's tone. "You drove from Illinois to California?"

"How do you know that?"

I roll my eyes.

My father states the obvious. "You parked your Ferrari in my driveway."

I place the crystal glasses on a tray and carry it over. The room's so quiet, you could hear a pin drop. I glance from my father to Emo, whose face is flushed with rage.

"You recognize my car?" Emo snarls.

Shit. Oh shit.

My father's eyebrows pinch. "Well, yes? Your uncle showed me pictures of it, but we also saw it—"

"I poured you a whiskey, too, Father." I cut him off, handing each mafioso a glass except for the man I shortchanged. "Oops," I murmur. "Must have miscounted."

No one's listening to me.

Emo downs his whiskey, slams the glass onto the tray, and then snatches the glass from the man next to him and polishes it off, as well.

Then he strikes. "I've a question to ask, the same question I've asked numerous men ever since your last visit with my uncle. I can fucking smell a lie a mile away, so choose your answer carefully."

"Okay ..." my father warily replies.

"Do I look like a cunt stud to you?"

My father jerks like he's trying to induce whiplash. "What?"

"Cunt. Stud," Emo enunciates. "Don't make me say it again."

"Well ... wah ... shit ... wado ... you mean?"

"I want twenty grand for the damages."

"Twenty grand?" Like flint to kindling, my father finds his voice. "For what damages?"

"To my car!" Emo roars. "In cash. Get it now, or you won't live to see the wedding."

No way will I be left alone with this madman and his men while my father leaves the room.

"Oh my God. Your language." I drop the tray and cover my ears. "Vulgarity isn't allowed in our house."

Everyone stares daggers at me.

"I need a broom for the mess I've made," I exclaim, then flee to the kitchen.

I hear my father loudly empathizing with the psycho. Sharing how his dear cherry red Mustang was recovered in the California desert with irreversible damages. How blood had ruined the custom leather backseat.

My father is the worm that survives a heat wave while lying on the California freeway. I wouldn't be surprised if Emo leaves empty-handed.

And there was mention of the wedding. I won't die today.

Act normal. Get through this visit. You can do it.

I enter the pantry off the kitchen to retrieve the broom. I've got the handle in hand when Emo fills the doorway, blocking out the light.

Stupid, stupid mistake.

I imagine him crawling out of the dark, wearing another man's skin, just to see who breaks first. A chill settles over me.

"Found it," I exclaim, holding the broom across my body like it'll protect me.

His eyes are dead. His smile pure evil.

He steps forward and wrenches the broom from my hands. I clatters to the floor behind him.

"But I need that to clean up."

He grabs me and slams me back into the pantry shelves. My arm is wrenched up and twisted behind me so fast I can't react. A jolt of pain shoots through my shoulder.

"What do you want?" I gasp. My chest tightens. Panic climbs, and I can't breathe right.

He says nothing.

Only silence and the sound of my own ragged breath.

Finally, he speaks. "You know what to do." A pack of cigarettes and a lighter drop onto the shelf beside my face. "You piss me off, you pay."

I try to placate him. "I'm sorry."

"Things will be different in Chicago. You drop a tray like you did tonight, and I'll leave burn marks across your body."

What can I say to make him release me, some line that will pacify him? "I'll be a new girl in Chicago. A good one."

He laughs, and it's vile. He's enjoying fucking with me.

His breath smells sour as his lips graze my earlobe. The urge to hurl is great.

"We'll practice tonight."

My brain scrambles to decode his words.

He thumbs his phone, the cigarettes forgotten. "You left an impression on me, and I've been thinking about this since your visit."

His tone reads eager. I'm terrified to learn why. "But I couldn't remember your size to prepare."

Prepare?

He presses play on a video.

What I see is worse than anything I could imagine.

I blink, trying to understand what I'm viewing. A person lies still on a cement floor, completely engulfed in a white latex catsuit. Only the eyes, nostrils, and mouth are exposed. She can't move. She doesn't even try.

The terror in her gaze is unmistakable.

Oh God.

She looks like something discarded. Not a person anymore. Just a shell.

"What is this?" I whisper.

He presses his erection into my back, and my stomach turns.

"Your future."

This excites him. He gets off on this. The control. The fear.

"But Carlo ..."

"I'll be our secret."

"Whatever you want." My voice quivers even though I want to scream. "I swear I won't say a word."

He punches me. Once. Twice. A third time.

The pain is searing. I double over, hugging my side.

"Get back in the living room and clean up your mess. Then you'll practice not being such a clumsy bitch."

He grabs the cigarettes and lighter, the video still playing on his phone, then vanishes.

You can do it, Fina. You won't be alone with him. The worst is over.

The men are seated when I return. Rolls of hundred-dollar bills on the side table nearest Emo.

I make quick work of the broken glass.

"Drinks, anyone?" Emo demands.

I don't wait. I push down the pain and return to the bar, pour four more whiskeys, place them on a tray, then serve the men. My hands are steady this time, but only because I force them to be.

"My uncle hates incompetency," Emo says. "Fill that tray with glasses and keep crossing the room until I say stop."

I glance at my father.

He says nothing. Just watches, forehead furrowed.

No outrage. No protection.

I'm on my own.

Tears threaten. I blink them away.

I carry the tray. I walk. I return. Over and over. My body screams, but I ignore it. I smile like it's a game. Cunt stud. Cunt stud. Cunt stud.

Again.

And again.

Until the pain blends into the rhythm of my steps.

Emo claps. "Faster."

I nod, moving quicker, though my ribs feel ready to shatter. He watches me like he's already got me zipped up in rubber. And I thought cigarette burns were torturous.

Time slows. It feels like this hellish nightmare will never end.

Then his phone rings.

His men's phones buzz too.

I'm twenty-one, and have seen so little of the world. Barely have had a taste of what freedom feels like. Just once, I want to be loved, happy, alive, *safe* ...

My gaze falls on Emo, then widens.

Gone is the coldness. In its place, a storm of disbelief and fury.

"Fucking strawberries?" he snarls, lurching to his feet, fists clenched, jaw grinding. "How did this happen? Why wasn't I called sooner?"

His men, phones lit up, exchange sharp looks.

"We need to get to Chicago."

They leave in a rush. No goodbyes. No thanks for the hospitality, the fun and games.

I trail after them and watch, overwhelmed with relief, as Emo and his men peel away in his Ferrari.

My father's on the phone when I come back into the living room.

"What happened?" I ask. I'm begging silently for good news, like Carlo's men were caught breaking into the Beneventi estate.

"Fuck, fuck, fuck." My father paces the room, much like I've been doing, except he's completely, utterly unraveling.

"Answer me," I insist. "What happened?"

"Carlo is dead."

7

Renzo

S andro glares at me from behind his office desk like I'm one of his submissives he's about to go alpha on. A pompous ass, in his slick suit and tie. Uptight still, despite the steady girlfriend now in residence. He doesn't hide his annoyance at my unexpected visit.

"Why are you here?" You'd think he'd be more delighted to see me, considering I took an indirect flight to Rome by way of Sardinia just to visit his charming villa.

"This place brings back fond memories." During my last visit, the sadistic fuckhead chained me to a bed for days and forced me to detox. An excruciatingly painful experience, the withdrawal *and* being in his company for that long. I refined the art of cliff jumping during my visit, a necessity to escape his men.

Good times.

You'd think he'd be pumped to see me here, willingly.

I dig inside my pocket, retrieve an envelope, and toss it like bait on a hook onto his desk. "Happy birthday."

"It's six fucking months away."

I roll my eyes. "Open the goddamn gift."

He's taken aback, hating feeling obliged to anyone, even me.

I snatch the envelope back. "It can wait …"

That makes him smile. "Dick."

"Asshole." I hand it back. He looks inside, expression changing from curious to puzzled. "A spa weekend?"

"At a swank resort in Sicily. Once you shed the suit, tie, and workaholic tendencies, you'll love it. Riley will, too."

Sandro softens at the mention of his girlfriend. He's tight-lipped about his relationship, but Riley shared with me how they fell in love in Sicily, so I thought it'd be a good gift.

"She'll fucking love this."

Perfect execution on my part, which I hope he remembers after he learns the real reason for the visit.

I adjust my seat, making myself at home, but as I do so, my foot collides with a metal bar beneath his desk. Curious, I repeat the action, kicking it a few times more until the answer dawns on me. "Is that a cage under your desk?"

"Where should I send your gift?"

I'm a kinky motherfucker, yet so is Sandro. Now why would he have a goddamn cage beneath his desk if not to scratch his need for domination?

"Your favorite rehab in Maine?" he continues, unfazed, focused on riding my ass rather than caging his girlfriend's. Riley deserves a spa stay after putting up with him.

"I thought I'd stick around for a bit."

"You thought wrong."

I smirk.

"Why are you here, Renzo? And don't say you miss me." He leans back, waiting.

I hesitate, because if I seem too eager, he'll laugh. I've spent years researching drone tech for covert surveillance, a resource that could elevate the Eleven in ways the old-school mafiosi can't even imagine. The possibilities are staggering; silent, untraceable air strikes and the ability to monitor our enemies' every move without detection.

Don Lucchese knew traditional mafia wars, where one kill sparks retaliation until bodies pile up and peace is finally brokered, would lead to the mafia's downfall. No civilian wants to see corpses lining the streets.

If Sandro can look past a drone's toylike appearance and recognize its lethal potential, he'll realize investing in the latest tech will put the Beneventis ahead of everyone else.

But misperceptions aren't about knowing too little—they come from believing in the wrong thing too much.

Like I'm the weaker twin.

Like Sandro can wear our father's shoes without tripping over his own feet.

"I've a plan," I say, short and simple.

His expression's smug. "You don't have plans."

"I need to borrow a million dollars."

His body goes rigid, like I shot a bullet up his asshole.

"Ten percent interest. I'll pay you back in a year."

"You fucking serious? Lend you a million?"

"Two, if you can spare it."

His lips curl cruelly. "To do what? Open a chain of kink clubs? Lorenzo's Den of Lust?"

"Sounds more like porn, not kink."

"Are you fucking serious?"

I brush fake lint off my pants, then offer up a partial lie, something believable his pea-size brain can compute. "I've been fucking around with the market and found some ripe tech investments." The ripe part is true, but I don't "fuck around" with the market, I dominate it. I've been a ghost investor since sixteen, mostly in tech, and have built a sweet nest egg. But it's nowhere near what my father has at his disposal and, as the Beneventi heir, Sandro has access to.

The way I see it, this fucker owes me.

"A million-dollar investment?" he repeats.

"Let's call it an even two."

"No."

I offer him a winning grin. "Fine. One and a half will do."

He stares at me from across his desk, reminding me so much of our father. Sandro was born to be the Beneventi heir. Doesn't fucking excuse him from stealing my destiny.

"You owe me," I say, the truth coming out of me whether I wanted it to or not.

"For what?"

"The bullshit you pulled in Rome."

His expression reads confused. The asshole's settled into the Life now, hasn't he?

"*You* shot Conti's uncle."

"What about it?"

I blankly stare at him, waiting for the assumption.

He doesn't disappoint. "You stood there with this stupid expression, like the night of partying had finally caught up with you. You froze like a pussy."

"I was manifesting the moment." Savoring the rush, the elation that took me by surprise.

He fucking blinks.

"You know, projecting an outcome you want and sending it into the universe. But you ruined it."

"I did what was necessary and covered your ass."

"You stole my moment to satisfy your raging hard-on to please our father."

He leans in. "You didn't have it in you."

"You have daddy issues."

That hit the mark. "You don't have the killer gene."

I stifle a laugh. I can't wait to prove this asshole wrong.

"Want into the Life?" he snarls when I don't give him the reaction he wants. "Focus on earning and not enforcing. The fall will be less messy that way."

He rolls back in his seat, satisfied he's out-assholed me.

"Fine," I say after a few minutes, curious if he understands how I manipulated the fuck out of him. "Float me the million and a half so I establish myself as an earner."

"Jesus Christ," he utters. It's followed by a long pause. "You really want in on the Life?"

I shrug.

"I'll float you two million with twelve percent interest. If the money ends up in your bloodstream or up your fucking nose, I'll beat the living daylights out of you."

I toss my information, which I wrote on a piece of paper, onto his desk. "Transfer the money to this bank account."

"Now?"

"No. In a fucking year from now."

He fiddles on his computer. A few moments later, a single satisfying buzz of my phone confirms the transfer.

Mission fucking accomplished—two million dollars is now at my disposal. "This is the smartest investment you've ever made," I murmur, a sliver of excitement coloring my tone.

He leans back, arms crossed. "You think you can give up the lifestyle? The partying, drugs, the excess?"

I tap my temple. "Mind over matter, baby."

"I hope you can do it, but I won't bet money on it."

I straighten, feeling more inspired than ever to prove him wrong. "Say hi to Riley for me."

He looks perplexed. "You're not staying for lunch?" His voice dips into something gruff, reluctant. "She'll want to see you."

I have a meeting with Dante tomorrow afternoon, something I don't intend to share. The less he knows about my movements, the easier it'll be to slip beneath our father's radar.

I smirk, because, bullshit aside and truth be told, I was hoping for the invitation. "I'd love to."

He studies me then, a pause heavy with scrutiny. His gaze sharpens, calculating. Is he catching on to my mindfuckery? Or sensing something deeper—the truth to why I'm in Italy and far away from Rhode Island ... and Chicago.

"Why ask me?" he finally says, voice edged with suspicion.

"Father would be thrilled you're taking an interest in the *famiglie*. Why not go to him for support?"

"Can't."

His expression tightens. "Why not?"

"I need to lay low for a bit."

A muscle jumps in his jaw. He wants to strangle me, and I don't blame him. For a man who surrounds himself with yes-men, puppets who never dare defy him, he's still so damn desperate to prove his worth to our old man. Ripping that gun from my hand and stripping me of my place within the *famiglie* wasn't enough to do so, it seems. Hate to tell him that it'll never be enough, not until he stops trying.

Where would he be without me keeping things interesting?

"Relax," I say with a lazy grin. "I'll be long gone before the call comes in." Pushing up from my chair, I stretch, rolling my shoulders. "Goddamn, after all this hard work, I'm starving. What's for lunch?"

A RED LIGHT BLINKS OVERHEAD. MY EXHAUSTED MIND struggles with what it might be.

Am I passed out on some seedy Roman side street? In a field, staring at a small drone hovering in the clouds? Did I fuck up again or, for once in my life, commit to a bigger picture?

I awake with a start.

Fucking hell, what time is it?

Sunlight offers me a stiff finger as I crawl out of the hotel bed. I was a good boy last night. Early to bed, early to rise—except mornings and I never agree, and evidently, this holds true despite being completely sober.

I flew into Rome last night like a goddamn gladiator ready to take on the world. So why mourn the death of the sins that used to make me feel alive? Because—not going to lie—it was a struggle not to indulge in one final celebratory evening. My last night to be anyone but Sebastiano Beneventi's son.

My demons were out in full force, beckoning me, tempting me. But I'm an asshole, not an idiot. Mind over matter, right? I'm in control.

I'm on a new adventure in life.

I'm the Beneventi about to flip the Life on its ass.

Guerrilla warfare, like the kind playing out in the streets within the Cosa Nostra, is so 1980s. Massimo Grassi, for all his education and tech talk, is still a barbarian at heart. It's clear I can no longer leave modernizing the mafia in his hands.

Still, I managed to fuck up and overslept. If it hadn't been for the fire alarm light blinking overhead, I might have missed my meeting with Dante.

The clock tells me I've fifteen minutes to haul ass across Rome. A quick brush of my teeth and spritz of cologne, and I'm on my way.

I move through the streets of Rome like a ghost retracing steps I barely remember taking. Everything looks cleaner now. Sharper. The air doesn't reek of piss and smoke like I remember, and the graffiti that once screamed from the walls has been scrubbed down to faint whispers. Perhaps it's the daylight, and how my prior experience with Rome was mostly at night in a part of town not mentioned in travel brochures.

Tourists wander past with gelato and shopping bags, smiling like this city hasn't chewed people up and spit them out for centuries. Cafés spill sunlight and laughter into the alleyways, and for a second I wonder if I've stumbled into the wrong goddamn Rome.

It's beautiful now, all healed from wounds I'm still bleeding from.

The memory slams into me: the gun in my hand, the sharp, electric, and addictive rush. The high of all highs. Then Sandro, yanking it away, stealing my thunder like it was his birthright. His betrayal cut deeper than the recoil. And my father's silence, heavier than a bullet to the chest. His disappointment's been clawing at me ever since.

I drag my hand along a pristine white wall as I pass until my fingertips are raw, streaking it with blood just to leave a mark. Proof that I'm still here. That this city, past and present, hasn't erased me completely.

Fucking hell. Sandro isn't the only one with daddy issues, is he?

My phone vibrates against my hip, jarring me back from the crippling realization.

Hand shaking, I retrieve it, preparing for Dante to tell me to fuck off because I'm officially late.

But it's a text from Sandro:

Carlo Accardo is dead.

I carefully type back, not wanting to get blood on my phone.

How?

Food poisoning.

With a little extra help from the thallium mixed in with his Pepcid pills. You bet I did my homework.

Father is demanding you call him.

I give the text a thumbs-up emoji. Avoiding my father until this passes over tops my priority list.

What did you do?

What did I do? Now that's a loaded question. Risk my father's rage? Risk the Beneventi name? Risk the Eleven's wrath if they ever learn I acted without their bullshit authorizations?

What I didn't do was murder Accardo to showcase my true nature. The ice in my veins. My lack of empathy toward most people. The devil I've dulled through sex and drugs, who's primed and ready to play as a made man. All that will come in time.

I killed him for *her*.

I send him a kissy-face emoji, then, glancing at the time, tuck my phone in my pocket. I'm late, but not that fucking late.

With fire in my stride, I push forward, because for the first time in a long damn while, I did something that fucking mattered.

I gave Fina a chance at a real life.

While I set off to become the monster no one sees coming.

8

Renzo

I MEET DANTE AT ZIA TERESA, A SMALL FAMILY-STYLE restaurant on the same narrow street as Dante's Club Tiberius. The place is empty except for our famiglie's second-in-command, the waitress seated on his lap, and one of the Italian Youngbloods, Luciano Santoro.

Dante neglected to mention he'd be here.

I stick out my hand for a firm shake. "Luciano."

"Lorenzo."

"You look like shit," Dante greets me, frowning as both men regard me skeptically.

I'm wearing an expensive designer suit I stole off Sandro, but the material hangs off my frame, making me look like a boy playing dress up. Looking at me, they're probably wondering if I have what it takes to fill my father's shoes.

Luciano makes a gagging sound. "And he smells like a French whore."

I smirk. "Rather smell like a whore than act like a kiss-ass."

His face turns red. Goddamn amateur. He's ambitious, I'll give him that. Doesn't explain why Dante invited him to our meeting, one I'd hoped would be private so I can safely pitch my proposal.

The gorgeous waitress leaps off Dante's lap and escapes to the kitchen.

We watch her go. Dante knows how to pick them. The asshole has a hot girlfriend in every fucking city. She's the perfect distraction.

I fall into a vacant chair. "You speak to my father?"

"Not today. Why?"

Yep. Perfect. I shrug. "No reason."

An older Italian woman approaches the table with a tray piled with steaming hand towels. I take one and rub the dried blood from my fingertips. When I look up, the trio is scowling at me.

"Sei una bestia," the older woman hisses.

"Mi sento insultato. Sono più un mostro che una bestia," I smoothly respond, warning the woman that I'm more monster than beast.

"Zia Teresa," Dante addresses her, placing his used towel on her tray. "Grazie."

I drop the filthy napkin onto her tray, then immediately hold my hands up, fearing she's seconds from smacking my head with it.

With a scowl, she charges off.

"Took you two minutes to piss off the best chef in Rome," Dante scolds, playing the big brother he never was. Years ago, my father struck a deal with Don Lucchese to protect Dante from the bloodbath that would've followed under the old rules of succession. By those rules, the Don's son should've ruled next. But instead, my father offered Dante mentorship and protection in exchange for one thing: his name at the top of the new election process. Like my father and brother, Hollywood—as we like to call him for his stylish clothes, razzle-dazzle, and split personality—is a dual threat. An enforcer and earner, exactly what I aim to be. Dante's been a reliable figure in my life and one of the few people I trust. He knows how to manage my father ... which, considering recent events, I'm going to lean heavily on for help.

"No Sandro today?" Luciano asks, in another lame attempt to piss me off.

"No pack today?" Pack being him and the two other Youngbloods.

"Off making money." He hesitates. Cocky fucker. "The arrogant asshole too busy to meet with us?"

Even if his depiction's spot on, insulting my twin can't go unanswered.

But in the Beneventi way, I make him wait for it until he's squirming in his seat, before striking. "Oiling his new chain saw, I suppose."

Luciano's eyes widen, with good reason.

My brother notoriously mailed the Eleven body parts from that weasel, Emilio Conti, after butchering him with a chain saw. We Beneventi earned quite the reputation for our creativity with small machinery.

Dante chuckles.

I wonder what part Luciano received? Ear, eye, or most likely dick?

A few awkward seconds pass—well, awkward for Luciano, anyway.

Ever the diplomat, Dante changes topics. "Zia Teresa makes the best spaghetti alla carbonara in Rome. Place is always packed."

Luciano drinks his wine before asking the obvious. "Aren't you biased, being a partial owner?"

I glance around, throat parched, searching for the hot waitress.

"I own the club straight-out but collect rents on the entire block; the apartment buildings, storefronts, and the restaurant." Easy, passive income the traditional mafia way, by fleecing owners and occupants in exchange for protection.

A different waitress heads toward our table. Dante looks past her, grumbling, "So much for a quick fuck after lunch."

She stops before us, then addresses us in English. "The usual?"

"The spaghetti alla carbonara," Dante tells us. "It's the best in Rome."

"Two," she says in English, looking from Dante to Luciano.

"Three ..." I begin. But she's already rushing away. "And bring wine."

My stomach grumbles.

Dante and Luciano's laughter fills the restaurant.

I relax in my chair, faking annoyance.

"The war is spilling out into city streets," Luciano comments. "Last night, Cassio's men barely dodged an ambush in Naples. They had no choice but to defend themselves and killed a few men."

Dante leans in. "We stay clear of the Cosa Nostra drama," he commands. "No more deaths, capisci? The famiglie will not take a side. Our suppliers are skittish enough, worried about retaliation if we side with the wrong family."

I snort.

Dante looks offended.

"We've a long-standing agreement with the Grassi family."

Dante jerks his chin at me. "I forgot you and Massimo are friends."

"We've a mutual respect for each other and share similar interests, is all."

"Same kinks." Luciano smiles like he's said something that might upset me.

I smirk back, unfazed. How the fuck did this numbnut pull off the most shocking initiation into the famiglie yet? "Dante likes quantity, I'm into variety, as is Massimo—even if he's old-fashioned at heart. But you, my friend ..." I pause for a few beats. "... get your kinks from being a bottom."

"Motherfucker." Luciano shoots out of his chair. "Where did you hear that?"

Dante, my source, subtly shakes his head. "Jesus," I mutter innocently. "What's the big deal if you lie back and take it? It's just a matter of perspective, with you ... looking up ..."

"Sit down," Dante orders. "You're causing a scene."

Luciano obeys. "Whoever started that rumor is a dead man."

"Enough. Let's get to the real reason we're here." Dante locks eyes with him. "I have a job. I want you to find out who's sabotaging my pistachio harvests."

His harvests, with Sandro's backing. I didn't laugh when my twin invested heavily in Dante's passion project. Everyone underestimated the emerging nut market, and pistachios turned out to be a gold mine. Puddings, syrups, even chicken recipes. They're the next big trend since pumpkin spice.

But Dante's behind. Knowing my brother, his men are already hunting the thieves.

"It's someone on the outside," Luciano tosses out, just to hear himself talk.

I'm not convinced. Feels too clean, too convenient. My gut says it's someone on the inside, and an Italian-based famiglie. And if we cross the Youngbloods off the list, that leaves only one name.

Vito Cardini.

"It's costing us a fortune, and good men have died." Dante's fist tightens, catching my attention. "Whoever is behind this is a threat to neighboring farms."

Neighboring farms. Right. Like Don Gallo's—and his lovely daughter's—farm. One right next door to the acreage Dante unexpectedly purchased. Do I doubt Dante's fooling around with Gallo's daughter? No way. Hollywood will tap anything with two legs. The only criteria is that they're good looking. Despite the age difference and Dante being much older, word has it that Luna Gallo harbors a huge crush on my father's right-hand man. Easy pickings.

So why the clenched fist?

Luciano straightens his shoulders. "I'll get right on it."

"Production's paused for three weeks."

"I'll have it dealt with in two."

I roll my fucking eyes. What I don't do is admit this won't be Luciano's moment but mine. It's the turning point I've been denied.

Another chance to showcase exactly what I am—ruthless, calculated, the worst of the Beneventi monsters.

No way am I letting another asshole steal my thunder.

Actions speak louder than words, and mine will land like a mortar blast.

The chef returns with three dishes. With a plop, she sets my meal before me, then leans in. "Boo."

My eyebrows rise. What the fuck?

With a vicious gleam, she stalks off.

I dig in, unperturbed, ignoring the laughter around me.

My warning about being a monster is genuine.

And now, more than ever, I'm looking forward to proving it.

"Seraphina. Hurry, or we'll miss the bus."

My mother's aunt Teresa is already halfway down the gravel drive, short legs pumping, her well-earned grandmotherly figure moving with surprising speed.

She lives alone on a farm tucked deep in the Italian countryside, surrounded by animals, grapevines, and the kind of silence that feels more foreign than the place I now reside in. A broad, still silence, like the countryside's holding its breath and waiting for me to finally exhale.

But I don't have time to relax. I'm about to miss the bus to Rome. And my no-nonsense great-aunt isn't about to wait for me to deal with the small problem blocking my exit from the front porch.

A rooster.

He flaps his wings, bobbing his head like he owns the place. His beady eyes lock onto mine. A fresh scar on my calf reminds me of last week's ambush.

"Shoo," I snap.

He stretches his neck and lets out a triumphant crow, chest puffed like a gladiator.

Lord, this is my life now, isn't it? To be brought to my knees by a dang rooster.

Why are the males in my life so relentlessly aggressive?

Still, I'm free. Gloriously, miraculously free.

The moment I heard Carlo Accardo was dead, I danced around the living room like a drunk cheerleader, fist pumps, high kicks, with a joy I'd forgotten I could feel. While my father panicked, I celebrated with strawberries and cream and toasted my freedom like a woman reborn. Then I vanished, exactly as planned.

He has no idea I was ever in contact with my great-aunt—my *prozia*—or that I'm even here. She was my lifeline. My mother's estranged aunt, from her mother's side. We connected a few years ago, quietly, and I never lost touch.

My father barely remembers my mother existed. He certainly wouldn't remember an eccentric aunt who never married, turned her back on the Life, and therefore holds no value in our world. A woman like that doesn't even register to men like him.

Grottaferrata isn't LA, not even close. But the village, known for its beautiful landscapes and wine—something I can fully get behind —is thirty minutes from Rome.

Big city excitement by day, quiet hills by night.

I gave everything up, yet somehow, against all odds, I'm riding a happy streak.

I've made friends.

I have a job I actually like and am good at. A job at risk because of this pint-sized feathered demon.

He crows again, full of attitude, daring me to step off the porch.

I retreat into the farmhouse, heading straight to the sleek, modern kitchen, and snatch two corn husks from last night's dinner. I wash my hands, grab my vintage purse, and step back onto the porch.

He spots me from across the driveway and charges back.

If my friends back in LA could see me now ...

I shove my handbag under my arm, narrow my eyes, and brace myself.

One.

Two.

Three.

I bolt off the porch, making a wide arc away from the beast as I sprint toward my great-aunt's fading silhouette down the drive.

He's on me. Wings flapping, claws scraping gravel, head lowered in attack.

Farm life has taught me a few things: Always shut your windows or prepare to wake with the early morning revellers. And always carry a weapon, stick, rock, or food, anything will do.

I wind up like a pitcher and hurl the husks at him. One clips his wing, breaking his momentum. He squawks, feathers flying, then drops to the ground and begins pecking at the prize.

I slow just enough to catch my breath, then see the bus. Aunt Teresa is already stepping aboard.

"Wait!" I yell. "Aspettare! Non andartene!"

Not wanting to disappoint her or miss work, I take off running.

The restaurant's alive with noise and movement, and I'm right in the middle of it and thriving.

"Posso prendere il tuo ordine?" I ask the three men just seated in my section.

"I'll have the American," one says with a smirk.

"With a side of beautiful," the second adds, tossing in a wink.

"And your number," the third finishes, grinning like he just won the SuperEnalotto, Italy's largest lottery.

Flirting is second nature to Italian men—an art form, really—and I can't say I mind.

I don't love attention, not when I've spent months trying to shrink into myself, but Rome is loud, sprawling, and teeming with Americans. I blend in enough to feel safe.

With a smile, I repeat their orders. "One cheeseburger," I write on my pad. "With a side of beautifully hand-cut fries." I pause and offer them a smirk. "And a big, fat, American-style tip."

"And your number?"

I flip the pad, scribble my response on a clean sheet, fold the paper, and toss it onto the table. "I'll bring three glasses of water while you men decide." Hips swaying, I saunter off toward the kitchen as they whistle in appreciation.

Camilla and Bianca are waiting for me. "Quegli uomini sono dei veri playboy," Camilla says.

"Manwhores, not playboys," Bianca corrects her. "Did you really give him your number?"

"I gave him a lucky number, but not my phone number." I grin. "I wrote Lucky 1. Hey, it's how I feel, like I'm the lucky one."

Truth.

Their laughter fills the kitchen. "They'll never leave you in peace now," Bianca says.

I shrug. If a bit of flirtation helps Aunt Teresa's profit margin, what's the harm?

"È una bella serata, no?" I say.

"Yes, Fina," they agree. "It's a great night."

Is it risky to go by Fina? Absolutely. But Fina is me—raw, unfiltered, untamed. Elia is the name my father picked, the one everyone else uses, the one that keeps me chained to his rules. Only my mother and my closest friends call me Fina because they see the part of me that won't be broken, the part that would rather burn the Life down than bow to it.

We banter back and forth in English and Italian, their English oozing sexiness while my Italian is rough around the edges.

Bianca's gorgeous, bold, full of life, and a warm welcome to Italy. Camilla's equally pretty, more reserved yet every bit as fun. Both are beautiful, ambitious free spirits living life.

Dolce Vita does exist outside the movies, I'm learning. There's a whole new world outside the Life, where a woman isn't an afterthought or a bartering chip.

I'm grateful, so damn grateful to have landed here. For their friendship. And for this lucrative job—Aunt Teresa's restaurant's always packed.

Bianca nudges me. "Are you ready for a taste of Roman nightlife?"

Her boyfriend owns a club that's literally a hop, skip, and jump away. He's handsome, older, rich, and a major player, Camilla tells me.

Bianca says he's hung like a goddamn stallion and makes her sit on his face while he eats her out.

My mind flashes to another man. Someone I thought I knew. But now, looking back, I'm not sure any of it was real. I saw what I wanted to see, painted him in colors he never earned and didn't deserve. I gave him my virginity. He gave me excuses and one hell of a vanishing act.

What remains is a bitter lesson.

Pleasure at his hands comes at a cost.

But the pain he brings for free.

"A night out is exactly what I need," I answer Bianca with more force than necessary. A new city, with new faces and new flirtations, sounds like the perfect escape.

An opportunity to forget him, and everything between then and now.

Renzo

The barber steps back, finished with brushing talc from my nape.

I stare into the shop mirror, looking more like Sandro than myself. Cropped hair, freshly shaven, draped in a new designer suit I purchased late yesterday afternoon, after the meeting at the restaurant. I look the part of a ruthless capo di tutti capi's son.

But there's a new spring in my step for a different reason.

This morning, I initiated my plan of modernizing the Eleven. I'm now the proud owner of a million-dollar kill box. I've stitched together a fleet of drones, half spy tech, half battlefield monsters. DJI Mavic 3s, with wide-view lenses for clean daytime surveillance. The Switchblade 300s, with thermal imaging for nighttime hunting and grenade-sized warheads for impromptu strikes. These babies don't just track, they end.

It's the Warmates I'm most excited about. Sleek, fixed-wing bastards that circle like vultures, silent and patient. They can stay in the air for over an hour, watch everything, strike hard. Doesn't matter if it's armored tanks, white cargo vans filled with stolen pistachios, or armed mafiosi vehicles on lookout. One press of a button and, poof, problem solved.

No fingerprints. No fucking DNA. No clue what just happened. *Was it a lightning strike? Bad luck, that.*

Who needs satellites when you've got death on autopilot?

My morning transitioned into an equally successful early afternoon. I hired my first team members, starting with a knobby-kneed sixteen-year-old tech wizard. Doubtful the kid or his friends even understand who I am or who they'll be working for. Book smarts, meet the king of streetwise. But green around the ears or not, their robotics team placed first in Italy with knobby-knees as pilot. And hey, I'm all about investing in the future generation.

In two days, surveillance begins on Vito Cardini.

Within the next two nights, I'll be a made man.

By week's end, shit will hit the fan. Because no one, especially not my father, likes a skimmer.

I rise from the barber's chair a new man. A horn honks as I exit the shop, as if Rome agrees that everything's at my fingertips.

It takes five minutes to reach the club. A woman on cleanup flashes me a smile over her shoulder as she wipes a table. I pause to admire the view before heading to Dante's office.

Smile in place, I push inside.

He greets me with a stare that doesn't blink, doesn't soften, just drills straight through me like he's contemplating ending me. At last, he speaks. "Do I have stupid *stranzo* written on my fucking forehead?"

I fall into a seat, then pretend to search his upper brow.

"The Eleven are demanding an investigation into Carlo Accardo's murder."

"Murder? I heard his death was an unfortunate allergic reaction to strawberries."

"You heard." He grunts. "Right."

"Who gives two shits if that traitorous fuck is dead?"

"The Eleven. *Your* father. You returning his calls?"

I sigh. "If I were, we wouldn't be having this conversation."

"His autopsy showed death by anaphylaxis caused by a severe allergic reaction to berries." He leans forward in his chair. "Fucking hell. You did it, didn't you? You somehow spiked that asshole's meal with berries?"

I smooth out an invisible crease in my new suit pants.

"They found traces of it in his goddamn beer mug."

"Handcrafted beer is fused with all kinds of shit. Though typically, it's not enough to kill anyone."

Dante stares at me. "Berries didn't kill him?"

I contemplate my choices, but they all boil down to this: my truthful admission in exchange for Dante's trust? Fuck, it's worth his rage.

"Though thallium, mixed in with his Pepcid pills, would."

"What?"

I wait, letting it sink in.

"You fucking didn't." Dante tosses a pen onto his desk. "There are rules."

"I broke one."

"You're unprotected. Not a made man."

"But I will be. Soon. Very soon."

"Thallium in his Pepcid pills." He leans back in his chair and scrolls on his phone. "Untraceable," he reads, "unless you're testing for it." When he glances up, his eyes are full of admiration. On my side, just as I was hoping. I'll need him to run interference with my father.

"Christ, you're clever. I'll remember not to cross you."

This is a taste of what I bring to the table. In two days, he'll get a fucking mouthful, and with my newfound success, I can finally return my father's calls.

"Clever, but there's a glitch."

I frown.

"Your father was dealing with Carlo Accardo."

"Dealing with?"

"Accardo's men broke into the estate." Dante's voice is tight with disbelief. "Your father's guards caught them soon after they breached the perimeter ... luckily the Beneventi soldiers were waiting for them ..."

Not luck.

Fina.

Her warning to my father comes roaring back—*If I were you ...*

She knew.

Of course she fucking knew.

"As director of the Midwest Real Estate Trust, Carlo played a critical role in financing the Midwest casino expansion. Eliminating him required careful timing. The Eleven sank significant investments into the trust, which is tightly regulated by state and local commissions. Pulling money out couldn't be rushed or it'd raise suspicions. Your father needed the famiglie financially fortified before carving Accardo out of the picture."

Well, shit.

"Everything's frozen, every cent. Multi-billion-dollar investments locked up tight. Construction in Chicago, Cincinnati, and Cleveland? Completely shut down." Dante scrubs a hand down his face. "I lost access to at least a billion. Because of you."

This is a goddamn disaster. "And I placed my father in a difficult position." Undermined his power. Gave the Eleven reason to question his decisions.

"If they discover it was you ..."

Yeah. Got it. I'm *dead.*

"I'll fix it."

"How?"

"I'll divert their attention elsewhere while I work on unfreezing the trust. Use my connections in Illinois to ease the commission's suspicions about shady activity or find the right incentive for them to turn a blind eye."

"And you'll call your father. Before he boards a flight to Rome and makes my life more miserable."

I grimace. "I need two days."

"Jesus. Fine. But no more, capisci?"

The tension in the room eases.

"You won't regret taking me on."

He sighs. "I already do, asshole."

Immediate crisis avoided, I roll out of my chair. It's time for me to make a name for myself. I leave his office just as he's muttering the question I hoped he wouldn't ask.

"Why in God's breath would you kill Carlo Accardo?"

Tina

"You look more Italian than we do."

Camilla meets my eyes in the club's bathroom mirror. My friends have highlights in their black hair, Bianca blonde and Camilla red, while mine's untouched. I'm what you call the antithesis of your typical California girl. Why be average?

"Are many women in Minneapolis dark-haired?" Camilla asks, smacking her lips with a fresh coat of lip gloss.

On the walk to Club Tiberius, they asked me where I was from. And I lied. This might be overly cautious since I blend in so well in Rome and the Life is far behind me. And maybe one day, I'll explain my lies. But for now, I keep details about myself vague.

"Minnesota has a huge Italian-American population." Never been, and know very little about the state.

Bianca wiggles next to me, settling her miniskirt higher on her thighs.

I love this girl.

"I'd like to visit the States someday."

I force a smile. "Sure. I'll show you around."

"It must be fun living in a big city," Camilla continues, three wines gone and clearly not letting the topic go. "Everyone knows each other here."

I roll my eyes. "Doesn't Rome have, like, two million residents?"

"Closer to three," Bianca chimes in.

"I mean this part of the city," Camilla explains. "They know everyone here."

My stomach drops. "They?"

She lowers her voice. "Bianca's boyfriend and his associates."

I watch my reflection as the blood drains from my face.

"Dante owns this part of Rome," Bianca declares.

"Dante?" Fear rolls up my spine. Because I know of a Dante with connections to Rome. Everyone in the Eleven does. Hard not to when he's the second-most powerful man in the Eleven.

Shit, oh shit. I didn't leave the famiglie behind. I fell into its lap.

Camilla pats my arm. "Don't worry. They're harmless."

"The mafiosi, you mean?"

Bianca and Camilla give each other a look.

"Does Zia Teresa know?"

"Of course," Bianca replies. "How do you think I met Dante? He eats at the restaurant all the time with his friends. He was there the day you were off, with two handsome associates. When he arrives at the club later, I'll introduce you."

I bite my lip, cursing my luck. My head spins with the weight of this revelation. I want to scream, to cry, to wave a magic wand and make the truth disappear. I never met Dante Lucchese. I couldn't tell you what he looks like, aside from being handsome and hung like a stallion.

How did I know intimate details about his anatomy but not Bianca's boyfriend's name?

It's unlikely Dante will take any real interest in me, no more than he would in any woman who happens to be friends with his girlfriend and related to Zia Teresa.

No cause to panic. That's what I tell myself, even though my pulse won't settle.

I need to talk to my prozia and ask her why she's rubbing elbows with the mafiosi.

Decide if I'm safe.

Or if I need to disappear, again.

11

Renzo

Interesting things happen in the dead of night. Especially when no one is watching—or so you believe ...

"Why are they hauling burlap sacks of pistachios into a shed in the middle of an olive grove?" the kid whispers.

We're belly-down in the dirt, tucked into the tall grass just outside Vito's property, running a damn-near-genius surveillance op on his secret side-hustle.

When my father shows the Eleven these photos, Vito Cardini is finished. Shame the greedy man won't live to see the fallout. Springing to my feet, I take out a roll of Euros and toss it on the ground in front of him. "Good work, kid. Now it's time to head home."

He gathers the Switchblade 300 beneath his arm protectively, and we walk back to the Vespas. As he secures the drone, I turn my motorbike toward Vito's estate. Photographs are one crucial part of my plan. But there's more I've got to do tonight to become a made man.

"You're not riding back to Rome with me?" the kid asks, finally noticing.

"You scared? Need me to hold your hand?"

He rolls his eyes, mounts his motorbike, and, flipping me the bird, takes off.

I must be rubbing off on the kid.

After two exhilarating hours of surveillance, I know everything I need to know to accomplish my goal.

I stop the Vespa and slip it between two ornamental bushes before heading up the driveway.

The guards are too busy arguing politics to notice me.

I move fast, pressing a gun to one's gut while covering the other's nose with a chloroform-soaked cloth. He drops like a stone. The first follows a heartbeat later.

No need to waste bullets, though I briefly consider making an exception for the one rambling about the pitfalls of democracy.

I bring the butt of my gun down on a third guard's head and step sideways as his form crumples across the grand foyer.

Italians have an aversion to air-conditioning—something I've learned the hard way. But open windows make for easy surveillance.

The drone slipped in without a hitch, so now I know exactly who's where inside the house, and more importantly, where Vito's sleeping.

Luck would have it that his wife is in a separate bedroom. He a snorer? Or just an asshole?

I set up my phone and hit record, then remove the portable unfolding handsaw, a sharper and more deadly version of a Swiss Army knife, from my knapsack before climbing over his body and straddling his hips. All it takes is a firm slap to wake his ass up.

Smile for the camera, motherfucker.

He blinks, struggles, and nonsense spews out of him. "You dare fucking breaking into my home. You know who I am?"

"Vito Cardini."

"You're a dead man."

He has no clue who he's threatening. Neither will anyone

viewing the video. Not until I tug off the black ski mask and show the world the truth hidden beneath it.

"Tell me about the pistachios."

He jerks beneath me, surprised. "What pistachios?"

"The pistachios you stole from Dante Lucchese. The pistachios you have hidden away in a fucking shed in the middle of your olive grove. Did you think you'd get away with stealing from the Eleven?"

"Who the fuck are you?"

I smirk. "I'm your worst goddamn nightmare."

He bucks beneath me.

I press the saw blade to his throat, slow and deliberate.

"Greed," I whisper. "That's what got you here. And you know damn well—stealing from the Eleven is a death sentence."

My hand doesn't shake. My pulse stays even. But inside, something electric surges—dark, euphoric. An endorphin-laced high floods my system, sharp as adrenaline, sick as pleasure.

This is my first kill.

And something in me snaps.

Mercy dies.

Conscience flickers out.

All that's left is the rush.

His anger gets the better of him. "You're a coward who can't even show his face."

I smirk, then rip off my hood.

He blinks, then blinks again. "Alessandro Beneventi."

"Close."

His eyes widen. And then he laughs. "Lorenzo Beneventi?"

"Correct." I pause. "Anything you'd like to say to Dante?"

"Fuck you, you pussy. Everyone saw you freeze. Everyone whispers about what a weak bastard you are." He tilts his head so the blade presses deeper. "What, was your brother not available?"

"Everyone's whispering, huh?"

I drag the blade across his throat, deep enough to make him gurgle, to paint the sheets in red. Not deep enough to end it. Not yet.

"Since you're my first," I murmur, "the one who earns me my place ... it's only right you hear the truth first."

I carve a second line, clean and parallel, beneath the first. His blood pulses out, hot and frantic. His eyes widen, pure terror blooming behind them.

"I didn't freeze," I say.

Then I smile.

"I was savoring the motherfucking moment."

I clamp my hand over his mouth and start sawing. Slow. Merciless. His body jerks. Blood spurts, coats my arms, soaks the mattress, slicks the floor.

I don't stop until his head is severed clean.

And then—like a goddamn medieval warrior—I rise, grip his hair, and step off the bed, dripping in death. I stalk toward the camera and lift the head high.

"For Dante Lucchese," I say coldly.

I wipe the blood from my face with the back of my hand, lean in close, and let my voice drop into a growl.

"Any more whispers about me being the weak Beneventi, and you'll be next."

Fina

"FINA. THE PEAS ARE CLEAN ENOUGH, DON'T YOU THINK?" Aunt Teresa calls out from her perch on a stool at the kitchen island.

I glance down at the water sluicing over the freshly shucked peas in the colander. I'm helping her prep for tomorrow's special, a simple pasta e piselli that her customers rave about.

Who knew I'd be the kind of girl who enjoys sorting a morning harvest in a sun-warmed kitchen? But here I am—hands busy, nails chipped, and somehow ... at peace.

In LA, dinner comes in sleek packaging with calorie counts, impossible expiration dates, and macronutrient buzz words scribbled like warnings. It's convenient. Soulless.

Here, everything's different. You can taste the earth in the food, sunlight in the tomatoes, rain in the herbs, something wild and real in every bite. There's no plastic packaging between you and your meal. Just time. Hands. Heart.

I shake off the water and return to the table.

My friends in Los Angeles would laugh at the sight of me at my prozia's kitchen table. But, although I miss them and can't correspond with them, I've no plans on returning. Which leads to the other problem at hand—how involved is Aunt Teresa in the famiglie in Rome?

"Did you know the mafia run a club near the restaurant?" I casually ask, not elaborating further about last night's unsettling discovery.

She pauses, fresh pasta between her fingertips. "Dante's club."
"Dante Lucchese?"
"He owns everything on the south side."
My eyebrows touch my hairline. "Everything?"
She pats my hand. "Even the restaurant."
Lord, I ran from the Eleven only to land like a dart in a bullseye. "I thought you escaped the Life?" Never once did she sound strange over the phone or worried. Never once did she complain or voice fear. Never once did she mention she's still part of the world I'm desperately trying to eradicate from my life.

"Fina," she sighs, noticing my distress. "There is no escape. Not really. You survive by being smart and by paying attention. Learn the rhythm of when to make yourself seen and when to vanish, when to speak and when to let silence speak for you. It's finding brief moments to shine, balanced by knowing how to move within the shadows. These mafiosi respect three things: brute force, money, and respect. Prove yourself in one or more of these ways, and not only can you survive but flourish.”

“My mother ...”

Aunt Teresa winces, sadness filling her eyes, her voice almost a whisper. “She shone too brightly.”

“You make it sound like she had a choice.”

She shakes her head, slow and heavy. “She didn’t. She caught the eye of a weak man who craved power. The kind of man who devours the little he does control.”

“I’m glad I left him with nothing.” No Accardo bankroll. No cash on hand, or inside his safe. No daughter to sell off. “Exactly what he deserves.”

Because no matter how much time has passed, there’s still a little girl inside me, pressed against the front bay window, eyes fixed on the road, hoping her mother might come home. I’d do anything to learn the truth, learn if the rumors are true.

Aunt Teresa moves away from the table, then returns with a bottle of wine. Silently and despite the early hour, she pours two glasses.

“Tell me about the Eleven in Italy.”

She shakes her head. “Italy, America, there’s no real difference. Sebastiano Beneventi still rules without question. You know that. You were at his wedding.”

The wine now tastes bitter instead of sweet.

“But Rome belongs to Dante,” she continues. “We’re lucky, in a way. The Italian famiglie—the Youngbloods, Vito Cardini—they don’t have Dante’s power, brains, or sense of fairness.”

Her gaze drifts, softens.

Oh no. She isn’t crushing on Dante.

“His good looks,” I add, “his charm, his big dick energy.”

“Elia Seraphina.” Her face flushes. And my friends and I thought her mind was on her sauce and not fine-tuned to our vividly descriptive discussions?

“Am I safe?” I blurt out.

She frowns. "Your father's proven himself untrustworthy. Odds are, he's not in regular contact with the famiglie anymore. No one will stick their neck out for him."

"And the Eleven?"

She studies my face—my worry, my panic. Because I don't want to run again. I like it here.

"Learn the rhythm of this life, Fina," she says gently. "Same way I did. And I promise you'll find peace."

Peace. Not safety.

And then my prozia does the most unexpected thing.

She reaches into the pocket of her flour-dusted apron, pulls out a small black object, and slides it across the table.

My jaw drops.

A gun, tucked in next to her wooden spoon and fresh oregano like it belongs there.

"Take my advice ..." she says, as calm as she is wise. "... and this." Like she's handing me a biscotto and not a firearm.

But at this point, I probably shouldn't be surprised.

This is Aunt Teresa, after all.

She pats my hand like a sweet grandmother and turns back to her pasta, humming softly as if she didn't just arm me at the kitchen table.

Just before the rolling pin hits the dough, she adds, almost as an afterthought:

"A woman in this world can never be too cautious."

12

Fina

"You look like a goddess," Camilla says, eyes wide with a mix of admiration and too much limoncello.

We're squeezed into the back of a taxi, limbs tangled and bodies slick with summer sweat, in tight dresses, towering heels, fake lashes, bold war paint, and wigs that whisper *dare me*.

My blonde wig spills over my bare back, sexy and sensual. Less goddess and more bombshell about to make questionable choices.

Camilla's edgy blue bob frames her sharp cheekbones like it was made for her. Bianca's wild red curls make her eyes glow. We're a three-alarm fire, and impossible to ignore.

I thank God for saving me, but I'm not cut out to be a nun.

When Bianca suggested dress-up, I embraced the idea. I can steal into the night, laugh loud, dance hard, live like I never almost lost it all, incognito.

Bianca's apartment is a short distance from Dante's club, but we cab it the few blocks. We can't let Camilla loose on the streets in stilettos, not with her tottering like a baby giraffe on cobblestone. We're ready to conquer Rome, not eat asphalt.

The club is alive and bouncing with an electric energy as we're ushered in.

Our first stop is the bar, where we order more limoncello shots. "One, two, three," we chant, and then—very American-style—slam our shot glasses upside down on the bar. Earning everyone's attention.

"Now we dance," Camilla proclaims, linking arms with us. We storm the dance floor like we're tonight's main event. And soon, I'm laughing and dancing like a fool, the strobe lights sweeping away fear, pain, and sorrow, pulverizing my heartaches into tiny colorful particles of light, then casting it into the stratosphere.

This is the life I dreamed about.

This is the joy I deserve.

Techno-pop has the dance floor vibrating, and a sea of moving bodies surrounds me. I've always been a good dancer, and tonight, I feel it, bumping, fist-pumping, alive. So alive.

An arm snakes around my waist, and I'm pulled back. I step on his instep and break free, then glance over my shoulder and realize I've nothing to fear.

Okay. He's hot. Strong jaw, a determined tilt to his lips.

He moves in again, and this time, I let him.

It feels nice, and I sway along with his movements.

We dance together for several songs until he goes in for a kiss.

I don't know why I balk, turning my head at the last second before stepping away.

Frustration surges, raw and aching. Followed by truth. If I'm truly committed to starting over, the past needs to stay in the past. I was slightly obsessed over one man for far too long. He has no right to be in my mind or heart. I never want to see him again.

And now, you never will.

I spin back toward my dance partner, driving all thoughts of him aside.

Only to find my dance partner locking lips with Bianca.

What the hell?

Camilla shoves between me and them, her voice cutting through the music.

"Come on. Fina. Bathroom!" Hand on my elbow, she drags me across the dance floor, then down a hallway to a bathroom. We wait our turn to enter, then once we do, Camilla locks the door behind us.

"Sorry about Bianca," Camilla says, now that we're alone.

For a busy club, the restroom is spotless. As I reapply lip gloss, I notice even the mirror's streak-free.

"You were vibing with him first."

She's more upset than I am.

I shrug. "He's just a stupid boy."

"It doesn't bother you?"

"I'm not the jealous type, especially not over eye-candy I just barely met."

"That's what Bianca was about." Camilla side-eyes me. "She was trying to make Dante jealous."

I stiffen. "He's here?"

"With another woman."

Well, hell with that. "Come on," I say. "We should rescue her before she does something crazy."

We retrace our steps down the hall, heading back to the dance floor.

Bianca is nowhere to be seen.

"Upstairs." Camilla points to a balcony, and I follow her to the stairs in the corner and blocked by security.

The mafioso asks for our names.

"Camilla," she offers before I can stop her.

He checks his list.

It's obvious my friend's never been to a VIP room before. What name will get us in? What name carries enough weight to make him step aside?

"Beneventi," I say, forcing the word through clenched teeth.

He waves us through without even looking down.

Camilla throws me a quick look, which I pretend not to see. Still, a cold prickle crawls over my skin because that was too easy.

We climb the stairs and step onto the balcony overlooking the dance floor. Everything is tastefully done. Burgundy curtains soften the industrial beams holding the loft in place. Plush sofas form intimate circles around low tables, grouped strategically for maximum privacy. The space feels expensive and deliberate. Dante has exquisite taste.

"Not crowded, like we figured," I say, eyes sweeping the room.

Camilla walks to the railing and peers down at the crowd. "I don't see Bianca. Or Dante." She sighs. "Probably off in some back office with Bianca's replacement. No wonder she's spiraling."

Laughter bursts from a group of women gathered around one of the large velvet sofas. The sound reminds me why I came. I'm about to tell Camilla we should head back to the dance floor, where Bianca's more likely to find us, when the women shift places.

And I see him.

Laid out like a king in ruin.

Suit jacket's balled beneath his head in a makeshift pillow. White dress shirt unbuttoned down to his navel. Chest rising and falling in slow, heavy rhythm. Eyes closed. Out cold.

Wasted.

A woman moves, exposing an open whiskey bottle on the table within his reach.

"God," Camilla mutters under her breath. "Him again."

No freaking way. How can this be?

Rage simmers just beneath the surface, boiling up like lava poking at a crack. "You know him?"

"He was at the restaurant a few weeks ago with Dante." Camilla offers a casual shrug. "Looked about the same. Like death warmed over." She even smiles. "He's quite the character."

A woman leans down and gives him a shake. Nothing. He doesn't stir. He's lights out, lost in whatever black hole he's crawled back into.

And all at once, the memories crash in—

Him swaying on unsteady feet.

Him chanting my name, like that'd make everything better.

Fina. Fina. Fina.

His lame excuses. My disappointment.

Take care of me? How could he when he can't even take care of himself?

I charge forward, push through the women, storm straight at him, and snatch the bottle.

Behind me, Camilla shrieks, "Fina, no—don't—"

But it's too late.

I empty the contents over his head, dousing him.

He jerks awake, coughing, sputtering, gasping for air.

I drop the bottle, and then slap him. The crack of my palm echoes like gunfire.

His head snaps to the side. He blinks, whiskey streaming from his lashes, dazed but not totally defenseless. And much quicker than I expect, he grabs my wrist, tight and fast.

"What the hell?" His voice is rough and groggy.

"Fuck you, Renzo, you promise-wrecker. No, fuck you twice—all the way back to Rhode Island. You don't get to ruin my new beginning. Go be reckless somewhere else."

He shakes his head and blinks rapidly, trying to clear his vision.

I don't regret what I've done, not in the slightest. He's worse than I remember, a mess of drugs and liquor and women who don't know any better.

I didn't either.

But now I do.

There's shouting. Security swarming and hands grabbing. Camilla's voice cuts through the chaos. "Fina!"

We're escorted away.

Out of the balcony.

Out of the club.

Away from the man I hoped to never see again.

Renzo

Y*OU PROMISE-WRECKER.*

I roll to my side, wondering why my mind's fucking with me. I made my peace, healed a wound that finally scabbed over, only to wake up feeling like it had suddenly bust open again. Booze, drugs, sex aren't to blame—I celebrated Vito Cardini's kill without falling back on destructive habits.

With a groan, I glance around. The club's quiet, and I'm completely alone in the VIP room. Fuck, the adrenaline had me soaring all night, then crashing like a child thrown into sleep, numb and blind to everything around me.

I sit up, my foot kicking an empty bottle, cheek stinging, while I shake off the buzz kill, then head downstairs to the bar for a much-needed caffeine fix.

Dante's already there.

"Espresso," I rasp.

The bartender gets to work. Dante looks me over and chuckles. "You look like I feel."

I grunt.

"Damn," Dante chuckles. "Was decapitating Cardini what you meant by giving the Eleven something else to think about?"

Christ, he's still celebrating? Wants all the gory details, does he?

The bartender places a small cup before me. I stir in two sugar cubes, then take a sip, sighing after the caffeine hits my tongue. "It worked," I finally say.

"But no chain saw?" Dante teases.

"I don't know if I've got the stomach to rehash all the minute details."

"I asked Luciano to handle matters." He smirks. "Still, you had to be the one to do it."

"Off Vito? Fuck yeah."

"Luciano will be pissed."

"Send him the video. He'll be less pissed."

I expect satisfaction to settle in, but instead my thoughts crawl back to the blonde. Like she never really left.

Go fuck yourself twice—all the way back to Rhode Island.

She knew who I was. Knew my name. And still came at me like I was a nobody. Like I was worse than nothing. "You see an angry blonde in a short dress exit the VIP room last night?"

"I was occupied."

I laugh. Sex is like air for this asshole. "Bianca's easy on the eyes."

My comment's met with silence.

"Not Bianca."

"No." He tosses back his espresso, then gestures at the bartender for another. "It got messy."

"Bet it did."

"Had to have her and her friends escorted from the club. A shame. I was digging the red wig she had on."

I frown. "Wig?"

"Yeah. She and her friends are into role-playing. Chick shit, you know."

Espresso sloshes over the rim, and I stare at my shaking hand.

"Adrenaline crash," Dante says, locking in. "You'll get used to it."

I say nothing. Let him think I'm coming down from a natural high.

Because the truth is the blonde triggers another memory.

Of the man I thought I left behind.

13

Renzo

Seven months ago

Hip propped against her car, partially for support, partially because the ground's spinning, I ambush her in a Whole Foods parking lot.

"Renzo," she breathes, coming to a stop a few feet away.

I straighten and lurch forward.

"Are you hurt?" she demands, her gaze skimming over me for signs of injury.

Yeah, I'm hurt. Fucking drowning in it, mixed with the liquor I've consumed and the drugs pumping through my veins.

It all ties back to Rome.

Rome. Rome. Rome.

"I expected you weeks ago."

My eyebrows pinch. Weeks? Is that how long it's been? Hard to distinguish between daytime and nighttime let alone between days ... weeks.

"Thank God you came. My father booked us a flight to Chicago for me to meet Carlo." She charges forward and grabs my elbow.

I sway on my feet from the contact.

"We can drive to Vegas right now and get married ..."

My foot catches on my ankle, and I tumble onto the pavement.

"Renzo," she cries out, falling to her knees. "What's wrong with you?"

I lie on my back and stare up at her. "I savored the moment too fucking long. And now I'm paying the price for it."

"What moment?"

"My destiny. I ruined it."

"You're not making sense." She stands and brushes dirt off her jeans, then glances around the parking lot nervously. "You have to get up."

"Can't. Not when I've fallen so far."

She sticks out her hand, insistent.

I take it and somehow manage to stand. "Fina ..."

"Don't," she mutters, her mind probably piecing together the truth, the reason I'm here.

"My father won't allow it."

"Your father will get over it."

I shake my head. If my father even knew I was in LA, I'd be done.

Her body goes rigid. "You promised."

"A lot has changed since I made that ridiculous declaration."

"Ridiculous?" She shoves me hard, and I fall back against a car. "My life, my happiness, my damn future isn't ridiculous."

"I'm not the marrying type."

She throws her hands up. "I don't care."

"Even if you're the only woman I'll ever want to marry." I'll give her this much.

Her eyes go wide. "If we elope ..."

I laugh, and it comes out hollow. "My father won't get over Rome. Why would he get over this?" My stomach curdles, and I'm six seconds shy of losing whatever food I've in me. But I can't remember the last meal I had. Life's been a fucking blur.

And now that I've told her, now that she knows the situation, I can get back to oblivion.

"Fina, Fina, Fina. I'm nobody's hero." I lean into her. "You might not know this about me, but I give out marriage proposals like bottled water. You're better off finding another asshole to marry. Or better yet"—I get in her face—"just vanish."

"You asshole," she screeches. "I'll ride every dick in Hollywood like it's my last fuck on earth, while you rot in hell, thinking about it." Tears roll down her cheeks. "I was counting on you."

"You're smarter than that," I mutter. "Smart enough to escape. Remember what we discussed." Hard to say if I'm reassuring her or myself.

"I hate you," she calls after me as I stagger off.

My mind spins as the demons beckon.

Can't hate me any more than I hate myself right now.

14

Renzo

"I UNDERESTIMATED YOU," MY FATHER SAYS THE MOMENT HE picks up.

No hello. No "How is Rome treating you?" Just that.

I savor the compliment like a rare vintage Chianti.

"Did you have to saw Cardini's head off?" he adds, dry as dust, like we're discussing another asinine political decision we've numbed our ears to.

"Would you prefer I left it attached?"

Dante, seated behind his desk, steeples his fingers and watches me like I'm both his greatest asset and biggest headache.

He's just glad I'm the one on the phone now.

"Some of the Eleven are pissed about that little threat you tacked on at the end of the video," my father continues. "But fuck if anyone's whispering that we're weak. Not anymore."

Annoyance sets in, as Dante chimes in, "Gave them something to think about."

I shoot him a look. If he were closer, I'd elbow him.

My father growls. "Other than the millions in frozen assets?"

I sigh. "My Chicago contacts are working on it."

"Fix what you broke. Capisci?"

Shit. Any doubts my father hasn't figured out what I've done go up in fucking smoke.

"Crystal."

"Good. Now tell me you had nothing to do with Elia Lombardi's disappearance. I told you to leave her the fuck alone."

I feel Dante's eyes drilling into my skull. I keep my face blank. "I haven't been in contact with her since that day in your office."

"You didn't marry her, did you?"

Jesus. Might as well toss all my dirty laundry on Dante's lap. "Still single, thanks."

"You know where she is?"

"No."

But the dark edges of my memory shift just enough to let a thought click into place. Shit, I might know. Still not telling, though.

"Her father's losing his shit, and his damn shirt. Without Carlo, he can't pay off his debts."

"Cry me a river."

Dante raises his brows, amused.

"Fuck off," I mutter.

My father goes quiet, and I immediately realize why. "Not you," I add quickly. "That was meant for Dante."

"I'm still going to beat your ass for the mess you've stirred up."

"If that's all I get, I'll take the beating."

"Have you spoken to Massimo Grassi?" Something in his tone shifts.

"No." I pause. "Why?"

"Dante, you hearing anything from Sicily?"

Dante straightens. "Should I be?"

My father's silence makes us sit straighter. "Don Tito Grassi was gunned down leaving Sunday mass. No one's claimed responsibility. Not a word from the Cosa Nostra."

Well, shit. Massimo is head of his famiglia now.

"I'll ask around," Dante says. "Find out which fool within the Cosa Nostra dares execute a Grassi."

I tap my fingers against my thigh. "It doesn't track. The Cosa Nostra loves theatrics and usually turns assassinations into parades. Why stay silent? You'd think they'd challenge Massimo's power."

"True." My father grunts. "But we won't take sides, not yet."

"Right."

"Renzo."

"Just checking."

"I'll amend. We use discretion. You need me to spell that out for you, you little shit?"

Dante laughs.

"I get it. No neon signs pointing our way."

My father grumbles something close to affection. "We'll talk again when we learn more."

The call ends.

The oppressive air in the room finally lifts, and I exhale.

But two thoughts linger:

Will Massimo retain power?

And why the fuck did Fina choose Rome as her new beginning?

Fina

"He's here," Camilla hisses, barreling into the kitchen like she's outrunning a tsunami.

Bianca freezes midchop. "Che cazzo? He has the nerve to walk into my restaurant and eat my food?" She slams the knife down. "Do I look like second best to you?"

"No," Camilla and I chorus.

Aunt Teresa shakes her head but keeps stirring her sauce. Tossing Dante Lucchese's cheating ass out of his restaurant isn't an option. He's lucky Bianca's not cooking tonight, or he'd be choking on clams marinara and regret.

"I refuse to wait on him."

"Fina and I will cover for you." Camilla helps clean the freshly chopped vegetables off the cutting board, and wisely moves the knife away from our friend. "You stay in the kitchen until he leaves. He doesn't get the privilege of your attention, not after whoring around."

We grab plated orders and head out. But the moment we push onto the floor, I stop dead in my tracks.

"Him again," Camilla mutters.

Renzo ... here?

No, no, no.

He's laughing at something Dante said, looking like sin in a suit. Clean-shaven, hair cropped short, his tailored jacket molded to his shoulders rather than hanging off his frame.

The world's most handsome heartache.

God's clearly still punishing me for stealing in His house. No man who ruins hearts with a smile and walks away like it's mercy should look that good.

I backtrack. "I'm not going out there."

Camilla glances from him to me. "He won't recognize you from last night."

"That's not what I'm worried about."

"Wait. You do know him?"

Does anyone know Lorenzo Beneventi?

"Cazzo," she breathes. "You do."

I thrust the plate into her hands before she can drown me in questions I'll never answer, then slip behind the kitchen wall, out of sight, unsettled, and burning with a curiosity I know will ruin me.

While I hide, Camilla plays waitress, delivering dishes with that effortless smile of hers. But when she circles back, she stops short near his table, glances at me, and gives a small shake of her head before moving away.

Bianca slides up beside me. "The balls on that man."

"I couldn't agree more," I mutter.

Camilla comes around the corner in a mad rush, grabs us both by the elbows, and drags us into the back storage room. She kicks the door shut behind us.

"What?" Bianca and I shout in unison.

"He's asking for the blonde," Camilla blurts.

My stomach plummets.

Bianca's face contorts. "The blonde from last night?" She snatches a clean knife from the storage room shelf and storms the door. "I'll carve him into pieces and add him as an anchovy appetizer."

"Wait, no!" Camilla lunges.

But Bianca's already halfway through the kitchen.

"Wrong blonde."

I freeze. "What do you mean?"

"Dante didn't speak to me. It was the other man, the one you assaulted last night."

My throat dries. "What did he say?"

"He asked for the nosy blonde with the wicked temper."

Oh, hell.

"I told him he was mistaken, that no one here fit that description."

"And?"

She gives a tight shrug. "He said blondes aren't really his type anyway."

I scowl, confused and insulted. But we don't have time to dissect his words because shouts erupt from the dining room.

Bianca.

We burst out of the storage room and into chaos. Aunt Teresa's already charging through the kitchen, with us on her heels.

I tuck behind the kitchen wall as Bianca's screams echo around the restaurant. "You playboy. Coming in here and throwing your other women in my face." In her hand is an empty plate.

Dante is on his feet, sauce dripping from his crotch.

Aunt Teresa's blotting the mess with a cloth napkin while Camilla, not knowing what to do, hovers beside her.

And Renzo? I expected his laughter, not his silence.

That's how I know this is bad. Boyfriend or not, you don't embarrass the second-most powerful man in the Eleven.

Aunt Teresa and Camilla are as white as the tablecloths.

Bianca steps back, realizing her mistake.

But Renzo? He's calmly speaking to the enraged man. Whatever Renzo says, Dante nods, and then sits back down like none of this happened.

"Nothing to worry about. Just a clumsy accident," Renzo declares, offering a lie, and a story the gossipers can whisper about. "Enjoy your meal. Dinner and drinks on us."

The guests return to their meals, and the shaken trio returns to the kitchen.

"You silly girl," Aunt Teresa scolds.

Camilla exhales. "Dante looked ready for murder. Thank God he stepped in."

Bianca is so quiet you can hear a pin drop.

I exhale. Crisis averted.

Except, is it really?

The rest of the evening blurs into motion, with Bianca leaving early and us covering for her. Camilla works the floor while I break down the kitchen, pretending I'm fine, though my mind won't stop circling questions I don't want answered.

Why was he here? Why ask about the blonde?

Rome is my fresh start, I remind myself. *That asshole has no business being here.*

It feels like hours before Renzo and Dante finally leave. I help Camilla clear the tables, trying to shake the weight of it all.

Which is how I end up standing here, hand trembling around an empty wineglass, staring down at the table they left behind.

His plate is clean—spotless—except for one thing.

Bright red. Juicy.

Not on tonight's dessert menu.

Oh, sweet hell.

A strawberry.

My obsession with Lorenzo Beneventi is pathetic.

I blame the renewed spark on the old Fina. The years spent tracking him, the adrenaline rush in watching him thumb his nose at the Eleven and do whatever crazy-ass things he liked, the bolder the better. Nothing ever worried him. His behavior enthralled me.

Until I ended up on the receiving end of his loyal-to-none philosophy.

He abandoned me. Fortunately, I wasn't stupid enough to rely on him completely and had an escape mapped out. The only issue with my plan had been money.

God, I'm sorry, okay? I had no choice.

If you want to damn someone, damn Renzo.

And that strawberry for sparking my temper.

How dare he play with me like nothing happened. How dare he walk into my restaurant, eat the food my great-aunt made with love, and toss out questions about some blonde who doesn't exist.

It's my day off. I should be anywhere but here, trailing him through Rome's most iconic spots like some obsessed tourist.

But here I am. Trailing after a man I never truly knew. Craving answers and revenge, yet too disgusted to actually confront him and his excuses.

He's led me on an aimless tour of Rome, ducking in and out of shops and trattorias, slipping through crowds near the Colosseum, weaving through ancient ruins like a man with no clear destination.

I follow, always steps behind.

We stopped for espresso, gelato, and a Supplì stuffed with mozzarella—where, each time, I mirror his order, then relish each treat. We visited the Forum, the Colosseum, the Trevi Fountain. I almost lost him at the Spanish Steps when a few flirty locals distracted me with whistles and bold compliments.

The lack of logic in the path he's carving through Rome is astounding. No pattern to his madness. Yet much to my annoyance, with each passing hour my curiosity grows.

We end up at the Santa Maria della Vittoria, and I discover him at the foot of Bernini's sculpture, *Ecstasy of Saint Teresa*. Quietly, I creep forward, partially concealed by the sheer scarf around my neck and a few other visitors.

I study him as he regards the statue, and note the changes in him. Gone is the fragile frame and in its place muscles. Massive, mouthwatering muscles, the kind you want to squeeze to test if they're real. His hollow cheeks are now filled in, and there's a healthy glow to his skin. My eyes rake over him, head to toe. He looks very different from the last time I saw him in LA.

What's the same is his dangerously erotic vibe.

He's staring at the nun like he understands her. The reverence and ruin. Bliss sharpened by a raw ache.

I stare at him, trying to understand him. *A hopeless task, isn't it?* I think.

He should be up there instead of Saint Teresa. Shirt unbuttoned, chest bronzed and glimmering in the soft cathedral light, his expression echoing the statue's aching hunger.

Admired but never to be touched.

It hurts to look too long at him, and I want to touch him. Slap him again. Grab him by the collar and shout, "What happened? Why disappoint me like that?"

So many unanswered questions. Did he follow me to Rome? Did he leave that damn strawberry as some twisted joke?

I drag my eyes away.

Fuck you, Renzo Beneventi.

Comforted by a familiar rage, I force myself to look away, anywhere but at him.

Then God reminds me my penance isn't over, and I spot the artist's name beneath the statue.

Gian *Lorenzo* Bernini.

Of course the asshole's named for an artist who immortalized agony and ecstasy, something this man practically bleeds.

I tell myself to walk away. Leave him to his aimless wandering, let him disappear into the city just like he vanished when I needed him most.

But I don't. Pathetic as can be, I trail behind him as we exit the basilica.

SHE HASN'T CHANGED.

I was wondering if she'd take the bait and confront me about that fucking berry, among other things.

Still relentless.

Still so fucking beautiful the cheek she didn't slap aches.

Joining Dante for dinner and clueing her in that I recognized her was a bad idea. It's better she remain under the illusion I completely abandoned her. Dark days are behind both of us. Why stir up shit?

And if my father discovers she's in Rome, whether it's my doing or not, I'm not just cooked but deep-fried.

But when I caught sight of her lingering by the club, fucking waiting for me, I couldn't help myself.

We played a game of hide-and-seek for most of the day.

Every city block, every step of the way, I made sure she found me. We practically locked eyes in Santa Maria della Vittoria. Did she really think I wouldn't recognize her hiding beneath that scarf?

But standing at the nun's feet, staring up at that little bastard angel looming over her and ready to pierce her heart, it hit home. Fina holds the arrow and has already driven it into my chest.

And hell knows, I love a little pain mixed with pleasure.

Fina's always understood my kinks. Craves a taste of that world herself. I had a vision, while we stood at Saint Teresa's feet, of forcing Fina onto the cold marble floor and worshiping her with my mouth until her ecstasy rivaled the nun's. Fuck the audience. They wanted to see a woman in the throes of an orgasm? Fina would come so hard, she'd forget every promise I shattered.

A throat clears behind me, and my attention snaps to my office door.

Dante stands there, watching in silence.

"What's up?" I ask.

"No one expects you to be an angel, you know."

Is Dante a goddamn mindreader now? "Yeah, an angel who'd jab a spear through your heart."

"No booze. No drugs. Are you even getting laid?"

I toss the phone I was scrolling through onto the desk. "You sound like my therapist."

He chuckles. "Your therapist wants you to get laid?"

I smirk, letting him draw his own conclusions. But the truth is, since that visit, sex has been me and my fist. I, a man with an anything-goes mentality and voracious appetites, have relegated himself to good, old-fashioned jerk-offs.

Now how the fuck did that happen?

"Maybe I used the wrong choice of words," he continues, crossing the room to take a seat. "An angel doesn't saw heads off men."

"You, of all people, should know, " I murmur, "light can kill just as fast as darkness."

"Yeah, I get that."

"Did you want something besides the pleasure of my company?" I ask.

Dante grows serious. "Yeah. Can you add or extend surveillance on our warehouses, particularly those near the port? Some fuckhead set fire to a lucrative weapons shipment."

I stare at him thoughtfully. "That makes no sense. Why torch arms when you can steal them and sell them on the black market?"

"Don't know. And after the example you just set, who would dare pull a stunt like this?"

"Right."

"Got to be a family in the Cosa Nostra. Makes sense considering how the violence is escalating."

"Right again," I add. "I'll need to expand my team and order additional equipment."

"Do it." He stands. "Your father said to give you whatever you need." With that, he straightens his suit and stalks to the door. But he turns my way, with one more thing to add.

"Our capo di tutti capi also wants men on you. You know, since things here are amping up."

He leaves the room—and me—wondering if I, the goddamn king of players, just got played at my own game.

16

Renzo

Ass up.

That sums up my night so far.

I'm being tailed, and this time by mafiosi. Normally, I could lose them without breaking a sweat. Years of slipping by my father's and brother's men made sure of that. But that's exactly why things have gone bottoms up.

My so-called security team spotted the tail and went full Rambo. Guns out, chaos unleashed. The streets exploded in gunfire, stone facades crumbled like stale biscotti, locals running for cover. But the mafiosi following me? They were sharp, trained, and vanished without leaving so much as a bloody shoe print behind. No one left to interview. No answers about what they want with me.

Dante tried to argue and thought I should keep the protection. But he knew I would shake them anyway, and eventually caved.

Didn't take long for the mafiosi to find me again. Now, as I lead them through the winding alleys of Rome, I get the sense this isn't a hit. They're not pushing, not closing in. I think they want to talk.

They're going to earn the privilege.

It's past midnight, and I've spent the better part of an hour toying with them. I play the part of an easy target, stumbling through the streets, half-drunk and unbothered. Now it's time to blow their minds; maybe they'll get a few other things blown too, if they're bold enough.

I lead them into Rome's most infamous sex club, La Vita Nera. The Dark Life. A place meant to mock La Dolce Vita, though I suppose it depends on how one defines pleasure.

The place is packed. The night's already in full swing.

I breathe it in, sin, spice, and everything not nice. A familiar hunger coils tightly in my gut. I ache for a taste, to sink my toes into depravity, to feel it under my skin, between my teeth, slick on my tongue. The thought of going into a scene sober is tempting, so fucking tempting. It'd be a novelty, something completely foreign.

But I didn't come to La Vita Nera for pleasure.

I head to the bar and order a vodka shot with two bottles on the side, sliding the bartender a thick roll of Euros. "Free drinks on me. I'll take the bottles filled with water."

He raises a brow, but says nothing, just nods and gets to work.

I dip two fingers into the vodka shot and touch them to my neck as if I'm dabbing on cologne. Just another layer to sell the illusion for when we finally speak, and they catch a whiff.

The scent hits hard. Familiar. Sharp. A promise soaked in heat and ruin.

An aching echo stirs deep within. Sharp, dangerous, familiar. It whispers promises I've heard before. *Just one sip. One taste. No one will know. Just a little fun, a small blur to soften the edges.*

It would be so easy.

Addiction doesn't bargain, it steals. One swallow and I'll ruin weeks of sobriety. And if that happens, I might not make it back this time.

I shake my head. No damn way am I fucking things up. I'm clean, and I'm staying that way.

You've got this, asshole. Mind over matter.

I grab the bottles, then stalk off, drinking from each as I go. The men step out from behind a red velvet curtain and fall in behind me. Just to fuck with them a bit more, I stop short and spin in their direction.

They dodge for cover.

Smirking, I sink into a velvet sofa shaped like a sapphire peanut. Then I drink, and drink, and keep drinking, flooding my bladder with enough water to wash away decades of damage.

Two gorgeous creatures wander over, naked as the day they were born, to sit beside me. I toss an arm around each of them.

"Perché te ne stai seduto qui, così bello, tutto solo?" I'm asked. Why am I alone? Technically, I'm not.

Her friend chimes in. "Sembri così delizioso da volerlo mangiare."

"Delicious enough to eat?" I pull them both in tighter. "Or violate?"

"Oh, he's dangerous, this one," she declares.

If they only knew.

This club is infamous for its back room—the Vault. A large area divided into a dozen private theaters tucked away behind heavy curtains and framed by oversized one-way windows. A voyeur's dream and an exhibitionist's delight.

Let's give these bastards a night to remember.

I stand. "Show me the Vault."

It takes time to cross the club with my half walk, half stagger. Once we pass security and are inside, I direct the two into a vacant room, while I hover outside in the large corridor, calculating how long it'll take for the men pursuing me to appear.

I'm raising a half-empty bottle to my lips when they push inside, and I hit the button to the curtains with my elbow.

Game on.

The two women appear, and the mafiosi practically piss themselves.

The corridor darkens as the women get busy. One of my ladies is dildo-ed up and the other wiggling her hips.

I can practically smell the sweat clinging beneath the men's tailored suits, desire a sudden slap in the face. Tension in the corridor builds as the moans through the open vents get louder.

Light abruptly interrupts the show, angering everyone, even the mafiosi.

The Vault door is hastily shut and the interruption immediately forgotten.

But they've had a taste, and I'm growing bored with the game.

I drop the bottles at my feet, shove off the glass, and stagger toward the emergency exit. Outside, I take a quick piss—no helping it. I'm tucking myself away when the door to the club swings open.

We've had our fun.

Now it's time to get down to business.

***

I MIGHT HAVE UNDERESTIMATED THEM.

They swarm me, pinning me against the building. All three mafiosi are built like tanks, but it's the biggest who grabs my throat, lifts me onto my toes, and presses a cold blade to my ribs.

"Lorenzo Beneventi?" he demands.

"Renzo," I slur, squinting up at him.

They exchange looks, disbelief followed by visible contempt. I deserve an Oscar for my bumbling act tonight, don't I? The man with the knife mutters something that makes all three shake their heads. "Ha detto che era furbo."

That gives me pause. Who the hell warned them I'm clever?

Another one snorts. "Sembra che le voci fossero vere. Selvaggio e fuori controllo. Alcuni dicono perfino che sia un codardo. Il Beneventi debole."

Translation? I'm a dumb fuck. The weak Beneventi.

Wrong assumption, motherfucker.

I flash them a crooked smile to hide the sting, the fact that the rumors spread this far. These three poked the bear now, and are clue-less to the danger they're in.

The knife pulls away, and I drop to my feet.

"What is this about?" I sway, trying to get a better read on them. "In English."

A fist slams into my gut.

I double over, dramatically, then grunt and look up. "Who sent you?" If a few punches get me answers, I'll take them. What intrigues me more is their restraint. They're holding back. Orders are to rough me up without serious harm. Whoever's in charge believes I'm worth more intact.

"He wants to speak to you privately."

Bing-fucking-go.

I squint at them, assessing each. All three are muscled and dressed like they've stepped out of a mob flick. Definitely made men. Cosa Nostra written all over them. Then I catch it, a black and red tattoo peeking from under a cuff. The base of a cross I recognize.

The Grassi crest.

Massimo sent them?

That's a surprise. The man has my number. He could've called. So why send muscle? Why the theatrics?

A sinking feeling drags through me, an answer that gives me pause. I test my theory. "Tell Massimo I send my condolences on his father's passing."

The silence resonates loudly. The big one tightens his grip on the knife. The other two look ready to pounce.

Holy shit. They think the Eleven killed Don Grassi.

"If we hear anything about who was involved, I'll be in contact."

Their laughter is bitter, sharp.

"He knows who did it," says the tattooed one, voice rough with contempt.

Well, fuck. That tone says it all. Things have turned sideways.

"Massimo believes my family murdered his father?"

The largest man steps in, his breath brushing my face. "My brother, as well."

It's been years since I prowled the streets with Massimo. We were close, brotherly, with common interests. Yet affiliated with different famiglie with different agendas.

"You'll live if you deliver two messages to Massimo."

They don't expect my calm.

"Live, motherfucker?"

"One," I say, voice even. "I'll meet with Massimo. Anywhere. Anytime."

They're listening, but words won't be enough. Massimo put hands on me, and no one, not even an old friend or a rival mafioso capo, threatens a Beneventi without repercussions.

I won't disappoint my father by being insulted this way.

This needs to be a message they'll remember. Then they can crawl back to Massimo and tell him exactly who I am.

I lower my voice, luring them closer. "Two. Tell Massimo ..."

That's when I see her out of the corner of my eye.

Fina.

Jesus Fucking Christ.

She's here.

Foolish and reckless. And in over her pretty head.

She's getting better at stalking me. Or was I too consumed with Massimo's men to notice her?

This changes everything.

They'll see her. When they do, she's dead.

I need to end this fast.

"And two ..." I slam my forehead into the big guy's nose. Bone cracks. Blood explodes.

The knife clatters to the ground.

Tattooed Guy lunges.

I catch his wrist and twist hard until it snaps.

The third man comes at me, blade flashing in the moonlight.

"Deliver my message to your boss before I really hurt you."

That pisses him off.

He points the knife at me, lips curling. "You're lucky I don't carve you into pieces."

I exhale. Crisis nearly averted.

"Hey!"

Her voice slices through the shadows. Everyone turns.

There she is. Fina, gun raised, eyes blazing.

Shouting erupts as panic spikes sharp in my chest.

Fina steps forward, waving the gun at the third man.

Then the big guy moves.

Crack. A deafening gunshot rings out.

I throw myself in front of Tattooed Guy, with barely enough time to react—if any of Massimo's men die, war will erupt between our families. Fire burns through my chest, but I push forward and grab the big guy by the throat. "Touch her, and the deal is off."

Our eyes lock, then I relax. He reads me perfectly.

"Let's go," he says to the men, voice calm.

The others hesitate, glancing from me to her, then follow him into the dark.

I fall to my knees, fading fast.

"Oh shit. Renzo ..."

I stare at her, eyes wide, mouth trembling, then smile.

She shot me. She fucking shot me.

I always knew she'd be the death of me.

Horrified, I stare down at his crumpled form.

If I don't do something, he'll bleed out.

I rip off my sweater and place it over his chest, trying to stop the flow of blood. "Asshole. Drunk fool," I mutter, pressing down on the wound. "Did you move to Rome just to torment me? Are you dead set on ruining my life?"

Blood soaks through the fabric, but it's slowing. He doesn't stir. A slight push confirms what I feared—he's completely out.

Too heavy to move. Too pale. Too still.

My chest tightens.

I fumble for my phone and call Bianca, my fingers slipping against the screen.

"What the hell, Fina. It's early—"

"I'll explain later. Please, I need Dante's number."

There's a pause, and I close my eyes, silently begging her not to say she deleted it.

"Are you in trouble?" she whispers.

"Yes."

"Okay." She sucks in a breath. "Okay. I'll text it. But be careful how—"

I hang up before she finishes. No time.

Dante answers on the first ring. "Who is this?"

"Renzo's been shot. He's in the alley behind La Vita Nera. He's unconscious ... bleeding."

Silence. I hear nothing but the ringing in my own ears.

I should run. I should disappear. But I can't. I won't.

Instead, I sit on the cold stone and lift Renzo's head onto my lap. My heart pounds as I gaze down at him. He looks heartbreakingly peaceful, even in this state. Even on death's doorstep, he's too damn beautiful for his own good.

"Don't you die on me," I whisper, smoothing his hair back with shaking fingers. "I'll never forgive you if you do."

I say it again, and again, desperate for the words to pull him back.

"You hear me, Renzo?" My voice cracks. "I don't care how infuriating you are or how angry I am. You don't get to die tonight."

I keep whispering to him, brushing blood off his temple, until a voice slices through the shadows.

"What in God's name—"

I freeze.

Dante.

Fear surges up my spine.

"You."

I blink as men rush me, lifting Renzo from my lap.

"Careful!" I snap, jumping to my feet. "You'll hurt him even more."

They don't listen.

I try to follow, but Dante grabs my arm, halting me.

"Not so fast. What happened?"

"Massimo Grassi's men attacked him."

His expression sharpens. "Grassi?"

"He believes the famiglie—the Eleven—murdered his father."

"What?" Dante curses under his breath and pulls out his phone, typing.

"Can't you do that later?" I say, exasperated and needing him to hear me out.

He glares but doesn't stop.

"Grassi wants a meeting with Renzo."

He halts his typing. "A meeting?"

"Yes."

"It doesn't make sense," he growls, his usual calm edge splintering. "Why would his men shoot him if that were the case?"

Oh Lord. Deliver me from evil.

"Answer me."

My heart hammers. My legs threaten to give out.

"I shot him."

Silence crashes over us.

Then, like a dam breaking, I confess everything. How I've been following Renzo. The sightseeing. Stumbling upon him tonight. Interrupting Grassi's men. My failed attempt at saving him.

How his stupid ass threw himself in front of the bullet like he has a death wish.

By the time I'm done, I'm breathless and shaking.

Dante watches me closely. Not blinking. Not moving.

"Jesus," he mutters.

"Please, it was an accident. The man had a knife. I didn't expect Renzo to—" My voice falters. "I didn't think he'd protect them."

I toss my hands up, trying to make sense of what's impossible to make sense of.

Dante's expression suggests he's doing the same.

"I'm Bianca's friend. Hopefully that's reason enough to keep me alive."

He steps forward.

I step back.

His sigh is long, sharp with frustration as he moves past me.

"If he lives, you live," he says over his shoulder. "But understand this: You can run, but you can never hide. You of all people should understand that."

He stops.

The air tightens, charged with the weight of something inevitable.

He turns, enough for me to catch the cold, merciless glint in his eyes.

"Isn't that right, Elia?"

—

Renzo

"Relax, and let the painkillers do their job."

My eyes snap open. The doctor on our payroll stands over me, needle in hand, smiling encouragingly at me.

"What did you say?" I croak, my words heavy.

"You'll feel more comfortable in a few minutes."

I try to sit up and take a swing at him. Pain shoots through my shoulder. He's got me on Dante's desk, shirt sliced open, pants shoved halfway down my legs.

"Mr. Beneventi, easy," the doctor admonishes. "I cleaned the wound, but still need to stitch you up."

"Dante!" I bellow, furious. So spitting mad I see red.

He walks in midcall, phone pressed to his ear.

"Hang up," I growl.

He disconnects, his eyes snapping from the doctor to me. "He tell you you're a lucky bastard? The bullet passed through your upper pectoral muscle, right below your collarbone, missing a major artery, veins, and the apex of your lung?"

"Fuck the medical jabber." I wave a finger at the doctor. "This motherfucker drugged me."

Dante looks as alarmed as I feel. "What kind? How much?"

The doctor's voice quivers. "Ten milligrams of oxycodone."

I swing my legs off the desk and yank my pants up, while the man stammers apologies.

"I'm sorry. Please, I thought it would help—he was in pain—"

"You're apologizing to the wrong man."

"Mr. Beneventi ..."

Mind over matter, right? I'm not losing my shit over ten milligrams of oxy. The pain, dizziness, hell, even the stench of vodka still clinging to me is temporary. I've survived worse things than this. "Just finish the damn stitches."

The doctor gets to work, eyeing me like he's expecting a punch as he digs his needle into me. I almost lean in with a playful "boo" like Zia Teresa offered me weeks ago, but the oxy's kicking in, and I've got shit to handle.

I lock eyes with Dante. "Bianca's friend. Is she okay?"

"You mean Elia Lombardi?"

A smug smile tugs at his mouth, testing me. He's like a dog sniffing out a juicy bone. "What kind of boss would I be if a rival capo's daughter moved into my neighborhood and I didn't notice?"

"Does my father know?"

He arches a brow, intrigued. "Should he?"

"No."

"Then we keep this between us."

"Thanks."

He runs a hand over his jaw. "When I found you, she wasn't exactly singing your praises."

"Where is she now?"

He shrugs. "Home, I imagine. Sleeping."

"And Massimo's men?"

"Gone long before I got there. She said they were delivering a message. Massimo wants a meeting."

I blink through the fog, vision swimming. "A text would've been the nicer touch."

Dante snorts. "You really have a gift for pissing people off."

Gift? I should have a trophy. "He thinks we killed his father."

"Why would we do that? Your father and Don Grassi were on good terms."

Yeah, so were Massimo and I—right up until he instructed his men to lay hands on me.

The doctor finishes the stitches and dabs antiseptic over the wound. "Bed rest."

I lean toward him, and unleash. "Boo."

He scurries away.

Yeah, it's a shitty move, and something Sandro would do. And I don't feel any better for it. Now that the doctor's done, I feel nothing. Just tired. "I'll meet Massimo," I say, the words slow and slurred. "Find out what this is about."

Dante shakes his head. I see two of him, like I'm stuck in some carnival fun house. "You should rest. Take a few days."

"Naooot happnin." Bad enough the bullet ripped through me without even clipping a vein and I blacked out like some weak-ass pussy. Me. A man who died on a cross and came back breathing.

Take a few days? Lie down?

Not a chance in hell.

18

Tina

THE BUS TO ROME WINDS THROUGH THE ITALIAN COUNTRYSIDE, past sun-drenched vineyards heavy with grapes, silver-leafed olive groves, and crumbling ruins. Midday light spills across the fields, warm and nurturing.

I see none of it.

Only his face—and his surprise the moment I shot him.

Bianca heard that he survived, though nothing more.

I try to pick up the pieces and slip back into the rhythm of my new life. Pretend I'm the same girl who fell in love with Rome and freedom's illusion.

But everything's changed, hasn't it?

I've been exposed. Renzo and Dante know exactly who I am. Worse, I'm entangled with two mafia families now. I shot at the Cosa Nostra, wounded a capo di tutti capi's son, and didn't just ignore Aunt Teresa's warning to not get noticed but turned it into a freaking spectacle.

Running's an option, but what good will it do without a plan in place?

Nearly three weeks have passed; I feel like I'm suspended in air, feet dangling after my shoes have already dropped. Still, there's no sign of Renzo or Dante.

Does he want me to let go? It seems that way.

A light rain falls as I exit the bus. Of course, I grabbed two corn husks instead of an umbrella when leaving the house, so I'm unprepared.

I tuck in my chin and, as the rain picks up, dash along the nearby sidewalk. Most people step inside, out of the elements. My prozia will be pleased—additional business is always welcome.

I'm two blocks away when a man slams into my side.

Then his arms wrap around me, and I'm being dragged into a narrow side street.

"Togliti le mani di dosso, stronzo," I screech, struggling to break free.

He loosens his grip just enough to slam a fist into my ribs, driving me face-first against the stone wall. Pain blooms across my cheeks, raw and burning. I gasp, desperate for air, my lungs screaming. My mind in a state of shock and outrage.

The stench of cigarette smoke clings to him, thick and choking. Triggering the nightmare I escaped, the burn marks on my skin feeling as raw as the day Settemo assaulted me.

You escaped him and his uncle, Fina. There's a way out of this, too.

Rain pours down in buckets, soaking my hair, my clothes. Undeterred, I brace my hands on the wall slick with water and grime.

Slide a foot behind his ankle.

And go slack, like I've given up, before he comes at me again.

It's basic self-defense 101. The oldest trick in the book.

I draw courage from my outrage at all the men who've touched me without permission, who underappreciated my worth.

"Ahhh!" I scream, raw and sharp, shoving off the wall with everything I've got, ramming into him.

He slams onto the cobblestones with a sickening thud, his right hand flung useless at my foot.

"Wrong woman to fuck with," I growl, seizing the moment.

I raise my leg and drive my heel down onto his fingers.

The crunch is cruel, and oh so satisfying. As is the scream that tears through the rain.

I bolt, heart hammering.

Thankful to have escaped with just a few scrapes and my dignity intact.

———

Dante Lucchese walks into the restaurant, and the place falls silent.

I pause midstep, then set two steaming plates onto the nearest surface before I drop them. His appearance isn't unusual, but his manner is, as is the fact he's alone.

This day keeps getting worse.

The couple at the table protest. "Tesoro, quella non è la nostra cena."

I'm too focused on Dante to care.

His eyes skim the crowded room until they land on me.

Oh shit.

He stalks toward me.

"Bianca isn't working tonight," I offer.

Without answering, he grabs my elbow and directs me into the kitchen.

My aunt stops stirring her sauce. "Dante," she exclaims, as surprised as I am by his appearance.

Still no response as he tugs me along into the back storage room.

The door slams shut.

He releases my arm, but I remain trapped beneath his ferocious glare. "What happened to your face?"

"Excuse me?"

He rakes his eyes over me.

My cheeks are scraped pretty badly. I didn't cover them with makeup, hoping fresh air will offer a quicker healing process. Like

168

everything, it's temporary, as will be the memory of today's attempted robbery.

"Nothing."

"Answer me, Elia."

"It's Fina."

"What?"

"My friends call me Fina." Not that Dante Lucchese is my friend, but I certainly hope he's not an enemy.

His lips tighten. "You avoiding my question?"

"A man tried to rob me on the way to the restaurant. Pulled me into a side street and threw me against a wall, where I scratched my face." I clench angry fists, so tired of men believing I'm their victim.

"What did he look like? What was he wearing?"

"Why?"

"I'll take care of him."

I sigh with frustration. "He wore black jeans and a black hoodie. That's all I saw."

"I'll ask around the neighborhood. See if someone knows anything."

"Okay ..." I say, unnerved by his kindness.

He pauses for a few seconds, like he's choosing his next words. "Has Renzo seen your face?"

"Renzo," I exclaim. "No."

"He hasn't been in contact?"

"Contact? No. I thought he was recovering."

"Damn it."

My stomach drops. "Are you sending me back to my father?"

"How about we make a deal?" he smoothly replies.

"What kind of deal? You want me to put in a good word to Bianca on your behalf?"

His face crunches, and I almost laugh. This big-dicked, talented-mouthed hunk has women falling all over him. The idea he'd need my help is comical.

"This remains between us, capisci?"

A nagging feeling settles in. "What did he do?"

"You'll be under my protection if you help me. Your father will no longer have a say over you."

Oh. My. God. He's handing me years of missed birthdays wrapped up in one enormous gift. No more running. No more being a pawn in my father's games. "One more thing." I force the words out. "My mother disappeared when I was five. I want to know if he did it, if he killed her."

"Done."

I'll finally know. And now under Dante's protection, I'll find ways to hurt Darling Daddy that would make any made man proud.

Dante silently watches me, waiting for my question.

"What's the deal?"

"Renzo. He's missing. And I need you to track him down."

Renzo

A red light blinks overhead like a heartbeat. My thoughts twist, trying to pin down what it is. Fire alarm? Drone sweeping the night sky?

No. Fuck, it's worse.

I see it clearly now. The flashing neon sign inviting me through addiction's gate. Welcoming me back. Wondering where I've been. As if it never believed I'd stay gone long.

I struggle against its pull.

This isn't what I want.

Poison floods my veins, cruel, twisted comfort.

Then.

Mind.

Over.

Awareness crawls in, slow and unwelcome.

Velvet sheets beneath my naked body. Music. Perfume. Hands I don't recognize, roaming over my flesh.

Not again ...

What the fuck have I done?

Not me—that motherfucking doctor.

He's why I'm here.

Anger claws at me, trying to surface. It's too much, though, and I sink deeper into the bed, into addiction's tightening squeeze.

It was all for nothing.

I'm the Beneventi they whisper about in shadows.

The unreliable fuck.

The weak link.

So weak. So fucking weak.

There's nothing left to prove, is there?

I lost.

I crossed the line for the final time.

And I'm never coming back.

———

"GET AWAY FROM HIM."

The mattress shifts beneath me as my bed-partners flee.

From *her* terse voice.

Fina.

I cling to the sound as it claws me from the void.

"Renzo, can you hear me?"

She touches my shoulders, then shakes me. Impatient. Demanding.

My limbs are lead. Cotton balls fill my mouth, muffling words that won't form. My temples throb.

The mattress sags once more, and she disappears.

Don't go.

My eyelids drag like they're weighted with sandbags as I pry them open. Her shape appears, haloed by too-bright light. Pain slices through my skull, and I shut them again, flinching.

None too gently, she places a cap on my head. "Keep your chin down, understand? No one can see you." I'm pulled up to sit. Every nerve screams, every joint stiff with agony.

"An Uber is waiting outside. Think you can wrap an arm around my shoulder, place your feet on the floor, and then stand?"

I nod, and the motion sends a nauseating wave through me. Still, I force myself upright.

She wraps an arm around my waist.

My knees buckle like they've forgotten how to hold weight. I collapse into her, breath catching as sharp, stabbing sensations ricochet between my ribs.

"Where ..."

"Where did I find you?" She scoffs with irritation. "Under a pile of bodies at La Vita Nera."

Well, fuck.

"You're lucky I don't put another bullet in you. It's what you deserve." Her body vibrates with outrage, and in some broken, messed-up way, it keeps me conscious.

I'll take outrage over absence.

We pass a few patrons, but the club is relatively empty. My gut twists, dread gnawing at the edges of my awareness.

How long have I been here?

I've lost track of time.

I reek of sweat, sex, and shame.

My foot catches on a crack in the floor, and we stumble. "God, how can someone so weak be this strong?"

Weak. Fucking hell. And exposed. Like a lamb headed to slaughter if anyone decides I'm not worth saving. If my enemies decide I'm worth killing.

Every step is agony. Muscles screaming, head throbbing, lungs too tight in my chest. And the worst part? The craving stirs, sickening and cruel.

"Motherfucking doctor," I grind out, my voice hoarse.

"What did you say?" Fina demands.

I grit my teeth, the effort making my jaw ache. I fucked up and am now fucked up. "Going to shove his freaking stethoscope up where the sun doesn't shine," I mutter.

"You're mumbling. But if you're asking me to let you go, the answer's no."

We exit the kink club through the back.

I'm shoved into the back of the Uber. The door slams. She crawls over me to the far side, like she can't stand to touch me any longer than necessary.

She doesn't tell me where we're going.

I don't ask. I just look at her.

Stiff-backed, jaw clenched, but breathing fire. A vision so beautiful, it makes every hurt feel like it can't compete.

So much to say. So much past to make up for. My voice rasps like sandpaper against my throat. "Fina, Fina, Fina."

Her temper flares. "Don't Fina me, asshole."

The words cut, but I deserve them. All of them.

I close my eyes, rest my head against the seat, and make a vow.

I've disappointed her for the last time.

Whatever it takes, even if it breaks me.

It won't happen again.

20

Renzo

I groan and try to move. But meet resistance.

What the hell?

Cold iron bites my wrists, sharp and waking. The sting settles into a dull, dragging weight that yanks my arms down. My fucking hands are cuffed, each wrist swallowed by steel, but there's slack enough to stretch, slap my cheeks, then test the pull.

Light bleeds through the wall slats, too bright and accusing, enough to see that my ankles are bound the same way, with shackles wrapped in leather, as if it were an urgent afterthought to ease the chaff against my skin. They're attached to a long chain trailing loose behind, so I can stand, kneel, even pace a few restless steps. The chain's bolted to a barn wall, tethering me like a dog on a leash. Room to move but no room to run—not that I'm in any shape to do so.

It's not the first time I've been restrained. My brother once locked me in a guest room when I hit rock bottom and ignored my sorry ass until the drugs worked through my system.

Looks like I've landed there again.

I'm drenched in sweat. My limbs jerk on their own, like my

body's trying to work something out. My stomach churns, and I swallow hard against the burn in my throat.

The physical withdrawal symptoms are familiar.

Where I'm at and how I got to this point are not.

I sit up, brush straw off my bare chest, and assess my situation. I'm in boxer shorts, on a straw bed inside a barn, with a round wooden stool to my left, straw piles to my right, and a woman in red high heels watching me at my feet.

Relief flickers, chased quickly by self-loathing.

Jesus, did she witness the entire thing?

"How do you feel?" she asks.

"Like shit."

"Do you know who I am?"

"Nope." I try to smile, but it falters. "But you look like my kind of woman—*trouble.*"

She doesn't react. Just stands there, arms crossed, taking me in like I'm something rotting on the sidewalk.

This is what dying must feel like. Me, at my lowest. Her, in her flower-print dress and red heels, forehead pinched and eyes branding me from the inside out. I was her salvation once. Now I'm her goddamn curse.

"Fina." I taste her name, slow, like I'm savoring a forbidden thing.

"Renzo," she snaps, voice sharp enough to cut.

A flush colors her cheeks, and she radiates a vitality that wasn't there before, like Italy breathed life into her and made her even more irresistible.

She takes a step and freezes. My gaze follows hers to the necklace I carried from Rome, now lying in the dirt. Fucking hell. I don't even know why I kept her pearls, why I hauled them around like some twisted good-luck charm. Maybe because they were a piece of us, a token of what could never be, a reminder of what I gave up.

My focus snaps back to her just in time to see it hit. Recognition slams into her, surprise hardening into raw, scorching fury.

"Are those my pearls?"

Shit. I must have shoved them in my pocket. A miracle they lasted this long. If I had been in my right mind, I would have done anything to keep them hidden. Deeply disturbed, I clear my throat. "No clue how they got there."

"Just like you've got no idea how you got here?"

Her hands are on her hips. Jaw tight. Chin tilted. She looks ready to spit nails.

God, she's stunning.

Our eyes lock, and something stirs. It always does with her. No one besides her has ever had this effect on me. Never has, never will.

"You stole them."

"So what? Or will you shoot me again for it?"

She glares at me. "It's crossed my mind once or twice."

"Hand me your gun. I'll save you the trouble." I lie back in the hay, suddenly exhausted.

"Don't you pass out on me," she growls. The hay snaps, and then she's in the dirt next to me. "We need to talk."

Persistent as ever.

I breathe her in. She's agitated, brushing loose strands of hair from her face, but underneath the fire there's a calm confidence, like she's finally settled into her own skin. And that body—Christ—she's more luscious than I remember, curves softer, breasts fuller, every bit of her begging to be touched.

Yeah, Italy's been good to her.

I've made a lot of shitty decisions in life. Killing Accardo wasn't one of them.

"Are you listening?" she snaps.

I raise my cuffs. "About the kidnapping?"

"Would you rather I left you?"

The answer's no. Although the circumstances could be better, I crave her company. Still, I say, "I didn't ask to be saved."

"Doesn't mean you didn't need it."

Damn it. Everything I've built—my shot at redemption, my name —might be trashed.

"You had to come to Rome."

"And you had to revert to your former antics by stalking me."

She flinches, but recovers fast. "My antics? Look at yourself and the state you're in."

She's right, take a fucking gander. You don't give a recovering addict a shot of painkillers and then leave him on his own. That part is that motherfucker's fault.

"You jumped in front of my target," she says. "Do you have a death wish?"

"If you killed Massimo's man, there'd be fallout. As it is, things as they are aren't adding up. I did what needed doing."

"So unlike you. You avoid messes."

That hits harder than I expect.

I point to her hand. "No ring, I see."

She stiffens. "Got lucky."

"That so?"

"I hate you."

Her voice cuts sharper than any blade. But it's the way her eyes linger, too long to mean nothing, too fast to mean everything, that gives her away.

"That why you dragged me here?"

"I didn't have a choice."

"Neither did I."

She's keen on fighting, like she's been saving it up for years. "You were too busy getting high and screwing anything that moved."

Shame floods in, fast and sharp. I allowed myself to be taken advantage of. Exploited. I chased what was painfully familiar instead of prying myself away from temptation.

Disgust is written across her expression.

It's simply a reflection of my own.

"Who knows about my fall from grace?" I demand.

"If you fell from grace, it wasn't off a ladder but a step stool."

"Shit, Fina. Answer me."

"Dante asked me to find you, with strict orders to use discretion.

No one else knows, not even my great-aunt—and you've been here a week."

Panic sets in. "A fucking week?"

"You were out of it."

Of all people, Dante sends *her* after me. I'll smash his face in for it after I thank him for covering for me. I'm a lucky bastard if, after all my bullshit, my reputation's still intact.

"Just to be clear, I did this under duress," she says, words clipped.

"And here I thought your obsession with me hadn't faded." I try to flash a smile, but it dies halfway there.

Her gaze sweeps over me, slow, deliberate, full of loathing. Then she exhales, sharp and resigned, and grabs a hay bale like she's trying not to throw it at my face.

"My LA girl feeding farm animals now?" I ask, voice hoarse.

"Something like that."

"Where are you going?" The question escapes before I can stop it. Restraints are more of a turn on when they're part of a kink scene, not when I'm chained up like a rabid dog.

"To work."

I rattle the cuffs. "You're leaving me like this?" I'm coated in sweat, shame, and seven days of regret.

"There's water and healthy snacks in the cooler over there. And, if you need to go, there's a bucket to pee in."

I find both within reach. "Don't go."

She pauses, biting her lip. That small gesture betrays her. But then, every muscle rigid, she snaps her armor back into place, like it's her against the world.

And knowing what she's been through, it has been.

"Zia Teresa's waiting at the restaurant," she says. Then, quieter but sharper, she cuts me into tiny bits.

"Unlike you, I keep my promises."

Blinded by Dante's offer, I clearly didn't think things through when I agreed to our deal. Did I really believe I could drop Renzo in a bale of hay, then walk away, leaving him to rot in his addiction, without it ripping me apart? Did I think I'd be unaffected? That I could chain the man I'd crushed on so fiercely that pieces of my heart broke, watch him unravel—twitching, sweating, moaning in pain like a ghost of his former self trapped in my barn—and feel nothing?

This past week has been hell. Watching him come undone, his body jerking through withdrawal, soaked in sweat, teeth chattering, eyes wild one second and completely vacant the next. Sometimes he'd thrash. Other times he wouldn't move for hours, just whisper, "Don't go. Don't go." Like I'm the one who left him. Like this is somehow my fault.

I've called Dante a dozen times, voice shaking. His answer never changes. Handle it. Help him through it. Don't make noise. Change the gauze on his wound. Keep the secret. Act normal.

But nothing about this is normal. Nothing about watching a man destroy himself feels survivable.

I hate Renzo for this. For letting himself fall so far. For dragging me down with him. For making me watch. For making me care when I've tried so hard not to.

How did this happen? How did someone as smart, as strong, as sharp as Renzo end up like this? Was he already spiraling when he abandoned me to my fate? Had the poison sunk its teeth into him even back then? Was there a trigger point, something that caused him to use?

I don't have the answers. And I hate feeling so helpless.

I shouldn't feel like I'm the one bleeding every time his body convulses.

All I can do is watch the drugs tear him apart, and pray he makes it through.

Yesterday, though, was progress. He was awake, coherent.

The angry part of me wants to unchain him, pat his back with "good luck," and just shove him out the barn door. And truth is, as ridiculous as it is, the more self-vindictive, self-destructive part aches to keep him chained to me forever.

"Are you cleaning out the barn?" Aunt Teresa asks as I scrub the varnish off the dinner plate I've been washing for several minutes. It's our day off. She spent hers in the garden, and I spent mine spiraling, worried she'd cross the yard, enter the barn, and discover I've a man chained to the slats.

"Why do you ask?" I manage, keeping my tone neutral.

"I haven't set foot in there since I stopped boarding horses. But there's a trail of straw in the driveway."

I force a laugh. "It keeps my feathered friend from getting too brave. He's scared of the stuff."

With good reason—having a large square projectile nearly flatten your feathered ass will do that.

She steps beside me, drying dishes with a clean cloth. "There's something I've been meaning to discuss with you."

My stomach drops. "Okay ..."

"I still keep a small apartment above the restaurant."

She's mentioned it before, usually as a complaint about how cluttered the space has become. A storage area that shouldn't be.

"This time of year, when business picks up, I usually stay in the city. No commute means more time to experiment with new recipes. I'd like to add a few summer specials to the menu. But if you'd rather not be alone out here ..."

"I can manage," I interrupt, grateful for the sudden luck. Keeping my secret just got easier. "Besides, who'll take care of your garden if not me?"

She studies me, then smiles.

"It's settled," I quickly say. "I'll stay and keep the farm running while you're away."

She pulls me into a hug. "Thank you, Fina. You've been such a help."

"Thank you, Aunt Teresa." My voice wavers. "I don't know what I'd do without you."

This woman, practically a stranger, took me in when I had nothing left. When I was at my weakest, and she helped me.

This same reason's why I won't turn my back on the man in the barn.

Even if the truth is more complicated than I'm ready to face.

21

Fina

Later that evening, after my prozia turns in for the night, I slip out the back door with a plate of leftovers and a pulse that's already misbehaving.

Even in the dark, I *feel* him. That stare—hot, steady, impossible to ignore.

"I thought you forgot about me," he drawls.

As if. As if I could erase him like a scuff mark on a shoe.

"My aunt was home all day," I say, walking closer and setting the plate down on a stool. "Hold on. There's an old lantern here somewhere."

I fumble around, cursing the pitch-black barn, until I find the lantern and light it. Warm light spills over him, and I stumble, distracted. Damn it, I should've kept us in the dark. Light makes things clearer, when all I want to do is keep my distance. In and out, a nurse with her patient. He thrives when things are murky, so who am I to change that? Better keep my distance. This way, he'll never disappoint me again.

By the time I reach him, he's already devouring the meal.

Guilt stirs in my chest, but I smother it. He put himself here. He deserves every last consequence.

I settle onto a nearby haystack and glance around. He's turned this place into a makeshift living space. Hay bales are arranged like a modified prison cell, complete with couch, table, even a high stack below a window he can't reach, being chained as he is. He's been busy and is restless.

A reminder that dangerous men don't do well in cages.

"I see you've been nesting," I mutter, my lips twitching before I can stop them.

He pauses midbite. A thick strand of fettuccine Alfredo clings to his lips.

My breath catches.

Even filthy, wild and half-feral, he radiates sex. It pours off him in waves. And I hate that my body responds like it's starving—for more than a lick of his fettuccine.

His eyes lock on mine, slow and sure as he drags the pasta between his lips. He licks the sauce away like he knows what he's doing.

And damn him, he does.

Heat rushes up my neck. I rip my eyes away, but it's too late.

He knows exactly his effect on me.

"Keep feeding me like this," he says, his voice gravel and honey, "and I might never leave."

"Thanks for recognizing my hospitality."

He snorts, unbothered, and keeps eating.

I wait until he finishes before revealing the dessert, two slices of orange polenta cake, rich and sticky with caramel drizzle. I'd lied earlier, claimed I was full when Aunt Teresa brought it to the kitchen table. But I saved a piece for me, and him.

Hospitable, I tell myself. I can't send him back to Dante malnourished.

His groan after the first bite nearly undoes me. "God, this is fucking insane."

"Coming from you, that carries weight."

He smirks like he knows exactly what I meant.

"What's the chance of a shower?" he asks, licking the last of the caramel off his fork.

"Tomorrow," I say too quickly.

I don't mention my aunt will be staying in the city. That it's just the two of us now. On this farm. Alone.

All day, starting tomorrow.

And all night.

A shiver slides down my spine.

He's filthy. Grimy. Gross. It's unnerving how every part of me is strung tight and humming.

We finish dessert in a silence that makes my heart pound. Him watching me. Me pretending not to feel the burn of it everywhere, my horror in myself growing.

The sooner he recovers, the better.

Then he can be on his way, and I can put my ridiculous obsession with him to rest.

Renzo

"Did Dante say how long I'm stuck here?"

She shrugs. "Until you're sober."

My jaw tightens. I've got shit to do. First, get to Massimo Grassi before he thinks I've ghosted him. Clear the garbage he's been fed and offer help tracking down who really killed his old man.

A day alone in the barn drove me batshit stir-crazy.

Worse still, having Fina close last night was a whole different type of torture. Why she'd saved a slice of cake to eat with me is puzzling. Hospitality, my ass. Either she's warming up to me or toying with me.

Doesn't matter. I crave her company.

"I need to speak with Dante."

Her hands find her hips, and for a heartbeat, I believe it's a no. "You can shower inside and use my cell phone. But I'm warning you" —she waves a finger at me—"don't even think about escaping. I've too much riding on you."

Sucking on her lower lip, she leans close to unlock my bindings.

"I'd rather you be riding me," I purr into her ear.

She jumps back like she's been burned, but in the light of day, her blush tells a different story. "Follow me," she says in a rush. Grasping hold of a hay bale, she stalks off.

I roll to my feet, then hurry after her.

Sunlight floods my face, a fierce warmth I've been starving for. I pause and inhale the fresh farm air.

Freedom from the barn and my bullshit hits like a clean shot of adrenaline. It feels fucking good. My body's lighter. My head is clearer. Nothing holding me down. No cravings chewing at my insides.

First thing I need is a shower. Second, a phone call. Third, burning these goddamn boxers before they start walking on their own.

She stops halfway to the house, shifting the bale in her arms.

I move in. "Let me get that."

She hugs it to her chest. "I'm good."

Something's off. Like she's alarmed, on edge, probably because I'm no longer chained ... "Look, Fina. I'm fucking grateful—"

"Hurry," she cuts me off, hauls the bale up the steps, drops it with a thud, and disappears inside.

I consider heading down the driveway and disappearing into the horizon. Bolting. But I don't.

Once inside, she leads me upstairs into a bedroom.

"Found some men's clothes that might fit." She rifles inside a drawer, and then tosses a sweater, sweatpants, and boxers onto the bed.

"I'm not wearing another dude's underwear."

Her expression fills with disbelief. "Unbelievable."

"No. Not happening."

"I found you at a kink club, half-dressed and buried beneath a pile of naked bodies."

"Still not happening."

"One of them was a dude."

Well, shit.

But something in her expression gives me pause, and I examine her more closely. Eyes darkening. Flushed skin. Jesus, she fucking loves the idea.

I test the waters, and share a truth. "Not the first time."

Yeah, I'm right. The dirty little kinkster.

She clears her throat, drops her gaze. "Shower's in there. I left a razor on the sink."

Then she surprises the hell out of me again by sitting on the edge of the bed.

I cock a brow. "You staying?"

"Maybe."

"You don't trust me."

"Should I?"

Ouch. But like respect, trust is earned. Don't I know it well? But Fina? Earning her trust will take more than extreme measures. It'll take something closer to bleeding out.

I've already bled for her once.

No stopping me now.

I turn away and strip down.

"The bathroom's right there," she says from behind me, voice tight.

"What did you mean, back in the barn, that you've got too much riding on me?"

She whispers her answer. "Dante offered me protection if I found you."

I frown. "The 'in his bed' kind?"

"Protection from my father. I'll never be at his mercy again."

"I'll protect you."

She sighs. "Renzo. You can't even protect yourself."

I'm butthurt she thinks so little of me. How quickly her perception would change if she learned about Vito Cardini. Would she believe I'm this fucking useless if she knew the truth behind Carlo Accardo's death? Naked, I kick away the offensive garments, and achieve a small victory as her gasp fills the air.

Likes what she sees? Good. She better buckle the fuck up. Call it spite. Call it payback. She underestimated me, and now she'll suffer the consequences.

I give her a show, wiggling my ass as I walk to the bathroom. In my present condition, I wouldn't wish myself on my worst enemy, let alone the misguided kinkster on the bed.

Shower first.

Show to follow.

I slide open the curtain, turn on the shower, then test the water with my hand before stepping into the tub. Hot water rains down on me, and I take my time lathering up, glancing her way a few times as she bites her lip and watches.

Always spying on me, isn't she?

"You there, babe?" I call out, pretending ignorance.

"I'm not your babe."

That's my girl. Not willing to give an inch. But fuck knows I'm all about taking a mile. Multiple, especially if the end result is getting off.

I wrap my hand around my cock and stroke. Rinsing off the dirt first, then adding pressure, squeezing, stroking.

A glance tells me she's still on the bed, knuckles white, eyes locked on me.

Eating this shit up.

My dick swells with goddamn pride.

"So, what would you like to do today?" I ask, cool as can be.

Her words are drunk slow. "Can't we chat ... um ... afterward?"

"Can't wait. Besides, my conversation with Dante will be predictably long." I thrust my hips, now riding my hand, intense pleasure taking over.

"You deserve his ... oh, OH!"

I relish her excitement as it bleeds into my own.

Eyes closed, I lean into it, fueling it with thoughts of Fina. Taking me deep. Letting me in. Taking what she wants. Letting go.

"Tell me to go harder," I command.

I'm met with silence.

Scattered like a little scared rabbit, didn't she?

I hear her clear her throat, then, "Harder."

I smirk. Thought I lost her.

Her next words are louder. "Harder, I said."

Fuck yeah. "That's right. Boss me around. Show me how you want it."

Her voice cuts through the steam. "I still hate you."

"Noted."

"Good. Now face me."

Eyes still closed, I turn.

"Hold it out. Like you're offering it."

I wrap my fingers around the base and extend it toward her.

"Now smack it into your palm. Hard."

I obey. Once. Twice. Three times. Each one driving me closer. My knees grow weak. It's been so long since I've felt this good. "You're in control. Say I can come."

"Not yet," she informs me. "Stroke it."

Control teeters. The burn is better than any high I've chased. I see her on her knees, lips parted, ropes biting her skin. "Jesus. Fucking hell," I groan.

"Okay. Come."

The breathless note in her command is the last push I need. Free hand pressed forward for balance, I spill, painting an *F* into the shower wall while groaning her name.

Minutes pass. I lean against the tile, panting, then call out, rejuvenated and ready to spar some more. "You still there, babe?"

Nothing.

She's gone.

But if she believes this is it, she's mistaken.

This is our new beginning.

22

Renzo

Invigorated, I find her in the kitchen, but before I can speak, she shoves her phone into my chest. Right. Business before pleasuring her. It's the way I'll balance the famiglie with my own.

Dante answers on the third ring. "How is he?"

"He's ready to reach out to Massimo."

"Renzo," he says, relief creeping into his tone. "How are you feeling?"

Humiliated. Humbled. Ashamed. "Alive," I smoothly reply. "I'll feel better once I talk to Massimo."

"About that ..."

I freeze.

"Grassi torched one of my fields, escalating the situation."

My grip on the phone tightens. "I still want to meet him."

"That's your father's call. And right now ..."

Goddamn it. The asshole briefed him?

Fina watches me closely, too closely.

I turn my back to her, swallowing the fury building in my chest.

"He wants you in Rhode Island."

"Fuck that."

Dante sighs. "Just until you're clean. He's lined up some Ivy League therapist—"

"I've got everything I need right here."

A dish clatters behind me. Proof she's hanging on every fucking word.

I stalk across the kitchen and away from prying ears.

"Yeah, and your father ripped me a new asshole for involving her," Dante mutters. "You made a deal with him to leave that poor girl alone? Hell, I've so many questions and can't wait to hear this fucking story. If I thought he gave a damn where she vanished to, I'd have told him myself."

Unease pulses through me. The last thing I want is Fina on my father's goddamn radar, and what happened? I put her front and center, right up alongside me.

"Since we're discussing your girl ..."

I scowl. Not sure if it's because of the label or his acknowledging Fina's not some random hookup.

"Are you aware her shithead father made a new arrangement with Accardo?"

I blink, caught off guard. "What? He leave a note on his gravestone?"

"Settemo Accardo."

Everything stills. "Go on," I demand, dead serious.

"He gave her to him in exchange for all his debts to his uncle be forgiven."

"Guess we put some feelers out and discover if he has strawberry allergies."

Fina gasps behind me. I cross the kitchen again, already protecting her. She'd be in tears if she overheard what her father has done. I'd rather she cry over his casket.

"Don't," Dante warns, his voice low. "Word is out that she's under my protection."

I stiffen with outrage. "Yeah, about that—"

He cuts me off. "Want my advice?"

My silence should be answer enough.

"Your father wants you in Providence ..."

"And you think I should tuck tail and crawl home? Leave my job? Ignore the shit brewing with Massimo?" I lean a hand on the counter, suddenly out of breath. Pissing me off even more. "Do me a favor, since it's *your* doctor who pumped me full of oxy—call my father and inform him that I give him my word I'll get clean for good. That Fina will help me."

"A good therapist ..."

"I'll see one after the bullshit with Massimo is resolved."

"Are you trying to offend me? Orders are to leave Grassi to me."

Not happening.

I can feel him on the other end of the line, grinding his teeth and dreaming up ways to force me to obey. His loyalty to my father is admirable, and a goddamn headache.

"I'll communicate your message," he grinds out. "Pass her the phone."

My hand trembles, my body betraying me. Reminding me I'm not at one hundred percent, despite trying to convince myself otherwise.

"He wants to talk to you," I say without turning.

From right fucking behind me and all up in my shit, she hooks an arm around me and snatches the phone from my hand.

I find the sink, crank the tap, and drink straight from it like a feral animal. I fucking feel like one, like I'd like to rip out my enemies' throats with my teeth.

"Okay," she says behind me, voice soft but steady. "But the restaurant's busy. I can still work, right?"

Whatever he tells her, she agrees. "I promise."

I count to three before I ask. "How long?"

"A month. Maybe more."

A fucking month? Massimo won't wait that long.

She draws up next to me. "What was that about strawberry allergies?"

I stare at the running water before turning the faucet off. "Not important."

Her sigh fills the room, then I hear her shuffling about, organizing pots and pans that don't need organizing. "You're stronger than you think," she blurts, the encouraging words spilling out before she can stop them.

"Did you read that in a fortune cookie?"

"I live by those words."

That catches my attention. I turn, narrowing my eyes on her.

Her hair brushes her shoulders as she shrugs, backpedaling like she's said too much.

"Don't knock it until you try it."

I don't tell her the problem isn't whether I think I'm strong.

It's about managing the egos of the men around me, all while trying to stop a goddamn war with the Cosa Nostra.

All while proving to every last one of them—my father, Dante, Massimo, Fina—that I'm the kind of motherfucker you sit back and take notice of.

Fina

I GO ABOUT MY DAY, DESPERATE TO SHAKE THE IMAGE SEARED into my brain. Squeezing my eyes shut only makes it worse. Renzo in the shower, stroking the thick length of his gorgeous cock, the flushed tip a sinful shade of pink. I couldn't look away if I tried.

That wicked man deserves to be immortalized, bare-assed for the world to worship. An Italian sculptor should carve him in marble—cock, smirk, and all—preserving every shameless detail. His head tipped back as water cascades over his chest, that taunting wiggle of his ass, the slow glide of his hands like he's performing for me alone. A scandalous exhibition of a scandalous man, and every one of my dirtiest fantasies brought to life in real time.

A man clears his throat.

My eyes flash open.

"Questo non è il mio ordine per il pranzo," the gentleman at my table comments, jarring me back to the present.

I bite my lip. I placed the wrong lunch plate on his table.

"Scusa," I offer, then take the plate to the correct table.

Lord, I'm a hot mess.

Inside the kitchen, Aunt Teresa's already on me. "Did you sleep enough, Fina? The farm is quiet at night, especially when you're alone?"

"No," I reply too fast. "I slept fine. Must be my hormones messing with me."

She wipes her hand on her apron. "Fresh air will do you good. The market is open in the square, and I've a shopping list. Would you be helpful and pick up what I need?"

"Of course." It's a gorgeous day. A walk will clear my head.

Rome has big-city energy mixed with small-town charm. In California, you'd sit an hour in traffic while driving to a bougie farmers market, where tables with fresh vegetables are nestled against trendy IV stations.

Los Angeles's farm-to-table trend has nothing on Italy's open-air markets. The food here hits different, less chemical-tasting, more salt-of-the-earth.

Basket swinging on my arm, I stroll through the market, ticking off my prozia's list, sampling as I go. A bite of fresh mozzarella, a sip of espresso handed over with a wink. Basil, rosemary, and grilled bread perfume the air. My senses are soon as full as my stomach, yet I feel lighter.

I'm at the last vendor when it happens. I swing my basket too hard, and a tomato leaps free. I stoop to retrieve it, laughing under my breath, until something shifts.

Out of the corner of my eye, I see a man dressed head-to-toe in black.

He's standing too still.

Watching too closely.

Then he disappears into the crowd like smoke.

The hair on the back of my neck prickles.

My hand goes for my gun.

He could be no one. Black is fashionable in Rome.

But my gut knows better. I've been around wolves my entire life. You don't grow up as Matteo Lombardi's sacrificial lamb without learning how to spot a predator.

And you sure as hell don't ignore one.

I call an Uber to take me the few blocks back to the restaurant just to be safe.

"Are dicks supposed to be pretty?"

Bianca and Camilla freeze like I just asked if pasta counts as a vegetable. We're knee-deep in decluttering Aunt Teresa's apartment, in the lull between the lunch and dinner, and I decide now's the time for a deep analysis of male anatomy?

Because obviously, nothing says productivity like chatting about pretty dicks while sorting lace doilies.

Bianca gives me a look that's equal parts amused and knowing.

Camilla drops a box of chafing dishes with a clatter. "Whose dick?" she blurts, eyes wide.

Our resident connoisseur smirks. "Handsome face, handsome dick. But if he's got yacht-sized feet? Game over."

We burst into the kind of laughter that makes your stomach hurt and your cheeks ache. Though seriously, if I hear about Dante's big dick one more time, I'll never be able to make eye contact without losing it.

"Fina." Camilla elbows me like we're twelve. "Spill. Whose dick?"

"It was just a general question," I lie, unconvincingly.

Camilla narrows her eyes. "It's him, isn't it? Dante's associate?"

Damn. My mouth really needs a better filter. "Who?"

"The guy you doused in booze and slapped like he insulted Zia Teresa's lasagna? The hot mafioso you ghosted last time he came to the restaurant?"

I fight the urge to groan. "I'm asking because I saw one online."

Camilla gasps. "You saw ... a pretty dick?"

"Porn?" Bianca's eyes gleam. "Love this for you."

I exhale. Crisis averted. Sort of.

Bianca pumps her fist in the air like she's courtside at a basketball game. "If she's into hung porn stars, I say cheers."

"I wasn't judging," Camilla insists, a bit breathless. "I was processing."

I get it. I really do. Especially since I've been mentally replaying Renzo's shower scene like it's my favorite guilty pleasure. Water sliding down every sharp line of muscle. His head tilted back as he strokes himself.

That dick is a dangerous weapon. And so is the man attached to it. A fighter. A charmer. A walking, talking bad idea wrapped up with temptation.

I already had a taste—a messy, deliciously wild dip into insanity— when he rid me of my virginity. It was a mind-blowing experience, one I've forced into lockdown and shoved deep into the back of my mind because what followed made the memory too painful to revisit.

Once was enough.

There's no reason to explore seconds.

"Break time," Bianca declares, and vanishes into the kitchen.

We abandon the boxes and flop around the coffee table, and minutes later, Bianca returns with three glasses of red from Aunt Teresa's stash.

"We have to work," Camilla grumbles, snatching her glass anyway.

Wine is exactly what I need to cleanse my palate and drive Renzo out of my brain.

We drink, talk, laugh. There's something magic about Italian women, the way they speak with their hands, wear their hearts on their sleeves, and live each moment with unapologetic emotion. But as I grow closer to these two beautiful human beings, I recognize that on the surface, we may seem different, but beneath the accents and customs, we are made of the same things. We love fiercely. Protect what's ours. Endure what we must. Don't take shit.

Our friendship flows as easily as wine. It's a gift, really.

After everything I've endured, after building walls so high no one could reach me, I didn't think closeness was possible. I was forced to keep people at a distance, to present the illusion of the perfect mafia princess while I slowly was dying inside.

But here I am, laughing without hesitation, sharing without fear. Somehow, in this new environment, I'm blossoming into the woman I was always meant to be.

Problem is, I'm lying to them. And it doesn't sit well.

The wall between my past and present has been breached. Dante and Renzo know the truth, and that's two people too many. Dante promised I'd be under his protection, but I've been in that world too long not to understand that things can unravel on a dime. I can't open up completely, not now. I won't risk everything I'm building, the life I'm making, their friendship.

My new life deserves to be unblemished by the past.

Damn you, Renzo, for making this impossible.

I drain my drink and place the empty glass on the table.

Camilla eyes me, amused. "Wow. You tossed that back like you have something to forget."

Currently, someone to forget.

Bianca scoots forward. "So, since Fina shared, I'll do the same. Guess what I'm into lately? Role-playing. So far, I've been a maid, a pirate, and a pole dancer."

What in God's name have I unleashed?

"I'm considering greeting the new guy I'm dating at my apartment dressed as Little Red Riding Hood. You know, wearing nothing but a cape, heels, and a basket." She drops her voice. "Well, hello there, you big bad wolf."

That night out in wigs definitely wasn't her first time.

"You think it's too much for a second date?" she asks.

"Ummm," Camilla hums.

But what does "too much" even mean? Who gets to decide where the line is drawn? People are complex. There's no cookie-cutter answer, no universal measure for what's acceptable.

Harder.

My cheeks flush. Bossing Renzo around was a rush I didn't expect. I tapped into something bold and unapologetic, a side of myself I never knew I had. And how could I have known? I'd been one week away from losing everything, including a part of me I hadn't even met yet. If Carlo's dinner hadn't included strawberries, I'd be his wife right now. Sex with a man like him wouldn't have awakened me, it would have erased me.

But fate intervened.

God spared me and gave me another shot at living fully, despite my desires being a little twisted.

You stalked him for years. And whether you like it or not, he's part of your new life. You basically shackled him to you. Why not ... "Why not explore it?" My heart pounds. "While you're young and eager to test limits. Why not be the Superwoman in your own bedroom?"

"You think so?" Bianca asks.

"I think you show that Big Bad Wolf exactly what you want."

Everything stills.

Why not? Why the heck not, Fina?

"Bondage is a huge kink," I confess.

Camilla gasps.

Bianca's eyes light up. "Have you been tied up?"

I bite my lip.

"She has," Camilla whispers, her tone full of reverence.

"Twice," I admit. "And once, I had my girlfriend tie me up so I could send pictures to a guy. Total thirst trap."

"Aren't you naughty?" Bianca purrs. "This is good."

"Did it work?" Camilla asks, practically vibrating.

"Work?"

"Did you get his attention?"

"Like a charm." I smile, remembering nearly running Renzo over in my father's car. I crushed on him so hard for years. He was my first. My only.

Until he wasn't.

But if that's true, why follow him around Rome? Why the urgent push to rush back to the farm?

"I like to watch," Camilla murmurs.

My lips part.

Bianca's eyebrows hit the ceiling.

We both stare at Camilla, who suddenly looks like she just shared the secrets of the universe.

"I only worked up the nerve to do it once," she shyly admits.

"There's this club with a back room ..." Bianca bursts out.

I only half hear her. My mind is tangled in a fight between "I shouldn't" versus "why not?"

He's the worst man to be in a relationship with—or nearly marry.

But the perfect man to experiment with.

If I can't tell my friends the whole truth, then at the very least, I need to be honest with myself.

Why not push boundaries with a man who has none?

EXCITEMENT LICKS UP MY SPINE AS I EXIT THE BUS. I HATE IT, almost as much as I despise the man handcuffed in the barn. Still, my pace doesn't slow until I'm standing outside, trying to compose myself.

You're better than this, Fina.

Breath finally calm, I push the door open and slip inside.

The smell of hay greets me, a fresh country scent I'm beginning to get used to. Sunsets amber rays filter between the wooden slats, and a momentary pang of guilt hits me. Penned like a dog and hours spent alone, he must be pulling his hair out.

I approach his form sprawled out in the hay. Even asleep, a soft smug smile softens his features. Withdrawal is brutal, but he seems at peace right now. For his sake, I hope his issue is more about getting clean than staying that way.

I drop the tote carrying tonight's special, a few side dishes, and dessert on the bench, then inch forward and nudge him with my foot.

He's out cold.

"Wake up," I demand.

Not even a flutter of his dark lashes.

I wait three seconds, then do it again.

He shoots up, grabs my ankle, and yanks me off-balance. My arms flail, a sharp gasp tears from my throat, and then I crash onto his chest with a thud. Before I can blink, he rolls and pins me beneath him, his weight pressing me into the straw.

His broad smirk is close enough to taste. "I'm awake now."

In that exact moment, I realize I need to rethink what I'm getting myself into. His pretty dick has made me reckless.

Hands on his chest, I prepare to shove him off. But he's warm, and muscled, and so sexy even my brain cells melt.

I hate that with one touch, he's got me dumbstruck.

His gaze flicks to my mouth, and time stills.

He's going to kiss me.

Do I want him to?

My pulse races, and I swear I'm sweating. Kissing is far too intimate, and exactly the opposite goal of my wining and dining him tonight.

What do I do? Slap his face? Grab his dick?

"Your dinner's getting cold," I lie.

His eyes light up. "The dinner you carried on a thirty-minute bus ride from Rome?"

Truth is, the tote is insulated and the food piping hot when I placed it inside.

He smooths an errant lock of hair from my cheek.

I still beneath his touch.

"You're gorgeous when you're flustered."

"Get off me."

"Kiss me first."

I stiffen. "Not on your life."

"Okay," he says.

I narrow my eyes at him. Impossible. It's not in his nature to give up so easily.

"If not on my life, how about my death?"

"What?"

"Because I'll die if you don't kiss me."

Unbelievable. "You're twisting a simple expression and trying to make it into some kind of cheesy pickup line."

"And?"

My heart thunders in my chest. This man, with all his antics, will be the death of *me*.

"Fina." He says my name with such relish, always has.

My response rolls off my lips. "Don't Fina me."

"I've spent the day thinking about you, here, taking advantage of me while I lie here helpless and vulnerable." He lowers his head and licks me from chin to ear. "You riding me," he murmurs, nuzzling his nose against my upper lobe and lightly flicking his tongue across the inner edge. "You being a naughty fucking girl using me while I'm shackled and powerless." He places a soft kiss against my temple. "Come on. I dare you."

I squeeze my eyes shut, trying to block him out. But he stirs something in me no one else ever has. Raw desire laced in kink, to be exact.

Should I kiss Renzo?

His eyes gleam with challenge, daring me to act.

This is a game. He doesn't think I'll do it.

Hell with that.

I snap my eyes open. His grin falters just before I lunge, my mouth crashing into his. I smile against his lips when he tenses in surprise. Our tongues collide, wild and desperate and filthy, and I lose myself in the chaos. I kiss him like he already belongs to me, like every inch of me has been waiting for this moment. He tastes dark and addictive, a flavor I've been starving for.

Is the kiss intimate?

If there were a Richter scale for measuring intimacy in a kiss, this one would shatter it. Nothing about it is gentle or hesitant. It's a collision of mouths and tongues, breath stolen, hearts entangling into one knot.

This is us in a kiss.

He growls, low and primal, then yanks me closer with those cuffed hands.

His cock presses into my stomach, sending a flood of heat between my thighs. But it's my name, which he groans like a man possessed, that does me in. "Fina."

My knees feel weak, like I'm going to swoon. Instead, I go to battle, rolling my hips, slow and deliberate, his body trembling beneath mine. "I should leave you like this," I murmur against his lips. "Hard. Helpless. Desperate."

His eyes darken to an impossible shade of blue. "You wouldn't."

"Wouldn't I?" I trail kisses down his jaw, then lick just beneath his ear.

He growls again, straining against the cuffs, and I swear the chains creak with how much he wants me.

Power rushes through me, egging me on. I slide my hand down his chest, slow and steady, grazing his abs until I reach the waistband of his pants.

Then his stomach growls.

I freeze.

He curses. "Fuck."

"You're hungry."

Our eyes lock. "Fucking starving."

Heat blooms across my cheeks. Does he mean for food or me? Because I need him to mean me. I crave that it's so. I dart my tongue across my lips, and his gaze follows the motion like he's tracking prey.

I can still taste him.

Suddenly, it hits me. No. No. No. One damn kiss, and I tossed my heart down the rabbit hole. I'm a lost and confused Alice, and he's for sure the Mad Hatter.

Let that kiss mean something more than a mistake.

"That was fun," he says, voice low, rough, and distant. Pulling away like what just happened was another day at the office. For him, it likely was. If he really, truly wanted me, he'd be thinking Fina and not pasta.

"Should we eat?" he asks. His question's a slap in the face.

He didn't kiss me back to claim me.

He kissed me back because it was easy.

A flush creeps up my neck, hot and sharp. I feel ridiculous. Angry. Twenty all over again.

What was I thinking?

Do I even know this man at all?

He's all rough edges and mixed signals. Every time I start believing something's real, he slips through my fingertips.

I offer him my frostiest look.

His forehead furrows into a deep V.

Good. Feel that.

My voice is calm when I speak, not reflecting the disappointment eating me up inside. "Your dinner is getting cold."

I came here simply for sex. Forgetting to consider one important truth: nothing between Renzo and me has ever been simple.

"KNOW WHAT YOUR PROBLEM IS?"

Fork raised, I'm midbite when she hits me with her question, as if she's laying a trap, as if her kiss earlier wasn't enough to drive thoughts of escape away.

I'm not going anywhere. Despite how it's taken the good part of an hour for her to stop tossing poison darts my way.

Fina doesn't understand the power of delayed gratification—not yet. Once I hose down, rinse off today's sweat and grime, and then bury my face between her thighs, she'll thank me for it.

Despite her displeasure, she's still here, "fulfilling her obligations" —which is what she so bitingly told me earlier—but mellowing as the light fades.

"My problem?" I force a laugh. "Pick one."

"You're too smart."

"If I were so fucking smart, would I be trapped inside a barn and pissing in a bucket all day?"

The key for my shackles is now inside my pocket, where I placed it after it fell into the hay while we were lip-locked. She's yet to discover it's lost. So goodbye bucket; I can escape at any time I want.

I continue eating, giving nothing away.

She continues prying. "No one's told you before?"

"Too many times I lost count."

She looks hopeful, the earlier spark in her eyes returning. But all this psychobabble and digging deep into my bullshit is uncomfortable, especially coming from a woman who's been riding my tail for years. "Smart is usually followed by ass." And then, in true smart-ass fashion, I gesture to her half-empty plate and repeat her warning from earlier. "Your dinner's getting cold."

She takes a bite of gnocchi smothered in a lemon butter sauce and closes her eyes as she chews, relishing the pasta-dumpling dish like it's a religious experience.

I'm instantly hard, the sight of her beautiful, reverent expression igniting something feral in me. I want to be the one who places it there, time and time again while I worship her body like the devil I am.

"You told me as much on the ride to Vegas," she says between chews. "How a brain like yours doesn't handle boredom well. So, I … um … looked into it."

Of course she did.

I pretend to be disturbed. "Fucking obsessed, aren't you?"

Yet calling her out this time hits different. I fucking love the balls on her.

She shrugs her shoulders, blowing off my accusation. Too caught up in the deep dive into my brain.

I wonder if I should warn her?

"People like you crave stimulation. You need to feel things. Test limits. Push boundaries. That's what gets you off."

I smirk. "Know what really gets me off …"

Jesus. I've avoided this psychobabble for years. I'm about physicalities. Filthy sex and bruised knuckles. A thick dick, a pair of cuffs, and the right woman on her knees. Deep internal reflection never crosses my mind. And when pressed, I typically deflect by doing something outrageous.

Which is why I'm humoring her and not shutting this shit down. Waiting for the perfect moment to act.

Bad decision, because she hacks through my bullshit with a goddamn machete. "Your father understands this."

Fuck, she's perceptive.

"My father?" I demand, irritated. She best be careful peeling back this onion because, surprise, surprise, what's on the inside also stinks.

"Why else would he allow you such freedom? Cover for your fights, the women, kink club escapades, run-ins with cops, pissed-off boyfriends ..." Her fingers roll lazily through the air like she's listing steps in a recipe. Part chef. Part fucking stalker. "He turned a blind eye to substance abuse, too ..."

Part boxer, because her jab is flawless. In my head, I finish the thought for her.

Until he couldn't.

I drag a hand down my face, annoyance sparking hard and fast. She recites my history like it's common knowledge, like she's memorized every fuckup and filed it away for moments like this. What pisses me off even more is how accurate she is with her sad portrayal of me.

"The condition is called dysrationalia," she plows on, relentless and unmerciful. "People doing irrational things despite having a high intellect. Normal bores people like you, so you take things to extremes to challenge yourself."

"Jesus Christ ..."

"Rules mean nothing to someone like you," she declares as my discomfort grows. "Not when you think you're smarter than everyone else. My father would've crushed your spirit. Forced the Life down your throat and watched you choke on it. Yours? He waited. Gave you time to figure out the truth."

Every syllable digs under my ribs, wedges itself where I can't yank it out. I turn away, jaw clenched, trying to steady the rising panic. She's not wrong, and that makes it worse.

I spent years pushing back, sure, but things only spiraled after Rome. That's when the rebellion turned toxic, driven by this desperate urge to become exactly what everyone already believed I was.

A good time.

Unreliable.

Weak.

The realization slams into me. My lips part, then press into a tight line. I shake my head, unsettled by the weight of it. Fuck. I never saw it this clearly until now.

Our eyes lock. Her soft smile says everything—she knows she hit the motherfucking bullseye.

Her voice dips low, velvet and lethal.

"You don't follow the rules. You rewrite them. And I kind of hate you for it."

Fuck me.

I shift on the hay bale and look away.

"You're embarrassed?"

How many poor bastards cursed with dysrationalia squirm at the thought of deep, soul-baring talks about intellect?

"I can't believe it. You are." She jumps to her feet, almost dropping her takeout plate. "The same man who wiggled your bare ass at me."

Finally, a topic I can get behind. "Same man who made an F into the shower tile with my come."

Her eyes pop out of her head.

Mission accomplished.

"You ... did?"

The tension in my body eases. "Practice," I simply say, thankful the little perv relishes my bullshit the same way she salivated over the gnocchi.

Her voice fucking quivers. "Practice for what?"

"For when I have you naked and tied to my bedpost and am decorating your tits and stomach with an R instead."

"Oh ..."

Bullseye for Renzo.

Her chest rises fast, and she doesn't say a word, but the way she squeezes her thighs tells me everything.

She's picturing it.

I spear gnocchi on my fork and finish the last few bites.

"I don't think so." She says it with such enthusiasm my brows rise as I look at her. "You're the one restrained, babe."

Holy fuck. Did she just babe me?

She ignores me, covering her dinner then placing the container inside the tote, every movement deliberate and sharp.

Stunned, I have to ask. "Why not?"

She stiffens, and then the verbal machete returns, sharper and ready to draw blood. "I made an agreement to help you, and that's what I'm doing. Otherwise, we're two strangers who happen to have a past ..."

"My dick was covered with your virgin blood—"

"Who don't even know each other—"

"You've been stalking me for years—"

"... and who, under normal circumstances, would never be attracted to each other—"

"Fuck normal."

The way she spits out her words, like she's trying to cleanse herself of me. And that won't happen. Not now. Not ever.

I stand, and the dinner container flies off my lap. She tries to jump out of reach, but she's close enough I can count the freckles on her shoulder. I wrap an arm around her waist and haul her into me. "Babe," I say, low and dangerous.

She squirms, trying to break free. "Don't babe me, asshole."

Oh, she wants raw? Let's go there.

"Now that we ate, let's fuck."

Her entire body goes slack.

"Here's how it'll play out. I'm releasing you and stripping. You're taking the hose over there and hosing me down. Then, you're riding my face and, when I say you can, my dick. Capisci?"

She's quiet for so long, I begin wondering if I imagined her earlier enthusiasm and the anger that followed when she assumed I was rejecting her.

Fina. Fina. Fina. You've so much to learn.

"This is casual sex," she states. "Don't be getting feelings for me."

I laugh. "Getting feelings for you?" *Already have them, babe.*

She jerks free of my embrace. "Asshole."

I'm not done stripping and still considering her reaction when a cold stream of water knocks me backward. I sputter, then glare at her.

Her smile is like a gift, and it lights up the barn.

I peel off my soaked sweatpants and boxers, drape them so the fabric swallows the chains, then stretch out with my arms and legs wide. "Do your worst."

And she does, letting me have it. Utterly delighted by making my dick and balls shrivel beneath the chilly blast. I count the cackles, ready to double the amount in moans.

She wants the full Renzo effect?

Then let's fucking go.

———

Fina

I DROP THE HOSE, LAUGHING SO HARD I'M CRYING.

Renzo just stands there—arms spread, legs apart, water dripping from his hair, his chin, his nipples ... and his maddeningly perfect dick.

Soaked to the bone and still sexier than sin.

Why not take what I want? He certainly plans to; his laughter when I said the sex would be casual was proof enough. That laugh stung, but I brushed it off. What did I expect, another marriage proposal?

Been there. Done that.

Epic fail.

"You gonna stand there staring at me?" he asks, one brow lifting. "Or get your ass over here?"

Nerves flutter in my belly, but I cross the space between us. He towers over me—he always has—but something about the way he watches me now makes my knees weak.

"Take off your dress."

My fingers tremble slightly as I reach the buttons. One by one, I undo them, feeling the heat of his gaze trace every inch of skin I reveal.

"Let me," he says, rough and commanding, stepping in and brushing my hands aside. He peels the dress off my shoulders, but instead of letting it fall, he lifts it like a sheet caught in a sudden breeze, then spreads it deliberately over the driest patch beneath us.

He wastes no time on my bra, stripping it away before settling himself on the expensive fabric, gloriously naked, arms propped behind his head, every inch of him daring me to look.

I bite my lip, suspended in that delicious, razor-edged space between fear and thrill, unable to tear my eyes away.

The air pulses, waiting for me to make up my mind.

Then he curls a finger.

Come here.

I step forward, his earlier promises still echoing; ride his face, then his dick, in that order.

He's the one restrained. At my mercy.

Wickedly willing.

I've always envied how wild he is. His reckless adventures. His total refusal to be caged. While I ... I've lived so little, so controlled, so muted. But not tonight.

All I want is freedom.

Why not start right now?

A wicked smile blooms. Little Red Riding Hood has nothing on me.

His gaze sharpens, locked on my mouth. He doesn't realize it yet, who's really in charge.

I kick off my heels, breasts swaying as I rise to my full height above him. He stills, pinned by my bold stare. His silence spurs me on as I step over his hips. From this vantage, I own him.

"How's it feel being my fuckboy?" I murmur. I crave the scrape of his mouth, the filth of his tongue, his worship given because I demand it.

He blinks, then his laughter rumbles low and dirty. "It'll feel a hell of a lot better when you're on my face."

His cock jerks hard, proof he means it. I've read most men dislike giving oral. Renzo? He worships the idea. The hunger in his eyes sends a jolt straight to my core.

I twist around slowly and unclasp my bra, letting it fall behind me. My fingers hook the delicate fabric of my thong, and I bend, shimmy, peel it down inch by inch, making sure he sees everything.

When I glance at him, he's stroking himself. "You trying to kill me?"

"Give me time."

His voice deepens, darkens. "Then let me die with your pussy on my tongue."

Lust slams into me. I step forward, positioning myself above his face, my thighs trembling with anticipation.

"Stop stalling," he orders.

I hush him with a finger to my lips. "I'm in charge."

And then suddenly, he moves. With a quick shift, he sweeps my legs out from under me, taking full control.

I land on my shins, hips forward, arms back, his nose buried in my folds.

Any thoughts about who is in charge vanish when he grabs my hips and positions me just so before his hot tongue plunges inside me.

"Oh my God," I gasp. Yes. This is what I needed.

"Miss me?" he demands.

He doesn't wait for my yes.

Every filthy memory I've stored, every fantasy I've secretly fed, collides in a rush as he unleashes on me. Tongue plunging deep, swirling like a cyclone before flicking over my clit in sharp, taunting strokes. Bold one moment, featherlight the next. Then a teasing nip. A slow lick. Pleasure vibrating through me with every touch.

I match the rhythm he demands until my body learns the tempo he's set.

No nerve goes untouched. No part of me safe from his attention.

I lose sense of space, of time, of myself. Then a flicker of panic slices through the pleasure, and I lift up fast, breath catching, afraid I might've smothered him.

But his voice rips through the haze, rough and hungry. "What the fuck are you doing? Ride my face."

I can't help the grin that spreads across my lips, my inhibitions gone. "When I come," I gasp, locking eyes with him. "I'm drawing an F across your face."

Despite knowing it's anatomically impossible, that women aren't built with the same equipment as men, his eyes flash with pleasure. "That's right, babe. Mark me as yours."

He tilts his head, then licks me from bottom to top.

My thighs tremble when I feel his finger at my folds. "No. I want your mouth."

"I haven't fingered you properly yet."

I shake my head.

He gives my hips a sharp tug, and I fall onto his face. Discussion muted.

This time, his movements are slow and gentle, forcing me to grind harder against him. It's the promise of what's to come that sends shivers up my spine, my climax building.

His hands cup my ass, and fingertips dip between my cheeks.

I'm frantic at this point, chasing my climax. So he catches me off guard.

Tthe tip of his finger push against my backside and I still.

"Renzo," I cry out.

He drives it deep, at the same time pitching me forward and impaling me on his tongue.

Holy shit. The pressure's exquisite.

I test the waters, shifting up and down. Then, I give over to it fully, frantically fucking his mouth and finger until I shatter.

He isn't done, though, sliding me back across his hips before thrusting up into me. Frantically. Furiously. Stretching me with his pretty dick and making me question why I hesitated to have sex with him.

How could I pass on this insane pleasure?

I roll up and place a palm on his taut stomach, balancing myself as I take back control.

"That's my girl," he growls. "Fuck me while I'm helpless and at your mercy."

Wrong words. I'm not his girl. As for helpless or at someone's mercy …

I allow my weight to take him deeper.

He hisses, and I smile.

My gaze drops. My dress is ruined. Straw clings to my thighs, his chest. But I'm more interested in how we're joined, and watch the way my flesh parts to accept him, how my clit is flushed pink, how wet I am, how good his pretty cock feels.

"You like what you see, dirty girl?" He flexes his hips, and I gasp. "You enjoying the view, and how well your tight cunt milks my dick?"

"Yes. Keep talking."

"Tell me to take your ass. Penetrate you with my finger and dick."

I'm already falling forward, and he's already sliding home.

"Wait until my dick's inside you. Wait until I've got you stuffed with dildos and my cock." He pauses, then in a sharp tone, says, "Look at me."

I lock eyes with him.

"You want another man fucking your pussy while I'm in your ass?"

God, he's filthy.

"Only if he sucks you off first," I reply.

Problem is, I don't want anyone else touching him.

"Just like with the boxers. Not happening, babe."

A sinking sensation takes hold of me. No. No. No. No. He feels just as possessive?

He thrusts, and I echo, until both of us are teetering on the edge.

"Not. Going. To. Happen," he chants. "You're mine, capisci?"

I gasp, from the second climax. From his declaration.

He clamps hold of my ass and releases into me.

I lie sprawled out on top of him, spent. Light shifts to shadows inside the barn as night approaches. I'm barely conscious, his heart beating against my chest the only sign he's survived, as well.

With the shadows, unease creeps in.

We didn't use a condom.

Aren't there insects in this hay?

He told me I'm his.

Shit. Shit. And double shit.

Casual sex, I said? With the most complicated man alive? And I actually believed I could walk away from this without getting attached?

I stalked this man for *years*. Reassuring myself I was only curious, and desperate.

God, what a fool.

What am I supposed to do now?

No amount of aftercare can soothe the fact she's freaked.

Truth is, I am too. Thoughts about a future with her keep slipping in. Days wandering Rome, espresso in hand, arguing about everything from the sun's place in the sky to whether two people like us can survive the Life and still thrive together. Nights with her tied up, folded over a spanking bench, completely immersed in our lifestyle and loving every second of it.

She's always been curious.

I've always believed I'd be the one to show her.

Jesus. My father will skin me alive for this.

Our eyes connect, and she flushes. Struggling to make sense of something that just is.

I pick up her thong. "Nice underwear."

"What?"

I hand it to her. "Italian?"

She gives me a strange look. Wild-eyed, like I caught her in a trap. "Yes."

I keep my tone neutral, playful. "But it's not pink."

"I hate pink."

Now that makes me smile. "You do?"

"Loathe the color. Almost as much as my father does."

I throw my head back and laugh. Jesus, she's one of a kind. "You're a piece of work, know that?"

"So I've been told." She smirks, and the weird vibe between us dulls. "Though considering how Carlo died, I've grown fonder of the color."

I cock my head. "How did he die again?"

She frowns, confused. Because she clearly heard me talking to Dante about this. "Allergic reaction."

"Right." I wink at her. "And then you fled, executing a brilliant escape plan."

She rolls her eyes. "Brilliant because you suggested it?"

I open my mouth to say yes because I'm a cocky fucker. But I placed a lot on chance back then and am well aware things could have turned out differently. "Glad you took my advice, Fina. You're safe here under my protection."

She is about to remind me it's fucking Dante who is protecting her.

I turn away to retrieve her dirty dress.

When I return, she's holding a hay bale.

I scowl. "Going somewhere?" I demand, not wanting her to leave.

"To bed."

"You're naked."

She shrugs.

I look her up and down, knowing without seeing. "With my come dripping down your thighs."

God help me. She hitches the hay bale to her hip, then touches herself only to confirm I'm correct.

I feel like pounding my chest and howling at the fucking moon. "I'll allow you to leave—"

"You'll allow me ..."

"If you don't wash it off."

My dick hardens, loving the idea. It's not as good as my initial imprinted on her skin but good enough.

"Deal."

What. The. Fuck?

"If you don't wash my juices dried on your face."

I'm all about pussy, in the moment.

She laughs. "Just as I thought."

With that, she leaves me to my own devices.

25

Renzo

Dante looks up, surprised to see me.

I drop into the chair across from his desk and watch him while he finishes his call. His suit jacket slung over another chair. Shirt wrinkled. Tie hanging loose.

What the hell have I missed?

"Is anything salvageable?" He listens for a beat, then curses under his breath and drags a hand through his hair.

That'd be a no.

"Keep me updated," he finishes, before hanging up and tossing his phone aside.

I tilt my head. "Let me guess. You haven't spoken with Massimo?"

He shoots me a glare.

"Why not?"

"I was told the window of opportunity has closed." He tosses his phone on his desk. "That motherfucker is costing me a small fortune in losses."

Well, shit. Massimo's too proud. We waited too long.

Because of me.

Frustration coils in my gut. A simple conversation might've changed everything. Now we're headed straight for war.

"Here's what I propose," I say, drumming my fingers on my thigh. "Surveillance every-fucking-where. On his holdings and ours, his place in Sicily, wherever else you want drones overhead. Let's see if we can catch whoever is responsible."

I'll swing by my apartment, see if my phone is there and not in a club or dark alleyway. Reconnect with my guys. Reignite the Sicilian team. Then it's back to the farm, where I'll slip the shackles back on and wait for Fina to get home, and for the video feed to start filtering in.

"About Rhode Island ..."

Jesus. My father's a demanding prick.

"I'm good."

"Are you?" I read the concern in his eyes, and shame hits deep.

"Just peachy." The lie tastes refreshing. Doesn't mean it's true. I understand how fragile sobriety is; one asshole doctor and I'm back at the bottom. One little taste and I'm zero to nothing once more.

She's seen me at my worst but has yet to witness me at my best.

Do I really want to drag her, everyone—even myself—through my shit again?

I stand.

"How about an early lunch?" Dante asks. "Somewhere else than Zia Teresa?"

I shake my head. "I've got to get my men and equipment in place, then get back to the farm before Fina returns home."

He grunts.

"What?"

"She's taken good care of you during your recovery. So much so, you almost sound eager to return."

Typical Dante. Lover to many. Loyal to none.

But my answer surprises him as much as it alarms him.

"She didn't just sober me up, she saved me."

Out of breath, I slam the barn door shut before the rooster can assault me again. Blood trickles down my calf where he struck. He's definitely left his mark.

The cocky feather-devil.

"What the fuck happened?" Renzo bursts out.

I didn't come racing back to the farm to be attacked by poultry. No. I came for sex, orgasms, and the thrill he always stirs up in me.

Talk about a buzz kill.

"Just another male trying to knock me down a peg." I remove a sanitizing wipe and Band-Aid from my purse, then dab at the wound like I'm not furious.

Chains rattle as Renzo tugs at them. "He's outside?" Concern echoes within his tone, but there's nothing he can do, not with those iron cuffs on his wrists and ankles.

"I left a hay bale in the drive this morning. When I came back, it was gone. He's scared shitless of them."

"An animal hurt you?"

I don't answer. He gets a star for answering correctly.

Silence stretches. I finish sanitizing my hands when he finally speaks, voice low and rough, causing my stomach to tangle in knots.

"Maybe the wind took it."

"Wind?" I laugh. Italy's in a heat wave. There's barely a breeze. "You hungry?" I ask, grabbing the tote and stepping closer, so done with this discussion and the feathered nuisance.

"Fucking starving."

Guilt tugs at me. If I open that cooler, I know it'll be empty. Not much to do all day but eat and sober up. But Dante gave strict orders.

One month. I won't break my word. I get busy laying out tonight's feast. An antipasto starter, grilled salmon with capers, fresh roasted vegetables, and cannolis Aunt Teresa made earlier this morning.

She questioned me sneaking double-portion meals into the bag.

I told her it was just an old LA habit, grab-and-go convenience. Nothing more.

"Fina."

The way he says my name, low and rough and ripe with hunger, sends a jolt straight to my core. I freeze midreach, the cannolis trembling in my hand as I meet his eyes.

"Dinner can wait."

My breath catches, and heat flares low in my belly.

I nearly drop the cannolis.

"I'm starving for you."

Chained or not, this man could ruin me. And Lord knows, I'm prepared to be ruined tonight. Completely. Thoroughly. Hands shaking, I set the cannolis beside the other food, taking time to summon my courage before facing him to spring my surprise.

But Renzo beats me to it.

He's stripped, his clothes draped over the chain as if he casually hung them on a clothesline, and wearing nothing but my necklace.

The pearls hang at his throat, soft and elegant against the brutal cut of his body.

A low hum resonates deep inside my chest.

There's something electric about pretty things on dangerous men.

His hungry gaze rakes over me, then he prowls forward, jerks me toward him, then dips his head and bites my throat first and nipple second.

I cry out, more shocked than anything else. This version of Renzo is my wildest fantasy brought to life.

I'm forced toward the hay bale, his hand clasped around the back of my neck.

"Bend over it."

No *babe*. No *Fina, Fina. Fina.* Just an order.

Impatient, he gives me a small push, and I fall forward. In an instant, he's thrust two fingers inside me.

I'm wet, and full, so full. My walls tightening around him.

"You don't come until I say so. Capisci?"

"Yes," I breathe.

His palm connects with my ass. His slap doesn't hurt, not with the leather straps across my bottom running interference.

He works a third finger inside.

"Please," I moan. "Harder."

"Jesus," he grinds out. "I've got to see you stuffed with my fingers." He withdraws, and I hear movement behind me before he flips my dress up over my hips.

Several tense seconds pass.

I grow impatient and wiggle my ass.

"Holy fucking shit."

Right. My surprise.

Bianca and I spent our break at her favorite boutique. I'm in black leather lingerie, with a sheer lace bra and underwear wrapped in leather accents. Leather straps crisscross my breasts, abdomen, groin and ass. The ensemble gives a total bondage vibe. My pulse hasn't slowed since I first saw it.

I wait, anxious for his next response.

The wait isn't long.

"You buy that for me?" he demands, tone deep and husky.

"Kind of," I admit.

I feel him stiffen.

"You," I whisper, "and me." Because we can't both be bound and tied at the same time. Because I love the thought of being completely, utterly subdued.

His breath dances across my neck as he arches over me and, in one fluid motion, rips my dress off. At this rate, I'll be replacing dresses like hair ties.

I'm lifted, spun around, and set on my feet.

One thing I'm instantly sure of—every Euro spent on this dress was worth it.

"You're fucking gorgeous."

My lips turn, and I bask in his praise.

"But asking for trouble."

I lift a shoulder. "We're past that now, aren't we?"

A low growl escapes his throat. "You don't want me to hold back."

"Well ... no."

"You trying to kill me?" he grinds out.

"Perhaps *later*."

His chuckle fills the barn. "Fine, babe. But don't say I didn't warn you."

Without warning, he hoists me and slams us into the nearest wall, then with one ferocious thrust, drives deep inside me until he's fully seated.

I anchor my thighs against his hips and hold on, pleasure wrapped in a sweet pain, the kind that comes from my tight body accepting his brutal intrusion.

He doesn't slow but pounds into me. Chains swinging, our hearts keeping rhythm.

I bite my lip. It hurts but feels incredible.

His hand slides down, and his fingers scissor my clit as he flexes his hips, so each thrust hits a place that makes me lose control.

I cry out, pant, and whimper. Tension building to where, within seconds, I'm ready to explode.

He curses and growls. "Don't you fucking come until I say so. Capisci?"

He pinches one nipple, then the other, making sure I hear him.

I do everything in my power to obey.

Except he's too much. I'm full of him, and not just his pretty cock.

His skin's a raging inferno against me, his heat matching my own. His muscles flexing around me, sexy as sin.

The pearls dragging across my collarbone, slapping my upper chest.

I hiss and squeeze around his massive girth, fighting for control.

It only sets him off, and his thrusts become more frantic.

"Renzo," I plead, needing his words. Then, when I don't hear them, I arch forward and bite his neck.

He's wild. Merciless. And just when I can't hold off anymore, incredible.

I cling to him as my climax hits me like an earthquake.

He drives deep three more times and then stills, unleashing inside me.

"Yes. Yes. Yes," I chant.

I'll be bruised and sore. Lord, I might be unable to walk.

"You okay?" he demands after a while.

I smile against his neck.

He tenses and jerks me back so he can look at me.

I want to joke and make light of what we've just done.

Instead, I answer truthfully. "Never been better."

26

Tina

THE SUN WELCOMES A NEW DAY BY THE TIME I GINGERLY EXIT the barn. I can't believe I slept with him. Inside an old barn, nestled on a hay mattress, his body half on me, half off, his arm flung across my chest.

Everything aches.

My heart most of all.

I didn't enter the danger zone. I kicked the door down.

I sigh. Casual sex and I don't seem to be vibing.

And ... I feel guilty. Because I lost the damn keys. I thought I'd release him so we could shower in the house, but the keys aren't inside my bag. I couldn't tell him his stay at the farm is indefinite now, until I get a replacement. How does someone even explain to a locksmith they've a man shackled inside a barn? Who reeks of sex and sin? Who has a just-been-fucked aura about him?

I'll open the barn windows to air the place out, and instruct him to behave. Play dumb to the locksmith and pretend I've no clue how Renzo got himself in this predicament.

I'm halfway across the driveway when my phone rings. My stomach drops as I release the hay bale and dig inside my purse for my phone. Panicked that something's wrong if my aunt's calling me this early.

When I look at my phone, I realize I'm being FaceTimed ... by Sebastiano Beneventi.

No. No. No.

Damn you, Dante—he must have shared my number.

I tug my torn dress tighter. What do I do?

The phone buzzes again, almost angrily.

Exactly as I picture the man at the other end.

I make the sign of the cross, smooth back my untamed hair, and answer the FaceTime call. Don Beneventi fills the screen, and a gasp escapes me. Eyes hard and lips tight, power radiates off him like a bull ready to charge. The man is just as terrifying on the phone as he is in person.

"Renzo still with you?"

I bite my lip, dumbstruck by his call, though that's not why I hesitate. I feel *protective* of the man chained inside my barn.

"Elia. Is my goddamn son with you?"

"Yes."

The muscles in his jaw jump as he clenches his teeth.

"He's okay. Better than okay," I reassure him. Because something's wrong, it's written all over his expression.

"Listen carefully and do exactly as I say. Get him to the town of Anzio, where a boat will be waiting to take him to Sardinia. Grassi's men will be anticipating that he'll flee to Sardinia but with luck will swarm the larger port at Civitavecchia instead. If he resists, tell him Grassi has Dante."

My lips part. "Has?"

"Ambushed him and likely has him locked up in a Sicilian dungeon. His men are hunting for Renzo right now."

My grip tightens around the phone, pulse pounding in my ears. "They won't touch him," I say, my voice low and sharp. "I'll do what I have to."

Don Beneventi tilts his head, studying me. "I get it now."

Before I can ask what he means, he cuts me off. "I'll hold you to it. Now get moving and call me from Sardinia."

I stare at the empty screen. Not because of his words, but because of what he left out.

It sounded like I'll be the one making that call.

Not Renzo.

I'll be on that boat, too.

My mind races. I need to call Aunt Teresa and alert her. But first, I've got to wake up Renzo and get us to the port.

I drop my phone into my purse, ready to do just that.

The stranger comes out of nowhere and slams into my side, taking me to the ground and knocking the wind out of me. Before I can scream, I'm punched in the side then head. Once. Twice. Three times.

He hauls himself off me, but not before I spy his hand, and the heel mark I made, deeper and uglier than the wound the feathered nuisance left on me.

Dread grips me. Lord, he's the same man who attacked me before.

I lie still, pain flooding every nerve ending, my mind scrambling for a way out.

He kicks me hard in the ribs. My vision fractures, my world spinning.

"You little bitch," he snarls. "Thought I wouldn't find you? Thought you could hide?"

Oh my God. It can't be...

"I own you," he roars, completely unhinged.

A psycho living up to his name.

I try to push up from the dirt, struggling to breathe.

Settemo towers over me, pure evil carved into human form. He drops a black duffel bag at his feet and pulls out the one thing I never wanted to see again. The white latex catsuit.

My stomach turns, and I fight off my panic.

He lunges before I can react, gripping my ankles and yanking them into the material.

I gasp and thrash. "Get off me, Cunt Stud."

Wrong word choice.

He flips me like I weigh nothing and drags me by the ankles down the gravel drive. Pebbles slice into my skin, the drive scraping my arms raw. My scream catches in my throat, choked off by terror.

I hear an engine running. He'll load me into a vehicle and drive off.

I'll break my promise to Don Beneventi about getting Renzo to safety. Joke's on me.

Renzo can't save me.

If Settemo gets me in that vehicle, I'll disappear.

Forever.

I claw at the dirt, screaming as rocks shred my palms. My knees knock against the ground, pain spiking with every inch.

He halts, moves to my side to glare at me. "You fucking around on me? Who did you wear that slutty lingerie for?"

Freaking psycho.

He grabs my hair and sends my head into the pavement. As the sun dims and my world spirals, I'm rolled onto my back. Helpless to do anything but survive and pray for a miracle.

Time and time again, it's proven that I have a funny relationship with God.

I hear my salvation before it strikes.

"Cakooo."

A battle cry from off to the right.

The feathered nuisance is charging straight at us.

Neck extended, wings flapping violently, he barrels across the yard like a demon possessed. Without slowing, he leaps, talons first, and slams into Settemo's face, spearing him in the eye.

The bastard howls in pain, clutching his eye, stumbling back. Blood trickles between his fingers.

I wiggle free from the latex, curl my legs and kick him as hard as I can.

It isn't enough.

He turns, focus back on me, fury twisting his features. But then suddenly freezes.

His gaze shifts to behind me. Something terrifies him.

And then he's running ... *away.*

He's halfway to the waiting white van when a shadow passes me.

Renzo.

Free. Wild-eyed.

Gun raised.

What the hell?

"You're fucking dead, motherfucker!" he bellows.

The crack of bullets pierces the air. Glass shatters. The van swerves.

Dirt erupts as Renzo fires at the tires.

The van accelerates in reverse, engine roaring, but Renzo doesn't stop. He takes off after it, relentless.

"Wait!" I scream, clambering to my feet, shaking off the latex completely. "Stop!"

He doesn't hear me. Or he doesn't care.

"Your father called!" I yell, stumbling down the drive after him. As much as I'd like Emo strung up and bloody, there's a more urgent matter to attend to.

"Dante's been captured!"

Renzo

Fina's scream will haunt me for years to come.

I couldn't unlock the manacles fast enough. My hands were clumsy, my panic clawing at my throat. She lay crumpled on the stone driveway, her face swollen, blood trailing down her legs. That white rubber suit bunched at her ankles like some grotesque costume. And standing over her, clutching an eye, was Settemo Accardo.

The image is burned into me, violent and permanent. Her battered body. His enraged expression. The sick silence only interrupted by the cackle of a nearby rooster.

Before I could deal with Settemo, she stopped me with news I never saw coming. Massimo took Dante, a man who's been a big brother to me and who I owe the fucking world to.

I've lived a life of chaos. I don't flinch. I don't stumble. I thrive inside it.

But I'm dealing with dual mindfucks. Both deeply personal.

I'll break Settemo Accardo.

Bone by bone.

Breath by breath.

Until nothing remains.

While weighing what's the best way to deal with the Massimo situation.

I held Fina in my arms the entire boat ride. Cleaning her wounds the best I could with the gauze and antiseptic my father's men had on hand. Refusing to let them touch her. Keeping her safe and protected, knowing I was almost too late.

We're in my brother's villa, seated in a chair across from him. She squirms on my lap, uncomfortable beneath his intense scrutiny. I don't release her, no matter how angry she gets or how the tension between Sandro and us builds.

"I want every man at your disposal hunting for Settemo Accardo."

She stiffens at his name.

Sandro stays quiet, taking it all in, missing nothing.

Rage has its claws in me and won't let go. The jagged scrape on her cheek from being dragged across the stone driveway stokes it hotter. The deep gash on her knee, bleeding through the bandage, sends violence pulsing through me. The raw, bloodied fingertips where she clawed at the ground to stop him have me strung tight as a drum, seconds from snapping. Every wince, every flinch, every sigh. I log them like I'm taking names. I won't rest until that bastard is dead.

"Not going to happen," my twin says. "In case you missed it, your friend Massimo Grassi has started a war." His gaze shifts to Fina, then back to me. "As for her, I want her gone."

Fina mutters something into my neck that sounds like asshole.

I want to pull her closer, replace Settemo's fingermarks with mine. Instead, I set her on her feet and then, without warning, launch across the desk. My hand locks around Sandro's throat, driving him and his chair back until we crash to the floor.

We start swinging.

Twins have their own language. Ours is brutal.

He lands a shot to my head.

I drive a fist into his kidney.

We've fought before, but this is different. I'm actually furious, when it's typically the other way around.

"Get the fuck off me," he growls.

"Tell me again you don't want her here," I snarl.

He stops fighting. Then laughs. It's sharp and throws me off. This fucker never laughs, and I don't understand what's so bleeding funny.

"What in God's name is going on?" a woman's voice cuts in. "Renzo, get off him."

Riley. Sandro's girlfriend.

She shoves me, and I roll onto my back, while he's still laughing.

"You must be Fina," she says.

"You must be the woman whose underwear I'm wearing," Fina replies, a smile in her tone.

I almost miss it, too caught up in the underwear part.

"You said to inform you when the doctor arrived," Riley tells Sandro. "I put him upstairs in my room."

"Your former fucking room," Sandro grumbles.

"Come with me ..." Riley gestures to Fina. "... and let these two ..."

"... fools wrestle like they're auditioning for WWE?"

Both women chuckle; their friendship's off to a fucking stellar start. Riley's great and a calming influence on my brother. Just what Fina needs after the shit she's been through, even my bullshit.

I spring to my feet. "I'll carry her."

"She can walk," Fina answers, exasperated. Similar to how she's been for the duration of our journey to Sardinia. Brave and courageous, while I spiraled into a deep hole where all I can think about is revenge.

"We need to talk," Sandro says, the chill back, then turns and, sweet as melting motherfucking butter, addresses his girlfriend. "Riley, mind showing her to the casita?"

"Will you two be okay?" she asks.

I offer him a hand up as proof.

He smacks it away. "We'll have a nice lunch tomorrow before shit goes down. Would you arrange that, too?"

Born from the same womb, my twin and I dance to the same rhythm. Move the same. Talk the same. But sometimes he does shit like this, and I've got to ask, *Who the fucking hell is this guy?*

Riley flashes a smile at him. She's too good for the bastard. "Sure."

But it's Fina's voice, drifting back toward us as they leave, that I cling to. "I'd rather eat dirt than have a meal with that A-hole."

"She hasn't changed much." Sandro moves to the bar. "Want a whiskey?"

"No."

I hear liquid pour into a glass. Are the cravings still there? Yeah. My demons will always torment me, and recognizing the fact is fucking progress. But a different kind of monster stirs inside, a hungry, violent fuck. A monster ravenous for another taste of Accardo blood.

"You look ... different," Sandro comments. "Is it the drink?"

I cross the office to sit on a couch, and Sandro follows, mirroring my every move like a shadow that never left.

"You know, I never thought I'd hear you turn down liquor."

"Yeah," I reply. "I never thought you'd act like a pussy-whipped dick, but guess everyone has their moments."

He glares at me, then softens. "Don't get me wrong. I love her. But pussy-whipped I'm not."

"If you say so."

"Says the black pot." He sips his whiskey, his fingers tightening around the glass like he's barely containing something darker beneath the surface. "So, Elia Seraphina Lombardi? Seriously? I expected you'd show up with a girlfriend one day but not that hellhound. Always up your ass. Always following you around like a lovesick girl. You couldn't shake her, and now she's here? You playing games or what? You trading in your sex club admission for idiot-for-hire?"

He's practically salivating, waiting for me to rise to the bait.

I don't ... can't. My emotions are shot to shit.

"Well, damn." He studies me intently, searching for clues without fully understanding the history between Fina and me, then lets it drop. "Father wants all resources directed toward Massimo."

I lean my head back on the couch, my eyes heavy. I fucked up. Missed a chance to correct this misunderstanding. And now shit's hit the fucking fan.

"How much time?" I ask.

"With Dante as collateral, I'm guessing a week? Father will want everything in place first."

Time for me to get busy. Situate my men in Sicily. Watch every frame of footage from our holdings and Massimo's and analyze each fucking detail for clues.

The cushion beside me shifts again as Sandro leans back. I glance sideways. His posture is almost identical to mine, legs sprawled, arms loose, breathing slow but controlled. Twin symmetry, which used to mean the world to me. We were close as kids, even as teenagers.

When did the cracks dividing us begin? Was it when his daddy issues kicked in? Was it after Rome, when my own began? When rumors about what happened began circulating?

Well, shit.

"You always wanted to be in the Life?" I ask.

"That's random." He turns his head to look at me. "I guess."

"You've built quite the reputation. It suits you."

He blinks. "You fucking with me?"

I give him a faint smile, tired, so damn tired. "Thanking you. For a long time, I blamed you for my shit when no one but my own twisted soul was at fault. You tried to help. Tried to cover for me. Tried to keep me clean. I just need you to know I see that now."

That lands harder than expected. His mouth parts, closes, then finally, he says, "You're my brother. There's nothing I wouldn't do for you."

The silence between us stretches, tense, raw, and oddly soothing. No bullshit, no pretense, we see each other clear as day.

Then his brows draw together. "I just got played, didn't I?"

"Nope."

"This isn't about freeing up a few of my men to sic on Settemo Accardo?"

I tense at the name, the thirst for Accardo blood alive and well. "It wasn't. But if you're offering ..."

"I'll be going against Father's order."

I stare at him, unwavering. Whether he sends men or not, Settemo's a dead man. I'll burn Italy to the ground until I find him. And when I do, I won't stop until he's screaming in agony.

"If Riley looked half as bad as Elia ... Fuck it, I'll have them report to you tomorrow."

"I owe you."

He rolls his eyes, but his voice softens. "Stay clean. That's all I ask."

I nod, the pressure in my jaw easing slightly.

"You know, something about this bullshit with Massimo is off," he mutters.

"Agreed."

"Massimo's a prick but a calculating one. Why kidnap Dante and not kill him?"

"To catch our attention."

Sandro scoffs. "Mission fucking accomplished."

"Who else has had their holdings hit?" I already know, but I want to hear him say it.

"Just Massimo's and ours. Dante included, but only investments tied to me, like the pistachio farms." His eyes sharpen. "You think we're being played? Pitted against each other?"

"That's exactly my thought." I lean forward, elbows on my knees, every cell on high alert. "I bet Massimo suspects it too."

"You both always had similar perspectives on things."

"I need to speak to Father."

Sandro sits up straighter, elbows on his knees. "Already handled. Conference call's set for tomorrow."

But as helpful as he's being, I understand how this ends. To Father, Massimo's motives are irrelevant. You strike at the Beneventis, you bleed.

What I need are eyes in the sky and a full picture of what we're dealing with. Yeah, reconnecting with Massimo is the priority, once I've men on the hunt for Settemo.

"Don't act on your own. Capisci?" my brother warns.

I ditched the drink and the drugs. Took to the Life better than anyone imagined. Shared a raw and long-overdue moment with my twin. But I'll never be the Beneventi lapdog.

"Yeah, I understand," I reply.

The question is: Will I obey?

IF THERE WERE A QUOTA ON UNPLEASANT SURPRISES, I would've hit my limit ten times over.

I touch the bandages on my cheeks and chin, feel the tight pull of gauze on my knees and thighs. Nothing's broken. Nothing permanent. Just torn skin, bruises, and nerves shot so raw they buzz under my skin.

I escaped Carlo by death. My father by careful, cunning planning. But if I'd known that psychopath was hunting me down, I would have torched the path behind me.

At least, that's what I tell myself.

Because nothing about Emo Accardo is predictable. His obsession with me is terrifying. The white catsuit he was manically trying to force me to wear was proof enough of that.

What kind of psycho wraps women in latex and tortures them for fun?

I wince, and pain flashes down my cheek. The doctor said the cuts won't scar, I've that to be thankful for.

Renzo looks at me like they already have.

He carried me from the farm like I weighed nothing. Held me on his lap the entire boat ride to Sardinia, tending to my wounds with antiseptic from the kit on the boat, which his father's men provided. I asked him to let me down.

"Not a chance," he murmured against my hair. "I'm never letting you down again."

In some ways, he's more wrecked than I am.

I breathe deep and soak in the silence of this bedroom, grateful for one moment without his heavy gaze tracking my every move.

I called Aunt Teresa first thing. Her voice cracked when she heard mine. She said Dante's men are watching the restaurant, guarding everyone affiliated or connected. I wanted to cry but instead warned her about Emo, gave her a description. She reassured me she's safe under mafiosi protection.

Bianca and Camilla got the same warning. Camilla told me the guards are keeping an eye on them. Bianca laughed and clarified, "Eyes, mouths, and very busy hands." I could almost see her wink.

After the calls, I washed up the best I could, then dressed in a loose pale blue linen dress from Riley's wardrobe

The room Riley placed me in while the casita is being "straightened up" is drowning in white. White walls. White beams. White furniture. Even the rug is white, and I've been pacing the same invisible line into it with my bare feet for the last ten minutes.

But my mind keeps dragging me back.

The scream trapped in my throat as Settemo tried to force that catsuit over me.

The panic.

The pure fear.

And then, of all things, the rooster. My little feathered hero, flying at Emo's face like a Fury from hell. I hope he clawed the bastard's eyes out.

I'll never throw a hay bale at him again.

Then came Renzo. Bursting from the barn like vengeance incarnate. Terrifying in his own right.

His rescue felt like a miracle.

But was it?

Because either he found some superhuman strength to break those manacles ... or he had a key all along.

Of *course* he had a key.

So why didn't he use it before?

I don't know whether to sob or laugh, whether to punch him or pull him close and whisper thank you into his chest.

What does it matter how he broke free? I'm here now.

Emo can't touch me in this place.

I glance at the door, wondering where Renzo's gone. Dreading his all-consuming tenderness and missing it.

With a sigh, I go and search for him.

Sandro's villa is spectacular, and very, very white. I'm upstairs on the mezzanine level, where the hallway forms a rectangle with rooms feeding off it, and the expansive open living area on view below. The stairway is majestic, like the kind a 1950s movie starlet glides down, ready for an audience.

I hear men talking in the distance, but the living area is empty.

My heart stutters in my chest when I catch sight of Renzo to my right, in the kitchen near an enormous island, drinking orange juice from a container.

By the time I reach him, I realize my mistake too late. He's not Renzo—but Sandro.

He pauses middrink, orange juice bottle midair.

I notch my chin upward. "Sandro." Twice in one day is two times too many.

His eyes widen then narrow as he takes me in. Like he can't make up his mind about me.

"Elia."

I sigh. This is his house, his mistress's ... girlfriend's ... fuckbuddy's ... clothing. "It's Fina."

"Settemo did quite the number on you."

"Something about me and men who like to put hands on a woman."

I swear he flinches. Human, after all.

"What was my brother doing on your farm?" he casually asks. Except there's nothing about this A-hole that's casual; every question sounds like an order.

I make dumb-eyes at him. "What farm?"

He scowls. I'm certain men quake beneath similar ones. "Shackled inside a barn, from what I hear."

"Prying for information is what I hear."

He doesn't like my response, or me.

We face off.

"If you have questions concerning Renzo, ask him yourself."

"Protective ..." he comments.

"Controlling ..." I mimic his condescending tone.

He screws the cap on the bottle and places the juice back inside the refrigerator.

I arch an eyebrow.

"What?"

"Anyone else drinking from that bottle? Or you starting a new batch of bacteria?"

He stares me down. "What I do in my villa, in my fucking kitchen, is no concern of any of my guests. Especially the nosy kind who can't leave well enough alone." He shakes his head. "Of all women, he brings you here."

I stiffen. "What's that mean?"

"Come on. You obsessed over him like a kid over a carton of candy." He cocks his head, arrogant as can be. "Let me ask you this: you follow him to Rome?"

"No."

"You hesitated—"

"I did not," I spit out. "Truth is, God's had it out for me ever since ..." Oh no. I almost handed him a loaded gun by offering a piece of my past best forgotten.

He laughs. "Ever since you stole from the wedding tributes?"

I pause like a deer in headlights.

"Listen, Elia—"

"Fina."

"Fina, answer this one question, the one I'm most curious about, and my father will never hear the truth from my lips of how an easy half million in tributes disappeared."

I try to bluster my way out of this. "Ask away."

"Did Accardo die from a fruit allergy or something else?"

"A fruit allergy." I bite my lip, my mind racing, trying to figure out why this, of all questions, has him so fascinated. "He was allergic to strawberries."

"Huh."

"What?" I exclaim.

"You don't know."

I huff. "I just told you. He died from an allergic reaction."

"And you split town, with no fiancé to worry about."

I draw in a deep breath. "I planned on disappearing anyway. It's why I took your father's money."

There. End of discussion. If he has a sympathetic nerve in his body, he'll drop it.

For a long time, the asshole simply stares at me.

Then he shrugs. "I'm not the only one with questions for my brother."

The casita is the size of a New York City apartment and decorated with the same luxury details as the villa.

Riley's been kind and sweet. Why she's in a relationship with the A-hole is beyond me. I adjust my breasts within the skimpy white bikini she's let me borrow, feeling more like myself after a solid night's sleep and the distance I've placed between me and Rome.

I make the king-size bed and straighten up, curious at Renzo's absence since I slept alone last night. But as I catch my reflection in the bedroom mirror, the answer's obvious. I look like Quasimodo and the bride of Frankenstein had a child.

Bruises will fade, and the scabs show healing. The emotional scars are what will take longer, especially with Emo still out there.

The heat has kicked up even in the early morning. Dipping my legs in the pool sounds like a good idea. I head to the open-space living room and, once more, stop to admire the furnishings. Off in the corner is the only out-of-place piece, a small picnic table with only one bench with a cushioned leather top pitched at a forty-five degree angle. Metal hooks have been fixed into the sides, and as I examine it more closely, I notice two leather straps casually dangling from parallel ends.

Is that what I think it is?

I cover my mouth with a giggle and whip out my phone, pulling up pictures of spanking benches. I skim through them until I find a near match.

I bite my lip, barely holding back a grin. Of course Sandro's into kink. Renzo is sex on legs, and they share DNA. But poor Riley, because it's definitely not Sandro who ends up facedown and tied up.

Still grinning, I glance around, then tiptoe to the bench like I'm sneaking candy before dinner. I flatten my stomach across the leather top and wriggle into position until it feels just right. I shift, settle, testing how my body fits. My lips part in a silent gasp.

I nibble the corner of my mouth. What would it be like to be strapped down like this, bare skin to cool leather, every breath spent waiting for his touch? My pulse quickens. My imagination takes over, bold and shameless.

A shiver curls up my spine, delicious and slow.

Yeah. I'm definitely feeling better.

I rise from the bench, smooth a hand over the leather one last time, then wander toward a massive painting dominating one wall. At first glance, it's just wild brushstrokes. But as I lean in, I notice the outline of tangled limbs. Bodies. Writhing. Intertwined. Lost in one endless, chaotic orgy.

I bite back another laugh. My cheeks flush, my thoughts even filthier.

Lord, I'm intrigued.

What else is hiding in this wicked little casita?

My gaze lands on an enormous armoire, oversized and elegant, better suited to a bedroom than a living space. It calls to me. I've always been curious by nature and not particularly good at respecting boundaries. Years under my father's rule taught me how to survive, not how to play nice.

Grinning, I grab the ornate handles and swing the heavy wood doors open.

My jaw drops.

Good Lord.

It's a sex toy chest. Not just toys. An entire wonderland. Every item is high quality and gleaming with promise. My pulse kicks harder as I scan the contents. Satin blindfolds. Candles, some half-melted. Butt plugs. Rope, soft and strong, perfect for shibari. Latex restraints. Leather cuffs. Hard metal cuffs. Adjustable straps. Vibrators of all sizes and shapes. Nipple clamps. Ball gags. Feathers. Floggers, so many floggers—long, short, suede, leather. Paddles. Belts.

And drawers I haven't even opened yet.

I'm vibrating. Like a girl locked inside a Rodeo Drive boutique, wild-eyed with my father's missing credit card in hand, ready to shop till I drop.

I close the doors slowly, savoring the possibilities, and lean back against the armoire.

Renzo has no idea what's coming.

And I can't wait to replace every bad memory with one I'll never want to forget.

I'm quickly learning, what Riley wants, Riley gets.

It's a surprising observation, considering the A-hole is involved. But I love Riley, and am silently cheering her on.

She joined me earlier, and we sat poolside, chatting about Los Angeles and New York, and doing an Olympic-level job of avoiding the ever-growing mafia population swarming the villa. Any mafiosi who so much glanced in our direction got barked at to get lost. Sandro's actual words: "Keep your dicks in your pants and your asses inside."

Charming, right?

Riley just rolled her eyes, used to his charm.

When Renzo saw me in the white bikini, Quasimodo's child or not, he froze, licked his lips like a hungry wolf, and proceeded to mentally undress me with such intensity I felt like dessert. I might be a bit beat up, but I've still got it.

"Wine?" he asks now, seated beside me, his hand casually claiming my thigh. I shift closer, loving his touch.

"Please."

His eyes twinkle with the knowledge I'm asking for more than wine. Our eyes lock, and for a second, everything around us fades. It's just the two of us figuring out what this is.

Sex, for sure. I lick my lips.

He squeezes my thigh.

But there's more to us than that. An undeniable attraction ... Some might even call it an obsession.

"I can't believe this," Sandro interrupts.

I glare at him, except he's too busy searching for Riley, who's gone to the bathroom.

Renzo grabs a butter roll and nails him in the head, stopping the search.

Lord, do I quickly collect the butter knives? Something tells me a food fight, Beneventi-style, gets bloody.

"Dick."

"Bastard," Renzo smoothly replies.

"Keep looking at her with those pathetic eyes. No wonder Alessia didn't want you."

Renzo stiffens.

"Alessia?" Only one Alessia comes to mind, and she's married to their father. "Didn't want Renzo? What do you mean?"

Riley appears, delaying Sandro's response, and takes her seat next to him. Noticing we're quiet, she asks, "What did I miss?"

"Nothing." Renzo waves a dismissive hand. "Just your boyfriend admitting he loved the spa at the Sicily resort. Wants to repeat the experience after we deal with the Grassi issue."

That's ... definitely not what we were talking about.

"Aw, I'd love that." She kisses Sandro, all sunshine and candy.

He grunts, then yanks her in closer for a kiss that's so intense, I look away.

I narrow my eyes at Renzo. "What am I missing?"

"Not important, babe."

Translation: very important.

"Your father's wife didn't want you?" I turn toward him, confused. "In what capacity—?"

"In the wedding."

"Oh." Make sense; he looked like hell warmed over at the service.

"The fair's back in town this Saturday," Riley announces, cheeks flushed and a bit breathless. "If you like antiques, you'll love it. I found a lamp last year that's like two hundred years old."

"Sounds ancient," Renzo comments, amused.

"Ancient and ugly as fuck," Sandro adds. "If I'm not around, my guys will go with you."

"And Fina?"

Renzo jumps in. "I don't know—"

"Fina would love to go." I answer for myself. Because yes, I want normalcy. Antiques. Wine. Sunshine. Bad enough the psychopath disrupted my life, no way will what happened ruin it.

"Don't worry," Riley says. "We'll be armed."

"Armed?" I echo. Because, unlike me, Riley doesn't seem the type to carry a weapon.

"Armed?" Renzo repeats.

Sandro grumbles into his drink.

"He makes sure stun guns are strapped under the front seats."

Renzo bursts out laughing.

"Why not actual guns?" I mean, I've got a pistol in my purse right now.

"Riley's too softhearted and refuses to aim to kill."

Renzo is still cracking up. "So you give her a stun gun?"

"Fuck yeah."

Okay. It's kind of adorable how much he wants to protect her.

Sandro throws his arms out like he's an open target. "Anything else anyone wants to throw at me?"

I grin, because how can I not? "Think that market has an antique bench like the one in your casita?"

Riley chokes on her wine like I shot it up her nose.

Renzo arches his eyebrows, intrigued.

Sandro doesn't even flinch. "You into benches? I'll introduce you to the one in my dungeon. Or have you already poked around the cellar?"

Well. Okay, then. Message received. Renzo's not the only Beneventi with kinks.

Renzo doesn't miss a beat. "Keep it up, and my girl won't be the only one I tie up," he says, stabbing a piece of pasta. "With a very different outcome."

Riley's mouth hangs open while mine is stuck on two words. My girl.

"Well then ..." Riley finally breathes.

The servers arrive, interrupting the awkward moment, though Renzo, not an embarrassed bone in his body, still feeds off it. "All this talk with all the *possibilities* has made me hungry."

I snort. Riley giggles. And just like that, the tension breaks.

We eat. We tease. Renzo torments. Sandro grumbles. Basically, lunch is a beautiful, feisty mess.

Then the conversation shifts.

"My team lands in Sicily today," Renzo tells Sandro.

"Let's hear Father's final plans before you act."

"I just want a casual look around before we send in the mafiosi cavalry."

"What are you talking about?" I ask.

They answer in stereo. "Covert drone surveillance."

"Your boyfriend thinks he'll modernize the mafia one toy at a time," Sandro says, tone sarcastic as hell.

"Oh yeah, because storming in guns blazing is so effective," Renzo shoots back.

Sandro waggles his fork at him. "Just run it past Father."

"What if I prefer to fly it by him?"

These two could argue about dirt.

Renzo grunts. "Did you even open the one I sent you? Fully assembled, so any idiot could use it straight from the box?"

"Nope."

Lord, they're seconds from throwing down, aren't they?

"Can you show me?" I ask, genuinely curious. Renzo hides the brainiac side of himself, but when it's on, it's such a turn-on.

"Me too," Riley chimes in. "I'd love a panoramic view of Sardinia."

Sandro grumbles, and Renzo's pleased as punch.

Then, the barbs, jests, and teasing continue for the remainder of lunch.

29

Renzo

As expected, the conference call later in the afternoon with my father is brutal and his idea of problem-solving all blood and bullets.

"My best shooters are en route to Sicily. We'll storm the house, flush him out, and take him down."

"Massimo will put a bullet in Dante the second it starts."

"If Massimo hopes to preserve the Grassi bloodline, he'll quickly realize the other Cosa Nostra families are behind us. So he surrenders, or we erase the Grassi name from the map."

I stare at the ceiling. Do I believe my father rallied the Cosa Nostra behind him? Probably. Their investments likely surged overnight with the promise of more wealth. Easy money is his specialty, when he's not butchering rivals.

Except he's underestimating Massimo. A lot can happen to change the outcome; Dante's death, Massimo pulling an ace card.

I can't pin down my old friend's play. They think he's lashing out and acting on emotion. I know from experience that man has the emotional capacity of granite. He wanted the spotlight, and now he's in it. To what purpose, is the big question?

I run my fingertips across my jaw. If I hadn't screwed up, I'd already have the answer. Let's hope his motherfucking window of opportunity is reopened, or my old friend will be whispering his secrets to the worms.

"When?" my brother demands.

"To be determined after the men are assembled," my father answers.

"I should be there."

"You and your brother both. The world needs reminding why you don't fuck with us Beneventi."

My brother and I lock eyes. This isn't just about eliminating an enemy. It's about sending a message. It's about us flexing and proving that the Beneventi twins are lethal in our own right.

We're not simply earners but enforcers. A double threat, and in more than one sense.

I dip my head at my brother, acknowledging I get it.

He nods back, hungry for another chance to prove himself.

Right—daddy issues.

But this time, I don't hold it against him.

This time, I acknowledge I carry around the same bullshit.

It's been a long day, and I'm coiled tight, knowing worse days are coming. The casita is dark and quiet when I enter. I'm exhausted after hours of listening to my father barking orders and laying out his plan to crush Grassi. Same old tactics. Nothing new and improved on.

I expect Fina to be asleep.

Am I tempted to crawl in beside her?

Hell yes. Lunch was torture. That tiny white bikini was a crime against my sanity. Every laugh made her tits bounce. Every sarcastic jab at Sandro made her glow. Every slow shift in her seat gave me a better view of her thighs. I've imagined using my teeth to peel that bikini off her and my tongue to trace its imprint.

I palm myself, hard at the thought.

But she's still healing.

The couch and my fist will have to do.

I cross the room, stripping as I go, clothes hitting the floor in a trail behind me. I'm about to collapse onto the couch when I hear it.

A whisper.

"Renzo."

I freeze. Her voice is soft, sultry, and close.

I reach for the light and flick it on.

Holy fucking shit.

Fina is facedown over the bench in the corner, still in that wicked white bikini. Her arms rest on the lower platform. Her ass, round and tight, is up. Her head turned just enough so our eyes meet. And on the floor, there's a lineup of toys: flogger, rope, blindfold, a small blue vibrator.

I'm thunderstruck.

God, she's magnificent. And just redefined every wet dream I've ever had.

What makes me even harder is the challenge and mischief in her eyes.

"Are you happy to see me, or is it just your dick?" she teases.

Her gaze drops.

The answer's fucking obvious.

"Oh, babe. You've no idea how happy." My voice is husky, raw. "But you're about to find out." I prowl toward her, slow and deliberate.

She bites her lip and smirks. My kind of woman, unafraid to ask for what she wants.

I grab the blindfold, the flogger, the vibrator, but abandon the rope. Restraining myself so she has time to heal, even though I'd love to unleash on her.

"Do you trust me?" I demand.

Our eyes lock, and a flicker of emotion crosses hers.

Her response is a punch to the chest. "Completely."

She's forgiven me.

I'm half-tempted to lift her off the bench, lay her out soft and slow on the couch, and make love to her until she can't remember anything. Whisper all the things I've never said out loud as I move inside her. That I've never wanted anyone else. That it's always been her. That she's mine. That she wrecks me in the best way.

How I fucking love her.

Well, shit.

The thought rocks me. I wait for denial to grip me.

It never comes.

"What are you waiting for?" she huffs, impatient. "Spank me already."

A grin spreads across my face.

She's tailor-made for me.

My girl wants to play?

Let's play.

I set the flogger and vibrator aside and curl my fingers into her silky hair. I give it a slow tug, testing her, guiding her into the game. "Tell me something dirty. The filthier, the better."

She gasps, half laughs, caught between nerves and excitement.

"I want the R."

The R?

"Make me your canvas. Paint my skin with your come. Brand me as yours."

It's not filthy but smart. Feeding my kink back to me and fueling every savage instinct in me.

I slide the blindfold down her face, letting it fall into place over her eyes.

Her lashes flutter against the fabric.

"Are you going to tie me up first?"

My girl loves her some rope.

I lean in and breathe against her earlobe. "When the time's right,

I'll bind you up beautifully and then suspend you from a hook. You'll scream. You'll come until you can't remember your name. But tonight, we compromise."

I brush my lips over her shoulder.

She squirms.

I land a soft smack on her ass. Not punishing. Just enough. Then wait for the anticipation to crawl up her spine. Five seconds. Ten.

She can't help herself and breaks, shifting her body.

I smirk.

She's mine to teach. Mine to torment.

I flick on the vibrator. The hum fills the air.

Her breath catches.

I smack her again. A little firmer. Then I pick up the flogger and move behind her, keeping her guessing.

Still, I wait.

There's an art to foreplay. And I'm named after a goddamn master of eroticism.

Tonight, Fina will fall apart so slowly, she won't know where she ends and I begin.

The bench has her at the perfect height and angle, and I take full advantage, running a finger from her knee to inner thigh, warming her to my touch.

She arches sideways, trying to get my finger on her clit.

I tap her inner thigh with the flogger's handle, signaling her to spread them.

She does, and I reward her with a light glide of the vibrator across her sensitive nerve bundle.

Her hiss is music to my ears.

I sink down, needing a taste, and lick the same spot, the thin white bikini a barrier between her sweet pussy and my tongue. I'm not having it, and do what preoccupied much of my earlier thoughts, nipping the material with my teeth and, with a backward tug of the head, ripping the bikini off her.

Then I go to town, alternating between licking and driving inside her warmth and rolling the tip of my tongue against her sex.

"You could do that all day," she moans.

Yeah, I damn well could.

I feast some more before amping up our play, stepping back, hiking her up by her hips and positioning her just so. I snap the leather flogger against her glistening lips. Her body jumps, nerve endings igniting into a coiled, delicious mess.

She gasps, a sharp, trembling sound that vibrates through me. Every shiver, every quiver of muscle, every small catch in her breath tells me exactly how she's burning—anticipation, defiance, hunger. Her hands flex against nothing but air, searching, testing, aching for the source of her delicious torment. The faint tilt of her head, the slight arch of her back, the way her chest rises and falls, all of it spurs me on.

I brush the handle against her.

The leather comes back wet.

With a wicked grin, I flick my wrist again and bring the flogger down across her ass, a second, sharper sting. She gasps, but before the sound fully leaves her lips, I slide the vibrator inside her, slow and deep.

She moans loud and primal.

Hard as steel, I let the toy hum inside her while I walk away, savoring her helpless little sounds. I check the drawers of a side table, rummage through a useless desk, then swing open the doors of the armoire.

Bing-fucking-go.

"Where are you?" Her voice trembles with frustration and need. "I want you. Not this toy."

I find what I'm after and head back to her, the lube in one hand.

"I'm close," she warns, voice high, breath catching.

I coat my fingers, before pressing one slick fingertip against the tight little star of her ass. "You're about to be full, baby. While that sweet pussy's still throbbing around the vibrator, I'm going to fuck your other hole. Unless ..." I draw the word out, teasing, "you'd rather I kept flogging you until you beg."

"No," she pants. "I want it. Please."

Her words light something savage in me.

I take my time, adding more lube, fingers working her open. My hand shakes with restraint. I grab her hips, position myself, and push in slow, inch by inch, her body stretching and welcoming me.

The tight heat swallows me whole.

I nearly come on the spot.

"You like being stuffed full?" I growl, rocking into her with small grinding thrusts. "That's your kink, isn't it?"

"I love the thought of you, Renzo, getting off, your handsome face filled with lust as women ... men ... line up to pleasure you."

Well, shit.

"Problem is"—her laugh is breathless and broken by a moan—"the idea of you with anyone else kills me. Do you understand what I'm saying?"

My dick thickens as my heart swells. "You're possessive."

"Yes," she admits, the word trembling with honesty. "So possessive."

"I get it, babe," I reply, voice raw with emotion. "So am I."

The truth startles me. A man raised in sex clubs, who was keen on keeping things detached and impersonal. Always moving on, always chasing the next thrill, boredom nipping at my heels.

But this is different.

My feelings for Fina run deep. Always have, even when she was breathing down my neck and not allowing me the choice.

I love her.

I want to tell her but instead show her, picking up the rhythm until she's arching her back and mewing my name.

Renzo. Renzo. Renzo.

I bury myself deep and hold, shaking from the force of it all.

She shudders, orgasm ripping through her like a storm.

Quickly sliding the vibrator free and easing the blindfold from her face, I fold over her, body soaked in sweat and pleasure, heart racing against her spine.

I may have blacked out, hard to say, but my pulse slows and the reality of where we are sets in. Her eyes flutter open as I scoop her up and carry her to bed.

"Renzo," she whispers, voice soft and dreamy. "I think ..."

I press a kiss to her temple. "Shhh. Sleep, baby. We'll talk tomorrow."

I settle her under the covers, clean her up gently with a washcloth, then take care of myself before crawling in beside her.

Wrapped around her, heart still pounding, I close my eyes.

The afterglow is warm, deep, and unfamiliar.

I'm content, in a way I've never felt before.

Tina

I can't keep my eyes off Renzo as he swims laps in the pool.

He glides through the water in a showcase of pure, brutal beauty. His muscles ripple, his back arches, and his shoulders cut through the surface like he owns it. I'm practically salivating. I want to lick the water beading down his chest, run my fingers through his wet hair, nuzzle into his wicked jawline. He's gorgeous, sexy, and radiantly alive. And healthy—the struggles he's endured long behind him.

I can't tell if I want to climb all over him, or drown in him. Maybe both.

"Think it's too early for a drink?" Riley asks. "You look like you need one."

"I think I'm in trouble."

"Trouble is that man's middle name." She laughs, then lowers her voice. "No offense, but his mind makes my nipples hard."

"You should see what his dick can do." With a shake of my head, I drag my eyes away. "But seriously, what do I do?"

"Do?" She spins on the lounge chair and lifts her sunglasses from her eyes, then waits for me to elaborate.

"It's complicated. Our history is messy."

She rolls her eyes. "Again, he's Renzo."

"Were things always so easy between you and the assho ... Sandro?" I catch myself. Because as sweet and kind as Riley is, she's crazy about the asshole.

"Easy isn't a word in Sandro's vocabulary. He hurt me, but hunted me down, refusing to let me escape." Her expression softens. "And what did I do? I melted like butter."

Biceps flexing, Renzo pulls himself from the pool. "I don't think I'm made of milk," I whisper. He straightens and, as if sensing my eyes on him, glances my way.

His broad smile has me grinning back at him.

Riley answers, her advice resonating deeply. "Then don't melt. You be the flame that makes him burn hotter, that makes him sweat." She shrugs. "Keep that beautifully wild man on his toes."

Noticing the attention, Renzo shakes his body like a wet puppy, sending water flying everywhere.

We laugh at his antics.

"Who's ready for a bird's-eye view of Sardinia?"

30

Renzo

Do I know I'm irresistible?

Abso-fucking-lutely. Women have always been drawn to me like I'm the center of their universe.

But I want to be Fina's world. By her side, inside her, above and beneath her, in every possible way and all at once. That feeling only magnifies as the day passes.

I spent the morning flaunting what I've got, teasing her until even Riley flushed. Midmorning, I gave them a break. While they took the long staircase from the pool deck to the private beach, I turned my attention to business. The kid had sent me a text, and I needed to see for myself what the clever little fuck meant.

Compared Naples warehouse footage to
Grassi feed. Same guys.

I settled into a pool chaise and opened the first link. Security footage from the Naples warehouse attack showed several shadowy figures moving in and out of frame, working quickly and efficiently as they spread gasoline around the perimeter. Job done, they climbed into a waiting vehicle off in the distance while the last man, dressed entirely in black from boots to ski mask, struck a match, tossed it, and sent our warehouse and a Beneventi associate up in flames.

The second feed is drone surveillance from a Grassi warehouse hit a week ago—the first real surveillance job my team had been handed while chaos erupted around us.

Six men. Gasoline. Same fucking scenario. Massimo's holding is torched, but this time two men are inside: a Grassi soldier and a Beneventi associate. Like we're amateurs who'd leave a man behind at a crime scene. Like we'd leave proof we were behind it. No wonder Massimo is convinced we're the enemy. Honestly, I'm disappointed in him. He's sharp enough to command armies and run families, and yet he didn't recognize this bullshit for what it is.

Whoever set this up has balls, I give him that. But his arrogance is laughable. He thinks pitting our families against each other means no one will connect the dots. He sure as hell didn't expect me to catch him on camera at an enemy site. I text the kid.

> How many Grassi holdings are we positioned at in Sicily?

I wait as he types his response.

> Seven. And we have feed from one more attack from three days ago.

> Keep a man at each, night and day, and immediately send whatever you have.

> On it.

Yeah, and I need to get moving. I toss my cell aside. Now that I have confirmation, there's no time to waste. I have to get to Sicily and reach Massimo before my father does.

Somewhere in the distance, doors slam. More soldiers arriving. All hands on deck.

I consider looping Sandro in, then dismiss the thought. He's like my father, and has zero interest in talking to Massimo, who sealed his fate the moment he kidnapped Dante.

If I find out he's laid a hand on Dante, I'll bury my old friend alive.

And yet, if he believes we killed his father, I can understand the fury driving him.

Fina will have to run interference while I vanish into the shadows, buying me the time I need before the Beneventi soldiers move into position.

I stand and, bathing trunks barely dry, make my way to Sandro's office, earning the curious stares of suit after suit. The box is exactly where I suspected, unopened in the closet. Hooking it beneath an arm, I retrace my steps to the pool, where I remove the preassembled drone from the packaging. I had a kid fine-tune it a few weeks ago before shipping it to Sandro. Typically, custom builds like this can take days to assemble, testing my brother's patience.

This particular drone's flight controller resembles a video game stick so the learning curve is easy. It not only has a high-tech camera for photography and video, but a special gimbal that holds the camera in place while the drone moves in different directions, making aerial shots commercial-grade quality.

From the top of the stairs, I send it soaring. My target glides through the sea below, beautifully unaware.

I ease it lower and lower, then forward, until I'm hovering over the spot where Fina vanished beneath the surface.

A moment later, she breaks through, hair slicked back, droplets tracing her cheekbones, long lashes blinking away water. She could be a fucking swimsuit model, her natural beauty outshining everyone else.

It takes her several minutes to notice the drone.

When she does, she paddles in a slow circle, tilting her chin toward it, well-aware who's operating it. Then, with a grin that could cut glass, she curls her finger at the camera.

I ease the drone forward, pulse kicking hard in my throat.

Her eyes glimmer with mischief as she traces her hands down her body. Without warning, she whips off her top, arching back into the water.

My grip on the controller tightens, heat surging through me as every muscle locks. The sunlight catches on her skin, and for a moment, I forget to breathe.

I fucking better have this on video.

Suddenly, my afternoon just got more interesting.

Ten minutes later, she and Riley return from their excursion at the beach.

Our eyes lock, and I contemplate dragging her into the casita and giving her some competition in who can be naughtier.

"Can you show us how it works?" she eagerly asks, as she and Riley pull two pool chairs beside my own.

"This baby is a quadcopter because it has four propellers. Unlike, say, an airplane with a fixed wing or a military drone, this has a motor that allows the rotary wing to spin against the air to create lift. As it spins, air molecules shift downward, which pulls the drone upward. Once in the air, it can move in four directions by spinning the four propellers at different speeds."

I pause, heat creeping up my neck because I've just geeked out on them. To my surprise, they're hanging on every word. I give a quick self-conscious smile and rein in the urge to go into detail about how military drones are usually fixed-wing, needing skilled ground operators, precise field data, and a maze of other technical systems to function. I keep to myself the fact they're also silent, efficient predators in modern warfare. "How about an aerial tour of the local attractions?"

Riley claps her hand. "They're setting up for the antique fair just south of here. Can we steal a peek?"

"Only if you promise to buy two more lamps? Hell, I'll pay for them."

She chuckles, and I can't help thinking my brother's lucked out with her.

Switching the camera to live feed, I send the drone into the air, keeping my eyes on their reactions instead of the screen.

"Wow, look at that view," Riley says, her voice full of awe.

"The sea and sky go on forever," Fina murmurs.

Finding the fair takes some time, but I know I've hit the mark when Riley claps her hands again. "See, Fina. It's huge."

Like most markets, it's set up in a local square, tables forming a rectangle around a weathered statue framed by old trees.

I keep the drone high enough that none of the vendors notice.

"The only street I've never been down is the one to the right. Can we check out the shops?"

I guide the drone along the narrow lane, gliding past a small café with bistro tables set out on the sidewalk, a butcher shop with a pig etched on the window, and a boutique that instantly lights up the women beside me. The street ends abruptly, spilling onto a sidewalk and then onto stone steps leading to an ancient church's tall wooden doors.

A throat clears.

All three of us glare at the man interrupting us.

"Sandro would like you in his office for a conference call," his soldier informs me.

I hand the controls to Fina, and almost curl up in laughter at her startled expression. "You trust me with this?" she bursts out.

I climb off the chaise, anxious to get the latest update over with. "Fly it over land," I reply with a wink, "and all is good."

"Everything okay?" I ask when Renzo returns to the casita.

He's been inside Sandro's office for a few hours with two dozen or so men, Massimo Grassi first and foremost on their minds. I can't imagine what Massimo was thinking, pissing off Sebastiano Beneventi and kidnapping his right-hand man. Does he understand he's in deep water? That the repercussions for his actions will be severe?

"Okay with the drone I pulled out of the pool or are we talking mafia business?"

I blink. "Is that where it disappeared to?"

He chuckles. "Considering you owe me now, can I ask a favor, one that will put you in an awkward position with my brother?"

I roll my eyes. "Sure."

"I'm flying to Sicily in an hour. Lie to my brother and pretend I'm still here for as long as you can."

"Okay." I bite my lip, then softly say, "You're leaving in an hour?" I don't hide my disappointment. I couldn't even if I tried.

"Against orders. I've got to sort this shit out with Massimo before war breaks out officially."

I nod. "Despite his men attacking you or what he's done to Dante, you consider him a friend."

He rubs his fingers across his jaw. So handsome. So completely male. "Yeah. But pray he hasn't fucked up, or that'll change rather quickly."

A shiver runs up my spine. The violence beneath the surface of this beautiful man always surprises me.

"Now let me say goodbye, properly." He grabs my hand and tugs me along into the bathroom.

"What ..."

His finger taps my lips. "Shhh ..."

He turns on the shower and tests the temperature until it suits him, then hoists me to straddle his hips and steps beneath the stream of water.

With one quick bounce, I lift into the air.

When I drop, he's inside me in one smooth thrust.

His pace is ferocious.

I love every flex, every upward drive.

We go at it, with me anchoring my thighs to his hips as leverage to lift, with his hands on my ass to keep me from falling.

He tears my top off with his teeth.

I laugh between moans.

His eyes pierce me. "Arch your back and let the water drip off your gorgeous breasts. Give me a repeat performance, dirty girl."

Fingers curled against his shoulder for balance, I do as requested. Rewarded by the feel of his dick swelling inside me.

"I'll never get enough of you, you know that, right?" he grinds out.

I giggle. "Right. That's your dick talking."

"Look at me."

His firm tone causes me to still.

"I'm going to marry you."

"What?" I gasp, completely thrown.

"Once this shit with Grassi is over, once that motherfucker who attacked you is dead, we're getting married."

I'm speechless, and blurt out the one question that comes to mind. "Why?"

"You trust me?"

"To marry me?"

So many memories, so much disappointment when he failed to follow through, so much anger that took years to release. Last night I told him I trusted him, yet here he is, asking again. Like my word is not enough, like my trust matters as much as my love.

I hated him for what he did. Hated his false promise, the way he backtracked, his endless excuses. He didn't just break my faith; he stomped it into the ground.

He was different then. Wild, strung out, lost to addiction.

I understand that now.

When did I let trust slip back in? Was it his confession in the barn? His commitment to get clean? Addiction is not conquered with a snap of the fingers. He will need support, even now. He will need therapy. I think he knows that.

Do I want to be there for him?

I tilt my head and smirk, because somewhere along the road, I decided to believe in him again. "I'll think about it."

He steps forward, pressing my back to the wall. "Maybe you need convincing?" His hips drive into me, forcing my body to slide up the wet tile.

"Maybe you'll actually propose?" I shoot back, gripping him as he fills me deep.

I fantasized about a future with him for years, beginning at thirteen when, as a guest at his Rhode Island estate, I spied him across the room, a tall drink of lemonade—the kind mixed with bourbon. My girl crush turned into a slight teenage obsession. Even at a distance, I tried to *know* him.

Still, this complex man is hard to nail down.

I never knew Renzo the way I do now. His passionate, inner-geek side, the brutal devil beneath the pretty, mouthwatering package.

"You need a proposal?" He grunts, enjoying this, the sex fiend another side of him I can't live without. "I'll do right by you, babe. And when I ask again, your knees will buckle. I promise you that."

"I won't hold my breath."

But I will ... I am. I've always done so, for better or worse.

I arch and close my eyes.

And give myself over to him.

Bodies colliding, our hearts tangled tight.

31

Tina

At exactly one o'clock the next afternoon, two men rush past my pool chair. Before I can react, they throw open the casita doors and vanish inside.

Minutes later, they return. One has a phone pressed to his ear.

Renzo left late last night, and all morning I've been feeding Sandro lies. That Renzo was sleeping in after a late night. That his twin abandoned me for the beach. That he was in the shower. Stalling, breathlessly anticipating the moment I'll be caught.

The man himself appears at the kitchen door, strides across the pool deck without a word, and disappears into the casita.

Half-amused, half-terrified, I bite my lip, knowing I'm in deep shit.

"Where the fuck is he?" he roars, pure fury, as he charges toward me.

I swallow and shrug.

"You want to play games?" He jabs a button, shoves his phone at me. "Lie to him, then."

My pulse spikes when Sebastiano Beneventi fills the screen. Even through the screen, he radiates a cold, deliberate danger that has me shrinking back. His voice is calm, almost soft, but every syllable drips with authority. "Renzo in Sicily?"

I feel like prey under a predator's paw. It takes everything not to answer.

"Elia ..."

"It's Fina."

His voice sharpens. "If you care about him, tell me his plans."

"I don't care about him." It's the biggest lie I've told today.

Sebastiano's eyes narrow. I've no doubt, if he could, he'd reach through the screen and wrap his fingers around my throat.

"Stop protecting him," Sandro snaps, then addresses his father. "I told him not to act alone, but he believes he can reason with Grassi."

"There's been a miscommunication," I add, coming to Renzo's defense.

"No shit," Sandro growls.

"Call him," Sebastiano orders, voice like iron.

I pass Sandro his phone, grab mine, and dial. The call goes straight to voicemail. "What do I say?"

"Don't," a woman's voice cuts in.

Sebastiano's head turns, his tone icy. "This is business."

"He's your son, Bastian."

"Alessia," he warns.

Unbelievable. The same Alessia who didn't want Renzo at her wedding is now defending him.

I speak up before the moment shifts. "Give Renzo a chance to prove himself."

The silence is suffocating.

Sandro studies me like I *am* Quasimodo's love child.

"Handing out more advice?" Sebastiano finally asks.

"Not really ... yes."

There's a long pause like Sebastiano's considering my words.

"He's a genius," I reassure him. "Cunning and clever. Add a give-two-shits philosophy and brass balls, and Massimo doesn't stand a chance."

Neither did I.

"He'll get himself killed," Sandro protests.

"He has one day."

Pride swells in my chest. I did it, I bought Renzo time.

"We still follow the plan, and our men will take position in case Grassi refuses the olive branch. If he listens, if Dante comes back unharmed, Grassi might live."

Off-camera, Alessia says, "Thank you."

Am I grateful? Yes. But the vengeful part of me holds a grudge on Renzo's behalf for her not wanting him at the wedding.

I imagine adding her name to my list, then erase it. Pettiness I can tolerate. Emotional and bodily harm, however, I can't.

Nor being victimized by men who view women as inferior and weak.

Only one name besides my father's belongs on my list: Emo Accardo.

Riley's an old soul in a young woman's body, and her excitement for tomorrow's fair somehow makes me care about dusty secondhand lamps. With only a few guards around, we settle into the theater room, wine in hand, popcorn between us, scrolling through Netflix thrillers. The danger Renzo and Sandro face is real. I've been in this world long enough to know Massimo Grassi isn't a man to take lightly.

Still, what I told Sebastiano Beneventi was true. I trust Renzo completely.

"How about this one?" I pause on a series about a kidnapped woman.

"Not interested."

"Right. Because there's a high probability she'll just sit there waiting for a man to save her. Gag me." I nearly did the same thing myself. Waited on someone else to save me. Then, saved myself.

Riley hesitates, popcorn pinched between her fingers. "He kidnapped me."

I blink. "Wait—Sandro?"

She nods. "We were romantically *involved*. I was unaware my boss was involved in shady business with the New York casino Sandro oversaw. So, Sandro took me."

"God, he's a first-class asshole."

"And no," she continues, ignoring my comment, "I didn't save myself. Renzo did. Well, tried to. Not from Sandro, but from this evil man who had it out for the Beneventi family."

My heart swells with pride. "Renzo did?"

"Don't you know he has a hero complex?" Riley chuckles. "He also tried to save Alessia from his father's wrath."

That name slams into me.

Riley smiles faintly. "He thought marrying her would protect her."

"Marrying her?" The popcorn bowl digs into my palm. "Renzo was engaged to Alessia?"

"Not officially. But he went to his father, demanding they wed. Set off a whole domino effect, too. But that's another story."

My voice is barely a whisper. "When?"

Popcorn slips from her hand to her lap. "Alessia's like a sister to them now. Don't be jealous."

I lean forward, my tone sharp. "When?"

"Almost two years ago. Sometime after their twenty-third birthday, I believe." She studies my face. "Are you okay?"

"He asked Sebastiano Beneventi if he could marry her?"

"Yes."

"He did that for Alessia?"

"Oh my God, Fina. What's wrong? It all worked out."

The world tilts. "No. No. No."

I push to my feet, fury and disbelief burning hot. His voice echoes in my head, the soft promise and later the excuses.

"My father will never allow it."

"I'm not the marrying type."

"You're the only woman I'd ever want to marry."

But that's not true. He was almost engaged to Alessia Beneventi, yet couldn't make the same commitment to me.

My ribs are closing in, crushing my heart. I nearly drop the wineglass as the room blurs at the edges, colors bleeding to grey until there is only his face, his handsome, treacherous face. Feeding me excuses.

Feeding me lies, lies, lies.

32

Renzo

It's been a long, violent night.

I grab the balls of Grassi's soldier and squeeze until his breath catches in his throat. He shuts up fast, while the other man—the same bastard who ambushed me outside the club and held a knife to my throat—stares wide-eyed, hog-tied, stripped, and curled like a baby in the fetal position.

Payback is a bitch, and that title I wear with pride.

My team and I are dug in on the Grassi estate. Beyond the stone walls, the Sicilian countryside stretches out in hard lines, dark olive trees and ancient farmhouses dots across the sunburnt earth. Citrus fragrances the air, but all I taste is a dry dust that scratches the back of my throat.

Midmorning's a bad time for this; the sun's too high, the air's lost its crispness, and the drone buzz carries farther than I'd like. But I defied my father to speak to Massimo face-to-face. Time's ticking, and initiating a conversation will require savviness, both his and mine.

First step, before shit begins, is to call my father. He picks up without a hello, and I swiftly get to the point. "I disobeyed an order."

Silence. The kind that weighs on your chest, the kind I've endured more times than I care to remember. I wait him out, focusing on the kids setting up the equipment next to me.

Finally, he replies. "What's your location?"

"South side on the hill."

"The worst place to be," he snaps with more emotion. "Get the hell out of there. Grassi has men crawling all over that hill."

"Not anymore."

It has been a night that tested the limits of my patience. I cleared the hill soldier by soldier, using every trick in my arsenal. Playing dead, springing up from the ground like I'm zombie hunting or in the remake of *Apocalypse Now*, stripping weapons from their hands before they could blink. Seven bodies neutralized, tied, gagged. My new pal, the man worried about his reproductive capabilities, is in charge. Every so often, I press a knife to his ball sack and make him report, "Nothing, boss."

Massimo likes clean and orderly. I made his morning spotless.

"Sandro has eyes on them." Pause, like my twin's relaying information to my father live. "You left his men naked?"

"The consequence of failure. Massimo will understand."

"If he's not already dead," my father grinds out.

I steel myself. "Ask me why I'm here."

"She already told me why, you little shit."

My brows lift. "Who did?"

"Elia Seraphina Lombardi. Turns up like a bad penny, hands out advice like loose change. Said this was your chance to prove yourself. Apparently, you've been denied that opportunity until now."

Rome hangs in the air between us. I grit my teeth and wonder if that day will ever be behind us.

"Next, you'll be demanding permission again to marry her."

"Since you brought it up ..."

"Enough." His voice is sharp enough to cut skin.

"I've proof someone is pitting us against Grassi." I forward two links from my phone. "Same clothing, same six men, same burn patterns, same style killings. Why else would Massimo escalate matters?"

His silence stretches as he watches the footage.

Impatient, I hurry him along. "I'll find Dante before I speak to Grassi in person."

"You're not entering his house without men."

"I'm not planning to." Not initially, anyway.

A low laugh rumbles through the line. "My money better work." Yeah, he understands what I'm about.

"If I had a military-grade drone, his entire estate would disappear with a single button pressed. You could do it from bed in Rhode Island, if Alessia can keep her hands off you long enough."

"Not another fucking word."

I smirk. He is always touchy about his sweet little wife.

"She said you were brilliant."

"Your wife's always been a fan."

"Not Alessia. Fina."

Well, shit. He used her name—*Fina*. Did I hear him right? They've been talking? Trading notes like old friends?

"Find Dante and report back immediately. I'll have my experts study the videos and see if they can manipulate the pixels for a clearer image of the vehicles."

It is a smart move, considering the poor resolution.

I wait for him to say more, but he doesn't.

I clear my throat. "She said I was brilliant?"

The line goes dead.

"Alright, kids." I grip the control board, and focus on the task at hand. They follow suit, eyes locked on multiple live feeds I've booted up onto a laptop. The drones rise, blades slicing the quiet morning sky, and vanish overhead.

"Showtime."

Massimo's estate is locked up tight—did I expect anything less?

I grind my teeth, scanning for weakness. Nothing. Then the kid crouched beside me flashes a thumbs-up.

Final-fucking-ly.

Eyes locked on the live feed, I send them off and slowly descend toward a window completely out of place. Not only is it wide open, but a knotted bedsheet dangles from the sill and down along the stucco facade.

"Looks like someone's escaping," the second kid murmurs.

"They'll break their neck before they reach the ground," the first mutters. "There's, like, a fifty-foot drop."

I glide inside, then freeze.

Cross-legged on the floor, surrounded by bedding, drapes, and clothes, is Luna Cecilia Gallo. Don Gallo's daughter is tying knots with the fury of someone ready to tear the world apart, her lips moving in a silent tirade. I watch, fascinated, as she offers the wooden door behind her the Italian salute, then, unsatisfied, hurls the fabric away, storms over to the door, and wrenches it open.

Dante fills the doorway. His expression positively livid.

Well, shit. This is better than the front row at a fight club.

"What the hell is happening?" a kid exclaims.

Luna barrels forward and throws a shoulder into Dante's body, knocking him back, then attempts to slam the door in his face.

Well, damn. Rumors don't lie. She's a firebrand.

To her dismay, the door bounces back open; he's stopped it from closing with his foot.

She tosses up her hands and charges off.

That's when he spies the drone.

Eyebrows pinched, he slowly puts the pieces together. When he does, he tosses his head back and laughs.

Luna spins around.

I'm fearful for my drone's safety.

The kid next to me wiggles backward, distancing himself from the laptop, fearing for his own safety.

"Shame there's no sound," the second comments, wide eyes fixed on the laptop.

Dante appears well. Other than messy hair from forking his fingers through it and a wrinkled shirt. No visible wounds or bruising.

As if sensing my concern, he signals a thumbs-up before pointing to the window, and shaking his head no. To emphasize the point, he draws a line across his throat.

Cut.

Don't attack.

I quickly text my father.

Dante fine. Signaling hold off.

"Boss," the second kid cries out beside me. "I've been made."

I hit send and turn to the feed.

"Fucking hell," I grind out.

But it's too late. From a balcony, Massimo aims a long-nose rifle at the drone and, with the press of a trigger, blasts it from the sky.

"Move. Before he reloads," I order.

The first kid's drone dives, skimming past Massimo and slipping inside.

Massimo follows, rifle ready, not giving two shits if he fires holes into the walls.

"Drop the note," I say.

What happens later hinges on this moment. Every mafioso in Sicily is watching and weighing whether I'm a man worth his name. Was that one-off with Vito Cardini a fluke? Are the whispers true? Can this wild and bent-in-the-head motherfucker deal with an enemy in a way that benefits everyone? The deciding factor balances on whether Massimo Grassi picks up that piece of paper. If he takes it, we talk. If not, things turn ugly fast and I look like a fucking fool. The weak Beneventi.

Massimo's gaze locks on the drone's lens, his eyes dark and unblinking, sharp enough to slice through steel. The muscles in his jaw flex. For a heartbeat, nothing moves. I can almost hear the decision grinding through his head.

Then, ever so slightly, he nods and picks up the note.

33

Tina

Escaping the villa is unwise.

But before I paint everything inside the villa red with my misery, I leave the whitewashed walls and white tiles behind and accompany Riley to the fair, the day in town a welcome distraction.

My heart is shattered into tiny irreparable pieces, each sliver sharp and piercing, small daggers keeping the pain alive.

"I'll do right by you, babe. And when I ask again, your knees will buckle. I promise you that."

Promises, promises.

I was a fool to believe him.

I've survived before. I can survive this.

Oblivious to my heartbreak, Riley's all excitement and light. I do my best to put on a happy face and not ruin her fun.

Sandro went overkill with security. Men in a car in front and behind us on the short drive into town. Men trailing behind us, arms stuffed with antiques, as Riley and I make our way through the fair. I force myself to relax and enjoy doing normal stuff. Failing beautifully, yet nevertheless, I persist.

"What about this?" Riley lifts a broken clock with a yellowed face. I didn't frequent antique shops in California per se, but the most hideous pink dresses in my wardrobe in Los Angeles came from thrift store racks.

Another time. Another life.

I thought the necessity of reinventing myself was behind me.

Wrong, Fina. Life without that liar in it is your next invention.

I flash Riley a forced smile. "You can put the clock on the nightstand beside your bed."

She laughs. "He'll kill me."

"Doubtful." I dig into my purse and withdraw my wallet. "My treat."

"But you already bought a lamp."

I hand cash Renzo left me to the vendor, ridding myself of it like I've done all morning, like I'm ridding myself of him. "You've been beyond kind to me, allowing me into your home and wardrobe."

"You're perfect for Renzo. I've never seen him so serious." She smiles, not realizing her words crush me. "I bet you get married before we do."

"How much?"

She blinks at my sharp tone. "You're fighting?"

I press my lips together, unwilling to drag her into our breakup.

"He can piss off the Pope, for sure."

Nope. Not saying a word.

She studies me closely. "I am loyal to him, and he's done so much for me. But the Beneventi men can be ... difficult. Please know I'm a friend you can talk to."

"Thank you," I mumble. Drawing a breath, I shove the ache down deep. "You know what might help?"

"What?"

"Gelato."

We cross the square to the small shop and, while security waits outside, make our selections. We settle at an outdoor table.

"It's the milk," I say between licks. "That's why it tastes better than ice cream from home."

"I think you're right," she replies, chocolate coating her lip. "Even beats the ice cream from my hometown in the Midwest."

I force my mind to stay present, my thoughts on Riley's easy smile, the vanilla cup, the busy market beyond.

But a sudden movement snags my attention. A flash of black over by the statue.

Goose bumps prick my arms, and the fine hairs on my neck stand at attention.

Riley tracks my gaze. "What's wrong?"

"Just paranoid," I lie, though my pulse hammers. "Must be tired."

"We can head back to the villa and doze by the pool?"

"Perfect," I reply, keeping my tone light. "But first, we'll redecorate."

Men in tow, we head back to the cars. I don't relax until the glass is between us and the street, and the cars are pulling away from the curb.

We're halfway around the square when the cars are forced apart by the Polizia Municipale, directing a chaotic swirl of pedestrians and traffic. A curse slips from our driver's lips as he jerks the wheel, veering onto the next street.

Riley's voice cuts through the tension. "There's the pink pig."

I catch sight of it etched on the butcher shop window.

"This road ends at a church," Riley warns the driver. "Dead end."

The man beside me places his gun on his lap, a cold calm settling over the car.

Don't panic. The driver will reverse, loop back, and we'll slip away. But a knot tightens deep in my stomach anyway.

I slide my hand into my purse, pull out my pistol, and tuck it inside my waistband. Maybe I'm overreacting. Maybe not.

At the foot of the church, the driver shifts into reverse. The moment we swing back toward the square, they move.

A dozen men in black, fast as shadows, sprint down the street. Guns raised, locked on us.

No. No. No.

"Get down!" Sandro's man yells.

Riley and I dive low, heads tucked tight as bullets tear into glass. The windows shatter but hold, but we're pinned down.

"There's no way out," the driver shouts. "Take them! I'll cover."

He spins the car hard, passenger side toward the church, then the door nearest me flies open.

"Keep your heads down until we're inside."

I don't wait. I'm on my feet before the words finish.

Riley scrambles, snatches something beneath the seat, then bolts after me.

We race slightly in front of Sandro's man toward the heavy wooden doors. Bullets hum past like angry hornets until a searing pain blooms in my arm.

I clutch it, fingers slick with blood. A nick or worse?

The few villagers unfortunate enough not to be at the fair scatter, parting like a broken wave. The dark figures behind gaining ground.

Suddenly, the man shielding us explodes, his head blasting apart and spraying Riley and me with brains and blood.

Neither of us stop. Neither of us cry out. She recognizes it as well. The Life is brutal, and the weak flounder.

Push back the fear. Stay strong.

Riley grabs my hand like she can hear my thoughts.

We sprint up the steps toward the enormous wooden doors.

Silence descends, thick with terror and ripe with fear.

At the top, panting, we shove open the doors.

I don't know if it's instinct or curiosity that causes me to glance over my shoulder.

The men pursuing us stand in an arc below, and several more race off to encircle the church.

My stomach drops. They're not firing. They're waiting.

"Riley, hold up!" I hiss.

Her fingers tighten around my hand as we're pulled inside.

Sunlight streams through the beveled glass, the scent of incense clings heavy, and an eerie quiet welcomes us ... just before the devil greets me.

"I've got you now, bitch."

34

Renzo

"WHAT THE FUCK TOOK YOU SO LONG?"

Massimo leads me into a dining room that smells like fresh coffee and polished oak. Without a word, he strides to the head of a long dark wooden table and sits, his presence filling the space like he was born to lead. One hand rests lazily on the arm of his chair, the other slicing through the air in a subtle gesture for me to sit. His gaze is steady, sharp, weighing every move I make.

"Been tied up," I say.

Mentally preparing for a chess match, not a breakfast buffet, I've already been frisked, stripped of my weapons, my team sent scattering into the brush.

The chef scurries forward, careful not to rattle the china as he pours steaming coffee into the cup before me, eyes darting between us.

"You were shot badly?" Massimo asks, voice low and deliberate, though I suspect his men fed him the juicy details.

"Something like that."

His eyes skim over me. For signs of injury? Or weakness?

I mimic his actions.

His father's been murdered, and his world's come crashing down, yet you wouldn't know the hurt he must be feeling by looking at him. "Sorry for your loss," I murmur. "My father enjoyed butting heads with your old man." My gaze doesn't waver—let him assess my sincerity.

We'd once been allies, real friends, before the Life swallowed us up.

His voice drops, edged with menace. "Don Tomarchio ordered the execution."

Cosa Nostra. Just like I suspected. "He envied your father for years. I remember you telling me about his Napoleon complex." I lean back. "But you haven't struck back."

Massimo's stare hardens. "Once I know who helped him, I will."

"It wasn't the famiglie," I reply, my tone like tempered steel.

"The rumors say otherwise. My men are dying. My holdings are going up in flames."

"Like you believe rumors over fact." My lips draw tight, and his attention narrows on them. He remembers me as a jokester, a good time, a challenge physically and mentally. What he's unused to is this take-no-bullshit side of me. "My father gave no such order. We've taken hits, too, with plenty of fingers pointed your way." I pick up the coffee and take a sip. The cream's absent, the liquid black like my soul.

"I brought you proof," I add, setting the cup down to fiddle with my phone. I slide it across the table, the screen playing out two brutal ambushes.

He watches in silence, every muscle in his jaw taut. "I've got similar footage," he finally says.

The chef reenters like a man tiptoeing across a mine-field, knowing he's standing in the middle of something dangerous, and sets down four plates with shaking hands. His eyes flick between us.

"We'll eat, then deal with this."

The phone lands back in front of me.

"Company?" I ask, nodding to the two extra settings.

"Unfortunately," Massimo says without looking away from me.

More plates arrive—eggs, bacon, hash browns, steak. Not a green vegetable or fruit tray in sight.

"Thought you'd appreciate an American breakfast."

Jesus. "You planned this?"

"Like I said, you're late. I was close to giving up hope you'd show."

I grind my teeth. Yeah, and I would've faded into the darkness if Fina hadn't stepped in.

"Eat."

I grab my phone. "Need to get word out I'm fine."

"Go ahead."

He agrees we've been set up. Has more video to review.

I pause. "I can extend the breakfast invite as a show of good faith?"

"Your brother out there?"

"Yes."

"Then hell no."

I chuckle and stab a fork into a steak. Cooked to perfection, the juice bleeding onto my plate. My stomach rumbles when the chef places a steaming pile of pancakes before me.

Out of the corner of my eye, I spot Massimo eyeing them as well.

A throat clears.

I spin to find Dante and Luna in the doorway.

"Ah, the lovebirds," Massimo says, sarcasm dripping from his tone.

Dante grunts. "Fuck off." Then takes the seat across from me.

Luna follows. But instead of sitting, she waits, eyebrow pitched in his direction.

Dante looks downright defeated and, with a grimace, stands and pulls out the chair for her.

I run my eyes over him, searching for injury now that I've had a closer look. Aside from a scratch across his collarbone, he seems fine.

Still, I ask, "Massimo treating you well?"

He nods slightly, answer enough. "Our men have the estate surrounded."

"Of course they do," Massimo answers. "What did you think, they wouldn't come to Dante Lucchese's rescue?"

"You're lucky a sniper didn't take you out."

Massimo's smile is quick. "Luck has nothing to do with it."

Luna snaps her fingers, catching everyone's attention. "Puoi continuare a discutere più tardi? Ho fame." She's tired of them arguing and wants to eat.

I offer her my hand across the table. "You must be Luna. I'm Renzo Beneventi."

Confusion shifts across her expression.

"Cut the bullshit," Dante grinds out. "Everyone knows you're fluent in English."

She straightens, shoulders back. "Everyone knows you've a huge dick. It's your brain size that's questionable."

Dante's killed more men than he's fucked women, yet she flashes him a smile, then ignores him to accept my hand. "I hope you're less of an asshole than your twin."

I smirk. "There's got to be a fucking good story why you're here."

Dante rolls his eyes.

Massimo grunts. "She came to save him."

"No shit?" I reply. Well, damn. The ice-cold killer's cheeks are pink.

"Charged in here, a one-woman cavalry show, and demanded I release him."

I grin at Dante. "Why'd she do that?"

"She," Luna growls, "got tired of waiting for you"—she waves a finger at me—"to save his sorry ass."

Enough said.

"You see the footage?" Dante asks between bites, eyes sharp. "Same men. Same style."

"Same transportation," Massimo adds.

"They use utility vans every time. Park them far from cameras," Dante says, his tone grim, as if he's been more co-conspirator than prisoner. By kidnapping him, Massimo sent a message—he wanted everyone to believe war was looming. Feeding into the game set by whoever is behind this.

"And the plates?"

Massimo shakes his head. "What plates?"

My father's men won't get far, then.

"Fiat Ducato vans," Luna adds.

I stop midbite, dread coiling up inside. Vans ...

We look to Luna.

"The FIAT emblems were removed, but you can tell by the hubcaps."

Dante slams his fist on the table. "We've been scrolling through these videos for a week. Why didn't you say something?"

"You told me silence was golden."

"Didn't stop her from speaking," Massimo growls.

I relay everything to my father.

Fiat Ducato vans. Check hubcaps.

Then stop short. "What color?"

"White," Luna says. "Common rentals in Italy."

Every thought in my mind freezes.

"White."

Massimo and Dante both frown. "What is it?"

Fear grips me, sharp and unfamiliar but settling in deep. "Settemo Accardo uses a white van."

"Accardo," both men say.

"My father is shutting down all Accardo businesses after men were caught on his estate."

Dante's lips tighten. "Your father butchered Carlo's brother. Settemo's father."

Massimo rises, motioning for us to follow him into his office as he makes a call. The conversation is quick, efficient, but full of weight.

"My father had issues with the Accardos as well. Carlo asked him to sabotage the Beneventi casinos, ruin their expansion plans. In exchange? Enough gold bars to build a wall around our estate. My father told him to fuck off. After your father killed Benny Manocchio for doing the same, Carlo refused to touch it. I thought it died with him."

I type a quick message to Fina, careful not to sound alarmed.

> Miss you, babe. Everything good?

No reply. Could mean nothing—her phone might be inside the casita while she's at the pool.

Panic twists inside me. I shoot a message to Sandro.

> Signs point to Settemo. Any word from the men you sent after him?

Dots appear. Then stop.

Seconds drag like hours. My breath catches. My hands tremble.

Then the message appears. And my world blackens.

> The motherfucker's at the fair.

"Settemo."

I spit his name like a curse, the syllables weighted with every violent memory. Riley's eyes flick to me, understanding in her gaze.

His fist crashes into the side of my skull, a brutal impact that sends me stumbling to my knees, the granite floor rattling my teeth. Pain blooms hot, but I ignore it, twisting my body to face him, my hand dipping beneath my waistband behind me toward my weapon.

I don't dare look at Riley frozen a few feet away. I'll do whatever I must to protect her.

"Who's your friend?" His voice is low, taunting.

"A local girl," I growl, locking onto him. Black clothes, shoes, and gloves. White gauze masking an eye. Whichever doctor treated him couldn't produce black? I listen for his men, but the church is silent.

Just Emo and his arrogance?

God, please say it's true.

He moves in on Riley, his shadow spilling over her. A gloved finger drags across her collarbone in a slow, deliberate line. "Pretty," he murmurs, his words sour, with an unhinged edge. Riley doesn't so much as flinch, but stares him down in a move Sandro would be proud of.

He sees the challenge, and is seconds from snapping.

"She speaks Italian, Emo. She doesn't understand you."

His gaze slices back to me. "What did you call me?"

"Emo. You know, emo—like when someone has too much emotion and not enough substance."

He jabs two fingers into my wound, then clamps down on it.

Pain rips through me, almost blinding me, before he jerks me upright.

"Move. The van's waiting."

I give Riley the smallest shake of my head as he forces me further inside the church. We're halfway across it when he stops short.

I stumble, horrified I nearly slammed into him.

"You," he bellows. "Dai, andiamo!"

No. I silently plead. Run.

But Riley, eyes frantic and looking utterly terrified, races to follow us.

"Good girl," he murmurs. "Maybe I'll keep you too."

We descend into the belly of the church. The air grows colder, heavy with stone, dust, and something older, deader. Tombs line the granite floor, more ancient than anything sold at the antique fair. My stomach churns as my eyes register the duffel bag set on top of the tomb closest to the door.

He catches my horrified expression and laughs, the evil sound bouncing off the walls so loudly, God couldn't silence it.

If we follow him outside, we're done.

If we open the door, we're done.

Psycho or not, he's one man.

My arm aches. The scar tissue from his burn itches. Every cut, every bruise, every time he's called me bitch. I'm done running. I'm done hiding. I'm done with arrogant men who get off on hurting women. I wait for peace to wash over me. For light to shine down on this moment of clarity like I'm guided from above.

But peace isn't what settles into my bones—rage does.

"You won't believe this, Riley," I begin, my grip tightening on my pistol. "But Emo gets a lot of drivers honking at him."

"He does?"

His eyes flicker from her to me. "You said she doesn't understand English."

I continue, unflustered, mind made up. "I can hear them now. Honk, honk. Hey, Cunt Stud!"

Lord, his outrage is a beautiful sight.

I smirk. "I did it."

The truth hits him before I even finish speaking.

"That's right. I carved Cunt Stud into your precious Ferrari's paint."

He loses his mind, charging at me like a bull.

I free my pistol and aim, but out of the corner of my eye, I see Riley moving fast—but with his damaged eye and emotionally charged state, he misses it.

Until she's right on him.

She jams a stun gun into his side, finger firmly pressed down.

His body jerks violently before hitting the floor with a sickening thud.

I kick him in his kidney, then bring a heel down on his hand, the crunch of breaking bone reverberating up my leg.

"Between the legs," I order.

She obeys, pressing the stun gun into him again.

His scream rips through the air, raw and animal.

We freeze. But the walls are thick down here. No one is coming to his rescue.

I strip his gun from his waistband. "Bring me what's inside the duffel."

Eyes on Emo, I hear her gasp. "What the hell is this?"

She returns with the white catsuit between two fingers, revulsion twisting her mouth.

"This," I say, my smile sharp, my tone ice-cold, "is sweet, sweet revenge."

Every move as a made man—and, if I'm honest, every choice since I could hold a gun—was driven by the need to prove myself.

But this right now is about me and my wife.

When this meeting with Massimo is over, I'm putting a ring on her finger and knocking her up, either order works.

Fina. I'm coming home, babe. You better be ready.

I'm eating pancakes, enjoying a rare moment of triumph, when the news breaks. Ambush. Guns. Chaos. Fina caught in the middle. Like distant thunder, I barely register at first what's happened. Then it lands, sharp and heavy, and everything stills.

That sick motherfucker went after my girl?

Massimo secures a private helicopter to take us straight away to Sardinia. Miles and minutes pass but the storm inside me doesn't move; it gathers strength. My heartbeat slows, cold and deliberate, while my mind catalogues every possibility: men, weapons, attack plans. Patience. Precision. Pain reserved for the right moment.

I don't say a word. Neither does Sandro, seated in the helicopter beside me. The tension between us is a living thing, thick and dangerous. Outside the window, Sardinia grows closer.

By the time we land, the streets around the ambush are frozen in a tableau of violence. Black-clad bodies litter the pavement. Two of Sandro's men lie broken, one slumped against an abandoned car, its doors wide open—Sandro's car ... *Fina's car* for the day. No sign of her. No sign of Riley. No sign of the dead man walking.

My hand closes around a wounded man in black, hauling him up by the throat until his feet leave the ground.

"Where are the women?" My voice rumbles low and sharp, a growl edged with fury.

He nods toward the church.

"And your boss?" Another nod.

I slam him down, smashing his skull into the pavement over and over until his brain stains the sidewalk.

"If they're harmed, if they're dead ..." Sandro pauses, then grinds out a warning. "I'll slaughter every Accardo breathing."

He'll have to beat me to them.

We storm the stairs, kick through the doors, and move through the foyer into the nave. Our men cluster protectively around us. Sandro barks orders, every syllable sharp, precise.

"You take one side, I'll cover the other."

I don't argue. I charge forward, every muscle coiled, every sense razor-sharp, ready to tear through anyone who stands in my way.

On either side of the nave, the aisles stretch long and narrow, framed by towering arches built to make men feel small. Light bleeds through stained glass, painting the stone in color. Incense clings to the air, thick and cloying. Alcoves draped with heavy curtains line the way, candles flickering inside, statues of saints staring down like cold judges on sinners rushing past. The aisles curve toward the back, funneling into shadowed corridors. I pull aside curtain after curtain, kick open closed door after closed door.

No sign of them.

I return to the group and catch Sandro's eyes, troubled and tense. He shakes his head, and I curse under my breath.

A man rushes forward, holding up a bag from the fair. "Found it near the bloodstain by the main door. It's empty."

A second man steps forward, ready to give up. "Maybe they're gone? We've checked everywhere."

I punch him square in the face, breaking his nose. "Look harder."

We were just warming up, Fina and I. Just starting a future. I hadn't even told her I loved her yet.

I arch my head back and roar, the sound bouncing off the stone and echoing through the shadows. "Fina!"

A runner approaches Sandro. "Boss, there's an empty van around the backside of the church, and the door into the lower level's locked."

"Show me."

They charge off as I still. I breathe deeply, calming my mind, panic clouding my thinking. I replay what I've seen, the alcoves, the back rooms, the corridors darkened by heavy curtains pulled tight.

I retrace my steps, this time yanking curtains aside until l find a stairwell leading below.

Fuck. How much time did I waste? How did I not find this sooner?

My footsteps echo off the stone steps as I descend into the church's bowels. "Fina," I call, throat hitching. I chant her name, push deeper into the room. "Fina. Fina."

"Renzo?"

Relief slams into me. "You okay, babe?"

"Nope."

My grip tightens on the gun.

Riley's voice trembles from the dark. "We're over here, Renzo. Is Sandro with you?"

I find them, shadows in a room filled with tombs. "Coming," I tell her, my focus locked on Fina. "You hurt?"

"I've hurt much worse than a bullet nicking me."

Something in her tone twists my gut, and I struggle not to lose my shit. "Where is he?"

"Emo?" she says calmly, like that motherfucker wasn't hunting her down.

What the fuck am I missing?

"If he hurt you—"

"He's right behind us. By the door."

I surge forward, gun ready, shoving the women behind me.

Suddenly, the door crashes open and light erupts into the room, Sandro hot on its heels.

Riley flies by me and throws herself into his arms. "Sandro. Oh my God, Sandro," she cries, then her tone pitches deeper. "Shhh. It's okay. I'm okay. I did exactly what you showed me ..."

I don't hear the rest of what she says.

My attention snaps to the man sprawled out on the church floor between us.

Emo lies there, bound in a cocoon of white latex, one eye gauzed, the other wide with terror. He looks like prey, wrapped up neat and packaged, and waiting to be killed.

I recognize the white catsuit, and slowly, ever so fucking slowly, realize what's happened.

Pride surges through me like a shot of adrenaline. Fina stands there, calm as can be, every inch the heroine in her own story. She didn't just survive—she put that bastard down. I fucking fall in love with her all over again. I want to grab her, crush her against me, tell her she did good.

Except she avoids eye contact.

"Holy fuck!" Sandro exclaims, his disbelief echoed in the expressions of every man entering the room.

But if Emo believes this delightful horror show is over, he'd better think again.

You should be afraid, motherfucker.

Your nightmare has just begun.

36

Tina

WHAT HAPPENS NEXT SHOCKS EVEN SANDRO.

Renzo doesn't just handle Emo, he owns him. Without a word and in a single brutal motion, he hauls Emo over a shoulder and stalks upstairs.

"Where is he taking him?" Riley asks.

Sandro grabs her hand and tugs her along, and I follow.

Men settle into the pews like spectators in an arena. I slide next to Riley, who's tucked away beside Sandro. We wait in a state of suspenseful anticipation, drawn by violence's magnetic pull.

A ripple of gasps breaks out at the movement in the choir loft high over the altar.

I blink.

Emo appears, his shoulder impaled by a steel cross as he's thrust forward, dangling like a broken puppet, blood soaking the white catsuit.

It's hard to say what's more shocking; Emo nailed by a cross, the now red catsuit, his precarious position, or Renzo's cold efficiency?

With every wiggle and squirm, the cross holding him over the altar buckles. Gravity and his weight reassure me he'll eventually fall, though unfortunately likely to survive impact.

Excitement grips the men around me.

"Do you see Renzo?"

"Bleeding like an open fire hydrant—how long do you think it'll take for him to slide off the cross?"

"Stupid traitor should have learned you never fuck with a Beneventi."

"Jesus, Renzo's only warming up." Sandro stands. "Come on, both of you. This isn't for your eyes."

Riley rises to her feet. "What's he going to ..."

"You hear me?" Sandro says to me, bossy as ever. "Let's go."

"The monster inside him doesn't frighten me." My heart pulls, sparking my rage. "My issue is that he's a goddamn liar."

Sandro pulls his head back like I punched him.

"If I weren't so exhausted, I'd plunge a cross through his miserable heart and give Emo some company."

He looks to Riley. "What the fuck?"

"I'll explain outside."

He pins me with a hard stare.

"Despite all this, I wouldn't miss this for the world."

"You're as bloodthirsty as we are." Admiration fills his tone.

My heart pinches while I watch him guide Riley away. The overbearing A-hole's actually kind of sweet.

I close my eyes, tired and ready for this to be over. Afterward, I'll check the car, that's hopefully still in the street leading to the church, for my purse. God, please say it is—haven't I suffered enough for what I did?

Either way, I'm returning to Rome. I'll pick up where I left off before Renzo fell back into my life.

I've earned a redo.

He's good at giving me nothing, and I'm banking on him leaving me the fuck alone.

A low rumble from behind has heads turning.

Then louder, the dangerous and unmistakable growl of a chain saw as it roars to life.

Renzo steps into view, shirtless, hair messy, and jaw set like stone. He moves down the aisle with a predator's grace, framed in a kaleidoscope of stained glass light, the antithesis of anything pure and holy.

Every step radiates raw dominance.

Every man sits straighter in his powerful presence.

The darkest part of me is turned on by the monster in the aisle. Curiosity about this violent side of him fueling the slow hum within.

He rakes cold eyes over us, until they lock on me. Dark, assessing, almost daring me to look away.

Heart pounding, I try, but fail, my own battle raging inside.

I inhale sharply, and am met with smoke, mixed with an odd chemical smell ... *plastic*.

My eyes rise.

Emo's on fire.

Everyone begins talking at once. "Covered that bastard in candle wax."

"Rubber suit will give before the burn sets in."

The chain saw growls in warning.

"With the way he's twisting and turning, my bet's he'll soon slide free."

Emo thrashes, while flames slowly, ever so slowly crawl down the catsuit.

Renzo reaches the end of the aisle, climbs the three steps to the altar, and faces us. With a quick flex of his fingers, the chain saw revs impatiently.

This isn't just vengeance; it's a cold, calculated *show*.

This is Renzo baring his teeth.

God help me, but he's horrifyingly hot.

"Can fear kill you?" someone murmurs, his tone awestruck.

"What's worse? Burning on a cross or getting sliced and diced after a bad fall?"

"It has to be by chain saw. It's the Beneventi way."

Renzo stands, arms folded, and waits.

And what do I do? Escape the church before Emo's completely dismembered? Spare myself from witnessing Renzo's brutality? Get a jump start and escape to Rome?

No, no, and no.

I soak it in. Every scream. Every cut. Every deadly slice.

Because it isn't the monster who is Renzo Beneventi that's driving me away.

It's the man who walked away from me first.

37

Fina

I'd like to say I got my happy ending. That after Emo's delightful demise and my return to Rome, life was all rainbows and butterflies.

But somewhere along the way, I fell in love with Lorenzo Beneventi. Worse still, I think I've always loved him.

That's what breaks me. For most of my life, I've only ever loved two people—my mother and him.

Bittersweet doesn't even come close to the feeling lodged in my chest. It's like sinking my teeth into the queen of fruit, a perfect strawberry, expecting a rush of sweetness only to taste rot at its core. No amount of spitting or water can wash it away. It's a fate almost worse than death.

Mix that with rage, and you have a woman in full-blooded turmoil.

It's no wonder my emotions are a mess. Renzo has always been a man of extremes, like molten lava shapes his iceberg heart. He can be charming one moment, lethal the next. Sometimes gentle. Sometimes a violent beast.

And with Emo, he had to unleash the beast.

Was I fascinated by the way he killed him? Absolutely. So was everyone in the church, and the whispers will haunt the mafiosi for years. The dark and twisted part of me felt a fierce, satisfying justice in it. Emo will never again get off on terrifying women. Enough said.

I'm strong. I've survived worse than loving a liar. Anger will fade. Bitterness will dull. Love will wane into a lull, never quite gone, just there.

He can go on dishing out marriage proposals like hollow mints.

While I build a life without him in it.

Stomach full, I inhale the aroma of espresso, and the garlic from the *linguine alle vongole in olio e aglio*, still lingering in the kitchen.

"It's quiet on the farm at night," Camilla comments, pulling me out of my head. Zia Teresa will reopen in two more days. My aunt's excitement is contagious. She even hung a sign on the window that says, "La famiglia ringrazia per la pazienza. Ci vediamo tra due giorni." Translation: *The family thanks you for your patience. See you in two days.*

Everyone in the neighborhood will understand which family she's referring to.

"We can play truth or dare," Bianca declares, "once we finish the dishes?"

Truth? I don't know if I believe in the word anymore.

Camilla and I shake our heads.

Aunt Teresa wipes her hands on her apron, then disappears from the kitchen. Leaving us to finish with the cleanup.

Bianca hip-bumps me, and I almost drop a soapy dish into the sink. "It's too quiet. How did you manage here all by yourself?"

I swallow hard. I never told my friends exactly how I came to arrive in Sardinia or the events that led up to it. The bruises from the attack are long gone and the threat buried. The burn mark on my wrist the only reminder. As for being alone ... the feeling's more intense now than ever before. Bittersweet.

My aunt returns and gestures us to the kitchen table. In her hands, she's shuffling cards. "Scopa," she announces. "Best two out of three."

Bianca and Camilla slide into their chairs across from me, Bianca giggling at the quirky suits on the cards and Camilla asking if the game is "like Go Fish."

Aunt Teresa's smile doesn't reach her eyes. "Something like that, tesoro."

The first few rounds are harmless enough; Bianca laughing when she accidentally helped Aunt Teresa win; Camilla making a show of overthinking her plays. Until the stakes started to appear, a folded note slipped toward the winner of each hand. Innocent little slips of paper.

The twinkle in my aunt's eye says otherwise.

"We can't have you girls bored," Aunt Teresa clucks.

They stare at her, wide-eyed.

For the first time in two weeks, I laugh.

"Redeemable for a favor," Aunt Teresa says when Bianca opens hers. "Any favor."

"What is this?" Bianca asks, staring at her in wonder.

"This is how we draw guests back to the restaurant."

"By my singing 'Mambo Italiano' while I'm on the floor?"

I laugh so hard my stomach aches.

"It's not even an authentic Italian song," she continues to protest.

Aunt Teresa gives Camilla a smile. "You're next, tesoro."

The game goes on, every note wilder than the last, every laugh convincing me that I'll be okay. That I'm not alone. That I have an aunt and friends who love me.

Still, the sweetness is tainted.

God, I hate you, Renzo.

Because what cuts the deepest, aside from knowing I wasn't the only woman he asked, is that the last time he promised me marriage, he was completely sober. He lied, fully aware. No addiction. No chaos. Just Renzo, his true self, serving me another broken promise.

"How are you?" the shrink with the Harvard degree asks. I'm in the same chair I occupied months ago, sucking on a stale lollipop I swiped from the container by the door. Same reluctance, same disdain for psychobabble.

What I'm not is the same man.

"Been better."

She smiles. "We're already off to a better start than last time."

I sink back, letting the sugar rush settle in.

"I was surprised when you called."

"Without my father demanding I be here?" No one knows I set up this appointment or the ones after it. The reason for the secrecy isn't because I'm worried about the same old whispers: Wild. Unreliable. *Weak.*

Trust me, that dying dog's been laid to rest. Oh, the fucking rumors still circulate, except now they don't bother me, now that they've got it right for once.

He's the most deadly Beneventi of them all.

But discussing mafiosi gossip, violence, or the Life isn't why I'm here.

The therapist crosses her legs, cheeks heating. "How can I help you?"

Sex isn't why I'm here, either.

"I'm in love."

"In love?"

The lollipop sours in my mouth. Not because what I shared is a lie. Because I blew it. I toss the lollipop into the bin. "You heard me."

"Well, okay ..."

"She's part of the reason I'm here."

Fina found out about my father's wife, my almost-fiancée. How I handed out marriage proposals like candy—just as stale, because the motive wasn't love. It was stupidity mixed with misplaced kindness, wrapped up in some fucked-up hero complex I've carried for years. I still carry it. What I unleashed on Emo proves that. The one time I actually was sincere about marrying wasn't a proposal at all, but a declaration.

An epiphany.

Fina is my girl. The woman I'll spend the rest of my life with.

But first things first.

Yeah, I'll always carry the monster within, and I fucking embrace him. He's my strength. He wins wars. Keeps the Beneventi name feared.

I'm here for the demon. He doesn't respect family or himself. He's pure hunger and chaos, and if I let him off the chain, he'll destroy everything I love.

The monster builds empires.

The demon burns them to the ground.

"I'm an addict," I say bluntly.

The therapist opens a file and picks up a pen.

"I'm here because I want to stay sober."

Tina

I SQUEEZE TOMATOES OVER A BOWL AND SCOLD MYSELF FOR thinking of him. If we're talking broken promises, I'm shattering the one I made to myself.

Camilla presses a wet kitchen towel into my hands. "Those tomatoes never stood a chance."

"Yeah," I sigh, the sound hollow even to me. "Happens to the best of us."

"Well, put the sauce aside. Bianca's about to perform."

I quickly scrub my hands clean because I cannot miss the thing that's become the pulse of our Saturday nights. Word spread through the neighborhood faster than cannoli cream spilling from a pastry and forced Aunt Teresa into accepting dinner reservations due to the bump in business.

Maracas in one hand, dishes in the other, Camilla and I sprint onto the floor. My smile is automatic as I serve the men at one table. I'll never tire of their flirting and compliments.

And then, we hear her.

"A boy went back to Napoli ..." Bianca begins, her voice close to a purr.

The restaurant erupts in delight.

Not to be outdone, Camilla and I join in, shaking our hips and maracas clattering as we weave across the floor.

Out of the corner of my eye, I catch the mastermind behind this, her apron dusted with flour and body moving perfectly in rhythm.

Joy like this was never supposed to be mine. Yet, here it is. And I'm grateful, so grateful to be surrounded with love right now.

I spin, tapping my maraca against my thigh, and drag Aunt Teresa into the center. The guests roar when she grins and then outperforms us, the real star in this restaurant.

Suddenly, everything grinds to a standstill.

I glance around. Every head is turned toward the same place—the front door.

No. No. No. Don't you dare.

I don't wait. I storm into the back room, heart hammering, nerves shot. There's no escaping him, so I'll need every ounce of rage to tell him to fuck off.

"Fina." Aunt Teresa's voice wavers with nervousness. "He demands to speak to you."

Demands? I grit my teeth. "Tell him I'm busy."

Her eyes flicker, worry flashing like a warning light.

"He's a Beneventi," I growl. "Not the devil incarnate." Wrong, wrong, wrong. He's definitely the devil disguised as sex on legs.

Her hands twist together, a rare sight of fear. "We have a few tables outside reserved for the *famiglie*."

While the restaurant was closed, Aunt Teresa had the outdoor space scrubbed, lights hung, and a few tables arranged out back in the cobblestone alley. A place for the *famiglie* to eat in peace.

With a small nod, I stalk off, grabbing a bottle of open wine and a glass as I go, then shove open the back door with my hip and collapse at a small table for two. I carelessly splash wine into the glass before drinking deeply, letting the alcohol calm me before he arrives.

A few minutes later, he exits the restaurant.

I refuse to meet his eyes. "I do not have time for liars."

His silence is loud enough to make my blood boil.

"You fuck me against a shower wall and whisper promises you have no intention of keeping?" My voice grinds low, rough as gravel. *"I'll do right by you, babe. And when I ask again, your knees will buckle. I promise."* The words taste like acid on my tongue. "Lies. All of it. How am I supposed to believe you? Am I supposed to forget the first time you proposed? Pretend you don't hand out marriage promises like party favors? Or did you think I wouldn't find out you asked Alessia to marry you, when you'd made the same promise to me?"

My chest is rising fast, each breath sharper than the last, but I push on. "Sure, I've got my kinks. But take a good look, asshole. Do I look like a goddamn sister-wife to you?"

"Cazzo. Can I at least sit down?"

My jaw drops. Not Renzo. Sandro.

"What are *you* doing here?"

"Fulfilling a debt." He smooths out his suit and sits across from me. "I didn't expect to step into a land mine. He fucked up worse than I imagined." Then, like a typical controlling asshole, he swipes my glass, helps himself to a drink, and stares at me with an unnerving calm I envy.

I scowl. "Bacteria breeder. I am not sharing."

"Play nice, and I will reward you."

I stiffen. "Go to hell."

He chuckles. "Renzo has his hands full with you."

"Renzo," I scoff, muttering the name like a curse, "will never know what a handful I am."

"Why am I even subjecting myself to his bullshit?"

"Then leave. Tell your brother I will fuck half of Rome before he lays a hand on me again."

"Only half?"

I glare. "Do you not have better things to do? Kiss Massimo's ass and make friends, maybe?"

"Dante's in California but sent a message."

My fingers curl tight. I know what this is, and if I'm honest, am slightly disappointed he's not here for Renzo. My entire life I've craved the truth about my mother's death, but how could I survive it? How could I live under the same roof, eat at the same table, breathe the same air, if I admitted the only family I had left was her murderer? I buried the suspicion so deep I almost convinced myself it wasn't true. But I can't run anymore. Not even from this.

"There is no gentle way to say this," Sandro warns.

Gentle and Sandro don't belong in the same sentence.

"Dante promised you an answer. Your father had your mother killed. Shot in the back of the head. Quick. Clean."

My eyes squeeze shut. The words crash through me, shattering what little hope I clung to. I always knew, somewhere deep down. But knowing and hearing are two different blades, and this one slices me wide open. I can feel Sandro's gaze on me as I splinter apart.

"Shit," he mutters under his breath while I struggle to find air.

"If it helps, Renzo got revenge for you."

My head jerks up. "What?"

"Dante is taking California from your father. Part of a deal my brother made with our father on your behalf. Your father's out. No longer part of the famiglie. Ruined."

A tear rolls down my cheek as my mind struggles to keep up. "Renzo did this?"

"Goddamn it. You fucking crying?"

"No."

"It looks like you are."

I blink back the rest of my tears to glare at the asshole.

He smiles. "Much better."

In the moment, he's so like Renzo, he's nearly likeable. My heart tightens at the thought.

"Look, Riley's upset for running her mouth."

"She only told me the truth."

"It was his fucking brilliant idea. He was never engaged to

Alessia. I was. And Riley wasn't exactly happy when she learned the truth."

"That the Beneventi twins are liars?"

His expression darkens. "Keep pushing, and I'll leave before clueing you in and giving you reason to thank him."

"Clue me in?" I demand.

"Why are you really mad at him?" he asks, eyes narrowing. "Don't tell me it's because he broke his promise?"

"Mad? I am outraged. Outraged for every woman. He promised to marry me, gave every excuse for backing out, and proposed to another woman without my knowledge then left me to Carlo Accardo."

"Bing-fucking-go." Sandro smirks, a grin that infuriatingly reminds me of Renzo. "You wanted Renzo to interfere."

I rise. "Are you smiling at my expense? I was days from marrying Carlo."

"Until he was poisoned."

My heart slows as my mind races to keep up. "What?"

"Who the fuck do you think poisoned that stranzo?"

"He didn't ..."

"Ask yourself why. Renzo wasn't a made man. With Carlo's help, the famiglie had millions tied up in a casino trust. Killing him risked everything, even my father's wrath. But he did it anyway—waited months, swapped Carlo's Pepcid with thallium, and made sure the staff staged it as an allergic reaction."

My world spins, vision clouding.

"That took careful planning and fuck-all cunning. No one but a few people know the truth. I'm trusting you to keep it that way."

"Months ..." My chest tightens.

Sandro moves to leave.

"Wait," I exclaim. "Where are you going?"

"I did what I came here to do—enlighten you. I've better shit to do than get involved in my brother's love life."

I jump to my feet, my mind in turmoil.

Renzo killed Accardo.

Renzo planned it for months.

Renzo didn't abandon me to fate, not completely.

"Why?" I insist.

"Come on, Fina. You're smarter than this. It's the same reason he took a goddamn chain saw to Settemo."

I search his face, dumbfounded.

"He ended Carlo Accardo because he loves you."

Renzo

I DIED ON A CROSS.

I drove a cross through a man's body and dangled him in the air with it.

But here, in the quiet stillness of an empty Roman cathedral, a strange peace seeps into my bones as I ask God to give me strength for what I'm about to do.

Then, it's time.

When I leave, my new motorcycle waits on the cobblestone road. Leather jacket zipped, helmet secured, I give the engine a few hungry revs and take off.

The ride to Grottaferrata should take thirty minutes, but I'm there in twenty. The road cuts through rolling vineyards and ancient olive groves, their leaves shimmering with dew and the early morning light. To my left, the sun edges over the horizon, turning the hills into a landscape fit for saints and sinners alike. Still, I can't reach the farmhouse fast enough.

I don't hide my arrival. This isn't about secrecy. This is me making a statement.

When Fina steps onto the porch, I stop breathing.

Bare feet. Tousled hair. Eyes still heavy from sleep. She's the most dangerous thing I've ever seen and has never looked more beautiful.

I expect fire, anger, rejection. But she just watches me as I climb the stairs toward her.

Did she believe I wouldn't come for her? Did she think I'd give up?

Well, I'm here now, and I'm not going anywhere.

We look at each other like it's the first time.

I open my mouth, because I've waited fucking forever to say it: I love you.

A crow of a rooster breaks the quiet, and in a flurry of flapping wings and evil intent, the feathered hellion charges across the yard.

I jab a finger at it. "Nail me with a spur, and I'll take you out."

It arches its head back, crows once more, and then runs off in search of an easier target.

Fina clutches her stomach, and laughter pours out of her.

The sound cracks me wide open. "Glad it knows who's boss."

"The look on its face ..."

"Yeah, I'm more interested in the look on your face."

That sobers her. "We're not fucking."

"Not what I meant, babe." I wait for her to correct the nickname.

She rolls her eyes. "Come inside. I'll make coffee."

I follow her into the farmhouse and kitchen, noticing she's lost weight.

That's going to stop. Fina's going to feast on food and love, and grow plump with the baby I fill her womb with.

She measures out spoonfuls of coffee grounds, then adds water to a stovetop coffee maker and ignites the flame while I lean against the kitchen table, soaking her in.

I hear her inhale before she faces me, eyes glistening with tears. "Why didn't you tell me?"

I give it to her, raw and honest. "This isn't an excuse, just an explanation. I was messed up. Period. I spent years avoiding the Life, sneering at the famiglie and convincing myself I was more clever and more deadly than they were. My father stayed patient with me until Rome. You remember, during our ride to Las Vegas, I mentioned that trip? It went badly. Everyone—my father, my brother, the Twelve at the time—saw me freeze and mistook it for weakness. My therapist calls it my trigger moment, and it was. I pushed back harder against the Life when deep down all I wanted was to be the son my father raised me to be. You got caught in the crosshairs. You, and Alessia."

"You proposed to her?" she quietly asks, but the weight of her question's heavy.

"More proposition than proposal, which we approached my father with. I did it because I was trying to help her, trying to do right by someone—if not you or even myself. Not only did my father shoot me down, I was neutralized and dragged off into rehab."

"Do you love her?"

My lips curl. "Yeah."

Fina hisses.

"Like a sister, even a mom. You will, too, once I formally introduce you."

Fina bites her lip, considering what I've told her.

I step toward her until our bodies almost touch. "Please tell me I didn't fuck this up. Please say we can move forward from our past."

"Renzo."

"Fina. I love you, only you. Always have but was too fucked up to see it. I had to learn to love myself before I could recognize it."

Her lips part, a sharp intake of breath trembling between us. Her eyes flash like she's been struck, my love bomb blasting away the lingering hurt and everything else holding her back.

I want to grab her and hug her so tight while the rest of the world fucks off.

Tears spill down her cheeks in quick, furious streaks. "Is that why you did it?"

"Did what?"

"Murdered Carlo?" Her voice cracks, shattering the air between us.

Well, shit. "Who told you?"

"Your brother."

My brows lift. "Sandro?"

Her soft laugh is edged with disbelief. "He came to the restaurant while you were in Rhode Island. Told me what you did for me. How you risked your father's reputation with the famiglie, the repercussions you'd have faced for killing Carlo and not being a made man. You gave me a chance at a new life."

"Yeah, I should have taken care of Emo Accardo too."

"Revenge made him unhinged. No one could have predicted he'd stalk me or try to take down the strongest capos in the Eleven and Cosa Nostra."

"My father appreciated the warning you gave him about his fence."

She swipes at her tears. "Advice, he calls it."

"He likes you." I close the distance and pull her against me. "I'm sorry."

Her head dips in a nod.

"Listen, Fina. A future with me means you're back in the Life. I've got demons I'm battling with a therapist's help. You witnessed my violent streak, how I coldly kill without hesitation. I'm twisted, bent, and nothing about life with me will be easy."

"Fine." Her breath warms my neck. "The answer's no."

"Is that right?" I demand. The answer is never no. I've a talent for wearing people down and, as stubborn as she is, I'm always up for the challenge.

"Can we start over?" Her whisper, fragile yet defiant, carries the weight of months lost. Like she's wavering between believing I'm the same man who left her and the one who now stands before her, heart in fucking hand.

"You can start over, babe. For me, you never ended."

She pulls back, eyes searching mine.

And then, her lips twitch.

"Is that why you bought a ring?"

What. The. Hell?

Yeah, I bought a massive, in-your-face engagement ring from a Roman jeweler days ago. Like I said, no isn't in the cards for us.

"You stalking me again?"

She shrugs, a hint of defiance in her eyes.

"You still got the hots for me?"

Her cheeks flush. "Maybe."

A growl builds low in my throat. "But you made me suffer, waiting until I came for you."

"I'm vindictive like that."

I scoop her into my arms and carry her to the kitchen table, before laying her across it. "I'm going to put a baby in you right now, so you'll never escape."

I'll get down on one knee later. Right now, I need her shaking with pleasure and laughing through tears.

Fina loops her arms around my neck and pulls me close. "Then show me. Over and over. Prove I'm yours and only yours."

Fina

I wait for weeks for Renzo's proposal.

It never comes.

He's wined and dined me, in expensive restaurants and small trattorias. One morning, he woke me before dawn and walked me from our new apartment, past the restaurant and club, to the river. He held my hand and kissed me as daybreak spilled color across the Tiber. Another time, he took me to the opera, which I adored while he endured for my sake. And once, at the old barn on the farm, I was sure he was about to drop to one knee ... instead, he chained me in the hay and fucked me until my knees buckled.

Be patient, I tell myself. He promised.

We've both been busy. Renzo's in charge of Rome now while Dante's in Los Angeles, running the West Coast in my father's place. That's right—Don Lombardi out, Dante in.

While Renzo charmed the Midwest Casino Trust into freeing the Eleven's investments, I set my sights on Sebastiano Beneventi. I coaxed, I provoked, and when his silence stretched long enough to rattle me even over the video call, I pushed harder, demanding a favor for taking Renzo off his hands.

Terrifying and calculating, the most powerful capo di tutti capi in the Life and soon to be my father-in-law, and I didn't flinch. Across the screen, I stared him down with every ounce of nerve I had, daring him to underestimate me. His low, amused laugh was music to my ears. "Cazzo. You two deserve each other." Then he gave me what I wanted: my father branded an embarrassment, stripped of his place in the Eleven, and banished from the famiglie.

In the Life, respect is worth as much as money, and now my father has neither. He's ruined. Alone. And I made sure of it. The last nail in in his coffin, hammered in by his own daughter.

Renzo's on a mission to knock me up, and I can't stop wondering what kind of parent I'll be. What I won't be is cruel or unfeeling, a hollow excuse for a mother.

My family is in Rome now, and I'm surrounded by people who love me here. Bianca's still a shameless flirt, Camilla's finally letting her hair down, Riley's nearby, and Sandro's almost tolerable when he isn't bossing everyone.

Do I miss the States? Sometimes. But we return often enough, the demands of the famiglie business pulling us back and forth.

Do Renzo and I clash, fight, laugh?

You bet.

We test limits. We fuck.

We love.

And Renzo always knows how to stoke my curiosity. My knees still ache from last night.

"Are you ready?" His voice brooked no argument, pure authority, as he set the scene. We're pushing boundaries before he softens our games with the promise of a baby.

"I'm about to lose my fucking mind," I warned. His muscles tensed, lifting me off the bed as the shibari rope bit into my breasts and thighs. Below me, the mattress was spread with every wicked toy imaginable, a sinful buffet that could rival Sandro and Riley's entire armoire.

"You're at my mercy now," he said, grinning, before suspending me in ropes and teasing me until every nerve in my body surrendered.

Renzo and I have been exploring Rome with a passion, too. Today, we're on a private Colosseum Underground Tour, winding through corridors rich with history.

Our guide leads us into the arena. The space is vast and ancient, the echo of the gladiators' footsteps shifting with the earthen floor. Sunlight slices across the weathered stones, glinting like it's spot-lighting every failure, every triumph etched into the ruins. In the Hollywood Hills, people "die" to get the right parking spot, to shop at the trendiest store, or to make the next great movie. Same illusion of drama with wildly different stakes.

I glance at Renzo, and notice the guide has slipped away. "Where did he go?"

He simply smirks.

My attention falls on something in the center of the arena. A small round table dressed with a red-checked cloth, two tall candles, a vase of red roses, and champagne on ice with crystal flutes.

"Is this part of the tour?" I murmur, caught between awe, disbelief, and the thrill of knowing he orchestrated every second.

"Hey, Fina!"

I whip around. Bianca's waving from the amphitheater seats,

flanked by Aunt Teresa and Camilla. Riley's there too, with Sandro of all people. They wave wildly, then point behind me.

Joy hits me like a punch. Everything I've been through, everything I dreamed about ... I've never felt so happy.

I turn.

Renzo's on one knee, ring in hand.

"Here?" I blurt. "Not the opera? Not some fancy restaurant?"

"This is the perfect place." His smirk curves into something softer. "Ask me why."

"Why?"

"Because we're fighters, Fina." His expression's fierce in a way I've never witnessed before. "And look at you. You don't stay down. You rise. You fucking thrive. I'm not just in awe, I'm proud. So damn proud." His voice thickens, my tears spurring him on. "Elia Seraphina Lombardi, will you marry me?"

"Yes."

He slips the ring onto my finger, pulls me into his arms, and kisses me. Cheers erupt from the seats, echoing off the ancient stone.

Love is like looking through a kaleidoscope. On bright days, light filters through, scattering soft, gentle colors across your vision. On dark days, colors clash and compete for attention, rich and saturated, intense and mesmerizing, beautiful in a different way.

And as I kiss my fiancé, my obsession, my heart, I know I'll never want it any other way.

EPILOGUE

Dante

I TAKE A LONG PULL FROM MY CIGAR, THE SMOKE CURLING SLOW and decadent toward the ceiling. My thighs spread wider, my hand fisting tight in the blonde's ponytail. I give a sharp yank, forcing her down until her lips are crushed to my base. Her throat works around me as she gags slightly, eyes watering, mascara bleeding into thick black streaks.

She looks like hundreds of women I've had. Hungry, depraved, ruined. She'll come back for more. They always do.

Dark hair, darker eyes, and a face that gets me into as much trouble as it gets me out of, I possess that Italian charm women eat up. I like expensive things; they like to be spoiled. I like to look good in tailored suits fitted to my muscular frame; they undress me with their eyes. My cars purr, and so do they, in my bed and around my dick.

My reputation is well-earned, and I live by one motto: Work hard, play hard, get hard.

It works for me.

As does California.

My new house sits in the Monterey hills where I can watch the

Pacific roll in or descend the steps to my own private cove. Glass walls face the ocean and drench the rooms in sunlight. I grilled a time or two from the deck off the living room, the taste of the salty air as invigorating as the steaks I enjoy. Inside my home, everything's black walls, oak wood, and white accents. Very male. Very me.

In the bedroom, a king bed faces the sea, but retractable blackout blinds block out the light when I need rest, particularly after nights spent in the best Los Angeles clubs money can buy. It's a waterbed with a thermostat that guarantees the perfect fit for my mood.

My Monterey home is my castle.

A place I never eat and fuck in.

Where I'm at right now, at my apartment in Los Angeles, is my fuckpad. I have them in other cities too, New York, Rome, Tokyo. Sebastiano busts my balls about it constantly. He doesn't get that I like my own space. My own sheets that smell like sunshine. A mattress that hasn't been fucked on by God knows how many strangers.

I like entertaining on my terms, with everything I want at arm's reach.

I tighten my grip on the blonde's hair and roll my hips deeper. Her moan vibrates around me. Blow jobs are my morning coffee. Fuels me for the day by taking the edge off. I don't skip them, ever.

At least, not by choice.

The only time I went without was when I was Massimo Grassi's "guest."

That is until Luna Cecilia Gallo inserted herself into my business once again.

I'd been locked in a suite on the Grassi estate, well fed and bored to tears, staring at the horizon and waiting for Sebastiano Beneventi to resolve the bullshit with Massimo. That's when I spotted two of his men cresting the hill, dragging a girl between them.

She fought like hell, heels digging into the ground, hair wild in the wind.

I stood in the motherfucking window, feeling helpless as fuck.

What was Massimo thinking? Kidnapping me was one thing. Throwing her into my suite and locking the door behind us was beyond cruel.

"What the hell happened?" I demanded the second we were alone. I'm not easily shaken, and my veins run cold. But now she was in fucking danger? I wasn't wearing a crystal ball—Massimo might actually have killed me, and in turn, her.

She straightened her dress and shot me a glare. "I heard Massimo kidnapped you. I came to help."

There were a few moments in life where I came close to strangling someone. That was one of them.

Un-fucking-believable.

She was a smokeshow, all fire and bad ideas. Barely eighteen to my thirty-seven.

Didn't stop her from stealing onto my property and invading my privacy while I swam naked in my pool.

Didn't stop me from noticing her curves every time she walked past my terrace.

I bought an estate next door to Don Gallo's as an investment property where I grow pistachios, unaware I'd be getting more than nuts in the deal.

And she makes me nuts. Insanely so.

The pull of the blonde's mouth drags me back to the present. My dick throbs, but it's not her face I see.

Fuck.

With a grunt, I shove her off me.

My erection softens instantly, angrily. "Go."

"Will I ... see you again?"

"Maybe."

She gathers her clothes from the floor and leaves me to my thoughts.

I almost call her back because this is becoming a problem.

I'm a man who loves variety. Always up for a good chase, always down for a naughty thrill.

Still, I should never have touched Don Gallo's daughter.

Allowed myself to be seduced by her, ignoring her lies.

Fuck her until my balls exploded.

Made her bleed on my dick, her virginity mine for the taking.

And the worst part about it aside from getting off on every second?

Now I'm shackled to her teenage ass.

The last thing I expected walking out of the Grassi estate was to be chained for life to Don Gallo's precious little princess.

THE END

DIRTY MAFIA SINNER

EXCERPT

Riley

HE'S NOT COMING.

My one-night stand, who turned into consecutive Friday nights and then into every night over the course of a few weeks. It was hardly the beginning of a meaningful relationship. People talk in healthy relationships. He said hello and goodbye, and between, fucked me six ways to Sunday. His touch was addictive. *He* was addictive.

His late-night visits became less frequent until they stopped entirely.

Three weeks now.

It's over.

I curl a tea bag around a spoon. It's two in the morning, a bad time for a caffeine fix. Except, I can't sleep, so what does it matter?

He left that night after our wild fling, and I thought that was the end of it. Then, a few days later, a man in an expensive suit showed up at my apartment to install a new lock. Ciro—when I approached him later about it—was dumbfounded, and I realized he was the wrong man to thank. Not fully comprehending I'd soon be doing so in person.

My buzzer rang, waking me. It was well past midnight, but I scrambled from bed to answer the door, believing guilt had driven Emily to come over to apologize for a fight we'd had over dinner. That, or because she'd left Ciro. Because who else would show up at this hour?

Except it wasn't Emily standing there, eyes smoldering and daring me, just daring me, to comment on his return. As if his presence didn't make my throat go dry and words impossible. He came every Friday night, then practically every night until his visits stopped altogether.

Now, it's over.

I squeeze the amber liquid from the tea bag. The tea's too hot, but I drink it anyway, welcoming the burn and the reminder that even something outwardly innocent like tea can still hurt you.

The things we did, the boundaries he pushed ...

He was everything I didn't know I was searching for.

Liquid sloshes across my T-shirt and kitchen floor. "Great," I mutter, setting everything on the counter before tearing off the shirt to rinse it in the sink. Once finished, I grab a towel, get onto my knees, and wipe up the mess, blindly making wide swooping arcs to reach liquid I can't see while I work.

Why is it so dark in here?

Big windows bookend my apartment's railroad-style layout, with plenty of natural light filtering in. The kitchen and small functional bathroom sit on one end, the living area square in the middle, and my bedroom on the other side. With renovations ongoing and the other apartments vacant, it's quiet at night.

"You live in a newly renovated NYC apartment rent-free," Emily informed me after I finally commented on how she'd bailed on being my roommate. One minute, she was crying over catching Ciro snorting coke like a character straight out of the movie *Scarface*, and in the next—after I suggested she move in with me "as planned"—she was defending him and attacking me. "Everything always has to be about poor, poor Riley, doesn't it?"

This from a friend who'd picked me up from the airport, dropped me off at the curb, informed me there'd been a change in plans and she'd moved in with Ciro, then, blurting out the entry code, drove off without the slightest remorse.

I'd stood on the sidewalk, in an unfamiliar city, in front of an unfamiliar building, two suitcases at my side and my one connection to home abandoning me. Left behind with an emptiness eating away at me.

"He could charge *thousands*."

"Is that why you're dating him?" I snapped, unleashing an anger that had been brewing for months. "For his money?"

Her claws came out to sink into my jugular. "I liked you better when you barely talked."

I stood up from the table, wavering somewhere between being the wrecking ball and the wrecked. "We'll talk when you're ready to hear the truth," I said in a flat voice before walking off.

But maybe I have changed. Still broken, yet not entirely defenseless.

I submitted to him yet discovered an inner strength long absent from my life.

With a sigh, I sit back on my haunches and toss the towel at the sink. "Why did he have to end it so soon?"

A grunt disrupts the quiet. A muffled sound, which has me falling backward. I search for the source, and find it at my kitchen table, a shadowy figure seated in the dark.

My eyes shift toward the door.

"Don't." *His* voice.

Fear quickly changes to indignation. "How long have you been sitting there?" The kitchen curtains are pulled closed, shrouding the table in darkness. I can barely make out his features.

I stand, arms folded, very aware how naked I am, wearing nothing but a skimpy red thong.

He doesn't respond. Typical. What else should I expect from a man who so reluctantly offered me his name. *Al*—that's all I got. "I wasn't expecting you."

"I know."

Three weeks, and he knows?

"Come here."

My stomach dips as I stand rooted in place, my hesitation shrouded by worry, because *that* voice is nonnegotiable. Yet he disappears and then reappears, and all he has for me is "I know"?

"Riley." His tone's laced with warning.

I close my eyes in defeat.

"Please."

Not once, in all the time we've spent together, has he ever used that word. I'm the pleaser. He's the taker. And never is the dividing line crossed.

He doesn't deserve my obedience, though I worry how he'll react if I completely disobey, so I meet him halfway, shuffling by him to open the kitchen curtain. Moonbeams dance across my skin, though he remains obscured by shadows.

"How did you get inside?"

"Used my key."

"What?" I gasp. "You have a key to my apartment?"

He counters my question with one of his own. "I've failed, haven't I?"

"Failed?" I stare at him, incredulous.

"At corrupting you."

A shiver races up my spine. That voice. That tone. He makes me forget my own name. "No," I whisper.

"Let me see," he orders. "Unfold your arms."

My skin heats beneath a flush. What a picture I must have made, bare-chested and crawling around on the floor. His lips have criss-crossed every inch of my body, so why this crippling shyness?

"Show me what you're hiding, baby."

Baby. The word feels like a soft caress from this harsh, no-nonsense man. Did he feel my absence, as much as I missed him?

I drop my arms, and my D-cup-size breasts bounce free. On my small frame, breasts this size appear bigger. And he, freakishly, loves them. Is borderline obsessed with them.

"Come here."

I step closer. My mema's crystal cocktail glass on the table, along-side a nearly empty whiskey bottle I don't recognize.

He had a few drinks the night we met, but I've never seen him drunk.

"What's wrong?"

His midnight black hair's mussed, like he's been running fingers through it. Scruff darkens his chin like he's forgotten to shave. I've memorized even the curve of his lips, the cupid's bow of his upper lip softening the rigid set of his bottom lip. I focus on the upper one, the antithesis of the steely force I've grown accustomed to.

How little I know about him, other than he thrives on control, domination, and filthy, dirty sex. He's always well-groomed, hair smoothed back and face baby-bottom smooth.

But tonight ... something's upsetting him.

"Say something."

"I'm here."

"I didn't notice," I quip. Such a liar. Because I notice everything about him. The spicy lemon cologne he wears. The tension sizzling between us. His face, body, enormous dick. The way Italian bleeds into his words, especially when he's bossy or extra dirty in bed.

"This is the last place I should be." He drops my cell phone onto the table with a clatter. Why did he have it? Was he scrolling through it?

As his comment registers, my earlier irritation reignites. Am I some magical, big-breasted siren who's lured him in? Does he actually believe, after weeks of relinquishing complete control, I have power over him?

"Then go," I respond, and mean it. I might beg him to fuck me, but I won't plead with him to stay.

The silence between us builds to a crescendo.

"You make my life impossible."

It's the only warning I get.

He lunges, knocking over his chair as he grabs me by the waist, hauling me off my feet, then rolling me back across the kitchen table. His arms wrap around me as he nuzzles his face between my breasts.

"I didn't mean it." I weave my fingers through his hair. Soothing him. Comforting him. "I've been waiting for you."

"Riley." He growls my name against my skin.

In moments like this, he allows me inside. Deepening our connection in a way words never could. His vulnerability as tangible as my fragile heart. I sensed the shift in him the week before his late-night visits stopped. Relentlessly overpowering me every way he could was normal but wrapping me in his arms afterward and praising me until I fell asleep was new.

What changed to make him stop coming?

His lips find my nipple. I smirk—they always do. God, I missed his mouth on me. Teeth scrape flesh, followed by pain softened with pleasure. I arch into him, relinquishing myself completely.

"Cazzo," he mutters then tenses. Just like that, everything shifts. "This shouldn't be this fucking hard."

His admission guts me. He doesn't *want* to want me. "You're breaking up with me." Hurt catches on each forced word.

He steps back—an answer in itself—and I hop off the table.

Tipping my chin up, I dare look at him. And immediately wish I hadn't.

His dark, brooding gaze locks on my face. Almost as if he was looking at a puzzle piece without a puzzle present to solve. Almost like we never stood a chance, but somehow we find ourselves in this moment.

"It's complicated," he grinds out.

"Explain it to me, then."

He stares at me. One second. Two. Then, he scowls and a steel wall slams down so hard between us, my teeth rattle. *Not today, Riley. Not ever.*

He disappears into the connecting bathroom. The faucet runs, and I listen to him splashing water on his face. I stand frozen. One part wanting him to leave; one part desperate for him to stay.

He returns, as cool, calm, and collected as the man I invited home that first night.

Silence thickens the air, but it's me who breaks it.

I pull my shoulders straight and draw on every ounce of pride remaining. "Am I just a fuck to you?"

"And if I say yes?"

His callous question is a punch in the stomach. This isn't within the rules of the games we play. This isn't me being a good girl or him pushing my boundaries. I might willingly, even eagerly, relinquish power, but what I won't do is be some doormat he can walk all over. "Go on. Leave. I've survived worse than you."

He frowns.

With a shaky hand, I gesture toward the door. If there's anything I know how to do, it's endure.

Everything pauses.

"Goddamn you," he growls, and before I can guess his intent, I'm swept into his arms and carried toward the bedroom.

ALSO BY MICHELE MANNON

Dirty Mafia Kingdom
Dark mafia romance
Dirty Mafia King
Dirty Mafia Sinner
Dirty Mafia Torment

Deadliest Lies Novels
Dark contemporary with *a lot* of suspense
Rogue
Mercenary
Hit Man
Player
Liar
Bastard

Worth the Fight Series
Sexy contemporary sports romance
Knock Out
Tap Out
Out for The Count

ABOUT THE AUTHOR

Michele Mannon has been writing romance since her first publication in 2012. A multiple recipient of Romantic Times Magazine's prestigious TOP PICKS award, Michele's books always pack a punch, leaving readers laughing out loud or swooning and biting their fingernails at all the appropriate times. Her books have been sold in print, digitally, and on Audible.

She loves the darker shades in romance; the anti-heroes and villains, the angst mixed with a heavy dose of unexpected.

Michele lives on a mountain overlooking the Delaware River, where she can be found with a glass of Riesling in her hand and a laptop on her lap.

For the latest updates on releases, join Michele's newsletter at
www.michelemannon.com

Follow Michele on TikTok, Instagram, and Facebook
@authormichelemannon